Ellen + Doug ~

With Love, With Connie

By

George R. Henaut

George R. Henaut

Thank you for sharing the journey!

ISBN: 1-4033-6449-4 (e-book)
ISBN: 1-4033-6450-8 (Paperback)
ISBN: 1-4033-6451-6 (Dustjacket)

Library of Congress Control Number: 2002093961

This book is printed on acid free paper.

Printed in the United States of America
Bloomington, IN

1stBooks – rev. 10/10/02

Dedication

With Love, With Connie is dedicated to:
my editor,
my inspiration,
my Rachel!

With Love, With Pauline!

Thank You!

A sincere thank you to:

my faithful readers/critics:
Edwina, Brenda, Neil!

Frances for clothing advice!

Prologue:

Among My Souvenirs - December 12, 1997

The festive season will soon be with us once again. Materialism and spirituality will clash as each promotes its message, its recipe for abundant life, its hero. Today is December 12. For many it is simply a benchmark on the road to Bethlehem or the Boxing Day sales. For a few, it will be a day to say good-bye and for two individuals a time to make sacred promises. For one individual, it is a day to commemorate her birthday, birthdays that have been celebrated, regretted or ignored since 1938.

Robert Mascaux is seated in an armchair near a wood stove in his den. He is reading his most recent diary entry while glancing at the numerous letters and other diaries that are lying on the table beside him. He rises, carrying his diary with him as he moves toward his cluttered desk.

How many times had he heard the expression, "All of us have within us at least one good novel just waiting to be written". He had always thought he would like to write that one novel but he knew that such a task would require talent, time, and experience. As a high school student in the 1950's, he was aware that for most of us, our personal narrative remains largely unspoken and inevitably unwritten. Among our souvenirs that we have gathered in a lifetime, there may be diaries, family albums, slides and videos; but few expressions in extended prose formats for wider audiences. He had always been aware that of the countless novels that finally are written, many are never published, and only a few published novels receive significant attention from the reading public.

As Robert leafs through a tattered copy of I REMEMBER MAMA, he recalls the plot line and textual notes in his grade 10 drama anthology. In the drama, Mama's daughter, Katrin wants to be an author. Mama seeks advice from a noted writer, Florence Dana Moorhead. Ms. Moorhead's advice to Katrin is that authors cannot write an effective story until they have felt what they write about. She also tells Katrin that authors must write about the things they know and have experienced. As a grade 10 student, Robert decided that he would need to record his experiences in a diary so that he would be able to recall the details that might be useful in his subsequent writing attempts.

Robert also knew that prose styles vary in their appeal. Not everyone could capture the minute detail of Dickens or Scott and still maintain readers' interest. Still others prefer the brevity of style expressed by Steinbeck and a host of modern writers. These were all considerations that influenced him as he faithfully recorded his observations from one diary to the next. Robert glanced at the faded rose on her desk, one of the many objects among her souvenirs. It was strange to have her things in his comfortable den, to have so many unopened boxes scattered throughout his usually tidy domain.

He carefully removed the lid of a banker's box that rested beside his desk. Here were the diary entries, newspaper clippings, memories that he had decided to use for his first venture into print. Some were his, but many were hers. Some were written by others who had shared their journey. All of them were private. Perhaps the fan club letters and photos did not have the expected intimacy of the other souvenirs.

Today was not the day to begin his narrative. A birthday party, a wedding and a funeral would be more than enough to occupy his time, but it was the perfect time to allow himself to recall the entries he had chosen as the essence of their story; a story that laid the foundation for the events of this special December 12.

Robert opened his first diary, the one he had begun as a Grade 10 student, following the realization that novels must come from the writer's experiences. He took this lesson literally and thus began his daily ritual of recording his joys and sorrows, his triumphs and his struggles, his fantasies and the harsh realities of the daily grind.

****

The December 1959 entries noted his growing awareness of pop music. There seemed to be so many new voices with a dramatically different beat to promote their lyrics. The term 'Rock and Roll' was becoming more common, even in the town of Northumbria in northeastern Nova Scotia. He had just discovered that the MacGuire Sisters were not singing such songs as "My Happiness" even though parts of the song seemed to feature more than one female voice. He had discovered Connie Francis and his life would never be the same again.

He was only 14 years of age when he realized that the voice delighting him with "My Happiness" was the same voice he heard singing "Who's Sorry Now", "I'm Sorry I Made You Cry" and "Happy Days and Lonely Nights".

The most treasured present beneath Robert Mascaux's 1959 Christmas tree was a record player. His first two record purchases were "Who's Sorry Now" and "My Happiness". The yellow MGM discs would become a familiar household treasure.

Robert's first diary characterized its author as a quiet, studious individual. His five foot eleven frame bore 155 pounds and slightly rounded shoulders. His hazel eyes were the gateway to his soul; they were warm and inviting, yet protected by a rather serious visage that screened entrance to his true self. He lived in a mining town, in a row of company houses. Each duplex with its peaked roof was the home of a bread winner who risked his life daily to provide for his family. The pick and shovel were passed from father to son, a legacy dug deep into their psyche. Coal dust, dampness, rats, explosions were all part of the ritual. Long hours in the mine seemed to dim their vision; for them the coal mine was life.

Robert was one of two sons born to Bertha and Camille Mascaux. Both parents had immigrated to Canada from Belgium to find a more secure life. Northumbria became their home after brief stops in Cape Breton, Alberta and an ill-fated attempt to settle in New England.

Robert was born in Northumbria. He was Canadian by birth. That did not prevent some of his peers from calling him 'bohunk' when they sensed they needed to express their superiority at his expense. He was of a timid disposition, passionate by nature and nonathletic; this made him the prey of the jocks at school. Because Robert was a loner, he was spared more frequent assaults on his Belgian heritage and his masculinity.

His elder brother had been killed during a cave-in at the end of a night shift. His father was the first to find the two young miners covered with coal and timbers. From that moment, his father was determined that his second son would never have his life cut short by the weapons of the cruel earth. His father's spirit was buried with his elder son, beneath the rubble of the coal mine; it would never be rekindled. He took early retirement long before it became fashionable and long before his household could afford the luxury.

Many of the Northumbria Belgians were successful grocery store owners. Bertha tried desperately to supplement Camille's monthly income of a $32 pension by operating a small grocery store, but her tendency to give liberal credit to those who were struggling to survive soon closed the doors of her shop. For a brief time, she sold some of her home baking. Robert recalled the aroma of freshly baked apple, lemon, and brown sugar pies. Her waffles, 'galettes', made in waffle irons heated on a coal stove were his very favourite dessert! The home baking venture failed when Bertha refused to use less costly ingredients and would not raise her prices. She then became a practical nurse in a local nursing home.

At age 14, Robert knew that he had to succeed at his studies; his mother expected it, his father demanded it. He also knew that the purchase of a record player was not without great sacrifice. He was not, however, ready for his mother's 1960 New Year's resolution.

Bertha had become increasingly dismayed by the mismanagement of the private nursing home where she worked. She was distressed by the owner's attempts to make a profit by serving unappetizing, sparse meals. Two cans of tomato soup and a loaf of bread could be stretched to feed fourteen. Cheap stale cookies from a local bakery served as dessert. The residents who received family care packages soon discovered that their goodies went missing; a delightful addition to the owner's table. On the occasions when Bertha was left in charge of the home while the owners spent the day visiting relatives in the capital city, she inevitably got into trouble when it was discovered she provided extra treats for the meals; treats which she had purchased with her own funds; often treats from her own kitchen.

Robert shook his head as he read an entry in his January 1960 diary; an entry with details of eating a meal at the nursing home. In the centre of the table, two lonely plates gave little encouragement for the appetite. On one plate were twelve pieces of bread; another contained twelve pieces of stale apple pie, one piece for each person seated at the table. The other residents were given their meals in their rooms. Sometimes their plates were devoid of the sparse luxuries shared with the dining-room guests. On this occasion, three cans of baked beans were being shared among the guests.

Robert had known that his mother could not continue to work twelve hour days, spend bus fare for transportation, purchase extra food and gifts for the manor guests and still balance her own household budget. Bertha's solution to the dilemma was received with subdued enthusiasm by both Camille and Robert. She proposed opening their home as a nursing home. The other side of their duplex was available for renting. They could easily accommodate eight or nine residents.

With reluctance, the men gave up their privacy to welcome seniors into their lives. For Robert, it was the gift of foster grandparents that transformed his life. He now had Connie, an extended family and a home with an adequate income guaranteeing that he would not have to descend to the black depths to earn a living. This realization pleased his father who had retreated into his own world of memories of happier days.

While many of Robert's peers might have had real-life experiences similar to the thoughts expressed in Connie's late 1959 hit single, "Lipstick on Your Collar" or shared the sentiments of "Among My Souvenirs", Robert's personal life remained untouched by the romance portrayed in the songs he listened to so attentively after he had completed his homework. His interest in real romance was overshadowed by his passion for Connie's world of love and heartbreak; an interest that extended beyond the lyrics themselves to a growing fascination with the singer herself.

In 1960, Connie recorded "Everybody's Somebody's Fool", "My Heart Has a Mind of Its Own" and "Many Tears Ago". Her career expanded from records to the nightclub circuit, and movies. Robert purchased entertainment magazines that featured his beloved songstress, but they failed to quench his thirst for information. In desperation, he wrote his first and only request to become a member of a Connie Francis Fan Club. Choosing the right fan club was given as much thought as would be required for a research paper. He wrote to a fan club in New England; the president was also a high school student who promised a starter kit with photos and a quarterly newsletter. She had met Connie at a recent concert.

On this special anniversary (December 12, 1997) of Connie's birth, Robert affectionately opened his first letter to Rachel. He had begun his letter with:

"I have been a Connie Francis fan for over a year. I admire her voice, her sincerity and her ability to deliver a song on stage (I have only seen her on television.). I have read a great deal about her in magazines, but I would like accurate, current information. It is hard to know what is truth in magazine articles. If you can promise to supply such information on a regular basis, please accept my request for membership..."

Little did Robert know back in 1960, that this letter would transform his life more than his passion for Connie or his relationship with his foster grandparents.

He waited four weeks for a response to his fan club letter, but what jubilation when he received his first brown envelope! Inside were three glossy pictures of Connie, a biography, a list of her hit singles and albums, a list of awards, and a two page letter from the president, Rachel Turner. It was more than he had hoped for. How many times had he reread this letter, looked at the photos while listening to the singer's records! Rachel apologized for the delay in sending the information, but she was swamped by requests for membership. She wanted to give personal service, so each kit was accompanied by her personal response to Connie and her career. Her first letter contained the following:

"Unlike many of her peers, Connie is destined to have a long career in show business. She sells millions of records, she is a great nightclub act and she is preparing for her first movie.

Her beautiful contralto voice can be heard around the world as she extends her fans by singing in various languages besides English and Italian.

It is my pleasure to share Connie's career with you..."

Robert slipped the letter back into the brown envelope that first carried Rachel to him. Thirty-five years had passed since he first read that letter. So much had changed in his life, in Rachel's life and indeed in Connie's life in those ensuing years.

Chapter 1:

My Happiness

On this long-awaited December 12, Robert was somewhat in awe of the day he was about to begin. There was almost an urgency to leave this sentimental collection of memories and take control of the day's agenda, yet he felt compelled to linger among his souvenirs. He needed to recall the legacy of their life apart in order to savour the beginning of their life together. He gingerly opened her 1962 diary recalling the captured moments, the nurturing of his happiness.

In just a year of correspondence, he had learned a great deal about Connie's career, and had slowly become familiar with Rachel's extended family. Her parents had been killed in a late winter car accident. She reluctantly went to live with her somewhat eccentric aunts in their mansion at Flanders Cove on the coast of Connecticut. After a year of business college, she began looking for a job, but the local business community was not looking for an inexperienced secretary.

Robert revelled in the detailed accounts of the three aunts. They were so alike and yet so dramatically different. Rachel's grandfather had called them his treasured bouquet: his tall Iris, full-bodied Daisy, and robust Rose.

Rachel's 1962 letters presented such graphic details of her life with the bouquet. Gradually they won her heart. Her letters revealed her grandfather's love of his family, his understanding of their unique qualities and how each contributed to the beauty of the bouquet...

- - - - - Flanders Cove, 1962

Rose entered the living-room with her customary pile of books, taken from their home library. She was an avid reader of classical, romantic and Victorian literature, and *The Bible*. Iris sighed at the sight of still another collection of books invading the formal setting of their

Victorian living-room. "Why can't you read those books in the library, Rose?"

With a hidden smile, Rose replied. "Reading is social, I need to read in the company of others, thank you." She carelessly dropped her collection on a rounded mahogany table located near her favourite Queen Anne chair.

Iris continued arranging her bouquet of cut flowers in a crystal vase resting on a marble-topped plant stand in front of the bow window. "Reading is social? I thought it was one of the final pleasures of life that required solitude for reflection. How can you concentrate on what you are reading with conversation all around you?"

"I shut out the intrusions, but process anything I think is worthwhile", said Rose as she reviewed her latest literary acquisitions.

Iris selected a pink carnation from her bouquet and passed it to Rose. "Papa and grandad loved flowers."

Accepting the carnation, Rose replied, "They also loved books, Iris, and that is why we have so many volumes in our library. These books will still be here long after our graves are sprouting bouquets for others to pick." Rose held up a beautiful leather bound copy of FLORAL DELIGHTS FROM SHAKESPEARE. "Thank you for the carnation, let me return the favour." She passed the copy to Iris. "The perfect book for you. If you turn to page 185, you'll discover this quotation from the bard's THE WINTER'S TALE:

The year growing ancient,
Not yet on summer's death, nor on the birth
Of trembling winter, the fairest flowers o'the season
Are our carnations, and streak'd gillyvors.

"Rose, you are remarkable, you always have a quotation at your command."

"It comes from years of experience." Suddenly she broke into laughter. "Actually, I was reading the book while watching you pick the carnations. I knew the quote might serve my purposes to advantage."

"And so it did, Rose. Papa always admired your scholarly interest. If you had been a boy, he would have sent you off to university. He knew you had great potential."

"Iris, he was afraid that I might learn the ways of the world from the academic community and leave his side forever."

"Rose, I think that is unkind! Papa was protective, but he wanted us to be happy."

"Yes, one big happy bouquet. Really, can you imagine anyone naming his four daughters after flowers, then calling them his bouquet?"

Iris stiffened her back to reply, "Papa was a rare individual who understood the world. He knew that we would flourish best under his guidance."

"We would bloom to reflect his likeness."

"Rose, you were always arguing with Papa. It never mattered what the subject was or who was present."

"I was the thorn in his bouquet."

"Yes, that may be, but despite the bandying of wills, you were his favourite. He knew your will matched his. He knew you were his intellectual equal. He knew..."

"Iris, he knew nothing of the sort. He favoured you, because you were the image of mother. You continued her legacy. You were the gardener. You and mother spent hours shaping the garden beds, pruning, arranging bouquets. Papa knew that as long as you lived, she would live. You were grace and poise; I was barbs and thorns. I could quote *The Bible*, you could live out that faith. Just before he died, he presented me with a copy of Wordsworth's poetry."

"You never mentioned that before."

"Oh, I thought I had. He reminded me that Wordsworth was England's nature poet, penning such lines as:"

Come forth into the light of things,
Let nature be your teacher.

"You and mother were so close to nature. I was always buried in books, his books. I believed that I could best know him if I read what he read, thought what he thought. But in the end, it was nature that won his heart."

"Rose, you are partly right. He loved nature, he loved his garden, but he equally loved his library. During the last snowstorm we had before his confinement to bed, he asked me to walk with him to the library. We spent three uninterrupted hours looking at his collection. He sat in his leather chair while I fetched each treasure for him to share with me. He told me that nature had created such beauty, but man's imagination was the greatest source of beauty. His library was his collection of the beauty spanning centuries, continents, nationalities, religions. He reminded me that mother had left us her garden, but he would leave us his library. Rose, you inherited his entire collection. That tells you something."

Rose who rarely displayed emotion, cleared her throat, smiled, then walked toward Iris, taking her hands in hers. "Thank you, Iris. Let me ask you one question."

Iris returned the affection of the moment by hugging Rose. "I was always the emotional one."

Rose released herself from their embrace. "And I the stoic. Iris, one quick question for you. What was Papa's favourite flower?"

Without hesitation, Iris replied, "The iris, of course!"

At that moment, Daisy and Rachel entered. Rachel carried a basket of mail. They realized they were intruding on a private moment.

Daisy apologized, "Are we interrupting your thoughts?"

Rose retorted, "You have and you are, but fear not, your timing was perfect. We were descending into sentimentality."

Iris smiled as she pronounced, "We shall rekindle the conversation at a later time."

Rose threw herself into her Queen Anne chair exclaiming, "Another basket of mail?"

Rachel smiled, "Forty letters today."

"Are they all fan letters?" asked Iris.

Rachel separated the letters into three piles. "There are thirty-six fan club letters, three employment rejections and…"

"And a letter from Nova Scotia, I presume,"declared Iris.

Rachel winked. "Yes, a letter from Connie's biggest fan. He never seems to get enough information."

Daisy looked at her sisters, "Information on what, whom?"

"Connie, of course", replied Rachel. "Oh, he does ask about all of us. It is interesting how we have begun to share family details with each other."

Rose brought the topic to a close. "It is good to have at least one sensible fan club member who has an interest in real people as well as cult glorification. Three rejections?"

Rachel picked up the three business envelopes. "The replies are so kind; they seem to be genuinely sorry that they do not have a secretarial position at this time. I had also suggested I would handle their bookkeeping duties as well, but they cannot afford extra help at the moment. I have had thirty-two rejections. I have nowhere else to apply."

Daisy motioned for everyone to find a seat. Daisy and Rachel sat on the window seat overlooking the garden. Iris sat on a Queen Anne chair facing Rose.

Daisy offered words of comfort to Rachel. "How many interviews have you had?"

Rachel indicated that she had had five formal interviews and three long conversations on the telephone.

Daisy who loved the theatre and was considered by her sisters to be an equal to Katherine Hepburn, rose to her feet. "Imagine you are in an office of a local business. I am the president of the company, this lady (pointing to Iris) is my partner and this lady (pointing to Rose) is my secretary."

Rose exclaimed, "Your secretary!"

Daisy raised her finger to her lips to curtail discussion. "Now Rachel, we are going to interview you."

Rachel giggled. "I don't need practice, there will be no more interviews."

Daisy continued, "Now, Miss Turner, we want you to feel comfortable. We have read your resume and checked your references. We know your aunts are outstanding individuals."

Iris laughed; Rose rolled her eyes.

Daisy recaptured everyone's attention by raising her voice. "Miss Turner, beyond the information contained in your file, what can you tell us that might cause us to give favourable consideration to your application?"

Rachel assumed the role of a confident, poised applicant. She blushed but began her interview. "I am pleased that you know my family background. Allow me to comment on that background. I will indicate the strengths that I have inherited. I possess the scholarly attributes of my Aunt Rose. I have her wit and ability to cut through formality, to get to the core of the issue. Like my Aunt Iris, I have learned patience, to nurture people as one would one's garden. I have inherited my Aunt Daisy's organizational abilities. Just as she can manage the household duties for 23 rooms, I can manage records, accounts, and secretarial routines."

Daisy asked, "Do you have experience as a secretary?"

Rachel responded immediately, "I manage a celebrity fan club with 600 members."

Daisy rose from the window seat, motioning for Rachel to stand. The remaining aunts quickly rose and approached Rachel. It was Daisy who made the announcement. "Miss Turner, we are delighted to engage you as our private secretary, bookkeeper and general manager of our household."

Rachel was unaware that she was in fact being offered a position. She extended the drama, by bowing. "Thank you, thank you. I know, don't call us, we'll call you."

Daisy realized that their proposal had not been clear enough. "Rachel, we are asking you to stay here with us, to work for us, to be our manager. Do you accept?"

Rachel was shocked. "But I can't work for you!"

Iris feigned agitation, "We're not that hard to get along with!"

Daisy took Rachel's right hand in hers. "We need you, we need to have a manager. James King, our trustee, has just indicated that he is retiring. We need to have someone who can manage our affairs. We have always trusted James, but we are hesitant to engage a younger member of his firm who is unknown to us."

Rose added. "You need a job, we have a job. It is that simple. You are qualified, and we know you can handle the responsibilities."

Iris hugged Rachel. "Help your aunts. We have already discussed this matter in detail with Mr. King. He will give you some help before he retires. He is confident that you can do it. Will you give it a try?"

Rachel was overwhelmed. "I want to say yes, but I don't want to disappoint you."

Rose brought the discussion to a close by assuring Rachel that the proposed arrangement was mutually beneficial to everyone. "Let us do the manly thing and shake hands to seal the agreement."

After shaking hands, Iris spoke to Rose. "The manly thing; what has shaking hands got to do with men? We have hands, haven't we?"

Rose continued speaking to Iris as they moved toward the French doors leading into the dining-room. Daisy and Rachel returned to their window seat. Daisy shared the details of Rachel's new position with her.

"I am overwhelmed, but most grateful. I'll do my very best. I think I might have to give up my fan club position."

"We have discussed that possibility. I think we have found a solution. Rose is interested in helping you with your duties."

"Rose! Oh, forgive me, but Rose has never indicated any real interest in the fan club. I don't think she knows who Connie Francis is."

"You're wrong! She told us she admires your ability to keep your membership happy. She has been reading copies of the fact sheets and newsletters that you send in the mail. She knows a great deal about Connie. In fact, she wrote to eight other fan clubs for information, using our mailbox in town to house the return mail. She is adamant that your club is the best one. Besides, she is interested in poetry and all these modern songs have interesting lyrics."

"Rose is interested in Connie Francis! Oh, it is so out of character. The lyrics from "Where the Boys Are" cannot possibly find accommodation in the same repertoire as Milton's *Paradise Lost*."

"They are different! Rose understands culture. She knows that each new generation expresses itself in different forms. She is not buried in the past."

"Oh, I didn't mean to imply that she was living in the past, but I never thought she was avant garde, either."

"Rose is a complex individual. The more you know her, the less you know her. I'm the simple one. I do the household chores."

"Don't underestimate your importance."

"Look, I have lived all my life with a father who was a successful business man, a mother who was the epitome of grace and poise, one sister who quotes classical literature, another sister who knows everything there is to know about gardening. What do I do? I do housechores. The only book I read is *The Bible* and I can only recognize five or six flowers by name."

Showing a maturity beyond her years, Rachel replied, "There are twenty-three rooms in this household. What would happen if the dusting were not done, if the meals were not prepared, if the laundry remained in the baskets?"

"I know the work must be done, but it is insignificant compared to their accomplishments. Father so valued Rose's intellectual ability and Iris's horticultural skills. He seemed oblivious to my contributions."

"You are correct. He did value your sisters' abilities, but he was fully aware of your considerable talents." Rachel rose quickly from the window seat requesting her aunt to remain seated. "Stay here, I will return in a moment."

She returned within a few minutes carrying an envelope. Opening the letter, she provided the following comments. "This letter was sent to me while I was on vacation in Maine." Before opening the envelope, she showed Daisy the return address. "This was the first letter I received from grandad after mum and dad were killed in that terrible accident. Let me read just one passage:"

"Rachel, no one can replace your mother and father.

None of us will try. My Lily is gone and so is her beloved husband. Lily was the peacemaker, the diplomat of the family. With just a few words, she could calm the household...We shall miss that influence. My bouquet will never be the same.

But the living flowers continue to bloom and to give us comfort. You have your grandparents for now, but my bouquet will continue to delight, comfort, guide you when we are no longer able to do so.

When you know your aunts better, you will come to understand how delicate they are, how resolute they are, and how gifted they are. You will come to appreciate the quick wit and the tender hand, but it will take you longer to discover the faithful one; the one who devotes herself to caring for the others. She cooks, she sews, she cleans, she loves."

Daisy began to cry as Rachel continued. Rachel consoled her by placing her left hand on hers. "Just a few lines more."

"The rose, the iris and lily are such distinctive flowers. They are prized for their beauty. They are cultivated at great cost. Ah, but the daisy grows unattended, unnoticed. The month flower of April is often dismissed as 'pretty', yet it adorns the hillside with its innocence and purity. It was the daisy that was included in Ophelia's garland in HAMLET. It was a flower to be valued. The more you learn of the daisy, the richer you will be. She is my steadfast delight! My home thrives because she devotes herself to the service of others. In serving, she

humbles all of us. She teaches us what the Master taught his disciples..."

Rachel returned the letter to its envelope, then with tears in her eyes she hugged Daisy. "Thank you for being here for all of us."

*** * * * * * * * * ***

Robert pensively closed Rachel's 1962 diary, tenderly returning it to the banker's box. He remembered his life in Northumbria during those early years of their correspondence. As 1962 drew to a close, he had awaited anxiously his return to studies after a year of working in the produce department of a supermarket. His first job had not been without its rewards. Although his weekly income was minimum wage, he was able to save enough money to ensure that he could enrol at the provincial teachers college for the fall term. He would qualify for a bursary and was eligible for a student loan. With his college financing secure, he had time to cultivate his interest in Connie, Rachel, and the bouquet. His happiness increased with each new recording released by Connie and with each letter from Rachel. The more he learned of these Americans, the more he came to treasure his own bouquet- his parents and the guests at the nursing home, the manor.

The most popular room in the manor was the sun porch. There was enough room for eight of the guests to relax in rocking chairs, wing chairs and other rather formal parlour chairs. Much of the furniture had come from the homes of the guests. It was eclectic style at its best. Robert was pleasantly surprised that none of the guests claimed a favourite chair. They always ventured to the empty seats nearest the window first. There seemed to be no territorial claims to sit in the chairs from their former homes or to claim any chair as their private domain. He had thought the elderly especially would be victims of practised and cherished routines. Of course, the guests surprised him in countless ways by their unexpected behaviour. But then again, his parents never ceased to surprise him as well.

The sun porch was delightful in all seasons. Robert liked to have one of the wing chairs envelope him during the first cool mornings of autumn. From the large picture windows, there was a view of his father's vegetable garden, his mother's flowers, and the magnificent oaks and white birches that adorned the edge of the driveway. The

manor was located on a corner lot; the sun porch provided a view of the two streets crossing each other as they funnelled their walkers and traffic past the dedicated viewers seated comfortably in their cozy observation room.

- - - - - Northumbria 1962

On this crisp autumn morning, Robert was enjoying the privacy of the moment to reread his latest newsletter from Rachel. He had just seen "Where the Boys Are" for the sixth time. It was great to see Connie starring in her own movie and to know that it was so popular at the box office. Rachel claimed that the movie would become a classic film for the college crowd who migrated annually to the southern climate for their spring break.

He was suddenly aware that he was not alone in the sun porch. Seated near him were Miss Brown and Gramma Horton. It was the sound of Mrs. Ford's cane that bridged his return to the sun porch from Florida, the setting of Connie's movie. Miss Brown, who had been a missionary in Africa, could quote THE BIBLE as eloquently as Rose; Gramma Horton had operated a nursery with her late husband. Their flower shop adjoining the nursery was still the most popular place in Northumbria to purchase fresh flowers and plants. Mrs. Ford's memory was in decline; she could, however, recall her past days as a school teacher and mother of three. She remembered fondly her beloved husband Alfred, but the recent past was never clear.

Robert had always been fascinated by the names that came to be used for the guests at the manor. Some were called by their last names as a means of respect, yet others inherited terms of affection such as gramma or aunt; a very few were addressed by their first names.

He had become increasingly aware of the similarities between the manor guests and Rachel's aunts. Her aunts' traits seemed to be dispersed among the manor guests. Perhaps that is why the bond that was growing between him and Rachel was so strong. They could easily identify with each other's home environment.

Mrs. Ford was standing near the doorway leading to the outside. As always, she was holding her cane as an ornament rather than a support for her trim straight figure. She knew she was supposed to carry the accessory but she dismissed its practicality. She always wore a hat when taking her walks, and sometimes through neglect, the hat was worn for hours in the sun porch or even within the privacy of her bedroom. On this occasion, she was wearing two dresses and a sweater. As she put on her second white glove, she spoke to Miss Brown.

"Have you met this lady, previously?" pointing to Gramma Horton.

Winking at Robert, Miss Brown replied, "We've not been formally introduced."

Gramma Horton giggled, "Perhaps you could introduce us."

Mrs. Ford stiffened her frame as she replied, "It would be a great pleasure to introduce you to each other, but I am about to go for a walk and I shall leave the pleasure of introductions to this young gentleman." Without a further word, she stepped out into the cool morning air.

Gramma giggled again. "I knew she would get out of the situation. She always does. I admire her ability to disguise her memory loss. It must come from years of working with students. I always thought teachers were great impostors!"

Robert came to the defence of teachers. "I think it is wrong to call teachers 'impostors'," he exclaimed before he realized he had taken her clever bait.

Miss Brown reminded everyone that Jesus was the Master teacher and hardly an impostor. "Remember that Jesus spent his active ministry in the role of a teacher. It is a noble profession."

Gramma, who greatly admired Miss Brown, but delighted in teasing everyone, replied, "Oh, the Lord was a master teacher to be sure, however, his disciples throughout the centuries have not all been faultless. Besides, are there not times when teachers pretend? What about drama?"

Miss Brown, who had grown fond of Gramma and who realized Gramma's gift for good humour, replied. "I see what you mean."

Gramma continued, "And I find teachers to be the most accomplished impostors!"

Robert who now realized he was the target of their game replied, "The famous deceivers have traditionally been females. Have you forgotten Delilah, Jezebel or Cleopatra?"

Miss Brown was quick to reply, "And let us not forget Judas Iscariot, Iago from THE MERCHANT OF VENICE and..."

"Touche!" conceded Robert. "I surrender."

Gramma drew everyone's attention to the window overlooking the vegetable garden. "I see your father is already in his garden. Is there a garden anywhere that receives so much care and attention? I love the raised framed beds and the narrow walkways."

Miss Brown added, "Very typical of European gardens, isn't it?"

"Father loves his garden, it seems to be his one final interest. He enjoys working the ground and has come to respect the earth for its ability to bring forth life..."

Bertha, Robert's mother entered the sun porch with an afghan for Miss Brown. "You may want this for your shoulders."

"Thank you, I was getting a little chilly." She leaned forward to receive the afghan.

Bertha looked through the window panes at the vegetable garden. "Wait, what is he doing?" Knocking on the window, she raised her voice, "Stay away from my flower beds."

Robert came to his father's rescue, "I'm sure he knows his boundaries!"

"I'm sure he doesn't. Yesterday while preparing the beds for the winter, he decided to extend his carrot patch at the expense of my bleeding hearts. I found my plants in the garbage container at the back of the garage. My bleeding hearts!"

Miss Brown asked quietly, "Could he have mistaken them for a weed?"

"A weed, never! He wants to get rid of my flowers to plant more vegetables." She moved toward the doorway. "I'll settle this." The outside door slammed shut as she made her brisk exit, moving toward the garden.

Robert confessed, "I love it when they show their Belgian tempers. Look at the hands flying."

Gramma responded, "I expect you would prefer that the plants receive the focus of their anger rather than yourself."

"You bet I would."

Miss Brown turned her attention from the window to Robert. "How old is your father?"

"He is 70, twenty years older than my mother."

Miss Brown, who appeared to be surprised at this disclosure, added, "He is so fit for his age."

Gramma sighed, "He is only five years younger than I am. And here I am spending my days in a rocking chair watching the world go by."

"Yes, but he hasn't had two heart attacks to slow his pace," Miss Brown reminded Gramma. "And let us pray that he will continue to enjoy his garden, even if he does pull up an occasional flower."

Robert looked affectionately at the two ladies, then back at the continuing battle outside. "I can't tell who is winning."

Miss Brown announced with assurance, "I don't think there is a loser, so there could hardly be a winner."

"Perhaps you are right, " acknowledged Robert.

At this point, Mrs. Ford returned from her brief walk. As she entered the sun porch, she meticulously removed her gloves, placing them on a table near the doorway. She placed her cane on the back of a chair and sat with her usual dignity in a wing chair. The hat remained untouched on her head. "It was a pleasant walk, but there are two people quarrelling outside. I couldn't make out what they were saying. French, I think. Serious business, though. Hands were flying. Is it the gardener and the cook?"

Miss Brown smiled, "Yes, the gardener and the cook. Just a mild disagreement. Don't worry about it."

Mrs. Ford drifted away in her thoughts to her days with Alfred while the others continued their discussion.

Gramma inquired, "Who is the new guest in the room off the dining-room?"

Robert confirmed that it was Mrs. Henderson who was 87 and very senile. She assumed she was still at home with her own parents as well as her daughter-in-law, Ester. She was continually calling out to Ester in language that was somewhat coarse for the gentler folks at the manor.

Gramma chuckled as she recalled the morning's conversation heard in the dining-room. "Mrs. Henderson has an extensive vocabulary."

Miss Brown added, "She does use interesting metaphors."

Robert recalled her favourite expressions: "Get here before the turkey chews tobacco," "As slow as molasses" and "No rude noises in public."

As if on cue, the sun porch conversation was interrupted by Mrs. Henderson's latest declarations: "Ester, get off your fat arse and help me. I suppose you're sitting in the kitchen smoking and drinking tea. I want to go home to visit my mother, so get in here to help me. And don't get your bloomers in a twist. What was that noise? No farting in public."

Miss Brown blushed as she reacted to Mrs. Henderson's expletives, "Robert, you were so considerate to substitute the euphemism 'rude noises' for Mrs. Henderson's coarser language."

With a twinkle in her eye, Gramma responded, "You have to admit her language is descriptive."

Robert enjoyed these times with his foster grandparents. He had never known his own grandparents and even though his father was now in his seventies, he had never thought of him as being near the age of the guests. He loved to listen to their stories of the past and yet see them so interested in the present. Like all families, they were protective of each other and quite often took time to allow newcomers to become fully accepted members of their fraternity. Mrs. Henderson would, however, continue to be the outsider for as long as she remained at the manor. They could enjoy her outrageous comments on occasion, but they could not consider her their equal. Her language separated her from them; they regarded it as language of choice rather than inheritance.

Miss Brown broke the silence that had bred itself since Mrs. Henderson's latest outburst. "Robert, I see you were reading your latest newsletter. What is happening with your singer friend?"

Robert delighted in sharing news of Connie, so he replied enthusiastically, "Connie has eight gold records now that "Where the Boys Are" has topped the charts. She has been named "Best Singer of the Year" by "American Bandstand" and she has recorded songs in eight languages."

Gramma questioned, "Is she married?"

"Not yet but the fan magazines say she and Bobby Darin are a twosome."

Gramma teased Robert further, "Perhaps there is still a chance for you."

Miss Brown imitating Gramma's intonation, "Maybe your affections should be directed to that young lady who looks after the fan club."

Robert laughed heartily, "We are just friends." He was somewhat surprised to hear himself use the term 'friend' in reference to his relationship with Rachel. In many ways he was closer to her than he was to any of his peers in Northumbria. Perhaps his friend, Leah, was an exception. He had always known Leah and if it weren't for her older brother, Trevor, they might be closer friends. Trevor had always disliked Robert and that dislike increased with the years. Trevor was an athlete who liked to work out with weights. He literally enjoyed throwing his weight around. Robert had borne the brunt of numerous challenges offered to him by Trevor, most of them in front of Leah.

Gramma picked up Robert's latest scrapbook and began leafing through the pages. "You certainly are faithful to put the clippings and photos in your scrapbooks. How many books do you have?"

"This is my third one."

"I don't think you should keep them in that cabinet." Miss Brown pointed to a corner cabinet that contained a variety of picture books and cherished curios. "Someone might remove them without knowing their real value."

"Oh, I'm sure they are safe. Unless the new guest proves to be a kleptomaniac."

The two ladies exclaimed, "The new guest!"

Gramma inquired, "You mean Mrs. Henderson?"

"No, we will soon have an elderly gentleman join us."

"How elderly?" asked Miss Brown.

"I think he is 76."

"You call 76 elderly?" asked Gramma.

"No, I mean, he is..."

"Too late, the damage is done, but we will accept your apology," teased Miss Brown.

Gramma wanted to know more about this mysterious guest.

"There is nothing mysterious about Mr. Gordon. He was a farmer, evidently quite an athlete in his day. He has a reputation as a ladies man and a gifted raconteur."

Gramma assured Robert that Mr. Gordon would be in safe hands with them. Robert realized that he had not heard any excitement from the garden within the last few minutes. Both his parents were originally from Charleroi, Belgium. The language they spoke was Walloon rather than Flemish that characterized the section of Belgium influenced by Germany. The Walloons were definitely French in language and mannerisms.

The Belgian community was overshadowed by the Scottish and English dominance in the coal mining town of Northumbria. Although they remained a close knit subculture, they were anxious for their children to be an integral part of the community. The children were encouraged to speak English at home, although the parents tended to speak to each other in their native dialect.

Robert had learned quickly that it was important to know what his parents were saying to each other, but he never considered speaking to his parents in their inherited language. He would later come to regret his failure to acquire the benefits of an extra spoken language.

* * * * * * * * * * *

Robert paused for a brief moment as he looked further into the banker's box of memories. He lovingly removed an envelope of photos. Here was the first photo he had received of Rachel and it was the first non-professional photo he had of Connie. Rachel had placed a copy of the photo in her newsletter to all of her club members. A friend of hers had taken a photo of Rachel talking to Connie after a star studded concert in New York. Robert was thrilled to receive a "real" photo of Connie, and had placed it immediately in a frame that adorned his dresser. He was also elated to have a photo of his new friend, Rachel. Rachel looked so tall in the photo. Of course her five foot eight frame did tower above Connie's five foot one. They both looked slim in their formal gowns. Both had dark hair, sparkling eyes and radiant smiles. Connie's hair was much longer and more flamboyant than Rachel's rather cropped pageboy look. In the ensuing years, he would come to treasure the gold framed photo that contained the two inspirations of his life. He carefully placed the photo on his desk and then returned to the contents of the envelope.

He was surprised to find within its contents a fan club letter and a personal letter from Rachel from the summer of 1963. He had not remembered placing these in the banker's box containing his most prized treasures. Before exiling them to another box, he glanced at the contents.

Rachel's newsletter contained a number of quotes from Connie:

"Life for me will begin at 40—a true private life, that is. Since I have set a retirement date, I'm in a greater hurry than the usual performer, because I want to squeeze as many new experiences as possible, before I bid adieu to the only way of life I've known since early childhood."

Robert vividly recalled his reaction to that quotation. Connie was 25 at the time. He felt a bit uneasy that in 15 years his star would fade from the spotlight, that new recordings would not be produced and fan clubs would obviously fade away. And yet he wanted not to be selfish; he wanted his star to enjoy herself, to find happiness in privacy, to be a 'real' person. After all, he had fifteen years to prepare for the retirement. Rachel had enjoyed his reflections on Connie's proposed retirement date. She was convinced that fifteen years might well produce circumstances that would alter that farewell to performing. Many other stars had notified the public of their retirements only to be wooed back to the stage or recording studio.

Robert appreciated Rachel's objectivity. She certainly had a head for details, a steel-trap mind! It was her business sense that proved a valuable asset as she assumed responsibilities as business manager for the bouquet. She presented Robert with a detailed account of her first meeting with James King when she was briefed on her aunts' portfolio. Nothing could have prepared her for the disclosures of that first meeting.

- - - - - Flanders Cove, 1963

Mr. King was a gentleman of the old order. He was soft-spoken and gracious. He was always impeccably dressed in a three piece suit; the gold chain of his pocket watch hung loosely across his vest. His silver hair and erect figure were striking features that one noticed immediately after being put at ease by his warm smile. Rachel liked him immediately. She knew that by reputation he was a man of integrity and compassion and as a host, he was obviously warm and amiable.

He had served as financial consultant for Rachel's grandfather since 1925. Her grandfather's will gave specific powers to Mr. King to handle the estate and its trusts. In 1925 the portfolio encompassed factories, warehouses, lumber mills and shipping companies. The home property included 500 acres of prime real-estate with shore frontage, forests, ponds and rivers, orchards, formal gardens and a twenty-three room mansion with stables, garages, a greenhouse and a guest house. The mansion was separated from the main road by a six foot stone wall that required constant attention to keep it from falling onto the roadway.

Rachel was aware that over the years her grandfather had sold his companies as he prepared for retirement. She also knew that the home property had gradually been reduced in size. She had wrongly assumed that these reductions were precipitated by a desire to be free from business responsibilities. She could not have known that her grandfather had fallen into financial difficulties, and that his salvation came from divesting of his business enterprises, and that slowly his own private property had to be divided into lots to satisfy creditors. Mr. King was given the authority to continue to sell portions of the estate as required to allow the aunts to live in the style to which they had grown accustomed. Mr. King was forbiddden to tell the aunts the true nature of their financial status. He was relieved to have a member of the family take over his responsibilities and to share with that person the declining value of the portfolio that he had managed.

The original estate had been reduced to 200 acres, all of which continued to escalate in value as city dwellers moved to the suburbs to build their summer and retirement homes. Flanders Cove was becoming one of the most exclusive areas in which to build executive homes on Connecticut's shoreline.

Mr. King and Rachel sat at a round table in his office as they examined the numerous documents that comprised the portfolio. Mr. King calmed Rachel after his initial disclosures saying: "I remind you that 200 acres is a large property. Most of the other estates do not exceed 10 or 20 acres. The aunts could not possibly notice the estate shrinking because the new lots are not visible from the main road and they never explore the sideroads nor the shoreline beyond their own beach area. There is sufficient land left to keep them comfortable as long as they live. You will need to get the best dollar for any land you sell while protecting the knowledge of the shrinking estate from your aunts. It is a delicate responsibility. Rose is more likely than the others to question you."

Rachel looked somewhat helplessly at Mr. King, "But I do not think I could actually lie to them."

Mr. King took her right hand in his and spoke affectionately, "It will be a sin of omission rather than commission. Your goal will be to enable your aunts to feel secure; it was your grandfather's wish that they live comfortably and in a protective environment. In many ways they are well aware of the world and its modern ways, but this knowledge is gained through reading rather than experiencing. They rarely come to town except to church and to shop. They are known in the community, but are not of it. They lead their own sheltered lives much the same as they did when your grandfather was with them."

Rachel responded, "I cannot believe that my grandfather did not share his financial arrangements with at least one of them."

Mr. King acknowledged, "He did share the entire portfolio with one of the sisters, here in this very office."

"But you said grandfather did not share the secret with the three aunts."

"That's correct. But there was a fourth aunt, your mother."

"Mother knew?!"

"Yes, your grandfather called her his diplomat and financial equal. It was your mother who once mentioned that one day you might help to manage the estate. It was on the basis of that discussion that I suggested to your aunts that they consider you as my replacement."

"I'm speechless. I am so thankful that you have shared all of this with me. I am daunted at the prospect of assuming the tasks that you have performed so faithfully and efficiently for so long."

"You will do what is best for the aunts. You understand the treasure which you are to protect. You know the legacy you have inherited and you have business sense. I checked with the college you attended and you were at the top of your class. Besides, you are running a very efficient fan club. Rose gives you straight A's!"

Rachel was intrigued by the thoroughness of the man who sat across from her. She absorbed his confidence in her. If he could trust her, she could trust herself! She looked affectionately at her advisor, "With your help, I will certainly try to do my best!"

Mr. King concluded the discussion saying, "Rachel, your aunts are fortunate to have you with them. I have one other disclosure that I want to share with you later, it is not a financial matter. However, I think you have enough to keep you occupied for the time being."

As Rachel departed from the reassuring smile, she felt a growing uneasiness about her ability to manage the estate in secrecy. She hesitated in her car, gathering her resolution before entering the house to meet the aunts who would probably expect a detailed account of her meeting with Mr. King. But she had forgotten the code of the household. Each person had an area of responsibility; it was enshrined with respect and confidence. No one questioned the delivery of the responsibilities.

Rachel was greeted enthusiastically by the aunts whose main goal was not to question her but to reassure her that they were relieved to have her as their business manager. She need not have feared maintaining secrecy; the aunts expected it. Their father and Mr. King had never taken them into their confidence; they expected the same from Rachel. Rose might be her only obstacle.

Once Rachel had retreated to her room, she sighed with relief and quickly replayed the afternoon's discussion in her mind. She carefully placed the portfolio materials in a strong box located in her desk. She locked the container and placed the key in a dresser drawer. It was only then that she recalled Mr. King's last comment: "I have one other disclosure that I want to share with you later, it is not a financial matter. However, I think you have enough to keep you occupied for the time being."

What did he mean? What disclosure could remain? Was it from her grandfather? If it did not relate to finances, what was the nature of this disclosure? She began to examine the possibilities until she was interrupted by Rose. For a brief moment, she feared that Rose had come to pry information from her. She welcomed Rose with a slight uneasiness.

Rose inquired, "I hope I am not preventing you from resting."

Rachel motioned for Rose to sit in one of two wing chairs near the window while she slowly sank into the other. With a faint smile she confided, "No, I was just reflecting on my meeting with Mr. King. I hope I shall be able to perform my duties."

"Of course, you will. Do you have any specific concerns about the portfolio?"

Rachel wondered if Rose knew more than Mr. King had assumed about her father's estate, but she was on guard not to betray a trust that had been given to her a mere two hours previously. "I guess all new tasks are daunting, but I'll spend some time reviewing the portfolios, make a list of questions and then meet with Mr. King to obtain further clarifications."

"If I can help, I'm here, don't hesitate to ask for assistance."

Rachel suddenly realized that Rose had not come to talk about her meeting with Mr. King. She seemed to have the wistful appearance that she often displayed when buried in her literature studies. Rachel hesitantly asked, "Is there something I can help you with, Rose?"

Rose retorted, "I don't think so, I just wanted to know how you were reacting to your initial meeting with James King. I..." She drifted into her own thoughts, forgetting for a brief moment the person she was addressing.

Rachel noticed Rose looking rather unsettled. She attempted to restore Rose's comfort. "I notice you have a leather bound book in your hand. Is it your diary?"

Rose continued in her own thoughts until Rachel touched her left hand. Rachel repeated her question.

Rose looked awkwardly at the book in her hand. "Oh, the diary! No, it is not...It is the type of book that all three of us use to record our exciting lives. I'm not sure why we all keep diaries. Perhaps we need to clarify for ourselves the events of each day. Perhaps it helps to return to these notes to recall the thoughts and feelings that shaped who we have become. Why am I rambling about diaries? This is a diary book, but the contents..."

Rachel looked at her aunt who was normally so definite, so self-assured and wondered why Rose appeared so uneasy at this moment. She knew that the solution lay within the contents of the book her aunt was holding. Trying to lighten the conversation and to appeal to Rose's wit, she questioned, " Is the book you are holding blank or filled with notations? Is it untouched by human script or filled with secret thoughts?"

Rose smiled as she began to relax, "It is not blank!"

"Ah, then it has notations."

"It has notations!"

Rachel leaned toward Rose, whispering, "Are the notations a secret?"

Rose leaned toward Rachel, whispering, "Yes!"

Both women laughed at the dramatic intensity of their charade. Rachel asked the inevitable, "Do you want to talk about those notations?"

Rose hesitated, then nodded in agreement. "Everyone in the household knows that I keep a diary and everyone knows I enjoy literature. They do not, however, know what I keep in this book. Nor do I want anyone to know."

At this very intimate moment, Daisy entered the room with a vase of fresh flowers. She realized that she was intruding and attempted to retreat as quickly as she could. "Iris arranged some flowers for your room. I'll leave you two to solve the problems of the world." As she started to leave the room, she noticed Rose was holding a diary book. "Rose, are you reading excerpts from your diary?"

Rose retorted, "No secrets here!" She rose from her chair and without further ceremony removed herself from the lost intimacy.

Daisy searched Rachel's face for a glimpse of revelation. "I am sorry if I interrupted a private moment."

"We were just talking about diaries and their value."

Daisy moved to assume Rose's seat. "I have kept a diary since I was twelve."

"What do you see as the value of diaries?"

"They are a storehouse, a treasury of thoughts and feelings that form character. I am a product of the notations in my diary. I can be honest with myself when I record my reactions to each day's events. Sometimes, I discover truths that surprise me. My diary is my companion."

Rachel confessed, "I guess I am too new at diary keeping, I rarely reread anything I have written."

"That comes with age. One day you will return to those notes. One day your memory will need to be refreshed. Diaries enhance memory, they enrich it with forgotten details. They recall reactions that have long been forgotten. Feelings recorded are feelings that will endure! We learn through recording. It helps me to decide what is important, what is worth remembering."

Rachel was pleasantly surprised to find herself engaged in this discussion with Daisy. She seized the moment to ask Daisy about the type of notations placed in her diary. "What topics seem to dominate your entries?"

"After I had kept a diary for over twenty years, I discovered that many entries dealt with my experience with reading *The Bible*, worship and church in general. As a result, I began keeping two types of diaries. One for faith-related experiences and one for everything else."

Rachel had not previously been aware of Daisy's dual diaries. She continued her inquiry. "Do your sisters know that you keep two sets of diaries?"

"Oh, yes, but no one except Lily..." She paused to reflect upon her audience before revealing her literary secret. "No one knows that I have extended my faith diaries into story form."

"Story form, you are writing short stories?"

"I don't think they are so much a series of short stories as they are memoirs in extended prose."

"A novel?"

"No, an extended story, I guess Rose would call it an autobiographical faith journey or something more trivial than that."

"I think Rose would be amazed to discover that you are venturing into authorship beyond personalized diary entries."

"No, she would be amused to think that I would assume that I could pen feelings and thoughts into anything beyond mundane diary entries."

"Forget about Rose, I think it is wonderful! What do you hope to do with your 'story'?"

"I know my limitations as an author. I have not read widely as Rose has. I do not have her extensive vocabulary, but I am confident that my reactions to my journey in faith might be of interest to others who share the same journey."

"I am sure that many individuals would like to know that they are not alone as they try to make sense of faith in changing times. Is your story primarily about Episcopalians or is it broader in scope?"

"My denomination shapes my experiences, but my reactions are hopefully of a more general nature."

The aunts never ceased to amaze Rachel. Daisy, the house manager was also Daisy, the author. Rose was the biblical scholar who claimed that Daisy was the one who lived out the faith. Daisy was the only member of the family who ever became involved in community life with her position in church government. She was very progressive in her views, revealing a genuine interest in the new translations, new music and new liturgies. Rose was anti-establishment, but Daisy was proactive in helping the establishment to return to its roots, to find a more meaningful form of worship. Rachel would learn a great deal about faith and be led to a fuller faith because of Daisy. At the moment, Rachel was overwhelmed by the events of the day. She needed to reflect upon the financial situation of the bouquet, Rose's diary and the budding author.

Daisy sensed that Rachel required space to be quiet. "Please don't mention my book to the family."

Rachel reassured her that her secret was safe, "Our secret. You'll have to come up with a name for your writing."

"I already have one. I call it, *With Love, With God.*" With that pronouncement, she quietly left Rachel's room.

****

Robert gingerly returned Rachel's letter to its envelope. As he placed the envelope in the banker's box, he retrieved one of his many diaries. His 1964 diary contained such vivid descriptions of his homelife, his first year at college, his growing relationship with Rachel and his involvement with Leah. He turned to a summer entry that recalled his continued fascination with Connie's career.

Rachel's latest newsletter listed the most recent hits by their star: "In the Summer of His Years" (a tribute to the slain President Kennedy), "My Buddy", "Blue Winter", "Be Anything but Be Mine" and the theme song from her latest movie, "Looking for Love". He was so anxious to see Connie in her latest movie.

The lyrics of Connie's songs had always haunted his thoughts. Each song provided a milestone in his journey with others. He was now 20 years old, enrolled in a two year program at the provincial teachers college. His friend, Leah, had also enrolled in the same program; this helped to strengthen their relationship. The teachers college was approximately 100 miles from Northumbria so that he and Leah were able to pursue their friendship without intrusion from Leah's brother, Trevor, who continued to bully Robert at every possible encounter.

Leah was a strong mathematics and science student; Robert's strengths lay in the arts. They made great studying companions, venturing to the college library most evenings. They travelled home by train or bus each weekend.

- - - - - Northumbria, 1964

It was during one of these late spring weekends that Robert found himself carried away in thought as he listened to "Looking for Love". He counted himself fortunate to have loving parents and such a large extended family. Rachel and her bouquet had become so much a part of the fabric of his life. He enjoyed his studies and he had become fond of Leah as they struggled with lesson plans, practice teaching and academics. He and Leah never dated although they did spend many hours together. On occasion, Leah dated another student, Big Al, as he called himself. Big Al was big in size and voice. He reminded Robert of Trevor; consequently they were not friends. He could never understand what Leah saw in Al, but he respected her right to select her own friends and was glad she was dating. He had, of course, considered asking Leah for a date, but he did not want to jeopardize their bond of friendship. He was not ready to go looking for love, but he was beginning to realize that there would be life beyond studies.

His thoughts were suddenly broken by Mr. Gordon's entrance to the porch. Gramma Horton and Miss Brown gave Mr. Gordon an enthusiastic welcome. Mr. Gordon had been with them for nearly a year. He came just after the sudden death of Mrs. Henderson who had passed away in her sleep. Her expletives no longer echoed within the walls of the duplex. Mr. Gordon had been a successful farmer and an athlete of local fame. He was also an historian and raconteur. He delighted the other guests with his tales of farm life, baseball, hockey and the early settlers.

Once a month, students from the nearby elementary school would visit the manor, bringing the guests treats and samples of their projects. Story time was always a delight. Mr. Gordon was the main attraction! He knew how to captivate an audience. With gestures and voice changes, he would mesmerize the children. Miss Brown and Gramma Horton were often fellow conspirators in his yarns. The truth might on occasion be stretched, but the audience was invariably satisfied.

Within a few moments, the sun porch was filled with seniors and elementary students. The children had shared a class story with the seniors, then it was the seniors' turn to entertain. Mr. Gordon was the featured storyteller. He asked the students if they knew when Northumbria became a town. "When was Northumbria incorporated?"

One student asked, "What does incorporated mean?"

Miss Brown came to the rescue, "Incorporated means when the town was born, when it became a town." That seemed to satisfy the inquisitor.

Some student guessed the town to be 50 years old, others 300 and even 1000. Mr. Gordon informed them that the town was born in 1884; in twenty years it would celebrate its centennial.

"You will all be about thirty years of age when the town is 100."

"Thirty! That seems so old!! responded a blond girl with pony tails. "My father is 35, so I will be awfully old when we celebrate our centennial. My father is real old."

Miss Brown winked at Gramma Horton. Gramma added her commentary to the discussion. "I'm looking forward to being 39 for a long time, even if it is old."

Another student asked Gramma, "Are you over 39?"

Gramma smiled, "Just by a few years."

Mr. Gordon coughed to bring the focus back to his story. "Over the years, many local historians have written about our town. They all tell of a town born on one of the richest seams of coal in the world, a town of smiles and tears. One dark, bitterly cold night in February, two elderly settlers were walking down a deserted road near the first coal mine in our district." He used his hands to draw the children into the story. The seniors leaned forward in their chairs; the students, many of whom were seated on the floor, moved closer to the storyteller.

"The two settlers were struggling on foot with the snow blowing in their faces. They became confused when they came to a fork in the road. Which path would lead them to a friendly home where they could find shelter til morning? Which path would lead them to the next town, an hour's walk in the blinding storm where they would face its full blast in open country. They couldn't decide. The storm intensified, yet they could not stay where they were. They prayed. They shouted. But the cold continued to dull their senses. Their skin began to throb."

"Just when they had decided to take the wider road, they noticed a faint light coming toward them. Someone was carrying a lamp. He drew near, then suddenly turned back in the opposite direction. They ran after him, but he remained well in front of them. They ran faster until suddenly they saw a house on the left, just behind a stand of fir trees. The figure in front of them was blurred by the snow. They ran up the lane to the house. Here they found shelter, a warm fire to greet them and spirits to warm their innards. They mentioned the strange figure with the lamp."

"The owner's son went to search for the person, to invite him to share their cozy nest and to thank him for helping the strangers find shelter from the storm. When he returned, he had a strange tale to tell."

"Shall I finish the story later?"

The children responded in enthusiastic unison, "No, now!"

"As you wish," said Mr. Gordon. "When the young man returned, he said he could find no trace of the man. There were no footprints. There were no footprints in the snow! During the young man's investigation, Sam MacGregor, the nearest neighbour came down the road in his horse drawn sled. He had seen no one on the road. Who was this stranger? Was it the ghost of Northumbria? Suddenly, the sound of the raging wind interrupted their conversation, followed by a loud haunting noise. Someone was knocking at the door."

At this appropriate moment, a loud knocking could be heard on the manor door. The children moved closer to their storyteller.

"Ah, is that the ghost knocking on the door to join us?"

Miss Brown went cautiously to the door, slowly pushing the curtains on the window panes aside. She peered outside. "No one here!"

The knocking occurred again, then faded. The children had not noticed that Gramma Horton had left the room. Mrs. Ford's cane often came to the rescue!

****

Robert delighted in the affection shared by the seniors and children. When storytellers get together, there is no age barrier.

His reflections were broken by the ringing of the telephone; the first intrusion of his privacy on this remarkable December 12. She was on the phone. She wanted to hear his voice. She, too, had spent the morning thinking about the bouquet and the life of Northumbria.

Robert thought of the secure life he had lived in Northumbria once his mother had opened the manor. His life had been filled with time to enjoy the people who shared his life. He studied, he wrote letters, he listened to Connie. It was a life devoid of the insecurity that had plagued his early years, with the threat of mine disasters and the financial uncertainly of the household. The early 60's were an idyllic time for him. As he read and reread Connie's book, FOR EVERY YOUNG HEART, he basked in the knowledge that his life was free from many of the concerns raised in the book. That was before the events of 1965! Just as his mother's New Year's announcement had so dramatically changed his life; the announcement from his friend would turn his life upside down, delay chosen paths, and provide him with a relentless foe. "My Happiness" was about to be shattered!

Chapter 2:

Everybody's Somebody's Fool

After talking to Rachel on the phone, Robert ground coffee beans to make a fresh pot of his favourite blend. With his mug resting beside him at his desk, he sat down to resume basking in the memories of the life they shared; separated by an international border, home responsibilities, and decisions that were thrust upon them.

Robert returned to his prized banker's box. This time he withdrew Rachel's 1965 diary; the diary that revealed the passion of the bouquet and Rachel's stewardship as a business manager.

- - - - - Flanders Cove, 1965

Rachel's 1965 diary noted her increasing role as confidant for each flower of the bouquet. Once Daisy had shared her secret writing with Rachel, they spent many afternoons discussing excerpts from Daisy's journey in faith.

Daisy stood in the doorway to Rachel's room, her five foot six frame blocking the light that streamed through the stained glass window at the top of the central staircase. The window featured a spring garden with flowers, shrubs and trees. Her grandfather had commissioned the window so that the garden would be with them throughout the long winter months. Although tulips, daffodils and other flowers were carefully etched in glass, the featured bouquet of violets, irises, lilies, roses and daisies adorned the large urn dominating the centre pane of the window.

Henry Thomas' beloved wife, Violet, was forever in his sight as he left his bedroom each morning to begin a new day. The window was his inspiration to survive without the influence that had dominated his personal and professional life. Her gentle manner had caused him to be more benevolent, more understanding and more patient than he might have been. The window was illuminated from the outside, so that after dusk the hallway was lit with a very different view of the artistry of the glass craftsmen and the flowers of endearment. Rachel's grandfather bade adieu to his bouquet each evening as he glanced at the stained glass window before entering his room; it was a ritual from which he never wavered. He privately confessed to Violet that her presence was still with the family, she was not forgotten and she was ever in their thoughts and hearts. It was not the confession of the rather ruthless businessman she had married so many years before.

The window occupied the two floors of the staircase, with a window seat at its base on the first floor. Bookcases flanked both sides of the window. Fresh flowers in season were kept on the shelves near the gardening books. Iris had inherited her mother's vast collection of gardening books; these treasures had never been a part of the more scholarly collection that were housed in her grandfather's library.

This was a shrine, dedicated to the memory of the bouquet, to flowers and books; the prized possessions of the household. The family crest was placed in the centre of the garden wall that stretched across the garden scene; the wall was not unlike the one that separated the mansion from the world. The window dominated the house, inside and out, night and day, season upon season.

Rachel was seated at her desk, looking at a photo that Robert had enclosed in a recent letter. The photo featured Robert and Leah; it had been taken during the Easter break from classes. Bertha had captured the two students doing research for a class project. Rachel noted how petite Leah looked with her long blonde hair hanging over her shoulders. Leah was definitely an attractive young woman. Rachel wondered why Robert had never mustered the courage to ask her for a date.

As Rachel studied the picture, she became disquieted. She sensed a growing anxiety within her. She wondered why she should feel such emotion. She was glad that Robert had a close friend. She dismissed the notion that she might be somewhat envious of Leah who shared Robert in a more intimate manner than mere correspondence. And yet his letters were her lifeline. He was becoming her confidant. She picked up the photo once again. Leah was so beautiful! Those blue eyes, that smile...But her imagination allowed itself to search beyond the surface of the glossy paper; Leah had a loneliness about her. Rachel saw it as she searched beyond the smiles.

"That must be an interesting photo, Rachel," whispered Daisy from the doorway.

Rachel glanced toward the doorway, her face betraying her mood. "Oh, just a photo from Robert."

Daisy moved toward Rachel, taking the photo in her right hand. "Robert and his friend, a recent photo, I assume. He must be six feet tall?"

"Yes, I received it yesterday. They were on Easter break."

Daisy noted, "Working on an assignment during their recess. Now that is dedication."

"They are lucky to have each other...to be able to study together."

Daisy discreetly studied Rachel's face searching for a confirmation on her appraisal of the relationship that appeared to be growing between Robert and her niece. "Are they just friends?"

"Oh, yes, they have never dated. Robert used to claim that Leah's brother prevented them from having a close friendship when they lived in Northumbria, but even with two years at teachers college, they seem to be just close friends."

"She is beautiful, isn't she?"

"Yes, very."

"But I see something in her eyes, they..."

"I know what you mean, I sensed it, too." Rachel was surprised to have Daisy confirm her assessment of Leah. She did not want, however, to pursue the matter further so she motioned for Daisy to sit near the window. She joined her in the other wing chair.

"What's the newest entry in, *With Love, With God*?"

Daisy opened her secret diary, "Do you have time?"

"I have nothing to do until my three o'clock appointment with Mr. King. Today is our final meeting. As you know he's been semi-retired for the last six months, this is his final week in the office and I do want to deliver his gift."

"I won't keep you too long, but I wanted to share my thoughts on our farewell party for our rector. He is leaving us after five brief years. But in those years, he has done so much to help us grow in faith. His influence is the focus of my latest chapter, entitled, "The Good Shepherd". Our church places so much importance on the rector's leadership, each follows in the apostolic hierarchy. This man has been a modern saint. His successor has such a rich foundation to build upon.

I've tried to capture his influence on our lives objectively, but my heart often wants to overrule my head. I am on the committee planning his farewell service and reception. I really hope we can have the perfect service!"

At that moment, Rose appeared in the doorway holding a diary in her hand. "Reading diaries. I guess we all have the same idea."

Daisy did not want to continue her discussion with Rachel now that their privacy had been disturbed, so she claimed that household responsibilities demanded her attention elsewhere.

"Would you like to chat, Rose?" Rachel asked while pointing to the chair that had so recently been vacated by Daisy.

"I am sorry to have intruded, we seem to do that to you and your guests."

"Don't apologize, no harm done."

"I have come to your door a number of times with this book, but I am reluctant to share my secret with anyone."

Rachel recalled several instances when Rose had approached her with her diary. Rose always appeared ill at ease on such occasions. What could she have in that diary that would cause her usual confidence to waver?

Rose leaned toward Rachel, "I haven't shared this with anyone in the family. They would find it so whimsical, so out of character."

Rachel rose, moved toward the open door of her bedroom, and closed the door quietly.

As she returned to her chair, she smiled at Rose, "We are alone, Rose, no further interruptions. I hope you will share your secret with me. I assure you it will remain with me."

"I know you will respect my privacy. You are aware that your three aunts like yourself maintain diaries. Everyone knows that my reflections are dominated by the world which I screen through my interest in literature. My books shape my view of the world. Of course, I do love the classics and that interest has caused some to assume that I appreciate only scholarly exposition, complicated poetry, and well-sculptured prose."

"I think you may have misjudged that viewpoint. Your sisters know you to be well-read, to have a broad appreciation for all literature. And they know that you have been an invaluable help to me in my role as president of Connie's fanclub. If you can appreciate the lyrics to

"Follow the Boys" I don't think anyone would accuse you of not being 'cool'."

Rose laughed at the thought that she might be considered 'cool' by anyone. "I have read widely and while I delight in reading Homer, Milton, Shakespeare, and Whitman; I do enjoy Ogden Nash, Lewis Carroll, and Mark Twain. I enjoy humour as well as serious writing."

Rose stood up, threw the diary into Rachel's lap, "There I am. My soul revealed. My great passion exposed. My concealed treasure. You have it in your lap. I pray you will read it privately, laugh at me if you must, but I do hope you will find merit in its content. I need to have someone I trust read it. I need to have a critic. Writing exposes the soul. I bare that soul to you. If you do not wish such responsibility, I understand, but I hope you will be kind enough to..."

Rachel assured Rose she would read the diary in private, that she would respect the bond between author and reader, and she would be a faithful critic. "I am due at Mr. King's office in a hour, so I will put your diary in my dresser until I return. I promise that we shall meet tomorrow to continue our discussion."

Rose placed her hands in her trouser pockets as she strode out of the room. "I'll await your appraisal of my work!"

Rachel regretted not having time to begin a cursory examination of the diary contents, but she faced a half hour drive to Mr. King's office and she did want to gather the notes she had made from her recent review of the household financial portfolio and to finish wrapping a gift. She was preparing to sell fifty more acres of land, and desperately wanted Mr. King to review her business plan.

As she drove to the office, her thoughts gradually strayed from the diaries of the aunts to their financial portfolio. She was uneasy about selling another fifty acres, but the mansion needed repairs and with increased taxes and rising prices, she had no other choice. Mr. King had never broached the "other disclosure that was not of a financial matter" with her. He had mentioned it during their initial meeting, but had remained silent throughout their subsequent meetings. She was unable to imagine what that disclosure might be. Surely, today, he would seize the opportunity to reveal this mystery.

Mr. King had the gift of making people feel comfortable. He was always so reassuring, and yet he was definite in his financial advice. He agreed with Rachel's proposal to sell another fifty acres. He did caution her to check with one other real estate company to see if she could get a better price. The company was a national one and might be willing to pay more for prime lots with shore frontage.

"You have a good business sense, I like your organizational skills, and you have learned the financial affairs of the household very quickly. Your grandfather and, indeed, your mother were concerned that your aunts live their lives without financial worry. You have embraced that responsibility so effectively. I am proud of you!"

Rachel knew that this was high praise from someone who was always diplomatic, but also always truthful. "I thank you for all of your years of dedicated service to our family. They were so fortunate to have had you as their financial advisor. I know grandad treasured your friendship."

Rachel placed a giftwrapped package on his desk. "This is a small gift from our household to you. Grandfather had two of these crafted. He was saving this one for someone special. We can think of no one dearer to the family than you. The aunts do not, of course, know the full extent of your contribution. But they have heard grandad sing your praises so often that they recognize the esteem with which he held you."

Rachel smiled as she continued, "And you know all too well, that grandad did not hold many individuals in high esteem."

Mr. King returned her smile, "Really, there was no need, but I am most grateful. I miss your grandfather, we did become more than business associates. He was a strong-willed man who built an empire and saw it begin to crumble. He never became bitter. He simply wanted to protect his family. I admired his devotion to your aunts. May I open the gift?"

"Please do."

Mr. King placed the gift in front of him on his desk. He methodically removed the ribbon, then the tape; carefully placing the giftwrap aside, he withdrew a velvet burgundy case from the box. He opened it delicately, staring intently at the contents. His face was without expression. There was no visible sign of his acceptance, his approval, his thoughts.

Rachel studied the blank visage. He continued to stare at the opened case. Rachel became aware that his eyes were moist and assumed that to be a confirmation of his approval.

"I am deeply moved. He lifted the pen and pencil set from the case. I have had numerous sets of pens given to me over the years, but this one is absolutely exquisite. The navy colour with gold borders is striking. But the pocket watch!" He lifted the gold pocket watch from the case, its gold chain sparkling in the light of his desk lamp. "This is a treasure, it is like your grandfather's. I remember now when he first wore it to my office. He said there was only one other like it in the world. I must admit, I was secretly envious of that watch. The Swiss craftsmanship is superb..." He paused to gain his composure.

Rachel leaned forward, holding up the watch and opening its cover to reveal an inscription,

"May I read the inscription?"

"By all means."

"Presented to James King for dedicated service. You are an honourary member of our family.

Iris, Rose, Daisy, Rachel - May 28, 1965."

Mr. King was deeply touched by the gift. He rose, walked over to his safe, returning with a small envelope. "And I have a 'gift' of sorts for you. It is a key to your grandfather's security boxes; there are two of them located in the attic, under the false bottom in the window seat that overlooks the front garden. I believe it is in the room you use as your fanclub office. The security boxes contain a number of personal papers that you will find most interesting. Unlike your aunts, your grandfather did not keep a diary, but there are personal reflections scattered throughout his record books. He wanted you to have these. He knew that you would be his only grandchild. He also has a burgundy case in that safe for you. Burgundy was his favourite colour, was it not?"

"I guess it was," mumbled Rachel. She was astounded at Mr. King's revelation of hidden security boxes in the attic. She had sat on that window seat so many times not knowing the real treasure it concealed.

"Your gift will be found in a tightly wrapped wooden box. There is a proviso. You may not open the box until the day you are to be married!"

"What!" exclaimed Rachel, foregoing her usual composure. "Not until I am married! I don't even have a boyfriend!"

Mr. King winked, "There is no one!?"

Rachel did not make the inference, "What happens if I don't marry?"

"There is no provision for that. If you do not marry, you may decide as custodian of the box, how best to deal with its secret contents."

"Do you know what is in the box?"

"I do and I can assure you that it is not a pen and pencil set, nor a gold watch."

"Your grandfather's legacy continues to influence the family even though he has been dead for five years. His influence will continue to dominate the household. He did what he thought was best for his family. He had great determination! He made friends but he also made enemies; he treated everyone the same. You will find his notations reveal his character. Much of what you read will confirm what you already know about him, but I assure you that there may be revelations in his records that will surprise you, perhaps shock you, and maybe some may disappoint you. Remember, he was a man of vision, compassion, and logic. He was what he was. He remained true to his commitments. You will discover that he was an anonymous benefactor for many charities. He also had political involvements. He was in the world and of the world. Yet he created a haven that is divorced from the world's influences."

"Are there skeletons in our closet?"

Mr. King chuckled, "I wouldn't say skeletons, but in time you will discover that your grandfather was a man of great principle who attempted to right any wrongs he may have done. He was his own worst critic. I leave you with a key to better understanding of the patriarch of your household." He passed the envelope to Rachel.

Receiving the envelope, Rachel smiled, "I thank you for this intrigue. I shall look forward to examining the records in the security boxes. Do my aunts know about them?"

"To my knowledge, they do not. There is only one key and you have it."

Mr. King rose, took Rachel's hands in his, squeezed them affectionately, "You are so young to be the custodian of so many secrets, but they are in safe hands. Although I will no longer be in my office, you have my home address. As a friend of the family who will wear your watch each day, I invite you to keep in contact with me. I am available for advice."

"I find that invitation reassuring. Thank you." She surprised herself by leaning forward and kissing him on the cheek.

Mr. King blushed, "Thank you my dear and God bless you as you continue to protect the bouquet. They are a delicate treasure."

Rachel quietly left the office, enjoying the drive back to the mansion. She was curious about the contents of the security boxes. A gift for her? Why must she wait until she was married? What if she never married? She was not dating! She only had one male friend, and he lived in another country. They had written, but never spoken to or seen each other. She had responsibilities that bound her to Connecticut; he was embarking on a career as a teacher that required him to be in Nova Scotia. And there was Leah.

As she drove up the lane to the house, she was unaware of the aunts seated in the screened gazebo in the front yard. She entered the main door, looking wistfully at her surroundings.

She looked at herself in the front mirror. She was dark with a page boy haircut. Blondes with flowing hair were so much more attractive. All the famous movie stars were gorgeous blondes, Marilyn Munro, Sandra Dee, Connie Stevens. Of course, Connie Francis was Italian! Definitely not a blonde.

She looked at the elegant silver vase on the oak table in the foyer. It was overflowing with fresh flowers arranged artistically by Iris. No florist could have done a better job. Each rose, each carnation, each piece of greenery was in its proper place. The symmetry was perfect.

She glanced at the winding staircase. How many times had she counted the 35 stairs that led to the bedrooms on the second floor. Today her eyes focused on the beautifully polished oak staircase. Oak was the dominant wood throughout the house. It covered the walls in the library, the kitchen cupboards, and served as the wood for most of the furniture in the house. The living-room was the exception where mahogany Queen Anne chairs and tables served to provide a warmth and richness that may have eluded the oak's dominance.

She hadn't really noticed that burgundy was the main colour for carpets and curtain treatments. If the background wasn't burgundy, there were traces to be found in the flowers or other designs that highlighted the fabric.

After mounting the 35 stairs, she continued to climb the 24 stairs that led to the third floor, the attic, her office, the home of the window seat. The home of the security boxes! The storehouse of secrets!

As she advanced to the window seat, she glanced out the window. It was then that she noticed the aunts in the garden, enjoying their high tea. Daisy would have prepared sandwiches and sweets to make the outside treat a special occasion. Undoubtedly she would serve English trifle to complete the celebration. The trifle would be laced with sherry; Daisy enjoyed adding a 'sparkle' to her cooking and baking.

She looked affectionately at her aunts. Daisy was wearing her usual apron, the symbol of her household responsibilities, her devotion. She always wore a plain housedress to cover her generous figure during the day. Rose was typically wearing trousers and a blouse over her athletic frame. Iris was wearing a fitted dress that always hung just above her ankles. Even when she gardened, she never resorted to trousers. What a trio they were. The scene could well be from a British movie. Iris was pouring the tea from a silver set with all the poise expected of a grand lady of the Victorian era.

Rachel's eyes drifted beyond the garden to the water of Flanders Cove. The cove was visible from three sides of the house. The water was green and calm. A few sailboats were lazily making their way to the mouth of the cove. Multicoloured gardens, green lawns, evergreens, and sparkling water combined to form a pastoral setting befitting the nobility of the aunts. They were a rare breed of individuals; the mould of their creation had been thrown away, never again would anyone experience their peculiar blend of elegance, wit, determination and innocence.

Rachel's mind flowed with the sailboats beyond the cove into the Atlantic Ocean. She could imagine sailing up the coast of New England, past the international border into Atlantic Canada, perhaps stopping in Northumbria for a brief visit.

The ringing of the telephone caused her voyage to take an abrupt change in direction. It was the local printer who wanted to verify a few items in the booklet that she was preparing to send to her fan club members. She wanted to include an updated list of Connie's achievements and reviews of her concert performances.

****

Robert shook his head as he closed Rachel's diary. 1965 was such an eventful year! Rachel was establishing herself as a worthy successor to Mr. King. She was learning more and more of the man she affectionately called grandad; a man whose work ethic and family values she revered.

Robert wandered toward the stereo, placing the album, "More Greatest Hits - Connie Francis" on the turntable. He glanced at the notes on the back of the album jacket. "Connie is as well known in Copenhagen as she is in Detroit, as familiar on the BBC as she is on tv channels in the States, as winning in Paris and Rome as she is in Chicago and New York." Connie was an international star. He recalled those days with fondness when each newsletter from Rachel brought new records broken by Connie, another first in a long line of accomplishments. His reminiscing was suddenly shattered when he realized the famous contralto was singing, "Yes, everybody's somebody's fool...and there are no exceptions to the rule." He retuned hastily to the stereo, forcefully striking the off button. He seized a few items from the banker's storehouse and flopped into his wing chair. His mood had changed. He was agitated and yet he was reacting to the past, a past that he now need not fear, a past that had made him stronger.

Robert was anxious to begin the first draft of his novel. Reviewing some of the material from the bankers' boxes was whetting his appetite to begin. However, he knew that she was entitled to his undivided attention. It was their day to begin a new life. The church was ready! The reception arrangements were complete! Finally, they would be one!

He knew that when he eventually did sit at his word processor to record his thoughts and feelings, to begin exposing their journey to the world, he would have great difficulty recording any further events of 1965. He did not want to cheapen their story by sensationalism, providing sordid details to arouse the interest of some readers who perhaps were more inclined to consider novels as a type of soap opera. He hoped his readers would be more interested in the innocence of youth struggling in a world where love does not always flow smoothly and unspoiled. He did not want his readers to focus on the dark side of the journey, on the moment of lust fulfilled at such a great cost, and yet the story would be incomplete without the incident that so dramatically changed all of their lives.

His diary was explicit, so were his letters. The memory of the incident was forever engraved in his memory. How could he ignore the details and simply say it happened...

----- Northumbria 1965

Robert sat alone in the sun porch, bringing before his mind's eye Connie's latest appearance on "The Ed Sullivan Show". Northumbria received only two television broadcasting transmissions. Both were Canadian. He often missed Connie's appearances on the American networks. The manor's one television set was always reserved for "The Ed Sullivan Show" when Connie was to be a featured guest. Silence would be maintained while Robert fixed his total attention on the 21 inch black and white screen. Connie's transmitted figure might be but a small object on the household television set, but her performance demanded unquestionable reverence!

It was the first week in June. He and Leah had graduated. He was pleased to land a teaching position at a local junior high school. Actually, he had had a choice of three different positions in two schools in Northumbria. His first position was to teach English grammar and composition to three grade seven and three grade eight classes. He was excited!

Leah had not applied for a position. That surprised him. He wondered if the two years of study had taken their toll. She seemed so unsettled since they had returned to Northumbria. The closeness they had shared at teachers college appeared to evaporate long before the train had pulled into the Northumbria station. Of course, Trevor was at the station to meet them.

Trevor seemed to become more aggressive and coarse with age. He was eight years older than Leah. His six-foot-two body was a well-defined muscular showcase. His job as a construction worker ensured that his muscles received constant stretching and he routinely went to the local fitness centre at least twice a week to improve his definition. Of course, his workouts at the fitness centre were intended also to display his body to others who were less gifted. His tank tops and t-shirts were purchased a size too small to make sure that his pecs, abs and biceps were given full exposure. Spring was heralded in Northumbria with Trevor allowing his shirt to flow freely unbuttoned so that his admirers could look at his washboard abs and chiselled pecs! He had developed a confident walk that allowed him to glide above any walking surface. He obviously studied the art of being a muscle machine. Robert was certain that Trevor never left his home without pumping his muscles in the workout room in the basement.

Robert's six foot body, covered with a mere 155 pounds, paled in comparison to the 190 pounds of solid muscle displayed by Trevor. He lacked confidence in his physique that caused his round shoulders to stoop even further than nature had intended. He had considered going to the fitness centre but the thought of being humiliated by Trevor discouraged that possibility.

Trevor's one redeeming quality was that he was devoted to his sister. He had appointed himself as her protector. Robert knew that he was not the only male to endure Trevor's scrutiny and abuse. Trevor obviously considered himself to be a man's man that few, if any, men could challenge. He enjoyed referring to Robert as "wimp, skinny, gutless," and didn't mind questioning Robert's masculinity. He had no respect for men who were engaged in paper pushing occupations. He had not been a good student and detested male teachers. His physical education teacher, who was a capable athlete, was a model for most of his students, but a threat to Trevor's need to be top jock. His fight with the physical education teacher had led to his dismissal from high school.

Today Robert's mind was bombarded with thoughts of school preparations, Leah's indecision, Trevor's hostility, his return to the manor, Rachel's bouquet, and Connie's career. There was so much happening. He could not turn off or slow down the turmoil that was erupting in his head. His mood plunged from elation to depression. He shook his head as if to refocus his attention, to delay thinking about his challenges and fears and to delight in the moment.

This was an exceptional day at the manor. Most of the guests had gone on a bus ride for the afternoon, stopping at a restaurant for dinner compliments of a local service group. Bertha had fed the patients who were confined to bed and therefore unable to travel on the bus. Today would be the first time in years that the Mascaux family sat down to dinner alone, without the extended family.

Bertha had prepared a special meal for the occasion although every meal at the manor was a carefully planned event. Bertha was known for her culinary arts. She didn't cook, she created! All her cooking was done on a coal stove. The manor could now well afford the luxury of an electric stove, but Bertha was adamant that no electric stove would be found in her kitchen. On this occasion, the dinner table featured red cabbage cooked with onion, apples and vinegar; mashed potatoes and turnips, peas and carrots, roast pork cooked with garlic and thyme, and of course, apple sauce. Fresh iceburg lettuce dripping with oil and vinegar was served with the meal. Brown sugar pie and the famous Belgian galettes were waiting to be served for dessert.

Robert loved his mother's cooking and nothing pleased him more than her galettes. All the Belgians made them. Each family had the basic recipe, but no one could equal the texture, the richness and the sheer explosion of flavour that his mother's galettes provided. Bertha's galettes were often included in her 'thinking of you' parcels that she frequently sent to family, friends, and shut-ins. Galettes were so much more practical and flavourful than greeting cards, and they were Bertha's signature. Anyone who received a basket of treats with galettes easily guessed the identity of the sender.

After Robert and his parents had gathered at the table in the large kitchen, Bertha asked Robert to say grace.

"Dear Father, we ask that You be the unseen guest at our table, fill our hearts with love and make us mindful of the needs of others. We thank you for all our blessings, especially this food, in Jesus' name. Amen."

Bertha and Camille responded, "Amen."

As the family savoured Bertha's offerings, they enjoyed the time of intimacy that was all too rare in the household. Camille was the listener, always the listener. Robert and Bertha loved to chatter.

"When are you going to visit the school?"

"I'll phone the principal next week. I think I'll wait until school is over. I am so glad to get a job in Northumbria."

"We have missed having you home. But you know that we are ready to see you leave home when you feel the time is right. We left our parents in Belgium to seek a new life here. One day, you will leave also, but I hope you will not have to go to another country."

"I don't think you need to worry about that."

Bertha looked affectionately at her son, "Perhaps you may decide to go to the United States?"

Robert laughed, "Who knows, but I needn't get my passport ready for awhile."

"How is Rachel? I noticed you received a newsletter yesterday."

"Rachel is so mature. She seems so much older than I am."

"You are both 20. I should be so old."

"I think that she has had to assume so much responsibility for her aunts. Being business manager is a big job. What an estate!"

"I guess the more money there is, the more there is to manage. No wonder we don't have such burdens."

"But the fascinating thing is that the aunts do not consider themselves wealthy; their needs are simple."

"Yes, Robert, but the mansion and property must consume a lot of money."

"A lot of money, but they are oblivious to that, protected from that reality."

"From what I know, Rose must know about the finances."

"If she does, she has never said a word to Rachel."

"What hired help do they have to run the estate?"

"Since Rachel assumed responsibilities, a gardener/handyman comes twice a week; his wife helps in the house on the same days. Years ago there were several servants, but during the last few years the grandfather was alive there was little assistance except for the seasonal gardener."

"Of course, everyone was younger then and the grandfather probably didn't want to waste money."

"Actually, I don't think it was so much an issue of money as privacy, but maybe the grandfather wanted to save as much of the family fortune as he could. Rachel is more interested in enabling the aunts to have time to relax and enjoy their beautiful surroundings. Daisy was getting tired performing the household chores plus the cooking."

"But the other aunts do help as well."

"Oh yes, each aunt looks after her bedroom. Iris always sets the table, Rose and Rachel clean up and wash the dishes."

Bertha looked at the table in front of her, covered with their department store stoneware and well-worn cutlery.

"I expect they set an elegant table."

"I know it is always tastefully set by Iris. They have several sets of good china, one Royal Doulton, one Spode, and one Royal Albert. The favourite pattern is 'Florentine', Royal Albert, I think. It features a raised turquoise flowered border."

"A bit more expensive than my department store Johnson's pattern!"

"But plates are just plates, the food could not equal this meal. I love roast pork."

"No, I'm not envious. Mind you, if someone wants to give me 'Florentine', I won't refuse it."

Robert exchanged a smile with his mother. She and Daisy were somewhat alike. Both served others. Both had big hearts. Both wore an apron with a bib to cover their oversized bodies.

Robert sighed, "The bouquet lead such a charmed life. I would like to meet them."

"And meet their niece?"

"Yes, and meet their niece."

Robert enjoyed talking with his mother. She was practical, calm and had a 'steel-trap' mind. She could analyse and synthesize, remain objective, and come up with possible alternatives for most of life's situations. She had created a successful home business, paid off the mortgage on the other side of the duplex, and had created an inviting environment for all the residents. The manor was everyone's home. Bertha was everyone's guardian angel!

Camille broke his silence, asking Robert, "How are you and the MacDonald girl getting along?"

"Leah and I are friends, but I haven't seen her much in the last few weeks."

"Did you have a fight?"

"No fight, I assure you. I don't like to go over to the MacDonald's when Trevor is there."

"Robert, you need to stand up to Trevor."

"Yes, stand up and be crushed. He's a bulldozer."

"I've seen guys like him fall easily. He's a muscle head. Use your brains to bring him down to your size."

"I don't have David's slingshot, but Trevor is certainly my Goliath."

"There's always a bully in life. Some use muscles, others use their heads. Brains are better than muscles. You can't back down. When I was working at the mine, there were always bigger men, but I stood up to all of them. It's the only way to get respect."

Bertha frowned at Camille, "Fighting is not the answer."

Bertha skillfully changed the subject, capitalizing on Camille's entrance to the conversation. "Robert, you missed having dinner at your Aunt Mary's last month." Looking at Camille, "Why don't you tell him about dessert?"

Camille laughed, "I don't think Robert likes prune pie."

"I know he doesn't like prune pie, but he might appreciate what you baked."

Staring in disbelief, Robert leaned toward his father, "You baked!"

Camille's face brightened, "Not really. Your mother has calmed down." Looking at Bertha, he asked, "Am I now forgiven?"

"Your father visited his sister on the morning of her annual family dinner. She tries so hard to please. You know, of course, she is not the best housekeeper in the world."

Camille added, "No, she's the worst!"

Robert could wait no longer, "What has this got to do with prune pies?"

"Tell him, Camille."

"I think we should hear your version."

"Your father sat at Mary's kitchen table watching her make the pies. She had to pit the prunes by hand. After she released each pit, she licked her fingers to clean them, then went on to the next prune."

"I can believe Aunt Mary would do that. Is that the story?"

"No, he (pointing to Camille) came home and told everyone about the prunes."

"There's more?"

"Yes! After we finished the first course of Aunt Mary's dinner, she proudly announced, 'I have prune pie for dessert.'" She brought two pies to the table and proceeded to cut them into large pieces. As she was cutting, your father began licking his thumb and index finger."

Robert burst out laughing, "That was terrible!"

Camille displaying a rare moment of amusement, "There was no harm done."

"And then, after the first bite, he announced to everyone, 'Mary, the pie is so moist.'"

"Dad, how could you do that?"

"With a straight face," retorted Bertha.

"But Bertha, you didn't have a straight face, more like a poker face."

"Everyone was trying not to laugh, not wanting to eat the pie, not wanting to hurt Mary's feelings. Your uncle sensed something was going on, but he decided it was the result of the drinks everyone had had before dinner."

Camille whispered to Robert, "Boy, did I get hell when we got home."

"Oh, and he was wasn't satisfied to leave it at that. There were two pieces of pie left over so he asked Mary if she would mind sending them home with your Aunt Oliva."

"Your mother is just annoyed that Aunt Mary's pies got more comments than hers."

"The finishing touch arrived the next morning. Your cousin, Roger, arrived here at 10 o'clock with a gift for your father from Oliva, a freshly baked apple pie. She included a note which read: 'I made this pie with fresh apples, I peeled each one, I hope you find it moist.'"

Looking at his father, "Did you eat the pie?"

"I certainly did, and it was moist."

The prune pie story had lightened the mood for the remainder of the meal. While eating a piece of brown sugar pie, Robert mentioned that he had received a letter from one of his professors who wanted to keep in touch.

Bertha was pleased with the professor's initiative, "I think you should be proud that Professor Jenkins wants to keep in contact with you."

"Oh, I am pleased, he was my favourite prof. I remember my first real conversation with him. He had asked us to write a brief autobiographical sketch. He personally sat down and discussed each sketch with its author. He claimed it was the best way to begin building rapport with his students."

"He was the one who was surprised that we were attending the Anglican Church of Canada or as I had referred to it in my auotobiographical sketch, 'The Church of England' instead of a Roman Catholic church. That really intrigued him."

"When we were in Belgium, we were all Roman Catholics, of course."

"It was Mr. Howard, the Church of England minister, who won you over, wasn't it?"

"We expected to continue being Roman Catholic, why wouldn't we? But we were not received with open arms by many of the Northumbria residents. The Belgian coal company was importing workers to help in their coal mines; the locals resented using foreign labourers."

Camille rejoined the conversation to say, "We were in a strange country, we chose to come here for a better life. We had nothing but the promise of a job."

Robert returned to Mr. Howard, "Mr. Howard was taking a risk to visit Roman Catholics in those days."

"I suppose he was, but his church was located below the tracks, obviously on the wrong side. Most of his parishioners were miners. His church was called, 'The Miners' Church'. He just wanted to be friendly."

"Did he try to convert you?"

"Never. And the Roman priest failed to visit us. We didn't attend any church for the first few months, but with Advent coming, we knew we had to do something. So we went as a group to ask Father Howard if we could attend his church. We have never regretted it."

Robert remarked, "Roman Catholics attending the Church of England!"

"It goes to show you how important a priest or minister is to a congregation."

"In her recent letter, Rachel indicated that Daisy is planning a farewell reception and service for their rector. She fears that his replacement will never provide the same degree of leadership. Yes, I guess the priest is important."

"Professor Jenkins recognized your writing ability from that first sample. He confirmed what I had told you all along, but you wouldn't believe me."

"You're my mother; you are supposed to believe in me."

"Don't you always claim that I am the objective one, the diplomat. I can tell the truth gently."

"Ok, you win. I guess I just needed someone who knew more about language to comment on my abilities."

"Writing is more than vocabulary you know. Language is the tool, but without ideas, emotion, story, language is a prisoner."

Bertha never ceased to amaze Robert. She had only a grade eight education, but she had developed a command of language that few of her peers could claim."

Their family sharing was interrupted by the ringing of the telephone. It was Leah. She invited Robert to go the beach the following day. She would drive her father's car. Robert longed for the day when he would have his own wheels.

As he hung up the receiver, the bus arrived at the manor, unloading its weary but enthusiastic travellers. Bertha stood at the door greeting her family's return. She had been particularly concerned about Mrs. Ford who seemed to be more confused recently. Her appetite had never been as keen as the other guests, but of late, she merely picked at her food. She had ceased going for her walks in the neighbourhood as had been her custom since coming to the manor.

"Welcome back, Mrs. Ford. I hope you had a nice drive in the country."

"Yes, and we had a delicious meal as well. Of course, it was not as good as your cooking, my dear."

Bertha was somewhat taken back by Mrs. Ford's comment. Often Mrs. Ford did not remember that Bertha did the cooking. Bertha wondered if Mrs. Ford had eaten at all at the restaurant.

Gramma Horton arrived in the sun porch on the arm of Mr. Gordon. Mr. Gordon announced to Bertha, "We got hitched this afternoon and you missed the big event. You didn't even come to the reception."

Gramma blushed, but enjoyed the game. "We had considered eloping, but we were afraid some might think it was a forced wedding, if you know what I mean."

"I do know what you mean." Looking fondly at the couple, she continued, "And his reputation would lead many to believe it!"

Gramma Horton leaned toward Bertha, "Mrs. Ford was strange today."

"Strange, in what way?"

"I know this sounds stupid, but she was so lucid, she seemed to be clear in her thinking."

Mr. Gordon whispered, "And she ate everything on her plate, including the french fries."

"French fries! She never eats french fries."

At that moment, Mrs. Ford who had moved into the sun porch, removed her hat while asking Robert, "No music today?"

Robert was somewhat surprised at the question, "Oh, yes, I was listening to my records earlier."

Mrs. Ford motioned for Robert to sit in the chair beside her, "I think you are fortunate to have your music. Music reaches the soul far faster than words. I hope it will always bring you comfort."

Robert could not believe that it was his dear Mrs. Ford talking to him. Certainly, she had shared profound truths with him before, but he had never really felt her comments were addressed to him. He always sensed that she was recalling someone from her past and perhaps sharing a memory with him.

She reached out and touched his shoulder, "You are the best grandson I have and we are not even related!" Without saying another word, she picked up her hat and wandered off to her bedroom.

Robert was deeply touched by the brief exchange. He could not understand it, but delighted in having shared such an intimate moment with his oldest and dearest foster grandmother. Mrs. Ford was always so gracious and elegant, gracious even when her memory failed her in conversation, still elegant when one of her two dresses she was wearing revealed the other garment's presence.

After the guests were finally tucked away in their beds for the evening, Bertha returned to the sun porch to relax. Camille was immersed in his favourite television programs. As she entered the porch, she found Robert looking at his Connie Francis scrapbooks.

"We'll soon need a new cabinet just to house your scrapbooks."

Robert blushed, "Oh, I think we are safe for awhile."

"Does Leah like Connie?"

"Not really, she doesn't like female singers, more interested in Bobby Rydell and Fabian."

"That makes sense. I'm glad Leah called you."

"Yes, I'm glad too, I've been worried about her."

"Why are you worried?"

"She seems so quiet."

"I have never known Leah not to be quiet."

"Sure, but there are different kinds of quiet."

"I understand. You father has always been the quiet one. But I never knew what quiet was until your brother was taken from us. I lost both of my men that night!"

Robert looked affectionately at his mother, "It has not been easy."

Bertha stiffened her shoulders, "It's life! The ground that your father nurtures to produce his garden is the same earth that took life. Seeds die to bring the harvest. Our dear Lord died to give us life. The pattern is woven into the life cycle. Someone is born; someone dies."

As so often happened in the household, Bertha was summoned to one of the bedrooms by a call from one of the guests. Robert returned his albums to the cabinet and slowly made his way to his bedroom where he found comfort listening to Connie's movie theme songs: "Where the Boys Are", "Follow the Boys" and "Looking for Love". He liked the beat of "Looking for Love." It always lifted his spirits. His mind wandered from Connie to Rachel and then to Leah. He had never really had an official date. He and Leah had gone places, but he had never asked any girl to go on a date with him. He wondered if this were normal. Most of the other guys his age in the neighbourhood had found themselves a steady girlfriend, a few had already gotten married. He knew he was shy about meeting people, and lacked the self-confidence to approach any girl and risk a refusal, but he had never really met someone he wanted to ask for a date. Then there was Rachel. He knew it was ridiculous to think about her romantically. They knew so little about each other. They had never met, had never spoken to each other. They were separated by an international border. She was an American, her family had wealth, and she had responsibilities that confined her. She was just a friend.

But his friend would not leave his thoughts. He tossed and turned in bed. He found himself smiling at Rachel, teasing her, laughing with her about the antics of the bouquet. He touched her hair, felt her body move closer to him. As he lay in bed, he realized that his body was responding to his fantasy. He felt uncomfortable, as if he had lured Rachel unwillingly into his embrace.

He closed his eyes again hoping that sleep would engulf him, but within a few minutes he was walking along the beach holding hands with Rachel, looking into her eyes, savouring every look, every movement. They were together. Connie's hit, "Together" drifted into his consciousness helping him to fall asleep with his American dream.

In the sunlight of early morning, he lay in bed thinking about his dreams. The lyrics of "Together" floated through his head, "We strolled the lane together..." Last night he had strolled the beach with Rachel; today he would walk it with Leah. As he became more aware of the sounds around him, he realized that something unusual was happening. There was so much movement upstairs.

From his bedroom in the basement, he could sense that something was different about the breakfast routine. He quickly got dressed, climbed the stairs, only to meet his mother at the entrance to the kitchen. Her face told him that something was wrong. Bertha approached him with tears in her eyes, "Robert, come with me to the sun porch."

As they walked in silence, Robert imagined all sorts of disasters, but he wasn't prepared for Bertha's news.

Bertha motioned for Robert to sit in a wing chair, and sat down beside him. "Mrs. Ford passed away last evening."

Robert looked blankly at his mother, "Mrs. Ford is dead! She died quietly in her sleep."

"Thanks for telling me. I think I'll go to my room."

Bertha knew that Robert would retreat to his room and there release the emotions that were building up inside him. Robert was ever the loner, his bedroom his sanctuary, his haven. She knew better than to try at this point to comfort him, that would come later. Now he needed to deal with it himself.

An hour later, Robert returned to the kitchen where his mother was preparing dinner.

"I never knew my real grandparents. And I loved Mrs. Ford..." He could not continue.

Bertha approached him and gave him a gentle hug..." And she was so fond of you."

"Last night she said, "You are my favourite grandson, and we are not even related."

"I cannot understand her behaviour last evening, but she obviously told you what you must have known for a long time. You teased her, walked with her, cared for her, and loved her. She sensed it and returned it."

"She talked about my music, too."

"Don't forget, she was a musician in her own right so she knew what she was talking about."

"I don't know how to say good-bye, to give up someone. I was so much younger when Arthur was killed in the explosion..."

"It is never easy, someone dies, someone is born. We learn to treasure our memories the older we get." She nervously adjusted the silver bracelet that she always wore on her left wrist. "Mrs. Ford was a lady who gave us so much, remember her elegance and grace. Remember those hats!"

Robert chuckled as he pictured Mrs. Ford wearing her hats, gloves and cane; walking so confidently. The neighbourhood would miss her.

"Robert, the cruel thing about death is that life goes on. I'm mourning her, but I'm getting dinner ready. Now, listen to what I am going to say, and please do as I say. I want you to go to the beach with Leah this afternoon."

"But I can't!"

"I want you to go to the beach!"

"If you stay here, you'll be in your room, thinking too much. You cannot bring her back by torturing yourself. Go to the beach, listen to your mother."

"I can't go to the beach!"

"Let me approach this differently. You say Leah seems quiet, you think she is worried. After weeks of silence, she calls you. You may be able to comfort her, help her sort out her problem, if she has one. You can't help Mrs. Ford and you won't do yourself any good, moping around here. Mrs. Ford's family will be here later, I need to deal with them as friends and we have business affairs to discuss."

"But what about you?"

"Robert, death is the ultimate test of faith. Mrs. Ford was a woman of faith. She has left the land of the dying to go to the land of the living. The Salvation Army officers call it, 'Being promoted to glory'. What more can we ask? She is at peace. She was 92!"

Robert weakened, hugged his mother, "I know you are right. I will go to the beach." Looking at his untanned arms, "I could use some tan." He retreated to the quiet of his room, waiting for Leah to pick him up. It seemed like hours before she finally arrived.

As they drove to the beach, he was so absorbed in talking about Mrs. Ford that he hardly noticed that Leah was pale and obviously troubled. Upon arriving at the beach, they found a private spot and spread a blanket on the hot sand.

"Do you want to walk along the beach?"

"Not now, perhaps later."

Robert continued talking about his lost grandmother. "Mrs. Ford was my favourite foster grandmother. Mom says that death is part of the life cycle. Someone dies, someone is born..."

Leah burst into tears. There was nothing Robert could do to calm her. Leah rose to her feet, "Robert, I'll be all right, just let me be alone for a few minutes, I'm going to walk along the beach."

"Let me go with you, I won't talk."

"No, I need to be alone, I'm sorry, just be patient." With those few comments, she turned and began her slow walk long the water's edge.

Robert was puzzled. He wondered why Leah had invited him to join her when she seemed to require privacy. He wondered if he had upset her talking about death. He looked at the ocean. The water was definitely blue, free from jelly fish, sparkling in the sunlight.

He knew he thought too much about everything. Bertha often said that he overreacted to things. She would smile and say, "Hey guy, stay cool." He always enjoyed Bertha's leap into the language of the 60's.

Leah finally returned to the blanket; her eyes were dried, but her face betrayed her faked smile.

As she sat down, Robert spoke tenderly, "Leah, something is wrong. You and I have been friends for a long time. You know you can trust me and I am a good listener."

Leah looked hesitantly at Robert, and she began crying again. She got up to leave. He took her by the hand encouraging her to return to the blanket.

"Leah, stay here, I won't talk, I won't probe, I'll just be here."

They sat in silence for an eternity until Leah looked at Robert with fear in her eyes, "Robert, I have a problem..."

"I know."

Looking shocked, "You know!"

"I know something is bothering you, I just don't know what."

Leah sat up and without raising her head, "I want to share something with you, but you must promise to tell no one, ever. Do you promise?"

"I promise."

"Robert, this is not a silly secret, I really mean it. You must promise to never tell anyone. Do you promise?"

"Yes, I promise!

After a brief silence, she continued. "I have rehearsed this for three days. I have to tell someone and you are the only person I can trust."

"You can trust me, Leah, I won't tell a soul."

"I want to tell you something, I hope you will not be disappointed in me, I hope you won't..."

"Leah, just tell me."

"I need to tell you everything, every detail, if I can."

"Whatever you need to say, say it."

"You will think it is something from a soap opera, from a "True Confessions" story.

"Never mind, just begin."

She sighed heavily, "You know Al?"

"Yes, Big Al. I know him."

Leah dissolved in tears again, but soon gathered her composure. "I will not stop until I have told you and I need to go into detail. Don't stop me until I'm finished."

"Whatever you want."

"Just after we returned to college at the end of the spring break, Al seemed to be more interested in me than before. We dated more frequently. I know you don't like him, but he was so gentle, so attentive. He must have read a book, if he can read. He sent me flowers, called me several times a day, walked me to the library. I loved the attention. I was flattered. Al was a good athlete and was so popular. I guess I liked being seen with him. I know that is a poor reason for being with someone. He and Trevor had met and they seemed to hit it off immediately. Trevor encouraged me to go out with a 'real' man."

Robert looked at Leah wondering where this 'story' would take them, but he was true to his word and said nothing.

"On the evening of the spring prom, Al invited me to his aunt's house for refreshments, said he could make a powerful milkshake. I had visited with him at his aunt's a couple of times; I really liked her from the first time we met.

"When we arrived, we discovered she was not at home, but Al had a key. I was a bit uneasy being in her home without her present, but Al was her nephew and he did have a key. Instead of a milkshake, Al asked if I would have a drink of wine. I hesitated, but agreed."

"We drank our glass together on the chesterfield in the living-room. I have never had much wine so I don't actually know what it should taste like, but it did seem powdery, a chemical taste. I wished that I had stuck to the milkshake."

Leah paused, "Robert, this is not going to be easy, so bear with me."

Robert looked anxiously at Leah, but said nothing. He wanted to touch her with his hand, but sensed that Leah needed to do this alone.

"Al encouraged me to finish my drink. I guess wine affects everyone differently. I became so sleepy. He moved closer, put his arms around me and quietly whispered to me. I fell asleep feeling warm and cozy."

Leah paused again, "Now don't stop me until I'm finished! Don't say anything!"

Robert was surprised by her firmness. He waited apprehensively for the conclusion, his mind creating a hundred endings for this disturbing story.

"Suddenly I woke up with pain shooting through my body. I couldn't focus, I couldn't fully wake up. Something was heavy on me. Something was...tearing me apart. I tried to move but couldn't. I could smell wine."

"I tried to focus, to get the strength to move, I began to realize that Al was on top of me. I could hear his breathing. He was shouting at me. Somewhere within me I realized he was...thrusting his entire body into mine."

"The pain was terrible! I cried. I tried to push him off. I scratched at him, but he was so strong. I faded into my sleep."

"It was early morning before I awoke. I found myself still on the chesterfield. The room was tidy and so was I. I wondered if I had dreamed everything. Al was gentle. He said he was sorry the wine had made me drowsy."

Robert looked affectionately at Leah, feeling her pain and yet he knew that Leah was not finished.

"Al was so gentle, but the pain was still there. I could barely walk. Al said that alcohol affects people differently. After I returned to my dorm, I undressed, and knew that I had not dreamed. I was covered with bruises, I smelled like lust. I knew I had been raped."

Leah looked at Robert, "Wait, don't say a word, I'm not finished. You will remember, I missed classes for a few days, the flu. Now you know, it wasn't the flu. And yes, Al didn't fall into the shrubs on campus after having too much to drink; I made those scratches."

For the first time, she had begun her story, Leah looked at Robert. "Robert, I'm pregnant!"

Robert started to speak, "Leah, are you..."

"Yes, I'm sure. Wait, let me finish."

"Now you know why I have been so quiet, why I haven't applied for a job. I have considered a number of options. I guess I will have to go away, I can't tell my parents. I feel so helpless! My worst fear is Trevor! He'll blame me."

Robert took Leah's hands in his, "Thank you for sharing this with me. It was the right thing to do." He tried to imagine what his mother would say if she were here.

"Leah, you are absolutely sure you are pregnant."

"Absolutely!"

"What options have you considered?"

"Robert, I have considered every possible option. No, I can't destroy the child, that would be murder, besides I don't have the means to do it. You know, we are Roman Catholic and I have..."

"Does Al know?"

"No, and he will never know, I haven't spoken to him since that night. He hasn't called! I don't want him to call."

Robert surprised himself, "Then you will have to get married!"

"Married!"

"Yes, married! It's the only solution."

"Al is not going to marry me, I would never consider marrying him. Why make the problem worse?"

"Leah, I wasn't suggesting you marry Al."

Leah looked at Robert, she instantly realized what this gentle man was proposing, "No way!"

"Hear me out!"

"The answer is NO! There can be no discussion. Do you think I want to ruin your life, too? Are you crazy?"

Robert moved closer to her, "Leah, we are friends, good friends, intimate friends."

"Robert, we have never dated. You are like a brother to me."

"Couldn't I be more than that?"

"Robert, you are talking foolishness. Never! No!"

The two friends remained on the beach for the remainder of the afternoon and well into the evening. They agreed to meet the following day for another trip to the beach. The pattern was repeated for a week. They met at the beach, spent time at the manor and Robert visited the MacDonald home when Trevor was at work. They spoke to each other on the phone first thing in the morning and last thing at night.

Leah applied for a job at a local elementary school and was hired.

* * * * * * * * * * *

Robert was distracted by another phone call. He reluctantly left the 1965 entries to return to the reality of 1997. The phone call was from the funeral parlour, confirming the last minute details for the service at the funeral home. He knew the call was necessary, he had been expecting it, but he needed to continue his reflections of the past, even if he had to relive the pain of it.

He returned to the 1965 entries, opening Rachel's diary again; this time he glanced at her September entries, the most painful entry of all confronted him.

- - - - - Flanders Cove, 1965

Rachel sat motionless on the window seat in the fan club office on the third floor. She looked at the cove, but she knew that her heart would never again float beyond the cove to the Atlantic Ocean on its journey to Nova Scotia. She knew that her romantic dreams were never to be realized. She knew that she had expected too much, assumed too much, dreamed too much. She knew that she had allowed her heart to create a relationship that never existed; she now realized that she would pay bitterly for her folly.

She held Robert's latest letter in her hand. It had been six weeks since he had written. She had imagined all sorts of explanations for his absent letters. The aunts had tried to console her. She had become agitated. She had decided to phone Robert and ask him if she had offended him, but they had never mentioned telephoning in all the time they had been sharing their lives.

She returned to the letter. It was so formal, so factual, so cold. It was not from her Robert. It was the end of her dream for them, a dream they had obviously not shared. She knew so little about romance, but now she began to sense the pain of rejection, isolation, and loneliness. She was now alone!

She reread the first few paragraphs:

"Rachel, I hope you and your aunts have been well since I last wrote.
I am sure that you will be surprised to learn
that Leah and I were married at the end of August.
We are living in an apartment in Northumbria.
Leah has a job at a nearby elementary school.
It was a small quiet wedding, our choice.
We toured Nova Scotia for our honeymoon.
Being married certainly is different,
but in time I am sure Leah and I will be very happy together..."

Rachel reread the last sentence again: "In time I am sure Leah and I will be very happy together".

She wanted to release her disappointment, her sorrow and indeed her anger, but she could not. She simply sat looking at the letter. It was in this state that Rose found her upon her entrance to the office.

Rose sensed that the letter had conveyed a disappointment. She moved beside Rachel on the window seat. Rachel placed the letter in Rose's lap.

Rose hesitantly picked up the letter and began reading. She gasped! She glanced at Rachel! She leaned toward Rachel to speak but was prevented by Rachel.

"Please, I can't talk. Tell the aunts my news, but please leave me alone for awhile. I'll come downstairs for dinner."

Rose left quietly. Rachel continued to sit without movement. Gradually evening descended upon the household. The light faded as her dreams had done earlier. Now she was shrouded in darkness!

Chapter 3:

If My Pillow Could Talk

Robert looked at the calendar on his desk, staring at today's date, December 12, 1997. He had recently been exploring the internet with his new computer. From the World Dates Archives he had retrieved a list of significant events that had occurred on December 12, including the birthday of Frank Sinatra, Bob Barker, Dionne Warwick, Edward G. Robinson, Ed Koch and a host of other famous individuals. It is also the date of numerous celebrations including Fiesta of the Virgin of Guadalupe (Mexico), Toronto Peace Festival, Independence Day, Miracle of the Roses, and National Ding-A-Ling Day. Numerous 'firsts' occurred on December 12: The first Trans-Atlantic wireless was sent, the first crossword puzzle appeared in a newspaper, the golf tee was patented, the first motel opened, and "Guess Who's Coming to Dinner" premiered. December 12 was selected as the date for their wedding for one reason only; it was the date of Connie's birthday. After all, it was Connie who introduced them; it was Connie who sustained them through their struggles, and it was Connie who would sing for them at their wedding reception. Of course, Connie was unaware of her influence. A soloist had been engaged to sing a medley of Connie's hits at the reception. Connie would never know how she had affected the lives of so many of her fans and certainly she would be unaware of her role as matchmaker and comforter for a couple she had influenced so significantly. How could she know how many times Robert and Rachel had listened to her records, watched her television appearances, read articles about her, shared in her journey to stardom and in her struggles to maintain a career? How could she know that each event in their lives was identified with one of her hits. "If My Pillow Could Talk" may have been a catchy title for Connie's 1963 hit, but its title was reflected in the silences Rachel and Robert experienced as they attempted to live their lives without their dream of "strolling the lane" together. Only their pillows and the diary entries they maintained could now reveal the pain of those "Happy Days and Lonely Nights".

They both tried to be happy, to get on with their life without each other, to make the best of life! But Connie's early hit, "Happy Days and Lonely Nights" characterized their existence. It was easier to pretend during the day. Their pillows received the silence of their hearts and the dreams they dare not dream.

Robert glanced again at the photo of Connie and Rachel taken so many years ago. They were all so young...

Robert placed the photo back on the desk. He selected his 1966 diary from the banker's box, gingerly opening to the January entries which described the young couple's first attempt to share the festive season.

- - - - - Northumbria, 1966

Robert and Leah were seated in the small living-room of their modest one bedroom apartment. He was in a rocking chair reading the latest newsletter from Rachel, Leah was seated at a table working on a jigsaw puzzle. Leah looked up at Robert who appeared to be absorbed in the contents of the newsletter.

"How does she find time to run that fan club?"

"Rachel is very organized and she does have Rose as her assistant."

"You didn't get a Christmas card from her, did you?"

"Not yet. She probably hasn't received mine either, I was late sending it."

"Rob, you should write to Rachel. I want you to continue your friendship. I know you both like each other very much and if..."

"Leah, we were and are just friends."

"Rob, you are not happy, are you? How can you be?"

Robert placed the newsletter on the floor beside the rocking chair. He looked affectionately at Leah. "We have discussed this a hundred times. Leah, marriage is an adjustment for all young couples. We weren't really ready for the big step, but it was the right thing to do."

"Rob, we weren't ready to leave our homes; you miss your parents, your foster grandparents, and the manor; I miss my family."

"Leah, we live only ten minutes away!"

"That ten minutes prevents us from being part of their daily lives. We now visit our homes, it's very different. Since we got married and now that everyone knows we having a baby, we are treated as adults."

"Leah, we are adults!"

"Yes, I know, but life is so different, just because of one drink of wine."

"Wine had nothing to do with it; Al would have accomplished the same goal if you had chosen a milkshake."

"Rob, here you are a married man, going to be a father. And we have never consummated our marriage. I know we agreed to wait until after the baby was born so that we could start afresh, and to give me time, but I know you are being short-changed."

"Am I complaining?"

"No, but it would help if you did. Get angry! Rob, you bother me, you are always so calm. Even when Trevor confronts you, you don't lose your temper. You must be bottling this up inside.You'll get an ulcer."

"Don't worry about my ulcers, Leah, you do enough worrying for both of us."

Their conversation was interrupted by Trevor's unannounced entrance.

"Door was open so why knock?" He walked over to Leah and gave her a big hug. "How is my favourite sister?"

"And your only sister!" Leah was very fond of Trevor. She secretly wished that he and Robert would be friends.

"Hello Robbie, how's the father-to-be?" Trevor was the only person who addressed Robert as 'Robbie' and he delighted in accenting the 'ie'.

Robert was always uneasy with Trevor. It was often difficult to remain calm in his presence.

"I'm fine. Would you like a drink of something?"

"Nothing stronger than coffee here, I suppose."

Leah replied, "Too many calories in anything stronger, Trev. You might put on weight!"

Trevor smiled as he flexed the bicep of his right arm hidden beneath his light winter coat.

"Hey, I'll risk it."

"Trev, what can we do for you tonight? I know you never visit, so you must have something on your mind."

"You must have ESP, Sis. I'm helping at the church, sorting junk in the basement. Looking at Robert, "Robbie, I actually came to ask a favour."

Robert was caught off guard, "A favour?"

"Yes, I found boxes of old books in the basement of the church. I think most of them are novels. I wondered if they might be useful for the school library. Would you come with me to look them over?"

Leah was surprised by the invitation but regarded it as Trevor's way of calling a truce to the struggle that had existed between her husband and brother.

Hesitantly, Robert replied, "Sure, let me get my coat and boots."

Within a few minutes, he and Trevor were walking to the church in silence. Robert wanted to initiate conversation, but he and Trevor had never exchanged more than a few sentences at any one time in all the years they had known each other and inevitably, Trevor had a series of insults to pass on to the "wimp".

Just as they approached the churchyard, Trevor pointed to a park bench, "Can we stop and talk here?"

"If you want to talk, why can't we go into the church hall where it's at least warm?"

Trevor seemed to be struggling to hold back his usual aggressive nature. "Robbie, I want to talk in private with you, can we do it here?"

"Sure, do you want to sit or stand?"

"I think I'll stand, but you can sit if you want."

Robert decided he had better not lower himself physically to the bench thus giving Trevor an apparent advantage in the conversation. "No, I'll stand as well."

"Suit yourself! Listen guy, we don't get along. We don't like each other! Something we got to live with. Am I right?"

"You're right."

"We have never talked about Leah, about your marriage and now this baby!"

"What is there to say?"

Trevor began to forget his forced politeness, "Listen here, guy. I didn't want you to marry my sister. You knew that!"

"Yes, but I proposed to your sister and she accepted and your parents had no objection."

"Accepted, what choice did she have? Guy, I know you think I'm all muscles and no brains. But it doesn't take a rocket scientist to know that you knocked her up and had to marry her."

"Wait a minute!"

Trevor moved closer to Robert, pushing him lightly, "You took advantage of her, my sister."

"Trevor, I would never take advantage of Leah!"

"Why can't you be a real man, and admit it? You forced yourself on her. You must have read a book on how to seduce a virgin." Trevor clenched his fists, his face reddened, he paced back and forth in front of the bench, then suddenly exploded into an onslaught of shouts and punches.

"You bastard, you faggot! I'll kill you."

Robert attempted to shield himself from the blows that tore at his chest and face, but he was no match for this powerhouse. Within a minute, he was knocked to the ground. Trevor proceeded to kick him over and over again. "You haven't seen anything yet, buster. I'm going to kill you, just wait and see. Now crawl back home. But some day, I'm coming back to finish you. You can count on it."

"I wanted my sister to marry a real man, someone like Big Al, but you got her pregnant!"

With this last outburst, he seized a handful of snow, throwing it in Robert's face. "Here's some snow to ease the pain. When I finish with that pretty face of yours, you won't recognize it. I hope the kid is a boy so I can teach him to be a man, something you wouldn't know anything about. I'm surprised you knew how to screw!"

Having accomplished his task, he left Robert lying in the snow.

Robert rose slowly from the frozen ground, trying to get his breath. Trevor's blows had been directed chiefly at his chest, although he had been kicked several times in the stomach. He managed to sit on the bench, feeling the intense cold envelope him. He decided that he would not tell Leah what had happened, but he was uncertain how he could conceal the obvious results. Trevor had verbally abused him for years, but this was the first time he had physically attacked him. It was also the first time he had threatened him. Robert took the threats seriously, he knew Trevor's reputation. On more than one occasion the local police had taken Trevor to a cell to cool off after a weekend brawl had erupted at the only tavern in Northumbria.

In the midst of his pain while seated on the park bench, Robert made the decision that he would never allow anyone to physically abuse him again. He was determined to put on weight, to work out and to learn how to defend himself. The local YMCA had good programs and the physical education teacher at the local high school ran a weight lifting program for adults at night. He would also invest in some weights for home. He would seek self defence courses to help him as well. All of this was planned within a few minutes as he waited for his body to signal to him that he was ready to leave this scene that would forever be fixed in his mind.

He knew that Leah was fragile. She had had to take early leave from her teaching duties because she was often sick in the mornings and too weak to cope with the children. Her mental health was more of a concern for Robert than her physical ailments. He was concerned that she constantly had nightmares, she was not eating properly and she seemed oblivious to her surroundings. He knew that Leah could not forget the invasion of her body, and the baby growing within her was a constant reminder of that night that had robbed her of her innocence.

Robert realized that his mother had been right. There are many kinds of silences. He prayed that the birth of their child would be the means of restoring Leah's confidence and security, giving her a renewed purpose in life. He hoped that together as parents, he and Leah could really become a family. He longed for the time Leah would welcome him as her lover. He had been so unprepared for his role of husband and now father. A husband and father before he was a lover. It was like reading a 'how to' manual from the back cover to the opening chapter.

Gradually he felt his strength returning. He managed to begin his walk to the home of his closest friend, Howie, who was married to one of Leah's cousins. Howie was an assistant manager at one of the local banks. His wife, Margie, was a nurse and church organist/choir director. Margie was probably Leah's only confidant. Robert often wondered how much Margie knew about their marriage. He had never told Howie any of the details; Howie would never probe, he accepted Robert's right to privacy. Margie was more curious, but definitely discreet.

Howie and Margie had stood with Robert and Leah for their wedding. Robert had noticed that increasingly Leah was hesitant to invite the couple to their apartment, although she and Margie spoke at length on the phone most days.

Robert knew that his encounter with Trevor would be kept in confidence and he needed to talk to someone about Trevor's threats. Howie had once suffered a few blows in a fight provoked by Trevor and he was surprised that Trevor had not gone further than verbal abuse with Robert. As Robert slowly walked to his friend's apartment, he thought about the changes that had occurred in his life since August. He did miss the closeness of family life at the manor. He refused to allow his mind to reflect upon his American dream. He had not kept up his correspondence with Rachel; he simply could not complete a letter to her. He had tried numerous times, but it was futile. He had stopped playing Connie's records; they were bitter reminders of forgotten dreams. He now felt more intensely some of the passion in those songs that had once touched his heart with a longing for romance.

Robert did not regret his decision to marry Leah. He was very fond of Leah and he hoped that they could eventually be happy together. He knew that Leah was suffering, that she needed time to forgive and forget the past, time to experience renewed hope and peace again. He wanted desperately to confide in his mother, but he had promised Leah that he would tell no one. He knew, of course, that Bertha was able to read him like a book so she was not unaware of what was happening and why it had to be so.

* * * * * * * * * *

As Robert replaced his diary in the banker's box, he recalled the years of devotion he had given to building a stronger, fitter, more attractive body. He had been true to that decision he made on the park bench. He looked at his 175 pound physique that was well-defined through years of exercise. Trevor had given him one gift, the motivation to become physically fit!

As he glanced around his den at the Christmas decorations and the clutter of banker's boxes, he marvelled at Rachel. After his marriage to Leah, she had gone seven months without correspondence from him; a brief, cold, formal Christmas card had provided no revelations of

Robert's new life or his previous interest in her and the bouquet. She could not, however, forget the dream she had allowed herself to create. She regretted that the marriage had destroyed even their friendship. She no longer had a friend and a confidant. She had lost her kindred spirit!

----- Flanders Cove 1967

Rachel and Rose sat at a work table in the fan club office; they both were stuffing envelopes with the current newsletter reviewing Connie's career in 1966. Connie had made numerous television appearances including: "The Andy Williams Show", "The Jackie Gleason Show", "The Tonight Show", "The Mike Douglas Show", "The Garry Moore Show"and of course, "The Ed Sullivan Show". She had made countless personal appearances including: The Sahara Hotel in Las Vegas, Eden Rock in Miami Beach and Blinstrub's in Boston. She had recorded albums in Germany and Italy. Her fourth movie, "When the Boys Meet the Girls" had been released, playing for months throughout the nation. Her 1966 single record releases included: "Love Is Me, Love Is You", "A Letter from a Soldier", and "Spanish Nights and You". Her albums, "Jealous Heart", "Movie Hits of the 60's", "Connie Francis Sings Songs of Love" and "Connie Francis Live at the Sahara in Las Vegas"revealed her versatility as a performer. With record sales reaching the 50 million mark, her career continued to blossom.

Rose finished stuffing the last of her envelopes, then began the tedious task of placing postage on each one. "I see you are sending one to Nova Scotia. You haven't mentioned Robert lately. Do you mind my asking about him?"

"No, it's all right. I did receive a Christmas card, with no real news in it. I guess married life is busy and, of course, he is involved with his school work and the church as well. They will soon be parents so that will be another big change."

"I am sorry that he hasn't continued writing, I thought that he would once he settled into his new life."

"I hoped he would, too, but some relationships are of a time and place. I guess our time is gone; he has so many new responsibilities that demand his time. I must admit, I do miss hearing about his family and Northumbria, but really I have become accustomed to his silence."

Looking affectionately at her niece, "I am disappointed in him, I felt sure he was more genuine."

Rachel came to Robert's defense, "Rose, we don't know all the circumstances, we don't know what happened."

"Defending Sir Lancelot, despite his betrayal."

"Rose!"

"Yes, I hear you! Next topic!"

"I think we could use a hot drink, not tea though; Daisy is planning a high tea for later. We don't have much more work to complete this mailing."

Rose left Rachel with the final envelopes to stamp. Rachel picked up Robert's envelope, gently pressing her lips to the envelope. She was devastated that their friendship had not survived the marriage. She wondered what she might do to let Robert know she was still interested in being a friend, but she did not know how to relate to a married man, especially one whom she had begun to fall in love with, someone she could not cease dreaming of. She was remembering with fondness some of Robert's most intimate revelations in his letters when Rose returned with a stack of correspondence, placing it on the tray on the work table, "Here is today's mail. Iris would like help in the kitchen, I'll be back later. Hope you will enjoy the hot chocolate, from a package, you know."

Rachel carelessly flipped through the stack of letters; she was surprised to see one from Canada with the familiar Northumbria address. She quickly tore open the envelope to gain access to the contents. She was startled to discover who the writer was!

Dear Rachel,

You will be surprised to hear from me. I hope you will not be
annoyed that I have written and that I have assumed you
may want to hear my news. I know that Robert has not written
to you for months and I am certain you are wondering
what is happening in our lives.

I will give you a few details of the manor later in this letter,
but I must ask that you not reveal to Robert that I have
written to you. Perhaps in time, he will return to corresponding

with you. In the meantime, I trust this letter will be some
comfort to you. Forgive me if I am taking liberties
that I should not.

You are entitled to know that in the years of correspondence
with you, Robert became extremely fond of you and
"the bouquet". He eagerly awaited each letter,
he constantly mentioned all of you in his conversations.
We teased him about becoming an American citizen!

Robert's marriage was a shock to all of us.
None of us could have anticipated it.
The courtship lasted only three weeks.
Now he and Leah are to be parents.
Leah is having great difficulties in her pregnancy.

Robert is busy with his school work. We see him for a few minutes
most days. Leah has withdrawn to their apartment
and seems to be ill at ease away from it;
this will probably improve once the baby is born...

Rachel found her hand trembling as she continued reading the contents. She had known that Bertha was a caring woman; she was overcome with gratitude that the "guardian angel" of the manor would reach out to her. It was obvious that Bertha knew the bond of affection that had existed between her son and Rachel. It was so comforting to have that bond confirmed. For the first time since she had received Robert's letter in August, she felt comforted; she felt that she had not been mistaken, she knew that she and Robert had been more than friends. He had felt that special bond, too.

She tried to not read between Bertha's lines, but she could not control her imagination. What had happened in August to bring about the sudden marriage? She wondered, too, about the baby so early in their marriage. She lingered over every paragraph, savoured each revelation, basked in the knowledge that she and Robert had been more than friends.

"You have a letter from Northumbria?" Rose inquired as she entered the room.

"You noticed!"

"There are few things that I don't notice."

Rachel looked fondly at Rose, "That I am well aware of."

"But it wasn't from Robert?"

"No, Bertha wrote. Here, there is nothing in the letter that I can't share with you."

"I always knew that Bertha was a remarkable woman, this confirms it. Now with a mother like that, there may still be hope for her son."

"Rose!"

"Yes, I hear you."

Rachel passed her the letter and returned to the postage of the newsletters.

After reading the letter, Rose looked tenderly at Rachel, "Quite a woman! And it is obvious that Robert was very fond of you. This is a strange marriage. I wonder if we will ever discover what really happened. I have a few theories."

"Next topic, Rose."

Rose passed the letter back to Rachel. "Bertha writes a good letter. Speaking of writing. I really appreciate the time you take to review my writing. It is good to have a critic. I remember the first day I dropped my secret diary into your lap. I was so apprehensive about having someone look at my thoughts. I was afraid that you would be amused that the 'scholarly' Rose would dare to write literature for children."

"I was surprised that you were interested in children's literature, assuming your only interest was the classics. Your expertise in the classics provides you with a richness that enhances your stories for children. Your stories are so tender, so captivating. They touch heart strings!"

"More, continue to flatter me!"

"Rose, you know how much I value your writing. You must gain the confidence you require to send a few of the stories to a publisher."

"I am certainly not ready to expose myself to that type of scrutiny, but perhaps one day."

"You should have a working title for your stories. They tend to be theme related, and they all fit together."

"I want a title, but I can never find one that is encompassing. I write the stories out of love; love of literature and my fondness for children. Our household has had too little influence of children, but I do enjoy them. I enjoy the wonder of children, their innocence, their ability to use their imaginations, their freedom, their trust. We seem to live in such a fast paced world and yet, children still enjoy the beauty of a good story. I must come up with a title though."

Rachel paused, then asked, "Perhaps you might consider, 'With Love, With Children'?"

"'With Love, With Children'. I like it. I like it a lot! Rachel, it is perfect. How did you ever think of it?"

"I won't take the credit, it is not really original, but use it if you like."

"'With Love, With Children'. I have my title. Thank you."

"I really enjoyed your last story about Rocky, the raccoon. He is a delightful character. His visit to a town's new subdivision was hilarious. You must have done a great deal of research on the habits of raccoons."

"Research is important, but we used to have raccoons visit us in our backyard; of course, that was well before your time. Since the city slickers have moved here, trees have disappeared and so have the animals."

"Rose, I have a favour to ask of you today. You are not the only author in this household."

"Oh, I know that. We all keep diaries, have for years. Your grandmother always kept one and she inspired us to begin our daily ritual as soon as we could write. Father was the only one who didn't keep one, claimed he was too busy with his "books" for the business. He did, however, record interesting notations in many of the books in the library."

"I'm beginning to think that grandad should have kept a diary. He also included fascinating notes in his business records as well. Some of them reveal his humour as well as his satire."

"You haven't mentioned that before."

"Much of the portfolio materials is dull reading, but I do enjoy the occasional rushed comment left by a shrewd businessman."

"Perhaps you might gather some of the better ones to share with your aunts?"

"A good idea, Rose. I'll do it! But I want to first inform you that I have been reading Daisy's diaries."

"Her personal diaries! She has shared them with you?"

"No, her church writings; she keeps them separate."

"She does, Daisy has two sets of diaries?"

"Yes, and she is very sensitive about her writing. I have asked her to share one selection with us after tea this afternoon. She is too timid to read it herself, but has asked me to do so. Please respect Daisy as an author who is taking a risk in having something she has written shared for the first time with an audience. Remember, soon you will want to take the same risk."

"Oh no. You know I write for a mythical audience, not for real people."

"Rose, your work is too good to be hidden away. Rocky is ready to be shared with the world."

Rose laughing, "I can see the headlines now: 'Aging spinster writes children's stories of raccoons frolicing in suburbia'."

The two were interrupted by the ringing of the bell used to announce that tea and meals were being served. It was a custom carried on from the days when servants would announce to the family that their presence was required in the dining-room or parlour.

As they left the fan club office, Rachel once again reminded Rose to be supportive of the fragile writer who was about to expose herself to her first critics. As they entered the parlour, Iris placed a package in Rachel's hand. "Rose must have overlooked this parcel which came in the mail today. I couldn't help noticing that it is from Northumbria."

"A parcel for me, from Northumbria!"

Daisy motioned for Rachel to sit in the window seat while the aunts took their customary places. "Perhaps we'll wait until Rachel has opened her parcel before the tea is poured."

"Oh thank you, I am anxious to see what is inside. It is from Bertha, I now recognize her penmanship. I received a letter from her today as well."

The aunts remained silent as Rachel tore at the wrappings; they did manage to steal quick glances at each other, but otherwise focused their undivided attention on Rachel. Rachel removed three smaller packages from the unwrapped box.

"A photo of Bertha and Camille and the residents of the manor. Oh, isn't that thoughtful! And she has everyone identified at the bottom of the photo." Rachel could not keep the tears from forming; she quickly brushed them aside.

Passing the photo to Iris, "Here is a photo of Northumbria, it is my first one of the entire family; well, there is someone missing but...How very kind of Bertha. Let's see what else is here."

Opening the second parcel, Rachel hesitated before showing the contents to the aunts. She dissolved in tears. When she had partially regained her composure she continued, "Bertha has included a piece of wedding cake with a note."

Rose broke the silence, "Why would she include a piece of the cake? It seems so cruel."

Daisy came to Bertha's defence, "I disagree, I'm sure she thought it would help Rachel to feel a part of something that she had been denied."

Iris responded, "I agree with Daisy; whatever the reason, Bertha must have decided it would comfort Rachel. May we inquire what the note says?"

Rachel passed the note to Iris, taking the opportunity to wipe her eyes and blow her nose.

Iris began reading, "Rachel, I have included a piece of the wedding cake. You were the uninvited but remembered guest at the wedding. We sent pieces of the cake to family and friends; I hesitated to send this to you, but felt that you had been denied what others had received. I hope you understand my motives."

Rose looked at Rachel, "This is an exceptional woman. Are you all right, Rachel?"

Rachel looked at her aunts with tears flowing down her cheeks, "Yes, it is so kind of her, and I do appreciate it. As a friend, I would like to have attended the wedding! I have felt so excluded, it does help." She could not continue.

Iris attempted to lighten the mood, "And I see we have one more parcel. Are we going to see its contents or are we going to guess what is inside?"

Rachel removed the wrapping to reveal a dozen of the famous waffles, 'galettes' as the Belgians called them. She dissolved once again in tears.

This time Daisy came to the rescue, "Tea is ready and I suggest we all have a galette, is that the correct word?"

Daisy reached for the silver tea set, complete with tea pot, milk pitcher, tea strainer, and spoons. High tea had its unique customs that the aunts rigidly adhered to. The cups were heated with hot water before being brought to the parlour. Milk, not cream, was used for the tea and it was always poured first. Loose tea was used for the afternoon ritual. Daisy gracefully placed the silver strainer over each cup before she poured. Silver spoons were provided, even though none of the aunts used sugar.

Today, Daisy had chosen to use pieces of the Spode "Buttercup" pattern for their china.

Complementary yellow cloth napkins with a delicate lace border completed the setting. Daisy had made chicken salad and asparagus sandwiches as well as her specialty, sausage rolls. She also included Spanish cream, fruit cake and lemon tarts to tempt the palates.

After each had received her tea and a galette, Rose lifted her galette in the air, "Here's to Northumbria. Thank you, Bertha."

Each tasted the galette in silence. Rachel was the first to speak. "Oh, they are so delicious!"

Rose closed her eyes as if to savour the delicacy without interruption, "It is sweet, but..."

Daisy added, "It doesn't taste like a waffle, at least not the waffles we have."

Iris looked at the galette in her right hand declaring, "This is a treat! I can't decide what it tastes like; it is delicate, the texture is wonderful, so light, definitely rich, exquisite. How many do we have?"

"Not enough! exclaimed Daisy.

The mood had changed, an extra gift from Bertha. Rachel gradually relaxed as the aunts chatted about Northumbria, returning to the photo, asking questions of Rachel about the manor and its guests. Each of the aunts could recall at least one amusing incident that Rachel had shared with them from Robert's letters. It was a time of healing and restoration.

When Rachel felt that Northumbria had received enough of their focus, she attempted to return to her agenda for the afternoon. She withdrew a folder from her attache case which had been resting beside her. "Ladies, I have something to share with you. You are all writers; you all keep diaries. Daisy has kept separate diaries of her church involvement. Daisy has given me permission to me to read an entry to you."

Rose smiled at Daisy, Iris looked at her sister in astonishment. Daisy gave each of her sisters a warm smile, then lowered her head to protect herself from observing reactions to the first public reading of her work.

Rachel continued, "I have chosen to read this particular selection because it is witty, contains satire, and reveals the gifts of an author who has much to share with us. This is tenderness with a bite! I want to read the entire selection before we pause for comment. It is entitled, "The Perfect Service". I know you will enjoy it."

"An Episcopal parish decided that it would have a service of worship that would be very special and long remembered as the perfect service. This service would be out of the ordinary, a real 'superspecial', a service to live in the hearts of parishioners for generations. Indeed, later generations would recall the service with such comments as: "My grandfather said that no service could ever surpass the one held in his day", or "It was the best service you could imagine".

One of the first decisions made by the parish in bringing the notion of a perfect service closer to reality was to request a full parish meeting one Sunday morning following church to discuss the proposed service. The 'blue haired' and 'no haired' parishioners turned out in full force, but there were a few young families present and even a few children. An idea was ready to receive its first breath of inspiration and life.

It was proposed by the rector, seconded by the wardens, and unanimously approved by those present that the theme of the service should be "That All May Be One".

Having settled upon an appropriate theme, the meeting enthusiastically settled down to wrestling with the basic ideas of the service.

The first detail to be discussed was the date for the service. Many felt that summer would be the most suitable time since the weather and roads were more predictable and energy costs were less. However, others pointed out that God traditionally goes on vacation for July and August and might not consider favourably having to tune in from above to such a service while possibly enjoying summer frolics. They also pointed out that parishioners often relaxed their church dress code in the summer. Some mentioned that too many of the teenagers wore low-cut dresses and shorts to church in the summer. Everyone enjoyed a comment from one of the eldest ladies, "Well, these young ladies are wearing biblical clothes." She paused for dramatic effect, then added, "Lo and behold". Everyone chuckled at the comment, more of a reaction to the speaker than her comment. Others pointed out that churches were too stuffy in the summer and wondered why others had not thought of such an important consideration. At this point, another group proposed a winter month be considered, but this soon received negative comments because it is too difficult to get to church with winter snow, ice and cold. Another group decided a compromise was in order and, therefore, suggested that either the spring or fall be considered. It was, however, pointed out that the fall is already busy enough with school reopening, Veterans'Day, Thanksgiving and then before you know it, Christmas. Likewise, how could anyone consider the spring with Spring Break and Easter taking up so much time and energy?

It was agreed to leave the selection of the season to a committee for consideration. There did seem to be general consensus that it might be desirable to have the service mid-way between Christmas and Easter so that some parishioners would feel more comfortable with poinsettias and/or lilies adorning the chancel, since many saw the church only when it was so arrayed. Someone suggested that the service be held to coincide with the red altar hangings because they were the most attractive."

Rose could no longer restrain herself, "Daisy, this is cleverly written and so believable. I love the gentle satire..."

Rachel raised her right index finger to her lips, "Shhh!", and she continued reading.

"The group then attempted to select the desired hour for the service. Some suggested nine o'clock as the best hour, but there were those who felt that this was too early for those who watched the late movie the previous evening or who had gone partying. It was suggested that it might be better to consider the traditional eleven o'clock hour. This brought forth some concern that such a service, if lengthy, might "cut in" to the midget hockey practice, the local flea market or other usual Sunday activities. The suggestion that the service be held in the evening startled many who had not realized that provision is made for evening services in the prayer book. This suggestion was soon abandoned since Sunday night television was family night with such favorite programs as: "Crime Today", "Desire on the Beach", "Take a Bribe" and "Lotto Today". This dilemma was also given to the committee for deliberation.

At this point, a small child seated with her parents was heard asking her mother, "Is it still Sunday?" The mother hushed the child, but it did prompt others to encourage the chairman to speed things up."

Iris clapped her hands in approval, "What a lovely touch. I can picture all of this."

Rachel raised her eyebrows and with an affected tone responded, "No interruptions, please."

"It then seemed appropriate to discuss the length of the service. Many felt that one hour was sufficent and that anything else would simply encourage the glorification of verbosity and redundancy. Some felt that a good sermon should only be five minutes in length; others disagreed. There was even a recommendation that the perfect service should be devoid of a sermon. One of the wardens indicated that sermons shouldn't be so long that it is difficult to stay awake, nor too loud to prevent listeners from sleeping. The group agreed that the length of the service would depend upon the individual items on the agenda and so moved on to consideration of the same.

The type of liturgy to be used was discussed in detail. It was recommended that the service be Holy Communion, yet there was strong resistance to this suggestion. It was pointed out that the service would be too lengthy. Some sage suggested that the rector be assisted in the administration of the chalice by laity, but there were those who would have none of that foolishness. The recommendation to invite a neighboring clergyman to assist did not bring favourable response either, since many felt that no 'outsiders' were required to assist them with their special service.

Someone suggested that a new liturgy be used for the service, but many wanted no part of that heresy. After all, this service was to be a time of reflecting upon the past glories and the use of modern language would be less suitable. Besides, most of the devout realized that Elizabethan language was infinitely more pleasing to God than modern jargon. It was good to see reason prevail."

Rose could not contain herself, "Ah, classical language, 'tis good to see reason prevail!'"

Rachel smiled, "May I continue?"

Rose replied, "By all means."

"Someone from the back row of the church hall suggested having a folk mass but no one really took him seriously. Such a notion smacked of the radical movement in the church; the organ was the only legitimate church musical instrument.

The group agreed that this important decision could not be sent to a committee who already had more than enough to consider. Consequently, the group favored sending the matter to the bishop and it was agreed that at least this would involve him in a matter that was relatively harmless.

The choir director asked for suggestions for special music. Some suggested there be a special anthem. Others felt no anthem would make it special. There was general disagreement on the choice of traditional or contemporary music. Many felt that only hymns written by Episcopalians should be used. There was a great debate about Beethoven's religious affiliation since many wanted "Joyful, Joyful, We Adore Thee" as the processional, although there were those who felt it would make a better recessional. It was agreed that this one exception be made to the Episcopalian authorship requirement; it would help to make the service more ecumenical.

The mere mention of the word 'ecumenical' brought forth many lively comments. The question of who was to attend the service then received attention. Many felt that only the faithful should attend. Some felt that other denominations might be invited to share the experience; however, many felt that "their ways are not our ways" and it might dilute the faith. After all, God was obviously Episcopalian, and He might not appreciate the inclusion of others.

As discussion began to wane, a former warden suggested that in order to provide a perfect service they should profit from past experiences. Obviously, they all knew what was NOT a perfect service. Immediately, everyone was given pencil and paper and an opportunity to list favourite 'beefs' with church services. The top five dissatisfactions were then recorded. These complaints were written into recommendations for the special service. These were the five responses:

1) No small children should be permitted to attend the service because they cause too much commotion. They can wait until they are adults.

2) The junior choir should not participate because they deprive the seniors of their seats, and after all, the seniors have earned their seats, they have sat on them much longer."

Iris laughed, "Well worn seats, indeed."

Rachel smiled, but continued.

"3) The rector should be careful to adjust his stole properly before the service begins; there is nothing as distracting as an uneven stole.

4) There should be no silences in the liturgy; silence makes people nervous.

Besides, the furnace can be heard when everyone is quiet."

Rose interjected, "Be still and know that I am God!"

"5) The entire service should be printed in booklet form so that no page flipping would be necessary with parishioners looking for the proper psalm, collect, responses, etc. Some parishioners get lost searching for the proper page and get so frustrated they tune out for the remainder of the service.

There did appear to be general satisfaction with the dissatisfactions! Consequently, the group moved on to the very serious consideration of a lunch. It was felt that a lunch of sweet breads would be most suitable as long as homemade jams were provided for freshly baked biscuits. The men agreed to serve if the ladies did the baking. There was a brief moment of discussion about stereo-typing in the list of duties for lunch, but this was soon forgotten."

Rose interrupted once again with, "Not much of a lunch, if you ask me. And you wrote this, Daisy?"

"Feeling that much had been accomplished, it was agreed to adjourn until reports were received from the bishop and the committee. As they were leaving the church hall, one parishioner was overheard saying, "I was really depressed in the middle of that discussion, but now that it is over, I'm relieved!"

It appears that closed door discussions in the committee room have not yielded a uniform position to date. As soon as the committee reports, all deliberations will be made available to you. It is important that we strive to be one!"

Rachel lifted her eyes to look at her audience, "That concludes "The Perfect Service".

Rose and Iris stood up and went over to Daisy to congratulate her.

"I would never have believed that you were writing such selections, Daisy."

"Actually this is not typical of my writing; I rarely poke fun, I am usually more serious, but..."

"I loved every bit of it. Anyone who has ever been involved with a church could identify with your account of that parish meeting."

"Does each selection have its own theme and title?" inquired Rose.

"Yes, each one is a separate story, but they all fit together. I call my ramblings, "With Love, With God."

Rose and Rachel exchanged smiles.

Rose repeated, "'With Love, With God.' What an appropriate title!"

* * * * * * * * * *

Robert smiled as he closed Rachel's diary, "With Love, With God", "With Love, With Children"!

The aunts were so unique, so gifted, so precious; treasures to be protected. He admired Rachel's ability to serve as their 'guardian'. She had been so faithful in allowing the bouquet to continue their charmed life in their declining years. He looked at the many diaries and letters that he had selected as resources for his first novel. The task that lay ahead filled him with excitement and trepidation. He was not certain where he would start, what approach he should take. How could he weave so many different voices into a coherent story? He glanced at the leather bound novels that adorned his bookcase. Most of the novels were British, American and Canadian classics: "Great Expectations, "Moby Dick", "Barometer Rising". He realized how important a title would be. In an instant, "With Love, With Connie" flashed into his consciousness. He knew that the title was perfect. He had his title!

He returned to his 1967 diary, recalling his first attempts to build a more powerful body. He had purchased weights which he set up in his former bedroom at the manor. He was faithful to work out whenever he visited the manor, and he had enrolled in the weight lifting program at the high school. He wanted his pursuit of a more physically fit body to be a guarded secret, in order to ensure that Trevor would be the last one to discover his goal.

----- Northumbria 1967

Robert relaxed in his favourite wing chair in the sun porch of the manor. He had just finished his exercise program downstairs and was now enjoying chatting with Gramma Horton, Miss Brown and Mr. Gordon. Bertha was standing in the doorway that led to the dining-room.

Miss Brown was watering the plants on the window sill, African violets, philodendrons and a few geraniums left over from the summer garden. "These geraniums have seen better days."

Gramma responded, "Haven't we all!"

Mr.Gordon retorted, "Speak for yourself, ladies."

Bertha agreed with Miss Brown, "I never know what to do with geraniums. Last year, I dug them up from the garden, placed them in plastic bags in the basement for the winter, then began watering them in the spring. But very few of them survived and none of them flourished the second summer."

Gramma Horton had operated a successful nursery for over 40 years and had a green thumb as well as experience with plants. "I have tried hanging the geraniums upside down in the dark for the winter and that seemed to work as well as anything. Most of the survivors bloomed well the second season."

For a brief moment Robert lapsed into his memory of the bouquet. The mansion included a conservatory, complete with ornamental trees, shrubs and numerous flowering plants. A grand piano and stereo gave the large bright room its musical flavour. This was the room to showcase Iris' winter gardening and it was here that Rose too infrequently gave piano recitals for her sisters. She was the only competent musician in the household although Rachel had studied piano for three years before coming to live with the bouquet. Robert recalled Rachel describing Iris' geraniums that bloomed all winter long in their protective environment. He deemed it inappropriate to mention such cultivation at this moment.

Bertha approached the window sill, "Perhaps I will try your method next year. I couldn't be bothered with them at the end of the summer with so many things happening." She paused as her eyes met Robert's.

Robert quickly changed the subject, "I like the African violets the best. They must like the light here; they never stop blooming. Miss

Brown, you must like African violets. Do they remind you of your missionary work in Africa?"

Miss Brown smiled, "African violets are to Africa what pizza is to Italy! If you understand what I mean!"

Robert chuckled, "I do know what you mean."

It was Mr. Gordon who asked Robert, "How is your singer friend doing?"

"According to the newsletters I receive, she seems to be doing very well."

Mr. Gordon confessed, "You know, I miss hearing her records; I grew accustomed to hearing her voice. Kept me young, you know, all that romance. With all these beautiful ladies here, a fellow must have romantic music to encourage him."

Miss Brown winked at Gramma, "As if he needed any encouragemnent."

Bertha looked affectionately at Robert, "You left all your records in your room downstairs, didn't you?"

"Yes, no room for them in our apartment. Besides, Leah is not fond of female singers."

Mr. Gordon commented, "Just play them when she is not at home."

"Leah rarely leaves the apartment. Some day, I'll have more space and time to play the records again, but..."

Bertha came to his rescue, "Robert, you wouldn't object if we played some of the more mellow Connie albums, would you?"

"No, please play them."

"The singles are too much of a nuisance, and the changer never seems to handle more than two records at a time, but we could put a few albums on at one time."

Mr. Gordon leaned forward to whisper loudly to Gramma, "We'll have Connie sing while we cuddle up under an afghan."

Gramma raised her eyebrows, "And Mr. Gordon, do you think I would cuddle up with someone who flirts with all the ladies at the manor?"

Miss Brown added, "And flirts with ladies outside the manor."

Mr. Gordon reached over to touch Gramma's right hand, "It's all just a warm-up for you."

Gramma gently pushed his hand away, "Then we won't need the afghan."

Bertha winked at Robert who was obviously enjoying this typical scene from the sun porch. He basked in the warmth, the humour and the nostalgia of his family. He knew that his self-imposed exile was his private burden to bear and he knew that his foster grandparents could not really understand why he had deserted them. Yet, the bond of affection between them continued to grow despite his move to an apartment. Leah rarely came to the manor; she was relatively unknown to the guests. Robert lapsed into the rhythm of the sun porch's warmth and cozy ambience until he was abruptly brought back to reality by his mother.

Bertha held up her left arm, "My bracelet is gone!"

Robert was startled to be awakened from his dream world, "What do you mean, it's gone?"

"I had it on just a few minutes ago, it must have fallen off."

As he got up from his wing chair, Robert suggested that his mother retrace her steps; he would search the kitchen and dining-room where they both had tidied up before coming into the sun porch. The search proved futile.

Later Robert and his mother were seated alone in the kitchen. It was obvious that his mother was distraught. He knew that the bracelet was a prized possession because she almost always wore it. He had asked about its significance throughout the years, but never seemed to get any satisfaction. Bertha seemed inclined to keep its real significance to herself. Robert did know that his father had not given it to his mother and it appeared not to be a family heirloom. Robert had asked his father about the bracelet on one occasion, but in typical fashion, Camille had told Robert to ask his mother for the bracelet's story. Bertha was normally calm and collected. Even when sickness and mishaps occurred at the manor with the guests, she remained in control, providing the strength that others needed. For some reason, this bracelet had a value that was well beyond its silver content. He needed to know this story, this secret that Bertha guarded so well.

"The bracelet will be found. It is just misplaced, but it is still in the manor."

"I'm sure we will find it, but I know I did not take it off."

"I guess I have forgotten the significance of the bracelet. Was it a gift?"

Bertha hesitated, "Yes, a gift."

"A gift from?"

"A gift from a stranger."

Robert teased, "The bracelet was given to you by a secret admirer?"

Bertha dismissed the teasing, "No, from a gentleman that you have never met."

"This is a mystery, continue."

"Robert, now is not the time to talk about the bracelet, but I promise I will tell you its story later. The bracelet has been a constant reminder to me that no matter how difficult life becomes, and our family has had its share of trouble, there are wonderful caring people to reach out with affection to ease the pain. The bracelet is an expensive one, it has always been here to provide me with a last resort. On more than one occasion, I have thought of taking it to a pawnbroker."

"After your father retired from the mine and before I opened our store, I did walk to the door of the pawnbroker in Halifax, but I could not sacrifice this piece of silver for a few dollars that would have provided only temporary relief."

"Robert, the bracelet is a reminder of all that is good in the world. When I despair with world news, with the bickering that goes on in a small town, and when I feel that life is consuming me, I have this bracelet to remind me that people can be compassionate, honest, decent, caring, loving; even to strangers. You are familar with the passage from the Bible, from Matthew's gospel, I believe:

When I was hungry, you gave me something to eat,
And when I was thirsty, you gave me something to drink,
When I was a stranger, you welcomed me...

There are such people in this world. Whenever I forget the good that is around me, my bracelet restores my faith."

Robert desperately wanted to have the mystery revealed, but he knew that his mother would only provide the complete details when she was ready. He was intrigued by this simple wrist decoration which he had taken for granted because it was always worn, worn for housework, and worn on special occasions. Its constant adornment of Bertha's wrist had ensured that it would be dismissed as ordinary by observers.

Bertha leaned over to give Robert a hug. "Well, my dear Robert, I have my secrets and you have yours."

Robert blushed as he nodded his head in agreement, "I guess we all have secrets."

Bertha smiled,"Perhaps I will share mine with you when you are ready to share yours."

Robert got up from his chair and embraced his mother, "We do need to talk, but I have made promises that must be kept."

"I understand. Sometimes, however, promises are best shared with loved ones."

"You may be right, but for the time being, I need to work things out."

Camille entered the kitchen to tell Robert that Trevor was on the phone with an important message.

Robert kissed his mother's cheek before hastily walking to the phone.

"Hello Robbie, Trevor here. While you were at the manor enjoying yourself, my sister began to haemorrhage. I had to rush her to Outpatients. When you have time, join us here at the hospital." He then hung up the receiver.

Robert stood for a moment, dazed, then quickly returned to the kitchen to inform his parents.

"I'll call you as soon as I have news." Within an instant he was en route to the hospital. He felt so guilty that he had not been there for Leah. He cringed at the thought of having to face Trevor at the hospital. Trevor had become his antagonist. Shortly after their fight near the park bench, he had begun to receive cards in the mail. One of them was a sympathy card with a blunt message: "Are you ready?" He knew that Trevor was trying to spook him and he hated to admit that Trevor was successful.

When he arrived at the hospital, Ellen and Ken, Leah's parents greeted him. Trevor had gone for coffee.

Ellen was crying as she hugged her son-in-law, but it was Ken's face that told Robert the news he feared.

"Leah has had a miscarriage." He placed his arm on Robert's shoulder. Tears formed in his eyes.

Ellen broke her silence, "Robert, it is just one of those things! No one is to blame. Leah is weak and her body just rejected the baby. We'll stay here in the waiting room, she's in room 305, go to her, she needs you; but she has been hysterical so expect the worst."

Ken grabbed Robert by the shoulders, "Son, you have been so good to Leah, I hope she appreciates you as much as we do."

Robert wondered if there was an unspoken significance to his father-in-law's comment but he was anxious to see his wife. His dream of having a child to unite them into a family was shattered, but he and Leah would still have each other and together they could deal with their problems.

As he entered Leah's private room, she greeted him with, "Rob, I want a divorce!"

"A divorce, Leah calm down!"

"I will never be calm again. Don't you see what I've done?"

"I don't think you have done anything. You had a miscarriage." He approached Leah to embrace her, but she put her hands up to prevent him from doing so.

"Listen to me, don't you realize what has happened? You were forced to marry me because you wanted to save my reputation, to give my baby a father."

"Leah, why bring that up now!"

"Because, it was all for nothing. There is no baby, there is no baby!"

"Leah, we have lost our baby, you are upset."

"Rob, I lost my baby, it was never yours."

"Leah, that is unfair, I would have loved the baby as my own."

"Yes, you would have, that is not the point, everything you sacrificed was for nothing, I miscarried. She could no longer hold back the tears. As she wiped her eyes, Robert seized her in his arms to comfort her. She cried uncontrollably.

"Leah, you are upset. I am upset. Our baby has been taken away from us."

"It is my punishment."

"Leah, you can't be punished, you didn't do anything wrong."

"Oh, yes, I did, I destroyed your life. Rob, you married me because of the baby, the baby is gone. My body rejected the baby."

"Settle down, let's just mourn our loss and then we'll talk about us. Nothing has changed. We will put our lives together. I love you, Leah. You know that."

"Yes, you love me, but you pity me. I know you loved Rachel, I know I destroyed that dream. I'm not the only one who doesn't sleep at night. I'm not the only one whose pillow has secrets. I know..."

Robert interrupted, "Leah, this is not the time to punish yourself; I didn't do anything that I have regretted. Can't we just have a good cry together because we have lost something very precious? Do we have to blame someone?"

"I am going to tell my parents the truth."

Robert was always gentle with his fragile Leah, but now he spoke aggressively to her, "Don't say anything to anyone now, take time to think this through. Will you promise me that? Will you wait? And if you decide to tell anyone, I want to be present, I want us to do it together. Do you understand? Promise me!"

Leah was surprised by Robert's forcefulness, "Yes...yes, I will wait."

****

Robert was overcome with the emotion of his memory. His Leah was so fragile. She could never forgive herself for their marriage. Nothing he could do would console her. The miscarriage was not the end of her suffering, but the beginning.

He returned his 1967 diary to the banker's box; these memories were too bitter, especially for today. He approached her large oak cabinet; it contained their joint record collection, their special collection. Only Connie Francis records would be kept in this beautiful showcase. He withdrew the hit single, "If My Pillow Could talk", it seemed such an appropriate song to summarize the pain of those early days of marriage. He and Leah lived together, yet apart. Their dreams were never the same dreams. They had tried so hard to reach out to each other, but it was too far to reach. He had been more successful than Leah in accepting the marriage and in attempting to find happiness together; Leah could not escape the shackles that her pregnancy had created. If their pillows could talk, they would betray their guarded dreams, their fantasies, their wildest nightmares; their desire to fulfil marriage vows, their inability to forget the lust that had denied them the time to become lovers. There were too few happy days and too many lonely nights!

Chapter 4:

Drownin' My Sorrows

Robert gently lifted yet another set of diaries from a banker's box; these were from 1970. He thought about his Camelot days at the manor, Connie, Rachel and the bouquet. It had been spring and very little rain fell on the kingdom. Connie's ballads sang of romance and young love.

The fast beat of "Stupid Cupid", "Too Many Rules", "Someone Else's Boy" and "Vacation" easily lightened his mood. The gentleness of "Together", "No One", "My Happiness" and "Among My Souvenirs" would slowly calm his troubled spirit. The emotional appeal of "My Heart Cries for You", "Second Hand Love", "Blue Winter" and "All the Love in the World" touched his heart with feelings he could only experience second hand. He knew that Connie's life in the early days was not always one of contentment. She struggled with her father who was overprotective. She had loved and lost Bobby Darin. And yet, they were all just growing up. The days of innocence were far too short. Connie's voice could tease, excite, calm, promise...

He often wondered if Connie spent much time playing her own records as she continued her life's journey. So many of her hits were supercharged with memories for him. When he first heard "Drownin' My Sorrows" he dismissed it as one of Connie's lesser triumphs. This hit had followed the extremely popular "If My Pillow Could Talk" and would be replaced on the charts by Connie's hit "Your Other Love". He thought of the significance of these three titles as they applied to his life in those days after Camelot was shattered. Dreams are hard to give up. He had briefly dared to have an American dream, then hoped for a Northumbrian dream. By 1970, both dreams seemed destined to be replaced with more pain than Connie could ever portray in her songs. No longer was it spring, no longer was there promise. It was a time of struggle, of trying to cope, of despair. As he read accounts of Connie's life, he realized that she, too, had not been denied the intensity of pain that Northumbria and Flanders were experiencing.

Whenever he played one of Connie's hits, he was transported to a time and place dictated by the song's bookmark in his life. Each song was related to a specific period in his life and each song carried with it an emotion that was linked with the events.

One of his junior high school students had chosen as the topic for an essay, "Life Sucks!" He had first reacted to the language used by the student in a formal essay, but as he stared at the title, he had to agree that life is not filled with tender ballads and light-hearted rhythms.

He opened Rachel's 1970 diary, flipping to the autumn section. He read some of the September entries, remembering the pain of that time in their lives.

- - - - - Flanders Cove, 1970

Rachel sat at her desk in her bedroom, examining her grandfather's earliest business records. She vividly recalled the last conversation she had had with James King in his office when he had given her the key to the strong boxes that were hidden in the window seat in her fan club office. She had learned a great deal about her grandfather through her careful examination of his business records. Mr. King was correct when he indicated that her grandfather was a businessman who made both friends and enemies. She had discovered that her grandfather began his career as a young entrepreneur with nothing but determination, energy and charm as his credits. His first job had been as a clerk in a shipping company. With his meagre savings, he purchased large areas of cheap land in which others saw little prospect for immediate development. After five years with the shipping firm, he became assistant manager. He lived modestly, investing everything he could save in forested land, waterside land, and neglected factory and warehouse buildings. The few associates who knew about his business investments secretly dismissed the investments as foolhardy.

The Great Depression had humbled many business tycoons but for Henry Thomas, Rachel's grandfather, it was a time when his investments were consolidated. He was able to purchase buildings and neglected land at great savings. By the time the depression had ended, he was manager of the shipping company. It was then that he met his beloved Violet.

In his struggle to save and invest, Henry had lost some of the gentler personality traits that had once endeared him to his friends and associates. Anyone who was not productive was a liability and soon dismissed. He gained control of the shipping company because of the ineptness of its owner. The owner had been too compassionate, too caring of his employees and as a result he fell into debt. Instead of coming to his aid, Henry profitted by purchasing the company at a cost well below the value of the business. Henry was becoming like Scrooge of Dickens' famous tale; however, it was not 'spirits' who transformed him, but a young lady who had little to offer for his advancement beyond her breeding, poise and love. For Henry, it was more than enough.

Their courtship lasted only three months. They began their married life in a humble apartment above the shipping office. It did not take Henry's employees long to discover that they had an ally in the boss' wife. She could be found in the offices, warehouses and on the wharf with freshly baked goods to supplement lunches. She visited the homes of the employees. She sent the families greeting cards. She became their means to gain a fair hearing with their employer. In time, Henry mellowed, he relaxed, he became more benevolent.

The business records bore numerous comments in Henry's script attesting to Violet's influence. His love for her never allowed him to regard her involvement as interference. He soon discovered the benefits of her kind acts. His employees responded to him out of respect for her. She was the ambassador, the diplomat, the gentle spirit who could quiet this business giant.

In later years, Henry anonymously funded numerous charitable foundations; his Violet managed all of these endeavours without pomp and ceremony. Few people in Flanders Cove would know that the local hospital, library and recreation centre owed the majority of their private funding to one major benefactor.

Henry had made enemies during his climb in the business world, especially in his earlier years. He regretted his treatment of the former owner of his shipping company. He was never able to gain the family's trust or respect despite efforts to do so. He did use his financial means to ensure that the children were able to receive scholarships to assist with their education; all of the scholarships derived from organizations funded by Henry.

After three years of examining the records, Rachel's affection for her grandfather had increased. She had also gained insights into the strength and warmth of her grandmother whom she had assumed to be simply a grand Victorian lady. She realized that all the strong traits of the bouquet were embodied within their mother. She was the diplomat, the manager, the intellect, the nurturer; she was definitely more than lace and poise.

Rachel's grandfather's records contained two mysteries she could not solve. She had discovered a few scattered comments that disturbed her. She had secretly collected them, placing them together in a notebook. She did not want to believe the conclusion that the evidence suggested, yet it seemed so obvious. She had found a key taped to the back of the 1940 ledger book with a note which read:

I think Violet would have understood, in fact, I know she would have.
Yet, I have never been able to tell her.
I feel compelled to record it, to confess it, and to justify it.
The key to my secret!

She had searched the house for another strong box, but to no avail. She had the key to solve a mystery and she was certain that the container was located somewhere in the mansion. As discreetly as possible, she had engaged the aunts in conversation regarding chests, trunks, storage boxes found in the attic and basement. Still the key remained without its home!

She held the key in her hand, wondering what secret it was intended to unlock. Part of her wanted to throw the key away and still another part of her wanted the mystery solved. After all, her grandfather had left a note with the key. He wanted someone in the family to know the secret, to put it to rest.

The second mystery dealt with large sums of money her grandfather had forwarded to a hospital. She wondered if the key would solve both puzzles.

Iris entered the bedroom with a vase of mountain ash berries, "Something to add a bit of colour to your room. They are a beautiful orange, aren't they?"

"Thank you, they are beautiful." Rachel discreetly put the key aside.

"Once we had an entire grove of mountain ash trees, but gradually they have died off. I suppose we should have replanted them. You have the best view of the trees from your window."

Iris walked over to the bow window, pushing aside the lace curtains. She knelt on the window seat as she looked out at the autumn scenery. "I love these bow windows; they provide the best view of the front yard, orchards and the harbour. Father knew what he was doing when he had the carpenters build bow windows and window seats so that we could enjoy the changing seasons."

"I have always felt guilty that I inherited the bedroom with the bow window."

"You needn't. This was always your mother's room and we all have our rooms which have their own rewards. Enjoy it."

"I hadn't actually thought about it, but of course, there are the three window seats, one on each floor, directly under each other." As Rachel shared this observation, she began to realize that she had overlooked an apparent clue in her search for the missing strongbox.

"Iris, were the three window seats built at the time the house was constructed?"

"Oh, yes, a master carpenter was hired to do the inside cabinets, closets, and window seats. Naturally they all contained a false bottom that served as a storage area for father's private papers and possessions."

"You know about the secret compartments?"

"Yes, of course, we all know. Father showed them to us on one occasion. He told us that we all needed to have our private places in the house. His library was his private domain as were our bedrooms ours. The window seats on the first and third floor were his private business storehouses. We were to simply forget the compartments existed. And we have respected his wishes. Did you not know about them? Didn't Mr. King mention them to you?"

Hesitating, Rachel replied, "Oh yes, he did mention them."

"The compartments probably contain nothing but outdated boring records, I suppose."

"That about sums it up, Iris. But the records are helpful in explaining grandad's business plan as it evolved over the years."

"I have no head for business, you and your mother inherited that talent."

Rachel glanced at the silver vase on her desk, "And you have enriched the household with your talents, Iris."

"Arranging plants and berries doesn't count for much, but thank you."

"But that is just the beginning of your talents."

"Now that Rose and Daisy have confessed their writing endeavours, I feel as if I have no talent to leave as a legacy of the past that we have shared here. Daisy has recorded our journey in faith; Rose has revealed life in Flanders Cove through the eyes of her animals. She is so clever to have written in modern fables the lessons we have all learned. My diaries are mere scratches, words, phrases; very few sentences."

Rachel got up from her desk, beckoning for Iris to follow her into the hallway. When Iris had joined her, she pointed to the stained glass window that graced one end of the hallway.

"Iris, this stained glass window is a testimony to the gardens on this estate. The window is the most striking feature of the house. It dominates the inside and outside of the house, both during the day and at night. You are the gardener, you and grandmother are responsible for this window; it is dedicated to you, to your love and devotion."

Rachel then turned to face the opposing wall, pointing to an enormous quilt that hung from a golden rod. The quilt was the same size as the stained glass window; it featured individual panels of the flowers that were maintained in the gardens. The Thomas crest was nestled in the centre panel.

"Iris, this quilt is the envy of everyone who has ever entered this house. You won first prize at the regional and state fairs. The quilt has appeared in several newspaper articles. It is an exceptional work of art. It is the legacy of this household. You have created a floral garden that will outlive us all. It contains our family crest, our names and so much more."

Iris looked at her creation, "I guess you are right, but it is only a quilt."

"Only a quilt that dwarfs any other quilt that anyone has ever seen. The size is enough to guarantee its legacy, but the workmanship is exquisite. You laboured over it for three years. You wouldn't use a panel until it was perfect."

"Yes, but embroidery and quilting are hardly talents to be compared with writing. Writing reaches so many more people."

"Do you know how many readers have seen the photo of this quilt in the state fair brochures?"

"Perhaps you have a point."

Looking at her aunt, Rachel inquired, "Would you object if I did a photo story on the quilt? I have never used my photography course that I took after leaving high school and I have been wanting to find a topic for my first venture into journalism."

"Don't do this just for me. There is no need."

"Iris, I'm doing this for me. It has been ten years since the quilt was the featured winner. I think it is time to highlight it again. We'll work on the project together. It will be our secret."

Iris kissed Rachel on the cheek, "You are just like your mother!"

"I take that as the supreme compliment. Thank you."

"I have some unfinished work in the conservatory. If I want to get my geraniums planted inside before frost comes, I had better get my trowel in action. Thank you, once again."

As soon as Iris had descended the steps to the first floor, Rachel closed her bedroom door and hastily went to her window seat. Why had she not considered the possibility of another hidden compartment in the other window seats? Why hadn't Mr. King mentioned the possibility? She removed the cushions, opened the top of the seat and held it with one hand. As she searched the bottom of the cabinet, she found the sliding panel that concealed the storage area. She was able to retrieve several boxes of papers and one steel storage box.

The storage box was quickly taken to her bed. She rushed to her desk to get the key. The excitement of the moment seized her as she fumbled to open the box. At last, she would know her grandfather's secret; at last, she would solve the mystery that had eluded her for three years.

The key turned easily in the lock. She opened the cover to reveal only a leather-bound book and a velvet box from a jeweller. She opened the jewellery box first, but to her surprise it was empty. She frantically flipped through the leather-bound book, searching for her grandfather's confession. What had he not told his beloved wife? Was he ashamed? What had he done in 1940 that remained hidden from those whom he loved, especially his beloved Violet?

Rachel was distracted by a phone call from the real estate agent who was handling her most recent sale of property. She answered the phone without her usual politeness.

* * * * * * * * * *

Robert left Rachel's diary open as he carefully placed it on the desk. He flipped the pages of his 1970 diary to the October entries, searching until he found the entries he wanted. As a student, he had always enjoyed such authors as Charles Dickens; especially Dickens' use of coincidence. Yet he knew that readers could only suspend their disbelief sufficiently to accommodate relationships that added a poignant touch to plots. He wondered if readers would ever believe the coincidence he could not ignore in his story and yet he questioned its inclusion. Daisy often spoke of coincidence as Godcidence. Perhaps their destiny had been established long before they knew each other. Indeed, he knew it had been!

- - - - - Northumbria, 1970

Robert sat at his desk in his classroom. The last group of students had left and so had the remainder of the teaching staff. He could hear the janitor moving desks on the first floor. He looked at the sealed addressed envelopes on his desk. To encourage his students to learn the basics of letter writing, he had engaged them in a project with practical applications. The class had examined famous quotations by authors. Each student had prepared a poster featuring a famous quotation, with an explanation of the quote and a picture to illustrate it. Each student was required to write a letter to two famous people asking them to share their favourite quotation. He had encouraged the students to consider writing to politicians and authors as well as sports heroes and rock stars. He would mail the letters on his way home.

He knew that he should be home with Leah at this very moment; however, it was Margie's night to visit; he wanted them to be alone. The miscarriage had not provided them with a fresh start. Leah felt that she was doomed to suffer for her sin. Nothing could change her mind. Robert had remained an Anglican even though they had married in a Roman Catholic church. He often attended mass with Leah. After the miscarriage, Leah ceased going to church; her spirit had been broken. Robert had asked Father Stevens, the parish priest, to call on Leah; the resulting visits were social but not productive. Leah would not confide in the priest and eventually discouraged him from visiting.

Robert was now almost 25 years of age. He had almost been a father, but he still had not found his way into Leah's heart; they had never been lovers. Leah had retreated into her own world. She rarely left the apartment. She had resigned her teaching position. Margie was the only friend who refused to be discouraged by Leah's remoteness; she phoned Leah every evening and visted twice a week.

Robert knew that Leah was attempting to solve her problems by drinking. He had found numerous empty bottles hidden in the garbage. He and Margie had discussed Leah's dependency on alcohol. They knew that Leah was far too fragile to be confronted and yet they knew that Leah could never drink enough to ease the pain she was bearing. Margie did not know about the rape and there were numerous occasions when Robert felt she should know, but he had promised Leah.

He looked at the handwritten letters on his desk. The penmanship varied greatly. Some of the writing and printing was barely legible. He looked at the return addresses featuring the names of the students. They were such characters; grade eight students, early teens searching for their identity, reaching for their goals. He wondered what dreams they would have to give up, how fate would trick them. Despite his problems, his faith had endured. He knew that his faith had not been a promise of a life free from problems but a provision of strength and hope to survive and eventually to triumph. He rarely fell into self-pity. He wanted to be a comfort to Leah and to help her family understand Leah's struggle. His parents-in-law were extremely supportive; they realized that Leah was struggling with her miscarriage and her alcohol dependency. It was Trevor who would not accept his sister's weakness; he blamed Robert.

The best news that Robert had received within the last year was Trevor's announcement that he was moving to Halifax. That would mean that Robert would be free from his interference except for the occasional weekend visit. Most of Trevor's visits to the apartment ended with a confrontation between the two brothers-in-law. There had been no physical expressions of their strained relationship since the encounter near the church, but Trevor never failed to remind Robert who was the real cause of Leah's problems.

As Robert held onto Trevor's image in his mind, he detested that smirk that dominated Trevor's face whenever he spoke to him. Trevor had continued to send notes and cards to Robbie. The letters were mailed to the school. Instead of a signature, the messages contained a large black dot. The first such signature featured an explanation reminding Robert that black was a death symbol and the dot was a hole, a black hole; graves were such holes. Robert often wondered where Trevor had found the idea of the black dot as an intimidation symbol. He opened his desk, removing Trevor's latest threat. The envelope contained newspaper clippings featuring people who had disappeared mysteriously. The message read:

So many have disappeared without warning
So many are soon forgotten
So many should fear the same
So many are just waiting their time.
Don't worry, you'll get what you deserve!

O

Howie was the only person with whom he had shared these threats; he took them seriously but he knew that Trevor would not fufil his hatred as long as he and Leah were together. He sensed that Trevor knew that Leah was dependent upon Robert even if Robert had been the alleged cause of her problems.

He returned the envelope to the back of his desk. He had decided earlier to visit the manor. He often had dessert there on the nights of Margie's visits...

Robert arrived at the manor long after dinner dishes had been washed and put away. Several of the guests were watching television, some had gathered in Mr. Gordon's room to have a game of cards, others were already tucked away in their beds for the evening. The sun porch was empty. Robert took his piece of freshly baked brown sugar pie into the sun porch. He enjoyed the solitude, watching the traffic and walkers pass along the streets. Several neighbours waved to him as he observed their passing. Bertha arrived in the sun porch holding an envelope in her hand.

"A letter from Rachel!"

"Why would she send it here?"

"Why would she send it anywhere else?"

"But she has been sending my mail to the apartment for over two years now."

"Yes, Robert, your mail goes to the apartment, mine comes here."

Robert became uneasy, "Is something wrong?"

"Nothing is wrong. It is time for me to confess. I have written a few letters over the years to Rachel and I have asked her to remain silent. You are not the only one who can keep a promise."

Robert had never thought of his mother writing to Rachel and yet it hardly surprised him. "So you correspond with Rachel?"

"Not often, but we keep in touch."

"I'm glad you do. Rachel and I write every two weeks. I enjoy hearing from her. I suppose you know all the bouquet news?"

"Just the highlights, I'm sure, but we do share the latest stories. Robert, has Rachel mentioned that she discovered the key to the hidden storage box?"

"Yes, I received the letter just yesterday."

"I guess we both received her letter at the same time. I want to chat with you about that letter. Let's go to your bedroom."

As they descended the steps to the basement, Robert wondered why privacy was necessary to discuss Rachel's letter. He sat on his workout bench while Bertha sat on the edge of his bed.

"Mom, I'm surprised Rachel told you about her search for the storage box."

"She felt that I could keep a secret. She didn't know that I was the only person who could solve her mystery."

"How can you solve the mystery?"

"I have a story to tell. It will equal any story Mr. Gordon has ever shared with you." She placed her right hand on her bracelet, twisting it nervously around her wrist. Extending her left arm toward Robert, she smiled lovingly, "The missing clue! No soap opera can match what I am going to tell you."

"I don't understand. What would you know that could solve Rachel's mystery?"

"Be patient! You know, of course, that your father and I travelled out West soon after we were married. There were reports of good mining jobs, but your father did not like working in the northern climate. We lasted only three months. After we returned to Nova Scotia, we were lured to New England by advertisements of prosperity for all. Your father managed to get several mining jobs, the climate was better, but the wages were low. We had spent our savings on travel. Life was hard. We rented one room in a long row of dreary apartments. I tried to get a job, but there were few positions available for inexperienced women, especially Canadians."

"I think I knew all this."

"I'm sure you did, but there is more. Once, we were in Boston while your father worked temporarily for a shipping company. He worked long hours, but the pay was reasonable. I often spent my time exploring the city. There was no extra money, but I could enjoy window shopping."

"One cool autumn day, I was enjoying the outside of the more exclusive shops, imagining what it would be like to walk into the shops and purchase some of their treasures."

"It must have been very difficult to look, but know you couldn't purchase anything."

"Yes, it was, but I was foolish to window shop in the richest area of town. I should have confined myself to Woolworth's or one of the other department stores."

"Everyone has the right to look and dream."

"I always resisted the temptation to enter the stores. I knew that the clerks would size me up in a minute and dismiss me as an intruder. But on one occasion I was gazing at the most exquisite jewellery in a window display and I couldn't resist entering the shop. I have relived that incident so many times in my memory...

As I entered the shop, a male clerk approached me immediately, 'May I be of assistance?'

'Thank you, but I am just looking today.'

'Just looking. You are aware that we do not sell costume jewellery. We feature only originals made on our premises by the finest craftsmen in New England.'

'I can tell everything is beautifully crafted.'

'Is there a price range that madam was looking for?'

'No, just looking.'

The clerk's tone conveyed his disinterest in me and his raised eyebrows to the other clerk, a woman with an even more severe face than his, told me that I was not welcome in the shop. Normally I would have quietly eased my way out of a situation that was so uncomfortable. I became so conscious of my worn cloth coat, my faded tam and scuffed shoes; but my Belgian temper took control and I planted my feet firmly in front of the showcase that featured what I thought to be the most expensive collection of rings, bracelets and broaches."

Robert smiled at his mother, "Good for you, you had every right to browse!"

Bertha raised her index finger to her lips, "Shhh!"

The female clerk decided it was her turn to deal with me.

'This collection of fine jewellery is well beyond the pocket book of most of our clients.' She selected a silver bracelet from the top shelf and placed it on a velvet cushion. 'This bracelet is our most expensive one. Is this the type of jewellery you wanted to look at?' As she placed the bracelet on her wrist, she winked at the other clerk who was serving a gentleman who looked as if he could well afford to purchase anything in the shop.

I decided to ignore the disdain I was experiencing. I methodically browsed through the entire collection, but I was drawn back repeatedly to the bracelet. I became aware of the gentleman who had also noticed me. I knew he must be ill at ease having someone like me sharing his browsing. He could obviously afford to purchase whatever he wanted, I could only look.

I heard the male clerk whisper to him, 'We can't refuse to let people like her enter; most of them leave immediately. She is a stubborn one.'

The gentleman was wearing a three piece suit underneath his unbuttoned overcoat. I noticed the chain of a pocket watch hanging from his vest. His voice was strong, commanding attention.

'I am looking for a special gift today, but I would prefer to have Mr. Johnson, the owner, attend to me. Is he not here today?'

The male clerk replied, 'He has gone to New York to collect a gold shipment; he will be back tomorrow.'

'Perhaps I will return tomorrow. In the meantime, I will complete my examination of your displayed items.'

The female clerk followed me with a dust cloth. As I moved on from one showcase to another, she would wipe away my fingerprints. It was humiliating, yet I would not leave. Finally, I returned to the showcase containing the silver bracelet. I boldly asked if I might examine it.

The female clerk frowned, but withdrew the bracelet from the shelf, placing it once again on the velvet cushion. 'Madam, the price has not changed. I am sure that you might find something more appropriate in other shops. Our clients can afford such luxury, I fear that you are...'

The gentleman interrupted the clerk and shocked everyone by approaching the showcase where we were examining the bracelet. 'May I see the bracelet?'

The clerk became politeness personified as she delicately passed the bracelet to a client worthy of the ornament's attention. 'It is an original, one of a kind. Most of our other silver bracelets are two inches in width; this bracelet is three inches wide; this provides for a more detailed pattern. The bracelet is entitled, "The Guardian Angel". The angelic design is taken from the artistic drawings of the mystical English poet, William Blake. I am sure you are familar with his poetry, sir.'

'Yes, indeed, *Songs of Experience, Songs of Innocence...'*

To see a World in a grain of sand,
And a Heaven in a wild flower;
Hold infinity in the palm of your hand,
And eternity in an hour.

As he concluded the quotation, he raised his head and looked at me. Our eyes met for a brief moment, he smiled, I returned the favour."

Robert looked at his mother, nodding his head, "A guardian angel bracelet! Why have you never told me this before?"

"Some stories are best kept as private memories. You should know about that. Let me continue."

The clerk was obviously impressed with the client's ability to quote Blake. 'The poet is as famous for his art as he is for his poetry. That was a lovely passage you quoted. Notice the guardian angel that rests over the clasp. The angel lifts up to expose the clasp. The angel, too, is based upon one found in Blake's art. There is also a safety chain to ensure that the bracelet will not fall off the wrist should the clasp come undone.' She then drew her client's attention to the inscription inside the bracelet.

'The inscription is from *The Bible*.'

His angel guards those who honour the Lord
and rescues them from danger.
Psalm 34:7

I was so intrigued by the discussion of the bracelet that I had allowed myself to forget that I was an unwelcome guest in the shop. The bracelet was so beautiful but once I heard its real significance, my foolish heart ached because I could never have such a piece of jewellery. I would never be able to afford such a guardian angel. I touched the chain that bore my crucifix hanging around my neck. I looked at this gentleman who could afford such luxuries. HIs appearance had softened, he looked far less austere than he had earlier. Once again we exchanged a smile. I realized that my intrusion could last no longer.

'Is there a tea shop in this neighbourhood?'

The male clerk approached the entrance to the shop, 'If madam will come to the sidewalk with me, I will show you the tea shop's location.'

I realized he was being less helpful to me and more inclined to rid himself of my embarrassing presence.

'Thank you, I shall have a cup of tea while I reflect upon your fine jewellery.'

As he returned to the shop, I overheard him say, 'Reflect upon the jewellery.' The comment was followed by a giggle from the female clerk. The door closed and my embarrassment ended. I suppose I might have felt anger had it not been for my interest in the guardian angel. As Roman Catholics, we did believe in angels. But to wear such a fine crafted bracelet on your wrist and to know that it had literary and biblical significance! To have it blessed by a priest. It would be more than any woman could hope for. I wondered if the gentleman did buy it for his wife.

I soon found myself outside the tea shop. I knew from its exterior that it was far too fancy for me, but I felt that I could at least afford a cup of tea. I would not even consider being tempted by any sweets that might be featured.

As I entered the shop, I was greeted politely by a young lady who had not yet learned to treat ladies with shabby coats differently than other patrons. I ordered a pot of tea and relaxed even though it was apparent that I was not the typical patron who frequented this establishment. To my surprise the gentleman from the jewellery shop entered the tea shop. I noticed he was not carrying a parcel. He had obviously not purchased the bracelet or he had placed it in the pocket of his top coat. He shocked me by approaching my table.

'May I join you?'

'Yes, of course, if you...yes, please do.'

He took off his top coat placing it on the nearest empty chair. As he sat down, he apologized for being so forward. 'I hope you don't mind this intrusion into your privacy, but I hate drinking tea alone.'

'Tea is a very social drink, it is good to have company to share it with.'"

Robert chuckled, "Oh, a chance meeting, is this the beginning of an affair of the heart?"

"Sorry to disappoint you, my son, it is not the story of a romance. No, it is..." She looked again at her bracelet. "Let me finish so that you may know the real beauty of this bracelet."

'Are you not having any of their famous pastries?'

'No...I thought I would forego the pleasure, diet, you know.'

Gently patting his stomach, 'You may be right, but on a cool autumn day, tea is so lonely without something to accompany it.' He lifted his pocket watch from his vest. 'Three o'clock. I really think that we should consider a few pastries. Please, let it be my treat.'

'Oh, I couldn't allow that, really, you are too kind.'

'I insist!' Without hesitation he caught the attention of the waitress and requested the pastry cart be wheeled to our table. The cart contained a pyramid of assorted cakes and pastries including: lemon tarts, glazed fruit tarts, scotch cookies; white, yellow, and chocolate sweet cakes, petits fours, and biscuits with jam toppings.'

'Just leave the cart, we will savour a few and I'll have the remainder packed for home.'

I stared at this stranger. I could not afford to buy one piece of pastry; he was purchasing thirty or more of them. Of course, it was obvious that he could well afford to buy a guardian angel bracelet as well. His pocket watch was stunning as was the diamond ring he wore on his left hand. I couldn't help wondering why we were sitting together in a tea shop.

Two hours later, we were still chatting. He was a business man. He was such a good listener. He apologized for the clerk in the jewellery shop. He recalled his days of struggle, providing me with hope that one day dreams would be fulfilled. Although we chatted for such a long time, we never exchanged names; it seemed that it was easier to remain anonymous. It was the best two hours that I had ever spent with a stranger and the only memorable moment of our trip to New England.

At five o'clock, he announced that he would have to leave. He thanked me for being so wholesome, so genuine, so refreshing. I wasn't sure if such terms were necessarily compliments; I had always considered 'wholesome' to be boring. He had the waitress pack the extra pastries in several boxes.

I retired to the restroom. When I returned, he insisted I take one of the packages of pastries home.

'I couldn't accept this, you have already been too kind.'

He thrust the box into my hands, smiled, 'Please take it, and as soon as you get home, be sure to open it and see that the sweets are placed in a cool spot. Thank you for a delightful afternoon.'

Without a another word, he walked away, and vanished at the first side street. I wandered home feeling for the first time in a long time that things would improve for your father and me in our struggles to make a living. When I got back to our apartment, I placed the fancy box on the wooden kitchen table. The box with its coloured ribbon and gold seal looked so out of place, I felt ashamed. I opened the box to see how the pastries had travelled. It was then that I discovered nestled among the cakes and tarts, the guardian angel bracelet with a brief note.

This is your guardian angel,
I hope you are not offended by my gesture.
Enjoy it, it was so obviously designed for you!

There was no signature. I was stunned! Why would he do such a thing? I cried. I laughed! I placed it on my wrist. I walked around the apartment, feeling it encircling my wrist. I looked in the mirror. I examined it, reread the inscription a hundred times. I said a prayer of thanksgiving for this unknown man. I did not even know his name. I felt like Cinderella!

I was still seated at the table with cakes, tarts, and bracelet when your father arrived home. We talked about the gift. There was never any thought of returning it. We knew that it was a kind gesture and we ought not offend the giver. We thought of a thank you note, perhaps leaving it at the jewellers, but we dismissed that idea. In the end, we decided to simply accept the gift as it was presented. Camille was not jealous, he had no reason to be and he did not regard the gift as a reflection on his inability to provide such luxuries. We have always been secure in our relationship with each other and we have always known that we can only do our best.

All these years, I have had a special guardian angel! It represents all that is good in the world! I could never dream that I would ever discover anything more about my benefactor. It all seems so much of a coincidence! Rachel's grandfather, Henry Thomas, and I met in 1940. Destiny is so interesting. And to think that you and Rachel have become friends."

His mother held up her bracelet. "One day, I shall return this bracelet to Rachel, but I can't part with it yet. First, I shall share with her the solution to her mystery."

"Wow! What a story! I can hardly believe it without the Rachel connection. But it is too much of a coincidence."

"I think I always sensed that the bracelet's story was incomplete, that some day, I would discover more about the benefactor. Of course, after thirty years, the likelihood of anything happening was remote. I knew by now that the gentleman had probably passed away. I wondered if he ever told his loved one that he purchased a bracelet for an immigrant worker who never had the opportunity to thank him. A guardian angel that became my treasured possession."

Robert rose from the work bench, approached his mother, giving her a bear hug. "Mother, it is a touching story! I now understand why the bracelet is so prized. I think we agreed quite some time ago, that one day we would share secrets. You have confided yours, now it is my turn to tell you mine."

"Robert, there is no need to do so now. You tell me when it is right for you."

"No, I think there will never be a better time. I don't want to go into detail, but let me give you a quick summary."

Bertha listened in silence, her heart breaking as Robert shared the secret that had separated them from true intimacy since August 1966. She waited until he had finished before responding.

Taking his hands in hers, "Robert, it is much as I had imagined. I am proud of you." She leaned forward to kiss him on the cheek. She wiped her eyes with her handkerchief. "You are quite a man; one in a million!"

"I wouldn't say that, and in the end, Leah and I have not found happiness. She is slipping away from me and from everything. She has lost the will to live. She drinks to forget but can never drink enough."

"Have her parents been supportive?"

"Yes, they have done everything they can. Margie has been the only person Leah will confide in, but she too, is now at a loss to know what to do."

"Have you tried AA?"

"Leah won't admit her drinking problem."

"Robert, is Trevor any help? Leah is so fond of him."

"I went to Trevor to ask for his co-operation, but it was useless. We almost came to blows again. He ranted and raved, called me names, accused me of destroying his sister."

"Don't you think you should tell him the truth?"

"No, it is too late for that. I don't want to break my promise to Leah, she is too fragile. I know my secret is safe with you; besides, Trevor would never believe me. In fact, it would make things worse."

"Is he still sending you threats?"

"At least twice a month. A card this week, but two weeks ago, I received a box containing a dead cockroach with a degrading message."

Bertha frowned, "You receive a cockroach for being a saint; I receive a bracelet for..."

"For being wholesome! Henry Thomas was a good judge of character. Now that was a remarkable man. Rachel will be thrilled to hear the story of the bracelet." He hugged his mother once again. "I feel better now that I have told you."

Bertha touched Robert's face, "I don't know how you cope with this. You don't complain, you..."

"Oh, I'm no martyr. Leah is the one in pain. It is such a waste. I do love her and yet I hardly know her. We have never been lovers. Does that surprise you?"

Bertha looked into Robert's eyes, "I guess it does. No, maybe it doesn't! Robert, you are so young to bear all this."

"Mother, Leah is the one who has lost herself, I am surviving! She has asked me repeatedly for a divorce, but I have made my intentions very clear. She is stuck with me for better or worse."

"How can I help?"

"There is nothing more you can do, I know you are here for me. Just continue to pray for us, we need every bit of prayer that can be raised. I think it was Tennyson who said, 'More things are wrought by prayer than this world dreams of.'"

Bertha embraced Robert as tears flowed down her cheeks, "You are ever in my prayers."

* * * * * * * * * *

Robert opened the top drawer in his desk, removing a jeweller's box. Opening the cover of the box, he withdrew the guardian angel bracelet; his mother's most prized piece of jewellery. Bertha had wanted Rachel to have it. Today would be the first time Rachel would place it on her wrist. "Something old..." Destiny would complete its magic; the bracelet would return to the benefactor's family. Henry Thomas' granddaughter would place the bracelet on her wrist before she made her sacred vows. He looked at the bracelet, tenderly remembering his mother who had worn the bracelet through a life filled with sorrow, struggles, joys and triumphs! He glanced at the guardian angel protecting the clasp.

"May you be our guardian angel as we begin our life together. If we can be half as worthy as Bertha and Henry, we will do well. Thank you, grandfather, thank you, mother."

He smiled with an inner warmth as he returned the bracelet to its home, recalling Rachel's shock at receiving Bertha's solution to the great mystery.

- - - - Flanders Cove, 1970

Rachel sat on her bed as she stared in wonderment at the letter on her lap. Her grandfather had once met Bertha. He had given Bertha a bracelet. Northumbria and Flanders Cove had already met, had already been united in sentiment. She felt that she had to tell her aunts and yet she could not do so. She sensed the dilemma her grandfather must have felt. Violet would have understood; so, too, would her daughters and yet, Rachel could not tell them. Revealing the secret would betray her grandfather. He could have told them, but chose not to. How could she do so? She had a sacred trust that she must protect. Bertha knew! She had a right to know, but it was all by chance, or was it destiny being fulfilled? Should she read more into this coincidence? Was there a further promise? Dare she dream again? No, she dare not!

She placed the letter on the bed, walked to her desk, removing the empty jeweller's box from the clutter that covered the desk. Holding the box in her left hand, she removed the cover. She would send Bertha the box so that the box would be reunited with its angel. She was relieved that her fears of a love affair between her grandfather and a mysterious lady could be put to rest. She regretted that she had even allowed her imagination to come to that possible conclusion.

Rachel thought of her photo article of the quilt and wondered if the bracelet might be a good follow-up article. She knew, of course, that the bracelet's story was guarded by an angel. It was a private story. But what a story!

She was enjoying her interest in photography. She had gone to the local photography shop to purchase a new camera and to get some suggestions to improve the shots she was taking. She was able to renew an acquaintance with the assistant manager of the shop, Derek Perkins, who had attended high school with her. She had never paid much attention to the rather overweight student who never seemed to take his studies seriously. She remembered refusing to go to the movies with him on more than one occasion. In the years since they had graduated, Derek had lost his extra poundage and had developed considerable charm. He knew his photography as well. He had just recently moved to Flanders Cove and had been unaware that Rachel lived in the area.

Rachel thought about Derek. He was very attractive and she had too few friends. He had come to the mansion several times to assist her with the light meter used for indoor shots. He also had considerable expertise in selecting appropriate angles to flatter objects captured by the lens. He had called earlier in the morning to ask her to accompany him to a photography seminar. She had accepted.

Rose was equally impressed with Derek and Rose was never easily impressed. She teased Rachel about the Tab Hunter of Flanders Cove.

Iris and Rachel had selected the photos they wished to use for the article on the quilt. Rachel had written the description in the article from the viewpoint of the quilt. The quilt spoke of its progress from pieces of fabric to a finished heirloom. The article captured the love and tenderness that had created it, the pride of workmanship, and the beauty of creation. It had naturally been impossible not to inform the other aunts about the project, especially when Derek began to frequent the mansion. It was no surprise that the article was entitled, "With Love, With Stitches."

Rachel was delighted that the bracelet mystery could be put to rest. Her search through her grandfather's records had left just one other loose end. She had found records of payments to a gentleman named, Samuel Franklin. The payments continued monthly for five years, from 1945 to 1950, then stopped without comment. She could not ascertain who Mr. Franklin was nor why the payments were made. There were several intriguing comments made beside some of the payment notations. She had collected them in her notebook. With her recent success in solving the bracelet mystery, she wondered if Bertha could be of further assistance, but easily dismissed this possibility. She had asked Bertha if she had ever met a Mr. Franklin, but was hardly suprised to discover that Bertha had never met such a person. She had also noticed frequent payments to a private hospital in Boston during that same time period and wondered if there might be a connection. She wanted to do a bit of detective work, but feared that she might become involved in the discovery of a family secret that might not be as heart-warming as finding a guardian angel.

Iris knocked on Rachel's bedroom door, pushing the door gently as she asked, "Is the envelope ready to send to the publisher?"

"Come in Iris, yes, I have it ready to post this morning."

Iris moved quickly toward Rachel, embracing her. "Thank you for taking so much time with the photos and the article. You have done a terrific job."

"It has been a pleasure to get back to photography and to try writing."

"You have two talents. If nothing happens with the publisher, I am glad that we recorded everything. The scrapbook you have prepared is wonderful, you took such time with it and your calligraphy is excellent."

"I must confess, we owe a great deal to Derek, he has been so helpful."

"Yes, that was an extra benefit of doing the project. He is a fine young man and so handsome."

Rachel blushed, "Yes, he's not hard to look at." She chuckled, "He's a nice guy!"

"I hope you will maintain the connection, he seems like a genuine person, unlike like many of the younger fellows one reads about in the local paper."

Preferring to change the subject, Rachel asked, "Iris, you are feeling comfortable with selecting "Better Homes and Gardens" as the first publisher for our project?"

"Yes, go to the top. They can only say 'No thanks'. What have we got to lose?"

"The real satisfaction comes from from knowing that we did our best. It is exciting enough to be making a presentation to my sisters at tea time this afternoon. I'm pleased that Derek will join us. I know your aunts will approve of the photo article. I am so grateful to you." She hugged Rachel once again, then quietly left the bedroom.

Rachel looked at the envelope containing "With Love, With Stitches" lying beside the guardian angel box. She smiled as she thought of the many heirlooms that filled her life. The mansion was a storehouse of treasures but she knew that its greatest treasures were her aunts. She had learned so much from them. Their lives were tranquil compared to life in Northumbria. She realized that one day, Flanders, too would have its share of sorrow. She could see that the aunts were aging and one day they would not be so self-sufficient. She had gradually managed to extend the gardener's hours and his wife's household responsibilities, but the aunts had not accepted the extra hours without comment. The aunts were careful not to challenge their niece's recommendations, just as they had never done so with their father. Rachel was the undisputed custodian of the mansion!

Rachel could hear music coming from the conservatory. It was a medley of Connie's hits played by Rose. Rose played the piano too infrequently and when she did so, she normally entertained with classical music. Rachel could hear "Together" being played as she tidied her room. She was lured to the conservatory by the medley.

As she entered through the open French doors, the scent of geraniums reminded her of summer. In the spring Iris had planted a number of shrubs in large terra cotta containers for the outside terrace facing the harbour. She had lovingly taken them inside for the fall and winter, placing them along the glassed wall adjoining the garden. A butterfly bush was still displaying its beautiful blue hue. Pink, red and white roses continued to produce scented blooms as reminders of their summer gifts to the household. All of the trees and shrubs were a vibrant green; no plants in any nursery were so pampered.

The black grand piano was situated in the centre of the conservatory with a seating arrangement of wicker chairs nearby. Rachel sat in a wicker rocking chair as Rose played "Drownin' My Sorrows". Rachel thought about the lyrics. She knew that Connie had tears she could cry and she herself had cried far too many. She was pleased that her friendship with Robert had been restored. She knew that he was not without pain; she knew that Leah was distraught. She thought of the bouquet and their charmed life. And she thought of Derek; it was so good to have a friend her age, someone who shared her interest in photography, someone who was fun!

****

Robert closed Rachel's 1970 diary. Rose playing "Drownin' My Sorrows" reminded him so vividly of those sorrowful years. He had been pleased that Rachel had found a friend. He placed Rachel's diary back in the banker's box. He hesitated as he lowered his diary into the same box. He really didn't want to read any further items from 1970; however, he relented, withdrawing his diary and opening to his November entries.

- - - - - Northumbria, 1970

Robert was working out in his bedroom when Camille entered the room. Camille was wearing his favourite blue cardigan, with his empty pipe and package of tobacco protruding from the only pocket in the sweater.

"Son, you are faithful to your exercises. You're looking good." He approached Robert, gently ruffling his hair.

"Thanks, it's routine now, I actually enjoy it."

Camille sat in a wooden chair near the benchpress. "How is school coming?"

"Fine, no complaints. I like it! Too much correcting, but that comes with teaching English."

"Hey, that's a good one! An immigrant's son teaching English to the locals."

"I hadn't thought about it, but you have a point."

"Your grandparents would be so pleased to know that you are a teacher. None of the family has ever been a professional. We were all labourers, most of us miners or farmers. We had one priest in the family."

"I really enjoy the kids and school keeps me busy."

"Keeps you busy. Son, we don't talk much do we? Your brother, Arthur, and I were close, both worked in the mine together. You and your mother are close, that is good, but I worry about you. I know I spend too much time mourning my loss, but you are here and...I..."

Robert was not prepared for his father's intimacy. He rarely had such moments with Camille. He knew Camille loved him, trusted him and was proud of him, but they never exchanged sentiments. Their love was unspoken, but clearly understood.

Looking at his father who looked as uncomfortable as he himself was feeling, Robert spoke, "Some things don't need to be said."

Camille shook his head, "Some things do need to be said while there is still time. Robert I am an old man. I don't have the energy I used to have. My body is telling me that I need to pace myself."

Robert looked with alarm at his father, "Are you sick?"

Camille smiled, "No, it's just old age."

"Now I never thought you would admit to being old!"

"Hey, I'll admit it to you, but no one else. Rob, your mother has told me about your sacrifices, your problems. You are the man that every father wants his son to be. I loved you when you were a skinny runt. I admire the body you have shaped. I respect what you have done for Leah. I am not good with words like your mother..."

Robert shook his head, "I think you are doing very well. Really you don't have to tell me how you feel, I know."

"I do need to. I am the quiet one, too quiet. That doesn't mean I don't think and I don't feel."

"I know you do. I thank you for all you have done for me." He rose from the workbench intending to hug his father, but he was interrupted by his mother and the police chief standing in the doorway. He read his mother's face; his heart beat uncontrollably.

Bertha looked at Camille as she walked toward her son. "Sit down." They both sat on the bed.

"Mr. Baker has bad news for us."

Mr. Baker was a friend of the family. He was a tall robust policeman who maintained his calm, collected manner in every possible situation. He had often been the bearer of bad news.

"Robert, Leah has been in a serious car accident. The car went out of control over an embankment near the old quarry. The ambulance has taken her to the local hospital, but she will need to be taken immediately to the provincial hospital in Halifax."

Robert stood up, "Leah hasn't driven for months. I have my keys in my pocket upstairs, I hid her set. Will she be all right? What happened? I must go to her."

"I'm here to drive you to the hospital. You can go with her in the ambulance."

Everything happened so quickly. The drive to the local hospital ended as the drive to the provincial hospital began. Leah was unconscious. Her parents followed the ambulance in their car to be met by Trevor at the hospital. After an emergency six hour operation, the prognosis was dismal. Leah had suffered spinal cord and brain damage. At best she would be confined to bed for a lifetime; her memory and speech had been affected. The medical staff could not be certain if her memory loss was permanent nor would they say with absolute certainty that her speech might improve. They attempted to provide the family with the most likely expectations for people who suffered such devastating injuries.

As the family dealt with the shock of Leah's injuries, they had to come to grips with the reality that Leah had been drinking at the time of the accident. Robert had thought that Margie was spending the evening with her, but Leah had telephoned Margie to indicate that she and Robert were going to a movie. Margie had been surprised but delighted that Leah would consider leaving the apartment. Leah had obviously planned her last drive. The car did not skid as it left the road. It seemed apparent that Leah had attempted to end her own life.

Trevor was uncontrollable when the doctors gave the family the results of the operation. He struck a blow at Robert, hitting him on the left jaw. Robert was able to protect himself and with the assistance of his father-in-law, Trevor was subdued. A doctor gave him medication to further calm him.

The medical staff recommended that Leah be transferred to a nursing home where she could have extended care. Northumbria provided few choices for the family. It was Bertha who solved their dilemma. She proposed having Leah moved to the manor. The MacDonald's would be close by to assist with Leah's care. Margie had agreed to help. Robert could return to his bedroom in the basement. The money saved by giving up the apartment would help pay some of the medical costs. Everyone welcomed the proposal except Trevor. He was adamant that Leah not be located near Robert, but he had no support from anyone. It had become apparent that Trevor's obsession had destroyed his ability to reason and to think of anything but feeding his anger.

Leah arrived at the manor on November 15. Her memory loss did not improve nor did she regain her speech. She lay in bed like a china doll, fragile but beautiful. She was surrounded by love. The manor guests were so good to her and Robert. They often took turns reading to Leah, talking to her, and scheduling gatherings in her room so that she would have company.

Robert was devastated. He blamed himself for not having hidden the keys in a better place, for not being there with Leah when she needed him. He felt for the first time that Trevor might be right in his condemnation of his brother-in-law. He began to retreat into his private world. He stopped working out, stopped assisting with extra-curricular activities at school and once again stopped writing his letters to Rachel. For six months he remained in this state of morbid seclusion from those he loved and who so deeply loved him.

He had taken a month's leave of absence from his teaching duties, but insisted that he was ready to return to school following the Christmas holidays. He taught his classes but not students. He returned home each evening to sit with Leah and to prepare lessons for his classes. The pattern was simple and rarely varied. Bertha wondered if silence would claim still another of her loved ones; it was her greatest fear.

Bertha wrote to Rachel more frequently than she had in the past and in turn Rachel wrote every week to Robert, but received no responses. Bertha began playing Connie's records in an attempt to get Robert to react to his environment, but she feared that her son had retreated so far within himself that he could not be reached.

All of the manor guests were fond of Robert, but the trio of Gramma Horton, Miss Brown and Mr. Gordon were Robert's dearest "grandparents". They felt his pain and were frustrated by their failure to awaken in their "grandson" the will to overcome the hardships that had befallen him. On May 15, they planned a special pre-birthday celebration for him in Leah's room. When Robert came to Leah's room for his nightly visit, he found the three of them already seated, comfortably chatting.

"Hello, I see Leah already has company."

Mr. Gordon spoke first, "Actually we wanted to talk to you and knew you would be here."

"Here I am, what's on your mind?" He moved to take an empty chair near Leah's bed.

Mr. Gordon pointed individually to his lady friends, "Miss Brown, Mrs. Horton and I have a presentation to make to you. Actually a pre-birthday presentation."

"That's great! I like presents and if they are starting a week before my birthday, it should be a great birthday week instead of a day."

Gramma Horton spoke, "Robert, enjoy your youth, when you reach our ages, birthdays are not so special."

Mr. Gordon grimaced, "Each birthday is one step closer to..." He raised his head upward and downward.

Miss Brown quickly interjected, "I think every birthday is a time of rejoicing; a time to celebrate the blessings of our past year and a time to look forward to continued blessings, to new adventures in the year ahead."

"You mean, I might finally get hitched this year!" responded Mr. Gordon.

Gramma Horton winked at Miss Brown as she responded, "Only if you can find someone gullible enough to fall for your proposals."

Robert enjoyed their bandying, it was part of their charm, their appeal.

Gramma Horton smiled warmly at Robert, "We each want to give you a gift. We have chosen to give you a second hand gift, one that has been well used. We hope you won't be offended by the fact that the gifts are neither new nor of great monetary value. Each gift is something we treasure, an object that has given us comfort throughout the years and which we hope will do the same for you."

Miss Brown continued, "At our age, we have given up most of the heirlooms that we collected during our life journey, but some objects are so precious that we cannot part with them. We have each selected one such object to present to you. You are the grandson I never had, and it is with great pleasure that I give you this gift." She passed Robert a brown paper bag.

Robert placed his hand in the bag, withdrawing a wooden plaque with the picture of an eagle on it; a biblical verse was carved in the wood, highlighted with gold lettering:

"But they that wait upon the Lord shall renew their strength, they shall mount up with wings as eagles; they shall run, and not be weary; and they shall walk, and not faint." Isaiah 40:31

"Robert, I received that plaque from a Sunday school class in a small African village. It cost only one dollar, but for those children it was a fortune. Their parents had to sacrifice to purchase that plaque, it is my greatest treasure. I have had it for thirty years as a reminder of those dear people who gave me much more than I could ever have given them. It is my favourite biblical verse. I hope you will read the verse often so that you may remember that there is a force that flows beneath the eagle's wings to allow him to soar, and you have that same force available to you."

Robert was overcome with emotion as he read once again the verse on the plaque, "Thank you. Are you certain you want to part with the plaque?"

Miss Brown smiled as she nodded, "It is now yours."

Gramma Horton passed Robert another brown bag, "I hope you like our fancy wrapping paper."

"Who cares about the paper when the gifts are so special? Now, let me see what this bag contains." He removed from the second bag a delicate miniature stained glass church window featuring praying hands surrounded by poinsettias, lilies and roses.

Robert shook his head at Gramma, "This is the gift you received from the Canadian Florist Association when you and your husband retired, I really can't take this gift away from you..."

"Robert, I want you to have it, I intended to give it to you one day, today is better than waiting. I hope you will enjoy it."

"Thank you, both of you. I know how precious these gifts are to you."

Mr. Gordon passed him the final brown bag. "One more gift, not a plaque and not stained glass, but I hope you will enjoy it."

From the bag presented to him, Robert withdrew a leather bound copy of "Shakespeare's Sonnets"; it was not a new copy but was in excellent condition.

"Robert, when I sold my farm and auctioned the things Sarah and I had accumulated in our lives together, I regretted having to part with my books, but there is a time to say good-bye to everything. I could not part with this volume of sonnets, it was given to me on my twenty-first birthday by my grandfather. I have treasured it and protected it and now I want you to have it. I know you appreciate poetry and Shakespeare, I hope you will..."

"I will treasure it."

Looking at his three "grandparents" with tears in his eyes, "You needn't have given me the birthday gifts, but I certainly am moved by the gifts you chose. I don't know what to say."

Mr. Gordon came to Robert's rescue, "Shakespeare gave us a simple thank you in his play, *"Twelfth Night*".

**"I can no other answer make but thanks,
And thanks, and ever thanks."**

Gramma Horton added, "My favourite thank you is from Barbara Bartocci:

"Thanks...Small word...Big meaning."

"You don't need to say anything more, this is our way of saying thanks to you," added Miss Brown. "Now we are leaving for Mr. Gordon's room so he can cheat at cards again."

"I never cheat, you ladies are just poor losers."

Gramma Horton slowly rose; approaching Robert, she kissed him on the cheek. "Happy Birthday."

Miss Brown followed Gramma's example. Mr. Gordon gave Robert a hearty hand shake. They disappeared leaving him with Leah, the gifts and the warmth of affection. He looked at the gifts, each a milestone in the life of the giver, each a reflection on what they valued in life. A missionary, a nursery operator and a farmer; friends, 'grandparents'. He was so fortunate to have them. He knew that the gifts were valuable in themselves but priceless with sentiment. He opened the collection of sonnets, flipping through the pages, recalling some of his favourites. He stopped at "Sonnet 18" in which the bard had ensured that the beauty of his lady would be immortalized by this sonnet:

"So long as men can breathe, or eyes can see,
So long lives this and this gives life to thee."

He tenderly closed the collection of sonnets, picked up the stained glass window, examined the detail of the composition, then picked up the plaque, reading the inscription once again. He looked at Leah, she lay in bed looking like a legendary princess waiting to be awakened by her prince. But no gentle kiss could awake her from her prison. She was with Robert, but so far away.

He reached over the bed to kiss her. "Leah, I love you. I hope you can hear me and that you know I'm here for you, now and for always." Leah remained with her eyes closed; she rarely displayed any emotion, any recognition of her surroundings. She was free from the pain that had driven her to her destruction. Everyone who loved her knew that she was seemingly at peace. It was they who now bore the agony of watching life continue without its ability to respond to the love around her.

Bertha arrived at the doorway of Leah's room as Robert sat with his beloved wife. Bertha was holding a plastic bag in her right hand.

"May I join you?"

"Please do." Pointing to his three gifts on the table at the foot of the bed, he smiled, "I suppose you know about these gifts."

Bertha nodded in agreement. "What a trio they are! They are very fond of you, Robert. But you knew that long ago. They are delighted to have you back at the manor."

"I'm glad to be back." He looked at Leah with sorrow in his eyes. "I know Leah is pleased, if she could only..."

"Robert, your twenty-fifth birthday is starting a week early. I wanted to get into the act so I have the first of seven gifts. A new Connie Francis album, one each day leading up to your birthday, then a final gift to you from everyone at the manor on your special day."

"I haven't purchased a new album in over a year."

"Exactly, and I want to hear them. We want to hear them. You need to hear them." She withdrew the album from the plastic bag. "I think you will like this one, "Connie Francis Sings Bacharach, Kaempfert, Last and Manccini", there are some great songs on it including, "Moon River", "Strangers in the Night" and "Blue on Blue". She held up the cover of the album to reveal a sensuous picture of Connie. "Now look at this photo, she's looking quite alluring, don't you think?"

Robert accepted the album, looking at the cover. "Hey, sexy is the word!" He chuckled.

"Can I take a picture of you smiling? You know, it happens too infrequently."

Robert hugged his mother, "I guess you may be right." His eyes filled with tears as the impact of the gifts reached his soul, comforting him, reminding him that he was not alone."

He picked up the plaque once again, showing it to his mother. "But they that wait upon the Lord shall renew their strength..."

* * * * * * * * * *

Robert left his desk to enter the living-room. The oak curio cabinet displayed a collection of their most prized possessions. He opened the doors of the cabinet to better view the gifts he had received on his twenty-fifth birthday. All of the gifts reminded him of the givers, but more importantly, they were reminders of the healing power of love. Surrounded by love and prayer, he had gradually been renewed in spirit. He knew that there was nothing he could have done to prevent Leah's accident; he learned that even in times of despair, there are blessings to be received. His parents, Leah's parents, his extended family and his friends had reached out to him, touched him with their concern. He realized he could not restore Leah by destroying himself. His students deserved his attention and he regretted having neglected them. He slowly began restoring his friendship with Rachel and he renewed his interest in Connie.

He glanced once again at Rachel's 1970 diary, noting the summer entries.

- - - - - Flanders Cove, 1970

Rachel sat on a wicker chair in the conservatory reading a number of Robert's letters. Rose was playing classical pieces on the piano. Rachel interrupted the playing, "Rose, please join me for a few minutes, I want to share something with you."

Rose sat in a chair beside Rachel. "I see you are rereading Robert's letters."

Rachel was holding a booklet in her right hand. "Yes, I think you might enjoy listening to some of these quotations."

"Are you quoting Robert?"

Smiling, "No, he had his grade eight students write to famous people, asking them for their favourite quotations. Listen to just a few of them."

Stephen King's Mom:

"It is possible for a man to stand, cringe, or crawl.
In your lifetime you will do some of each. When possible, I hope you will stand."

"Rachel, I like that one, can't say I'm fond of Stephen King's writing though. Maybe his mother should have been an author."

Rachel continued. "Prime Minister Margaret Thatcher shared this one:"

"So when the world is asleep, and there seems no hope of waking,
Out of some long, bad dream that makes her mutter and moan,
Suddenly, all men arise to the noise of fetters breaking,
And everyone smiles at his neighbour and tells him his soul is his own." (Kipling)

"I would have thought Margaret Thatcher would have selected a quotation that used inclusive language, but I suppose she has other more important issues to fight."

"I think you will enjoy this one from one of Canada's celebrated authors, Margaret Atwood.

It is from the speech of a famous Canadian suffragette, Nellie McClung:"

"Never retract, never explain, never apologize:
get the thing done and let them howl."

"I like that one! 'Let them howl!' Now that is my kind of woman!"

"You admire Edward Kennedy, he responded with this quote from Cardinal Newman:

"God has created me to do Him some definite service.
He has committtted some work to me which He has not committed to another.
I have my mission...I shall do good. I shall do His work."

"Yes, I greatly admire Mr. Kennedy and I love the works of Cardinal Newman."

Rachel passed the booklet to Rose. "Keep the booklet for a while. I think you will enjoy the quotes. It is a great project."

"Thank you, Rachel, I'll finish reading the quotations after dinner. I had better check with Daisy to see if she needs help." She left the conservatory, carrying the booklet.

Rachel continued looking at her letters. She enjoyed Robert's letter describing his week long birthday celebrations, including the photos that accompanied the letter. On May 24, Robert had received his special gift from the manor, a 11X15 inch collage of Connie's photos with a special greeting from the singer herself: "To Robert, thanks a

million!" On the back of the collage were three photos including the latest photo of Bertha and Camille plus the other manor guests, a photo of Robert's in-laws, and a photo of Robert, Leah, Howie and Margie in happier days. The collage was intended to stand upright with the support of a wooden frame constructed by Mr. Gordon. The title at the top of Connie's collage was borrowed from one of her hits, "Among My Souvenirs"; another Connie title, "All the Love in the World" was placed at the bottom of the family photos. The titles were done in precise calligraphy by Miss Brown. Gramma Horton and Bertha had assembled the photos.

Rachel was pleased that the photos she had sent Bertha had been useful, especially the one she had sent to Connie for a personal greeting. She and Robert were friends once again. They had survived two periods of silence, but perhaps that strengthened their relationship. They were now just friends, there were no dreams of a life together. Robert had his Leah to care for and yes, she had Derek who was becoming such a close friend that she dared to hope again.

Chapter 5:

Your Other Love

Robert heard the grandfather clock in the foyer striking nine o'clock. He realized that he had spent far too long among his souvenirs and yet, he could not leave his memories. He searched for Rachel's 1975 diary but could not find it during his initial search. Eventually he found it a banker's box containing mementoes relating to Connie's career. He opened the diary to the summer entries. Life in Northumbria remained relatively calm. Robert assumed teaching responsibilities for English Language Arts at the high school level. His interest in drama, especially Shakespeare, was given ample opportunity to develop. He enjoyed teaching library research skills as he prepared students for future academic work beyond high school.

Leah's health was stable, but she remained confined to bed with no mobility in her lower body and very little arm movement. Her speech and memory did not improve. It was difficult to know if she really understood where she was and what was happening around her.

Trevor continued to be Robert's adversary. Robert did, however, appreciate Trevor's devotion to Leah. Trevor visited his sister faithfully every second Sunday, bringing her flowers, stuffed animals and her favourite candy. Trevor spent most of his vacation time in Toronto; consequently, many of the gifts bore Toronto logos. He was a fan of the Toronto Maple Leafs hockey team; Leah had been a devoted fan as well. The blue maple leaf was a frequent adornment to many of the gifts.

Trevor's visits always followed the same pattern. He arrived at Leah's bedside, shed a few tears, then became the older, protective brother, recalling with Leah and guests the fun that the MacDonald family had shared in the past as the children were growing up. By the end of each visit, Trevor would seek out Robert to remind his brother-in-law who was responsible for his sister's downfall. Trevor continued to send parcels and letters to Robert; some were sent to the school but others to the manor; all of them contained the infamous black dot signature.

Robert looked lovingly at the diary in his hand. When he would eventually settle down to write their story, this diary had special entries that could not be ignored. 1975 was the year that the bouquet dared to invite the world to visit them in their private domain. Rose and Daisy were published authors; both books had gone into second printing. The popular monthly magazine, *American Estates* had featured Rachel, Iris and Derek's photo article celebrating the heirlooms and gardens of the estate. It was also the year that Rachel realized wedding bells were ringing for her and Derek. It was definitely Camelot time in Flanders Cove.

Robert withdrew a photo from Rachel's diary. It was a photo of Rachel and Derek at the beach. Rachel looked so happy; she had found her prince charming. For over four years she and Derek had been friends, sharing their lives with the bouquet, Derek's family and a few close friends. Romance had come naturally as they shared their days with each other. They had rarely talked seriously about marriage, but its promise was never far away.

Robert knew that Rachel was supremely happy in her relationship with Derek. He rejoiced that Rachel had found someone to love, someone who would love her for a lifetime. He had had to deal with his feelings for Rachel; feelings that had lain buried far too long. He knew that he had always loved Rachel and yet they had never met, never spoken on the telephone, never exchanged gifts. He often reread her letters for comfort. He did have moments when he wanted to hate Derek for daring to love his Rachel, but her happiness was more important than his selfish hoarding of a dream that would never be fulfilled. In the end, he was pleased that someone as sensitive as Derek had fallen in love with Rachel. He thought about Connie's hit single, "Your Other Love". Rachel had her chance for the love that he had been denied; he wished her and her other love, happiness forever!

- - - - - Flanders Cove, 1975

Rachel was seated in the library with her aunts. She sat behind her grandfather's oak desk; her aunts were seated in burgundy leather wing chairs arranged in a semicircle in front of the desk. Everyone present had pen and paper and extensive notes taken at previous meetings.

Rachel was the first to speak, "This July 4th will be like no other for us! Are we ready for this?"

Rose spoke confidently, "Now that we are over the shock of the decision we have made, I am excited! It's the best thing we have ever done!"

Iris added, "We may be out of our minds, but I know father and mother would be proud of us. We could never have done it without you, Rachel. You inspired us to write and to share our gifts. We thank you."

Rachel shook her head, "No, you have done it all, each one of you. I am proud of you. I know, too, that opening our home to the public is not easy for you. I applaud your decision to do so. The estate is unique and it was meant to be enjoyed and now others can discover the treasures that the estate wall has protected for so many years."

Daisy looked at her sisters, "Personally, I am overwhelmed at what we are doing. I am frightened that we will be invaded by people we have never known and will never see again. The thought of cameras snapping pictures inside and outside seems to rob me of something that has been ours and ours alone. I feel as if I am losing something that we have jealously protected all these years."

Iris patted Daisy's hand, "We all feel those sentiments. There is a sense of being violated! We have gone through all of this, but we have decided that we cannot hide our talents and gifts under a bushel. Daisy, you are the tender one, you are the one who dared to share her faith with the world. That was the big step in faith; this project is anticlimatic! You are now a published author. Your book and Rose's are in thousands of homes, your readers will delight in knowing something about the writers they enjoy."

"Yes, I know you are right and yes, we have all agreed to this. Let's get on with it. I'll be all right."

Rachel assumed the leadership role for their discussion. "We have a month to prepare for our reception. There are five hundred guests expected. Derek and his friends are looking after the tents that will be set up outside. The speeches will be given in the main tent with seating for everyone."

Rose inquired, "Where did they find a tent large enough?"

Rachel responded, "From the state fair committee who were only too glad to donate it to us for the day; some of the committee members will be here to help set it up. Everyone has been so co-operative. Let me review the agenda for the special presentations. As the master of ceremonies, Derek will introduce our senator, governor, mayor and the new rector of the parish; each will speak briefly. Then Derek will provide a few comments concerning ***With Love, With God***, followed by your reading of a two page excerpt from the book, Daisy. There will be a microphone so everyone will hear you."

"I think I'll faint reading in front of all those people!"

Rose interjected, "Listen Daisy, if I can stand up and read two pages about a raccoon frolicing in our backyard, you can read something more sedate."

Daisy laughed, "You have a point there. Are you going to use Rocky, the raccoon puppet, with your reading?"

"I certainly am. Charlie MacArthur, move over!"

Everyone enjoyed Rose's humour. Rachel reminded the aunts that the publishers would present Daisy and Rose with special monogrammed copies of their books, immediately following each reading.

"Once the readings are complete, the editor of *American Estates* will present a framed picture of the cover page of their September issue to you, Iris. We may have been rejected in 1970 in our first attempt to get published by a national magazine, but five million readers saw our gardens and treasured heirlooms featured in a ten page spread. I still can't get over it. After you receive the picture, Iris, we will conclude with a benediction by the rector and he will offer grace.

Rose glanced at her sisters, "Rachel, you may find this hard to believe, but the three of us have decided to speak to the audience just before the rector concludes."

Rachel looked rather surprised. "Well, sure, that's no problem, what should we say in the programme? 'Comments by Iris, Daisy and Rose'."

Rose spoke on behalf of the sisters. "Just leave the programme for a moment, I'll get back to you on the precise wording we want."

Daisy held up a letter she had received from Bertha, "I have Bertha's recipe for the galettes. The caterers have agreed to make enough to serve all our guests; I know that no one will have tasted such delights before."

Rose responded to the news by saying, "I am not all that fond of sweets, but I really do enjoy those Belgian delights. Read the recipe for us, Daisy. I'd like to know what I'm eating."

Daisy sought permission from Rachel before taking the time to read the recipe. "The recipe calls for:

1/2 pound of soft butter
1 cup brown sugar
1 cup white sugar
6 eggs
2 cups flour
1 teaspoon baking powder
pinch of salt
1 teaspoon vanilla."

Rose exclaimed, "Wow, they are rich; ah well, they're worth it. I hope we'll have plenty of leftovers from the reception."

Iris asked, "What is the procedure for making them?"

Daisy continued, "It's quite easy. Cream butter and sugar, add eggs one at a time, mixing well. Then add dry ingredients and vanilla. Bake in waffle irons and enjoy."

Rachel assumed her leadership role by thanking Daisy for sharing the recipe with them, but reminding everyone of the deadlines they had to meet.

Derek entered the library wearing a bright multi-coloured summer shirt, white shorts and sandals. "Sorry to interrupt, but I need to talk to you, Rachel, about the caterers for the reception. Can you join me on a telephone extension? I have the manager on the line. This is the biggest event they have ever done, so he wants to check numbers with us."

As Rachel rose from her chair to join Derek, Rose whistled at Derek and mimicking Mae West said, "I like that shirt, fellow, and the contents aren't too bad either!"

Derek blushed but he had grown accustomed to the aunts and enjoyed Rose's wit.

Iris smiled, "Derek, don't let Rose embarrass you, but you do look smashing in that shirt."

Daisy joined the game, "Derek, the only good looking legs we've seen in years have helped prop up the dining-room table. Nice to see real ones for a change!"

Rachel took Derek's hand in hers, "You ladies are shocking! I don't know if we can trust you to behave for our invited guests when you are so free with your comments about Derek's clothes."

Rose quickly added, "If he is going to wear such attractive outfits, then he'll have to suffer the ladies eyeing him and those legs!"

The aunts' laughter could be heard as Rachel and Derek left the room.

Following their telephone conference call, Rachel and Derek walked in the front gardens. The gardens were exquisite. Violet had planned them well. Each bed contained a specialized grouping of plants which was noted by a name plate. Rachel and Derek lingered among the flowering shrub beds, the rock gardens, the five perennial beds, the numerous annual beds, the pond with water lilies and acquatic plants, the iris beds, rose beds, daisy beds and the ornamental trees. The estate contained many varieties of trees, but oaks, maples and mountain ash dominated. The vegetable and herb gardens as well as the orchards were located at the back of the property behind the former stables.

Rachel and Derek stood back to look at the house. The painters had completed the six ornate wooden pillars of the front entrance the day before. The brick construction was highlighted by white shutters and large window boxes. The window boxes were spectacular with trailing white and blue lobelia; white, purple and lavender alyssum; pink impatiens, geraniums and fibrous begonias.

They strolled among the sculptured flower and shrub beds, past the pond with its flowing fountain, beyond the gazebo to their favourite spot, a bench beneath two chestnut trees. The lilac and honeysuckle were in full bloom filling the June air with their fragrance. Derek had taken the liberty of carving their initials on both trees. They sat together on the bench looking at the finery that nature had prepared. The gardens were manicured, the lawn freshly mown, and the view of the harbour was breathtaking with numerous white sails framing the horizon.

Derek looked into Rachel's eyes as he had done so many times. "Rachel, we have known each other since we were in high school. Remember when I was the overweight kid who tried desperately to persuade you to go to the movies with me?"

"Let me assure you, Derek, it was not your weight that caused me to refuse you!" She hugged him. "I dated no one!"

"Hmmm! It must have been my lack of devotion to studies. I had no time for memorizing all those dates, writing those senseless essays! Such a waste of time. But once I became interested in photography, studying was enjoyable."

"You are a good photographer!"

"You are just saying that because I assisted you and Iris and now our photos are in a national magazine. Business at the shop has improved dramatically since our photos were published."

"Undoubtedly the reason you were promoted to manager. How many outlets does the company have?"

"Fifty-six shops in the New England area." Looking intently at Rachel, he kissed her lightly on the cheek. "I actually have two things I want to share with you this afternoon."

"My, this sounds serious!"

"Rachel, we have become very close. You know I love you and we are good for each other. I have become very fond of your aunts and I think they like me."

"When the aunts can tease you about your legs, you can be sure they have accepted you."

Taking her hands in his, "Rachel, every time we begin to talk of a lifetime commitment, we reach a barrier that we have not been able to push aside. It is time to discuss us. I want to marry you! But you already know that."

"I do know and I...I want to say, 'Yes', but there are so many things to consider."

Rachel looked lovingly at her Derek. He was so considerate. She gazed into his hazel eyes, seeing the depth of his tender heart, knowing that he deserved to have the full expression of her love.

"Rachel, we have discussed the obstacles a hundred times. We can live here, I have no problem with that. If your aunts can accept me as a member of their family, I will gladly live with them and help you look after them."

"I know you will. I'm not so sure that beginning a life together here is fair to you."

"Only I can be the judge of that. I tell you, it would be super to live here. Hey, this is the estate the world is coming to. Do you want to deny me the privilege of living here?"

Rachel smiled affectionately as she looked at Derek, "I guess I shouldn't. But you have an opportunity to move to an executive position with the regional office of your photography firm. Are you willing to give it up to settle down in Flanders Cove?"

"It is not a decision I have to make. Sure, I'm interested in the promotion, but I am more interested in being your husband. Maybe one day, another opportunity will come up. In the meantime, we can plan other photo articles."

"Derek, there has always been the unspoken barrier between us. We have alluded to it and we have on occasions skirted it in our discussions. We need to talk openly about it now. Please be patient with me."

"I know this is difficult, but we do need to talk about it. Our entire relationship has been shared with another person."

Rachel hastily defended herself, "Oh, I have not shared our private details with anyone! Really I haven't."

Derek paused, "Rachel, you once loved Robert. I know that! You have been perfectly honest. I know, too, that your affection for him remains an important part of your life. I can never replace that affection; it is yours and his alone. I respect you for your honesty. I have never felt in competition with him."

"He is not your rival, I assure you. He is a married man."

"Robert is married, but you know that there is a part of you that will always love him. I understand that. I just want the rest of your love."

Tears formed in Rachel's eyes as she placed her head on Derek's chest. He placed his arms around her.

"Derek, I do love you, how could I not?"

"Rachel, there are many types of love. You love your aunts; you have loved me as a friend. We have become more than friends. I am thirty years old. Getting to be an old man. As you know I have never been with a woman." Smiling, he added. "Too fat when I was young and too busy with career until I met you."

Rachel sat up on the bench, looking again directly at Derek. "You have been very patient with me. I thank you for that. I do love you, you know that."

"I am going to arrive on your birthday with a ring for you; you need to decide what your answer will be. We are busy with the big event but you will have six weeks to think about my propsoal. Nothing like giving lots of notice." He leaned forward, taking her in his arms, kissing her with all the depth of affection he had for her.

As so often happened in the household, they were interrupted, this time by the approach of a truck coming up the long curved driveway. It was local nursery workers who were helping the gardener prepare the grounds for the big event.

****

Robert set Rachel's diary aside with a bookmark placed at the June entries; he would return to it in a few minutes. He wanted to spend a few minutes reading the thoughts he had recorded in his June 1975 diary. He easily found the diary but was dismayed to have opened it to the June 13th entry.

- - - - - Northumbria, 1975

Robert was seated at his desk in his classroom, correcting senior high research papers. His students had been requested to write an extensive research paper on the life and writing of their favourite novelist. The assignment also required the students to have read at least two novels by the author and to show how the novels reflected the elements of biography and style that they had discovered from their research. Although he had provided assistance through each step of the research process, the final paper required careful correction.

It was June 13; Robert was not superstitious by nature but today he felt uneasy, expecting something to break the calm that had existed in his world during the last few months.

He had begun a master's program through the extension department of a local university. Weekend trips to the university library and summer programs would fill his free time for the next two years. Leah remained unchanged; he felt that a master's degree would not only benefit his knowledge base, but the accompanying increase in salary would be a help in meeting the medical expenses that continued to rise at an alarming rate. His studies also filled a great void that existed in his life. He had no social life.

His only community involvement centred in church related activities. He had returned to his Anglican parish. He was in the senior choir and had taken training to be a lay reader. He had always realized that faith was important and it was only after Leah's accident that he had wandered away. He had become interested in the evangelical and charismatic sections of the church. Robert would never have considered himself 'a new-born Christian' but like Daisy, he believed in a living faith. He had also begun exploring the healing ministry as part of the charismatic movement in the church.

He gathered the unmarked essays, placed them in his briefcase and returned home for the weekend. After helping with the supper dishes, he took his essays and mail to Leah's room. As he entered Leah's room, his father was just leaving.

"Leah sleeps a lot these days, Robert."

"Yes, but even when she is awake, it's hard to tell if she is with us or not."

"Margie has been good to help, hasn't she? She comes most days now. Good to have a nurse in the family."

"Yes, she's been a real friend. Howie and Margie have stuck with Leah and me through all our struggles and now they are the only close friends we have. As you know, Leah has other cousins, but they have stopped coming to visit, except for birthdays and Christmas. I guess some people just don't know how to cope with Leah."

"Son, Leah and I just sit in silence together, but I think she knows I'm here. I don't talk much, so I found a good partner." He looked at Leah affectionately. "She looks so calm."

Robert looked at Leah lying in the hospital bed with her upper body elevated. She was wearing a blue satin bed jacket with a blue ribbon in her hair. She looked younger than thirty, but when her eyes were open, there was no sparkle, no happiness to comfort the guests who came to visit.

"Dad, I see you have been working on the roof of the garage. Don't go on the roof again until I can go with you. It takes two to handle those shingles."

"Don't worry about me, I can look after myself; I have been doing it all my life."

"Oh, I know, but I need the exercise."

Camille grabbed Robert by his right arm, "Feels pretty firm to me!"

Robert laughed, "Yes, but I need exercise from real work, not just from a workout on the bench press."

"Maybe so, but you are too busy. Leave the roof to the expert."

"I want to help, so call me in the morning before you go out to finish the roof."

Camille pointed to the essays Robert was carrying, "Let me know if I can help correct these papers."

Robert pushed his father through the doorway, "Sure thing, but I want to keep my job!"

As he sat down at a table near Leah's bed, he placed his essays in front of him. The first essay was entitled, *Jane Austen's World*. He stared at the title, reflecting upon his enjoyment of Austen's domestic novels, in particular, *Pride and Prejudice*. Austen's world was restricted to such a small area in the vast universe, yet, the author describes the setting with such warmth and affection. Robert realized that novels did not need to travel the globe to capture a reader's interest; ordinary events can reveal character and captivate readers.

He pushed the essay aside for a brief moment to look at his mail. There was a large brown envelope with a Halifax postmark. It was probably from his brother-law and it would undoubtedly be disturbing, but he opened all of Trevor's letters hoping that one day there might be a resolution to their conflict. He was tired of Trevor's constant harassment. He had thought of challenging Trevor to a fight, but he knew Leah would not have approved, so he attempted to keep the peace at any cost.

He withdrew a letter, newspaper clippings, and a smaller bulging brown envelope. He glanced at the newspaper clippings which featured pictures and stories of Connie Francis' rape on November 8, 1974.

Robert and Rachel had been shocked when the event was made public. Connie had been raped in her hotel room in New York after a performance at the Westbury Music Fair, the beginning of a cross country tour. Some of the headlines in the clippings leaped out at Robert, reminding him of Connie's night of terror: *Scream, and I'll Kill You!*, *Connie Francis Raped*, *Singer Tied and Raped*, etc.

He felt sick as he read portions of the articles which revealed the singer's ordeal at the mercy of her violator and her subsequent struggle to recover from the nightmare. Why would Trevor send him these clippings?

He opened the letter; it was short but brutal.

Hi Guy!

I know you like this chick so I thought I would send you a collection of articles about her.
Guess you knew she was raped. Did you do it?
I know you have experience. Leah can testify to that.
I guess Connie didn't get pregnant, better luck than the first one!

I have extra copies of the clippings and a letter to send
your American girl friend. Time she knew what you are.

I enclosed a gift for you, use them the next time!
Be safe with your favourite sport.

O

Robert carefully opened the small envelope. He often wondered if one day one of Trevor's parcels would contain a self-explosive mechanism. He pulled three condoms from the envelope with a note.

"If you had used one the first time..."

He looked in disgust at the clippings and condoms. How could anyone want to hurt him so much? How could anyone be so cruel? He looked at his angelic Leah and thought about Connie. They had both suffered so much. Connie apparently had been able to overcome her dark night of pain; Leah had not been so fortunate.

He took Leah's hands in his, tears forming as he thought of that night so long ago that had changed their lives. His Leah and his Connie had both experienced a pain that lasted far beyond the brief defilement of their bodies; their souls had been ravished. Robert kissed Leah's cheek.

Suddenly panic seized him! Trevor was going to write to Rachel. He wasn't sure how Trevor had managed to get her address, but it was possible that he would write. He thought of calling Rachel, but they had never resorted to telephoning although he had often thought of it. Now that Rachel was dating Derek, he felt awkward about calling; he didn't want his motive to be misconstrued. He had to write immediately to help Rachel understand.

He thought that he could understand Trevor's hatred for him, but why would Trevor decide to write to Rachel? Trevor could not really know much about Rachel; he obviously wanted to strike a deeper wound into Robert than he had already done. "This was the unkindest cut of all."

Robert left the bedroom to find some stationery. When he returned to Leah's room, he began a detailed letter to Rachel, hoping that he could avert any misunderstandings and pain that Trevor might cause. He knew his letter was long overdue; he hated writing it as damage control. He also was conscious of the timing of the letter. He knew the Flanders Cove celebrations were just two weeks away and he sensed that this summer might see Rachel and Derek make an announcement. However, he must protect Rachel and it was to this end that he began his letter.

****

Robert looked anxious as he placed his diary on the desk, returning to the bookmarked passage in Rachel's diary. Rachel had just received his letter. She understood perfectly Robert's motive in writing, but the letter would have a dramatic effect on their lives.

- - - - - Flanders Cove, 1975

Rachel, Rose and Derek were seated in the library reviewing the guest list for the ceremony and reception. Rachel and Derek were dressed in shorts and t-shirts, Rose was wearing light-weight trousers with a floral blouse.

Rose used a notebook as a fan, "It is so hot today, I might almost be tempted to wear shorts myself. Notice, I said almost."

"Rose, you could borrow a pair from me, we are about the same size."

"I don't think the world is ready to see these legs." Rose jested, raising both legs in the air.

"I still think you have the best pair of legs I have ever seen, Derek."

While Derek enjoyed all of the aunts, he particularly appreciated Rose's clever wit. He delighted in her teasing and liked to engage in a game of upmanship with her.

"Rose, I hear *Vogue* magazine wants you to do a photo session for their winter issue, *The Classy Lady in Slacks*. Is that right?"

"Definitely, but I had to refuse a *Playboy* spread, at least for the winter issue. I might agree to the summer issue."

Rachel enjoyed the game but wanted to finish the guest list. "Your attention, please. We are reviewing the guest list, not legs or complete exposures."

Rose chided, "And who said I would bare all?"

They all enjoyed a moment of laughter, but settled down to the work at hand.

Rose looked worried as she addressed her two co-planners, "I hope Daisy will be all right for this ceremony. Do you think she can do it? We're not spring chickens, you know. Daisy is 67."

Rachel paused to reflect for a moment, "I am a bit worried as well. She hasn't been feeling well the last few weeks; perhaps it is just the tension."

"Remember, my dear sister is the one who worries enough for us all. She is also the most timid. Whenever she is anxious, her angina reacts. She will be fine, I know. We just need to make sure that she relaxes and lets the caterers do all the work."

Derek added, "Rachel, the Cleaning Wizards will come before and after the reception to dust, vacuum, and clean. I have requested them to be here to help on the day of the reception. They will do the heavy work and clean up anything that the caterers won't have time to do. We have enough help to ensure that Daisy will have few responsibilities."

"Yes, we have lots of help, but that won't stop Daisy from worrying, will it, Rose?"

Rose nodded in agreement.

Rachel reviewed her list of guests, noting that they now had 467 accepted invitations. She held up three pieces of loose leaf. "Here are three lists of the guests who have not responded. If we each take a third of the names we could call them today and complete our guest list by the week-end. Agreed?" She passed Rose and Derek a list.

Rose looked at Rachel. "Have we forgotten any one?"

"I don't think so, we have reviewed the names so many times before."

Rose sat erect in her chair, "I wondered if...just a thought...but Rachel, had you considered inviting Connie to the ceremony?"

Rachel was somewhat startled by the question, "No, not really, it never crossed my mind. She really doesn't know me."

"My dear niece, you have been a fan club president for over a decade. No one has been more faithful than you. Why wouldn't you invite her?"

"I know we met briefly after a performance in New York and I have asked her for a few personal signatures over the years, but she has so many fans and I'm sure she would be forced to write a polite refusal wondering who I am. Besides, she is still attempting to get her life back together after that terrible night."

"I understand, but it sometimes doesn't hurt to ask. Connie has been a great influence on our lives. I've actually grown to like her!"

Rachel giggled, "Wow! That is high praise! Maybe I should invite her to meet her former critic and current admirer."

Derek shook his head, "What about inviting Petula Clark, now that would be something!"

Rose looked questioningly at Derek, "Petula Clark." Feigning a southern accent, she continued, "Now, listen here partner, we Americans need to stick together. We're being invaded by the Brits. We won the last war with them, so let's not lose this one. We want a belle from New Jersey not from England. Do you understand, dude?"

Derek could not restrain himself, "I understand Charlotte, the plantation must be defended against foreigners. Yanks are welcome, Brits ain't."

"Enough, you two, we have work to do. Derek, you and I should go to the caterers; Rose, you can begin phoning."

Rose stood up immediately, saluting, "Yes, madam, whatever you say." She marched stiffly out of the room, turning as she left to bow to them.

Rachel smiled as she turned her attention to Derek, "You two are impossible together."

"And you and I are definitely possible together. Remember, after the ball, the big decision."

"Yes, I know." She kissed him on the cheek. "First things first."

Derek looked serious as he tapped his pencil on his guest list. "Rachel, I have a question to ask about the guest list. I have wanted to ask numerous times before, but it never seemed the appropriate time. I know we have just decided that there are good reasons why Connie has not been invited. It makes sense, of course. She doesn't know you or the aunts even though she has been an important influence on your lives. Is there someone else who has been forgotten?"

Rachel pondered, "I don't think so, the aunts and I have gone over the lists a hundred times."

"The aunts and I have one name that we all thought of. Your aunts were reluctant to mention him, wanting to be respectful of my feelings."

Rachel gasped as the realization struck her, "Oh, Derek, you would think of Robert. Yes, I have thought of him, too. I must be honest."

"I understand you were not invited to his wedding."

"That's right, but circumstances were so different then."

"Perhaps two wrongs won't make a right!"

Rachel became agitated, "Derek, I think it is sweet that you would want us to consider Robert. No, he won't receive an invitation!"

Derek took her hands in his, gently holding them on his lap, "Don't get upset. I just want you to know that I won't be annoyed if he is invited."

Rachel sighed, "Derek, you are a saint. Oh, it is so complicated. I suppose he should be invited, but we have never met..."

"He is free to come, school will be out."

"July the fourth is a special day for the aunts, it's their day. You want us to consider a commitment shortly thereafter. And you know that I have my personal struggles. I don't want to complicate things. I will see that Robert receives a parcel of souvenirs from the ceremony and the reception. But..."

Derek came to her rescue, "Rachel, I only wanted you to consider the possibility of inviting him; you have, and I support your response. You stay here, you have so many other things to check on. I'll go to the caterers', I have the checklist to review with them. I'll also go to the nursery."

Rachel put her arms around Derek, kissing him. "'You are the wind beneath my wings.' Thank you for being you! I love you."

Derek returned the moment of tenderness, holding her close as he kissed her on the forehead whispering, "I love you and want to be with you forever. Now that we have planned this bash, the wedding will be a snap."

Rachel gently pushed him aside, "You are impossible! Taking advantage of me!"

Derek sat up, "Now taking advantage of you is one crime I could never be accused of!"

They stopped their jesting, gazing into each other's eyes, foreheads resting together. It may have been a moment, it could well have been an eternity. Love has no time limits when its full depth is shared.

Iris rushed into the library as the couple enchanged expressions of their love. "Rachel, Derek! Oops! Sorry!" She blushed. "Oh, I am dreadfully sorry. I..."

Derek smiled, "Perfectly all right, I have had better kisses!"

Rachel swatted him on the head, "From whom, may I ask?"

"Naturally from you, dear."

Rachel asked Iris, "Is there a problem?"

"I don't know if it is a problem, but the caterers called to say that they need to change some of the hors d'oeuvres we ordered."

Derek got up, taking his notes with him, "I'm just on my way to the caterers; Iris, please call them and tell them I'll be there in twenty minutes." He threw a kiss to Rachel as he rushed out.

"We seem to be using a common title format a great deal in this house. Someone should write a book entitled, *With love, With Interruptions*! I apologize, the caterers seemed so alarmed. I know it's their first major reception."

"It's fine, Iris. He was just leaving."

"The mail has arrived, let me bring it to you." She returned with numerous letters including one bearing a Northumbria postmark.

"Thank you, Iris, I notice I have a letter from Robert." She began to open the letter with her grandfather's brass letter opener bearing the family crest. Iris excused herself, claiming that garden duties required her attention.

Rachel carried the letter to the conservatory and sat in her favourite wicker rocking chair facing the outside gardens. The sky was perfectly clear; she hoped July 4th would be such a day. Robins could be heard near the fountains, several were having a bath. She paused to enjoy this ideal setting. She thought about Derek and the love he offered her. She had known him longer than Robert. In fact, she didn't really know

Robert. They had never met. She knew she was now being given a second chance to live happily ever after. Derek was the Robert she had dreamed of. He was tender, patient, and so caring. He was a tease! He made her laugh! She had laughed so little in a lifetime of missing her parents, caring for her aunts, worrying about finances and losing her dream.

She opened the letter, wondering if Robert had expected to receive an invitation to the ceremony.

Dear Rachel,

I know you must be very busy with your preparations for the big event.
I hope July fourth is a bright sunny day and that everyone
will enjoy the readings and presentations.
You must be so very proud of your photo article.
We have all enjoyed looking at it many times.
We have six copies on display.
We have read and reread *With Love, With God* and
With Love, With Children.
What an incredible family you belong to!
The mansion is beyond description. Gramma Horton loves the stained
glass window, Miss Brown wants to touch the quilt
and Mr. Gordon wants to claim the gardens for himself.
Mother and father are in awe of the size of the
estate. The famous bracelet has taken on new meaning.

From your letters, I know that you and Derek are enjoying
sharing your lives and I hope it works out for both of you.
You deserve to have happiness.

Leah remains the same. We can expect no improvement.
It is a constant struggle to keep her body free from bed sores
and to keep her from losing all reaction to her surroundings.
She sleeps most of the time, apparently at peace.

I am writing to share something with you that I should have
communicated years ago. The revelation is now forced upon me.
I regret its timing, but I hope you will understand. I will be brief.

You may remember me mentioning Big Al who attended teachers' college with Leah and me. I never liked him much because he reminded me of Trevor;
big, aggressive and coarse. I think I mentioned that he and Leah dated. He drugged Leah one night and raped her. They had no contact following that night. She became pregnant.
We married to solve her problem. It was my choice;
I had a difficult time convincing Leah that it was the right thing to do.
We have never consummated our marriage. Leah needed time to forget the past and to deal with the baby.
I was certain that the baby would help us to become a family, but the miscarriage changed all that.
Leah lost herself; and in the process we lost each other before love could blossom and bind us together as one.

I tell you this now because Trevor has sent me clippings of Connie's rape, threatening to write to you. He blames me for destroying his sister. Yes, I have thought of telling him the truth,
but he would never believe me. I believe he and Al are friends although Al lives somewhere in Central Canada.

I know how upsetting it must have been for you to learn of my sudden marriage. I tried to write to you, but words would not come.
I had promised Leah I would tell no one the reason for our marriage.
Eventually, I did tell mother; now I find myself betraying Leah's confidence again.

I wish you and Derek the happiness that eluded me.
I have had two romantic dreams that have not been realized.
It is interesting how Connie's life has been filled with so many heartaches. To think that her misfortune would be used by someone like Trevor to inflict pain on others is beyond me.
It is frightening to have someone hate me that much.
To think that he would also want to cause you pain because you and I continue to be friends is also inexplicable.

Please forgive the timing of this letter; I hope it will alleviate any misunderstanding that Trevor's letter might produce.

Best wishes for July fourth. I will send a telegram on the special day so the aunts will know that I am thinking of them.
You would already know that Flanders Cove will be in my thoughts...

Rachel felt a chill move through her entire body. She was not actually surprised by Robert's confession. She admired him so very much. Derek reminded her of Robert. She continually had to ask herself if she could ever give up the Northumbria dream. How could she continue to dream of Robert, a married man with an invalid wife? They had only shared letters. She and Derek had known the joy of holding hands, embracing, feeling emotions swell within them. They had embraced, felt the need for intimacy although they had never allowed their emotions to lead them beyond the limitations they had established. Derek wasn't a dream, he was a reality. He wasn't a promise, he was a certainty. He would love and cherish her.

* * * * * * * * * *

Robert was distracted by the sound of the doorbell. It was Howie checking on final details for the wedding and reception. After Howie had left, Robert wandered through the living-room looking at the eclectic arrangement of furniture. It seemed so strange to see those mahogany Queen Anne chairs in the Northumbria setting. He sat in one of the chairs, continuing to recall the details of his June 1975 diary without having the diary in his hand.

\- - - - - Northumbria, 1975

Robert got up early to help his father with the roof repairs. After a week of rain, the roof was finally dry enough to continue shingling. He discovered that his father had already gone out to continue the project. As he left the manor through the sun porch exit, he met Mr. Gordon rushing toward him. He knew instantly that something was wrong. Mr. Gordon was staggering, puffing, trying to point to the garage.

"Your father...your father has fallen...he's behind the shed."

"What! No! Oh no!" He rushed to the garage to find his father lying on the ground, still conscious, but badly shaken."

"Lie still, I'll call an ambulance!"

"An ambulance! I don't need an ambulance! I'm all right. Just had a fall...out of breath. Give me a minute."

"Look, don't be stubborn! Don't move! I'll go to the house."

At this point Mr. Gordon returned with Bertha and several of the manor's guests.

"Camille, didn't I tell you not to go on that roof! Didn't I warn you about falling! You are so stubborn."

Camille had recovered his second wind and was able to raise his head. "Yes, you told me. Yes, I'm stubborn."

Bertha knelt down beside him, "Are you hurt?"

Robert looked at his mother, "He's just fallen off the roof, of course, he's hurt."

"I know he's hurt, but can he move? Did he break anything? Here, let me examine these old joints." She carefully felt his limbs, using her years of experience as a practical nurse to ascertain the damage done to her Camille.

"I tell you that I'm all right!"

"Robert, help your father up. Lift him under his arm, I'll lift this side."

Camille was able to stand with assistance.

Bertha looked sternly at Camille, "Now see if you can walk."

Camille was able to walk with their assistance. He was taken into the sun porch, placed in a wing chair.

"Robert, stay with your father while I call Dr. Clark."

"I don't need a doctor. He'll tell me to take aspirins and go to bed."

"I am calling the doctor. You stay here and don't you dare move." Looking at Robert, "Keep him there until I return."

As she left for the telephone, she was able to calm the guests, asking them to wait in the living-room rather than their usual meeting place in the sun porch. As soon as the phone call was complete she returned to the sun porch to find Camille standing near the wing chair.

Looking at Robert, she raised her voice, "Didn't I say to keep him in the chair?"

Robert half smiled as he replied, "Yes, but he is stubborn, more stubborn than I am! He wanted to stand to show me that he is all right!"

"Look, I'm just a bit stiff, with a few bruises I suppose! I may not work out on the bench press, but I am fit!"

"Camille, you are 83 years old, your bones are fragile, you fell from the roof."

"Yes, I fell! Hurt my pride more than my bones."

Shaking his head, Robert stared at his father. "You are the limit, really you are."

"Hey, son, is that a compliment?"

Bertha revealed her annoyance, "This is serious, you could have killed yourself. You're not 30 years old!"

"No, I'm not thirty. Good thing, wouldn't want to be married to someone your age, if I were."

Bertha frowned, "Camille, be serious!"

"I am, I like women closer to my own age, never fancied the really young ones. I could use a cup of coffee and a galette."

"Coffee and a galette!" exclaimed Bertha. "You are impossible." Pointing to the wing chair, "Sit here, this time don't move." Looking at Robert, "Watch him, don't let him move. I will get your coffee. Dr. Clark will be here in a minute."

As soon as Bertha had left the sun porch, Camille pointed to a nearby chair for Robert to sit down.

"Women are always fussing! It's the way they are. When you work in a mine, you sometimes fall, you pick yourself up. If something falls on you, you lift it off and keep going. And sometimes you do this in total darkness."

"Yes, but you were a lot younger then. You know you shouldn't have been on the roof alone."

"I just got dizzy for a minute, I'll be all right now as soon as I get my coffee. I want to finish the roof today."

"You are not going to finish the roof. Howie and I can finish it. Now that is settled, no argument."

"Boy, you are as stubborn as your mother."

"No, I am more stubborn than you when I have to be."

Dr. Clark did arrive within a few minutes and pronounced that Camille had not been seriously injured in the fall from the roof; just a few bruises and a sore head. He ordered Camille to rest for a week, no gardening, no yard work. Camille reluctantly agreed to the restrictions.

Howie and Robert completed the roof repairs, not without much direction from Camille.

While working on the roof, Howie and Robert discussed their involvement in the Order of St. Luke healing ministry. Robert was pleased that Margie and Howie were as interested in the Order as he was. Margie claimed that there was a growing realization that body, soul and mind must be in harmony and that the link between the spiritual and physical had been largely ignored by modern medicine.

Margie was lay co-chair of the Northumbria chapter of the Order. Her interest in healing extended beyond her nursing career and her involvement in the Order to her passion for gardening. She had collected a great deal of research supporting the use of plants and, in particular, herbs for medicinal purposes.

Margie had always been slim; she worried about Howie's extra weight. Finally she convinced him to begin an exercise program similar to Robert's. She watched his diet and encouraged him to go swimming at the local YMCA with her twice a week. It had not been an easy battle to win, but eventually Howie lost weight and gained more muscle. He and Robert often worked out together at the manor or at Howie's new bungalow and were able to go to the fitness centre without having to worry about Trevor's interference. Margie was quick to remind both of them of the merits of working in her garden.

Howie stayed for a late supper at the manor after the roof repairs were finished. Margie joined them for coffee at eight o'clock following her shift at the hospital. The evening discussion dwelled on the common topics of interest they shared; family, church, music, Robert's Flanders Cove connection, diet and exercise, and the healing ministry.

Margie was seated on Leah's bed holding a copy of *With Love, With God* in her hand. "Daisy's book is remarkable. She talks about her congregation's struggle trying to find a balance between traditional and contemporary music in the church. She's right when she claims that a hymn book that is over twenty-five years old is long overdue for replacement, especially with so many new hymns being written today."

Robert nodded in agreement, "I guess Daisy has recorded the reactions most of us are experiencing in the church as we attempt to make worship more meaningful. Church is not a museum! Why did we think we had to be so morbid when we worshipped?"

Howie was the son of a minister and like many young people, he had wandered away from the church following his high school graduation. It was Margie's ministry of music that brought him back to regular church attendance. He had little patience for the barriers that prevented congregations from experiencing the worship of a living God.

"The churches have faced an exodus for the last two decades and what do they spend their time doing, arguing about whether King James' language should continue to be used in our liturgy."

"You are right, Howie," responded Robert, "but there are parishioners who are so stressed by all the changes occurring in their lives, that they find comfort in experiencing continuity in church."

"But do they understand the liturgy or is it just familiar?"

Margie held up Daisy's book, "The author discusses with great sensitivity the patience and understanding congregations need in order to help all worshippers experience the joy and peace they are searching for."

Howie reached for the book, "I guess I should read this!"

Robert looked at Margie, "I think you will agree with me, Daisy's language is simple, but the struggles she presents are the real issues we all face and she makes sensible suggestions based upon her own congregation's experiences. When she doesn't have a solution, she is honest."

"Yes, I agree, Rob, the book is really helpful. Daisy includes a chapter on the healing ministrry that we should read at our next Order of St. Luke executive meeting. She mentions the Order of St. Luke. Howie, turn to the chapter on healing and read her description of the Order."

Howie checked the table of contents to find the correct page, then flipped through the appropriate chapter until he found the required passage. "Well, she doesn't really dwell on the Order but here's what she says:"

"The Order of St. Luke, the Physican healing ministry is the outgrowth of the Fellowship of St. Luke which was established in 1932 by the late John Gayner Banks, an Episcopalian priest. It is now an interdenominational organization with a belief that all humanity is the creation of a loving God who wills for everyone wholeness, health of the total person, body, mind and spirit. The goal of the healing ministry is to see the total person restored to wholeness in all of life."

Robert agreed, "Daisy isn't a member of the Order, but she does appreciate its work. She mentions several healing ministries in that chapter. I think it is a good idea to recommend the chapter as a reading assignment for the executive."

Margie reached into her oversized handbag, withdrawing a copy of *Romeo and Juliet*. "Do you fellows remember this book?"

"Yes, I loved it!" replied Robert.

Howie frowned, "And I hated it!"

As Margie opened the drama to Act 11, scene iii, she reminded her husband and dearest friend that the healing ministry was nothing new. "We have heard so many speakers tell us about the threefold ministry of our Lord; teaching, preaching and healing and there have been so many stories of healings throughout the ages. Society is finally getting back to a recognition of the healing properties of nature, uniting body and spirit. I picked up *Romeo and Juliet* to read the other night. I was fascinated by this speech by Friar Lawrence:

O mickle is the powerful grace that lies
In plants, herbs, stones and their true qualities:
For nought so vile, that on earth doth live,
But to earth some special good doth give...

"People are returning to the healing powers of nature and to the healing that only the Creator can offer." She looked at Leah lying still in the bed beside her, "You know, we have talked about the healing ministry, we have attended healing services and yet we have never tried for ourselves the laying on of hands."

Howie looked questioningly at Margie, "Yes, but we need to know a lot more about healing before we can go to someone and lay on hands."

"Howie, what else do we need to know? You and Robert have attended the healing workshops with me. We've read several books on healing. We regularly read *Sharing* magazine from the International Order of St. Luke healing ministry, what more do we need? Will we ever be ready?"

Robert supported Margie, "She's right, Howie, we can all be channels for the Holy Spirit. None of us is a healer! We are just agents!"

"I know all that! But I think there is a readiness stage that has to be reached."

"Husband, dear, you sound like a banker! And you are the one who is so impatient with the church. Come on, it's taken us a few centuries to get the healing ministry back in the church, how much longer do we have to wait."

"Margie, we can't just go up to someone and ask, Hey, do you want to be healed? Then throw our hands on them."

"Howie, I think we need to practice first!" Looking at Leah, "Let's begin here, right now with someone we love."

Robert was surprised but agreed, "You know, that is a good suggestion. Why not?"

"Oh, I don't know, I feel uncomfortable doing it. Should we get permission?"

"Go ahead, Howie, ask her husband."

Robert and Howie exchanged smiles as Howie responded, "All right, all right! You win."

The three friends gathered around the bed, placing their hands on Leah's head. Margie led the simple prayer. Tears filled their eyes as they united their spirits to their God, praying for peace and health for their loved one. They knew that prayers for healing were often as beneficial to those who prayed as they were for the ones for whom prayers were raised.

During the laying on of hands, Leah opened her eyes and smiled at the three friends, but despite the faith that could move mountains, no instant healing occurred.

As they returned to their former seating arrangement, Margie asked Robert, "May I borrow your copy of *With Love, With Children*?"

"Sure can, we have several copies. The stories and songs are terrific; the illustrations really appeal to young readers, very clever."

"I thought I should begin reading to the baby!"

Robert was startled, "To the baby! Whose baby? You're not! Howie?"

"Yes, Rob, Margie and I are going to be parents! We just told our parents this morning. We wanted to be together to tell you."

Robert rushed from his chair to embrace Margie, then hugged Howie." "Congratulations! I am so pleased for you!"

"Rob, if it is a boy, we are calling him Robert; if it is a girl, Leah!"

Tears formed in Robert's eyes as he looked affectionately at his dearest friends, "Oh, thank you so much, Leah would be so pleased. I'm so pleased for you!"

Margie placed her hand on Leah's right arm as she looked from Leah to Robert "Rob, you know the MacDonald's have a history of miscarriages; Leah was not the first, so pray that this child will be born and will be healthy."

Looking somewhat concerned, Howie smiled, "Don't even talk about the possibility! The baby will be all right. Hey, the Patterson's have strong babies! No need to worry."

"How long will you work, Margie?"

"Howie and I have agreed that I will stop in my sixth month, I'm two months pregnant now. I don't know what I'll do after the baby is born. Howie wants me to stay at home, but I love nursing, so we'll see."

"I'm so happy for you, really I am. I remember how excited I was about being a father..."

Winking at Robert, Howie said, "Uncle Rob, you and I can take the little guy fishing."

Margie quickly responded, "Little guy, careful, who said it would be a boy and does that mean you wouldn't take our daughter fishing?"

"I knew she would take the bait, Rob!"

Robert excused himself for a minute, returning with a book under his arm and a puppet on his right hand. "Meet Rocky, the raccoon. the central character in Daisy's masterpiece. Consider the puppet and book to be the baby's first gifts."

Accepting the book, Margie kissed Robert on the cheek, "I'll treasure this and read it many times."

Howie placed the puppet on his left hand and using the puppet said, "Thanks, guy, you're cool!"

Robert always enjoyed Howie's sense of humour. So often Howie could bring relief during times of stress.

Robert thought of the many ways that Northumbria and Flanders Cove were united. Here he was giving Daisy's book and puppet to his best friends. He wondered if the bond of affection would survive Rachel's pending marriage. Would he and Rachel continue to share their special moments with each other? He had become so dependent once again on her letters; she was his lifeline; but they were simply close friends. He was married and she would soon have her own husband to love and cherish her.

****

The sound of the telephone caused Robert to abandon the comfortable reflections he had enjoyed in the living-room. The latest interruption was Howie who was calling from the bank. Howie was confirming the items on his best man checklist as methodically as he managed the demands of his banking responsibilities. He wanted to know if Robert were nervous. Robert sensed that Howie was, in fact, more anxious than he was.

Robert desperately wanted to complete his 1975 memory journey because it was the year that Rachel had made a painful crucial decision that had so profoundly affected their lives. He returned to the den, picking up Rachel's 1975 diary to once again recall the details of the July 4th celebrations.

----- Flanders Cove, 1975

July 4, 1975 was a perfect summer's day in Flanders Cove. The sky was clear, the temperature was forecast to be 80 degrees with little humidity. Rachel and Derek had just toured the property to ensure that everything was in readiness for the three o'clock ceremony.

The gardens were glorious with an endless variety of iris blooms, pinks, sweet williams, pansies, day lilies, foxgloves, petunias, impatiens and every possible colour of rose.

In the centre of the front garden, extending around the gazebo was Iris's triumph; the garden that she herself tended with no help from the gardener. It featured the family flowers; lilies, roses, irises and violets. Iris had also included larkspur, Rachel's birth flower, in the prized bed.

Rachel had extended the gardener/handyman's employment to full time beginning in May in order to see that the grounds were ready for July fourth. He was assisted by a crew of four young people from the local nursery who helped with the extra planting, trimming, pruning, and mowing.

It had all been worth the cost! Rachel had struggled with the projected cost of the event. The nursery bill alone was staggering, not to mention the carpenters, painters, caterers, cleaners and the promotion of Daisy's housekeeper to full time employment.

Following their tour of the grounds, Rachel and Derek checked the kitchen to ensure the caterers were ready. Extra refrigeration had been installed to accommodate the menu. Long silver trays of hors d'oeuvres, sandwiches, savouries and sweets could be seen everywhere. The featured dessert was English trifle; Daisy was careful to supervise the caterers as they prepared the spirited treat. Sixty dozen galettes had been made using Bertha's recipe; they were featured plain or with various homemade jam toppings with just a touch of whipped cream.

As they concluded their tour, they were summoned to the gazebo to give final instructions to the string quartet who would provide the music for the afternoon.

The aunts assembled in the living-room to await their entrance cue from Derek. They attempted to comfort each other, but only succeeded in making each other more apprehensive.

Daisy stood by the front window watching the guests drive up the winding driveway, past the front door, stopping near the stables to park. Two attendants were on hand to help with parking.

Daisy delighted in announcing who was arriving. "Governor and Mrs. Wallace are arriving. She is dressed in green, wearing a large brimmed summer hat, very stylish. Oh, and here are our neighbours, the Johnson's. He's wearing a blue suit; she's...oh, my, she's wearing slacks!"

Rose rushed to the window, "Good for her, I approve!"

Iris strolled to the window, "I suppose slacks are acceptable!"

Rose pushed the lace curtains aside to get a better view, "Here are members of the town council, travelling together for protection, no doubt. Probably afraid of us!"

Iris shook her head, "Rose, just because we have had a few arguments with the council about rezoning, I hardly think they are afraid of us."

Daisy drew their attention to a white limousine that had just pulled up to the front entrance. "Who is this? The governor and senator have already arrived. Can you see, Iris?"

"Yes, I can see, Daisy. It's the editor of *American Estates*."

Rose patted Iris on the shoulders. "He's not bad looking, maybe you can persuade him to take you for a drive following the reception."

Iris chided Rose for being so frivilous, then reminded her sisters that the appointed time had arrived for them to join their guests.

At precisely 2:45 p.m. the three aunts made their appearance on the terrace and were escorted to the reception tent by Derek. Daisy and Rose had chosen to wear full length summer dresses with lace trimming the collar and three quarter sleeves. Daisy's yellow dress contained delicate white daisies on the bodice, Iris's pale blue dress featured mauve irises on the sleeves. Rose had chosen to wear full length pink culottes with no floral imprint. The aunts looked radiantly Victorian as the sun sparkled on their accessories. They wore their favourite necklaces and bracelets, all gifts from their parents. Daisy had summer flowers in her hair; Iris had chosen to wear a corsage on her wrist. Rose was the non-conformist in dress as in manners; she would not even consider wearing a flower.

Rachel's multi-coloured dress extended just below her knees; like Daisy, she wore flowers in her hair. Derek told her she reminded him of Ophelia from *Hamlet*. Derek looked smashing in his white double-breasted sport coat with navy trousers. He had a small pink rose as a boutonniere.

The opening ceremonies were filled with glowing compliments by the dignitaries. Everyone was impressed with the estate and the attention to detail in the day's events. Senator Brown remarked on the beauty of the gardens, declaring that they rivalled any of the state's public gardens. Governor Wallace was in awe of the magnifiicent heirlooms found throughout the mansion, in particular the 200 year old grandfather clock and the famous quilt. Mayor Graham focused on the extensive library, reminding everyone that the collection contained some rare editions of Connecticut's heritage. The Rev. Simms graciously thanked their hostesses for having invited everyone to spend an afternoon among their treasures, reminding everyone that the ladies were by far the greatest treasures to be found on the estate.

Daisy appeared confident as she moved toward the podium to speak to the audience. She opened her copy of *With Love, With God* to the bookmarked page, looked at the audience, smiled and proceeded to speak in a calm, clear voice:

"I have chosen to read the lyrics of a hymn that I consider to be the theme of my book.

In composing the hymn, I relied upon a familiar passage from the gospel of St. Matthew:

When I was hungry, you gave Me something to eat,
And when I was thirsty, you gave Me something to drink.
When I was a stranger, you welcomed Me,
And when I was naked, you gave Me clothes to wear.
When I was sick, you took care of Me.
When I was in prison, you visited Me.

I thank the Flanders Cove Chamber Ensemble for providing background music as I read and three members of St. John's Episcopal choir for singing the chorus between the verses."

On cue, the ensemble began playing as Daisy eloquently recited the first chorus of the hymn from memory then turned to her book to read the verses.

Chorus:
Spirit, Spirit of Love Divine
Searching the hearts of all, looking for love.
Spirit, Spirit of faith expressed
Move me to action, Lord; Lord, let me serve You!

I gave you My blessings,
I gave you My love.
I gave you your wealth.
I gave you My dear Son,
I gave you My Spirit,
I ask you to love Me
Love My people, too.

My people are wounded,
My people need love,
My people need someone,
My people need you.
My people are hungry,

My people are cold,
My people need someone,
My people have you!

I live now within you,
I am that still voice,
And I ask you to serve Me,
To help all in need:
The hungry and naked,
The lonely and blind.
Give them my love,
The love I give you!

After she had read the final verse, the stately 67 year old closed her book as the trio sang the final chorus. The guests immediately rose to their feet to give this woman of faith an ovation for her courage, her talent and her inspiration.

Rose arrived at the microphone carrying Rocky, the raccoon puppet. She had decided to share one of her favourite legends with the audience, adapting the language to suit the adult audience. She placed the puppet on her right hand, lifting Rocky so that he could bow to the audience. Without a word of introduction Rocky began talking, captivating the guests with his whimsical presence.

"Hi, my name is Rocky; I'm a raccoon, but I bet you already knew that. Humans are quite intelligent. Have you ever wondered where raccoons got these famous circles around our eyes?"

"Oh, I know you humans don't like to have dark circles around your eyes, but we raccoons love them. It gives us that look of mystery and some people even think the circles make us look naughty."

"Of course, I have noticed women in particular using black paint around their eyes and people in sports often paint black lines under their eyes; I guess the raccoon look is catching on."

"But you must have wondered why raccoons were created with these special dark circles around our eyes. Remember the eyes are the gateways to our souls."

"My grandfather told me the legend of the famous circles; the legend had three explanations. I'll share just one with you today."

Rocky leaned forward, clapping his paws together and nodding his head at the audience. The audience was enthralled!

"My grandfather told me that raccoons were created with no circles around our eyes. It wasn't until a young raccoon about my age was wandering in the forest when he came upon a frightened child. The child had become separated from his family at a picnic and soon became lost. The parents were frantic. Soon a search party combed the forest searching for the child, but after five hours, the child had not been discovered. Nightfall slowly descended as the forest prepared for its cool damp air to refresh the vegetation that had experienced the heat of the afternoon sun."

Rocky perked his ears as he asked the guests, "Hey, do you mind if we call the raccoon Rocky?" Looking at the audience who had given their approval by nodding, he waved to them. "Thanks!"

"Rocky approached the child defensively because he had never seen a human before. The child was delighted to have company and ran to Rocky, picking him up, patting him on the head. They were instant friends."

"Rocky sensed that this human was looking for his parents. He had noticed some grown-up people back in the clearing. He decided to lead his new friend to safety. He leaped out of the child's embrace and started running toward the clearing. The child followed. After a few minutes the child stumbled, falling into a bog composed of heavy black clay. The child began to sink deeper and deeper into the bottomless pit. Rocky noticed that the child had dropped his hat before falling into the bog. He grabbed the hat in his mouth and began running toward the clearing. He was met by the parents and members of the search party who followed him to the bog just as the child's shoulders were being devoured by the consuming earth."

"The child was pulled to safety and immediately broke free from his parents to rush towards his new friend. With hands still covered with black clay, he hugged Rocky and looking into his eyes, he pressed his nose against Rocky's and took his little hands and traced clay circles around the raccoon's eyes."

"Rocky licked the little boy's face and broke free from his friend's embrace. He had had enough of humans for one day. He dashed for the freedom of the forest, allowing the night to envelope him."

"In the morning Rocky went to the river to have a refreshing bath. He missed his new friend and hoped that he might meet him again some day. After he had jumped into the cool stream, he used his paws to wash his face and in particular his eyes. He discovered that the black circles around his eyes could not be removed no matter how hard he scrubbed."

"The circles were a part of him; his good deed and the child's love would forever be with him. Little did he know that all raccoons would thereafter wear with pride their circles of love that reminded them of their companionship with their human friends."

Rose moved Rocky closer to the microphone for him to whisper. "Remember, that is only one of three stories in the legend. To discover the other two, I suggest you read *With Love, With Children*."

Rocky threw kisses at the audience, then bowed.

The guests who had earlier responded to the inspirational, now jumped to their feet to applaud this 66 year old who had enchanted them with a puppet and a legend. Rocky was the symbol of the young and the young at heart, the whimsical!

The editor of *American Estates* requested Iris to come forward to receive her special gift.

"It is with pleasure that I present to Iris Thomas, this commemorative framed photo of our September 1975 front cover. The inscription reads as follows:

The heirlooms featured in the Thomas collection are priceless. They represent some of the finest pieces we have ever featured in our magazine's thirty year history of publication. The floral bouquets captured in stained glass and fabric are classic American heirlooms that represent everything heirlooms should be. Heirlooms are best featured in their natural setting by Americans who treasure them and whose very souls are linked to the sentiment that produced them. We are proud to have had the pleasure and privilege of featuring the Thomas collection.

He presented Iris with the framed photo. Iris moved toward the microphone to speak to the guests.

"Our home is the legacy we have received from our parents, Henry and Violet Thomas. They instilled within their children and grandchild a love of our country and the appreciation of craftmanship. We are pleased to have shared our treasures with *American Estates* magazine and to have you with us today. We do extend a warm invitation to all of you to explore the grounds and our home.

Looking at her framed gift, she continued, "This photo reminds all of us of the treasures that are our legacy. We need to respect them, preserve them and yes, share them with others. My sisters and I have much to learn about sharing our treasures, but with your help, I am sure we can learn the stewardship we require to allow our heirlooms to speak to others. Thank you!"

Once again the audience rose to their feet as the eldest sister smiled warmly at them before returning to her seat.

Derek waited until the audience had had the opportunity to fully express their appreciation before he requested that all three sisters return to the microphone. Rose stood in the centre of the three, moving toward the microphone.

"Thank you for sharing this day with us. At our age, it is humbling to suddenly be recognized for our writing, gardening, quilting and collecting of American treasures. None of this would have come to fruition without our niece, Rachel. She has been our inspiration, encouraging us take risks, enabling us to do what we would have considered impossible just a few years ago. We want all of you to know that contrary to public opinion it is possible to teach old 'cats' new tricks!"

Rose paused as the guests enjoyed her humour.

"My sisters have a locket to give to Rachel to show our gratitude for her love and her encouragement. The outside of the locket features the Thomas crest; the inside contains a photo of the covers of our two books and *American Estates* magazine. The inscription reads as follows:

To Rachel, You are our treasure!
Iris, Daisy, Rose

Rachel was overwhelmed as she accepted the gift, receiving loving embraces from each aunt. Rose requested Rachel to remain at the podium as she continued speaking to the audience.

"The organization that was required for today's ceremony and reception was under the direction of Rachel and Derek Perkins; we thank both of them for donating their time and talents to ensure that today would be a success. We ask Derek to come forward."

Iris moved to the microphone to make the presentation; Daisy held the gift wrapped boxes in her hand.

"Years ago, my father had watches crafted as a gifts. We have been able to have the same Swiss firm duplicate those watches. The originals were pocket watches; these are wrist watches, one more delicate than the other. It is with our deepest appreciation that we present these gifts to the two individuals who made this day possible." Daisy kissed Rachel and Derek as she presented the gifts.

Following the benediction and grace, the guests enjoyed the delicious fare that the caterers had prepared. It was past ten o'clock when the final guests had departed. The aunts were exhausted, but thrilled with the day's activities. Rachel and Derek were able to spend a quiet hour in the conservatory unwinding and enjoying peace and solitude after a day filled with detail after detail that had demanded their undivided attention. In the following days, the family basked in their accomplishment; they had dared to invite the world to come to them and they had survived.

Rachel had not worried as much about the big event as she had about the decision she could no longer delay. She was haunted by the realization that she had to choose between a dream and a reality. She loved both Derek and Robert. She had lost Robert forever and yet part of her clung to the dream. Derek was everything she had wanted. Derek had won the hearts of the aunts who obviously had already accepted him as family. He shared with her a prized gift from the aunts.

Derek and Rachel spent a great deal of time together in the days following the ceremony and reception. There were numerous details that required attention to conclude the paper work.

On July 21, Rachel's birthday, Derek arrived at the mansion with a large cloth bag filled with gifts. It was Rachel's birthday; it was also decision day. The aunts were aware of the significance of the day and were conveniently absent when Derek arrived. Rachel had not revealed to anyone her decision although the aunts knew that she was struggling within herself.

Rachel welcomed Derek with a kiss and a hug, then led him into the conservatory. They sat together on a wicker love seat facing the garden.

Derek stared at Rachel hoping to discover an indication of what he might expect, but Rachel appeared to be guarded against such revelation.

Derek pointed to the bag he had placed beside him on the floor. "I have some birthday gifts, but we need to chat first. I have waited for this moment for so long. I suppose no guy has ever been positive that his loved one would accept his proposal, but I am almost afraid to ask. Rachel, I want to ask you, but I don't want you to have to refuse."

Looking concerned, Rachel spoke softly, "Derek, I must tell you first how much you mean to me. I have fallen in love with you for many reasons. You are tender, sensitive, caring! You are so good to the aunts."

"Rachel, this sounds like a speech offered to a big brother. Am I not something more than that?"

With tears in her eyes, Rachel tried to smile, "You have conquered my heart because I long to be with you, to feel your warmth, your strength, your love. Yes, Derek, I love you. That has never been the issue and we have discussed this before."

Rising from the love seat, Derek knelt in front of Rachel, "I guess this is how they do it in the movies. Rachel, I love you, I want to marry you. Will you marry me?"

Rachel dissolved in tears, reaching out to draw Derek close to her.

"I want to say, 'yes', I want to be with you, but..."

"But the invisible man is still there." He got up from his kneeling position, resuming his seat beside Rachel.

Derek was filled with emotion that could only be expressed with tears, tears which he tried to control, but had to release. They embraced each other, crying uncontrollably. Finally, it was Rachel who drew herself apart from Derek.

"Derek, I am...I am tortured by my inability to say 'yes'. You mean so very much to me. I know I am throwing away a lifetime of love, but it would be wrong to marry you knowing that part of me was trapped in a romantic dream that should have been put to rest years ago. How can I explain what I don't understand myself? I love a man I have never met."

Derek took Rachel's hands in his. With tears flowing down his cheeks, he soothed her.

"Rachel, I respect your honesty and courage. You have always been straightforward with me. I came today not knowing what the decision would be but fearing that a refusal was inevitable. The values that have caused you to make this decision are the same values that won my heart. Damn, I wish that it were otherwise."

"And so do I."

"Rachel, I did come with two speeches. May I go to the bathroom to freshen up before I give you my second speech, the runner-up one?"

He left before Rachel could say anything. She dried her eyes, but no sooner were they dry than they were moist again.

Derek returned looking solemn but wearing a frozen smile. He sat beside Rachel, withdrawing a jewel box from the cloth bag. "Rachel, this is your birthday. It is the saddest day of my life." His voice quivered with emotion but he forged ahead. "I have lost an opportunity to be your husband, I don't really know how to deal with it. I want to remain your friend; we are friends, nothing can change that." He threw his arms around her to feel her warmth, to convey the depth of his feelings.

"Derek, we are more than friends and will always remain so."

Derek passed her the jewel box. "This contains my final personal gift to you." He paused, but quickly regained his composure. "This is not quite as exquisite as Bertha's but I hope you will appreciate its significance."

Rachel opened the box to discover a three-inch silver bracelet with delicate angels engraved among larkspur, Rachel's birthday flower.

"I wanted you to have your own angel bracelet. I hope it will remind you of me and the love I have for you."

Rachel shook her head, placed the bracelet on her wrist and kissed Derek's cheek.

"I love it! I will wear it as faithfully as Bertha has worn hers, I promise." She pushed the clasp closed. The noise seemed to echo throughout the conservatory as if concluding the emotional struggle of the two lovers who were agreeing to part and be just close friends.

Derek placed his hands on Rachel's face. "I have enjoyed being with you so much, the sound of your voice, the touch of your hand...I have loved you with my whole being. I understand, I don't like it, but I understand that you must do what you must do."

"I guess I am lucky that you do understand, especially when I am so confused and upset myself."

"Rachel, the job at the regional office is still mine if I want it; I am going to take it. I think we need space before we can hope to be just friends."

"Derek, I think the job is something you will enjoy and will be a stepping stone to other career advancements for you. You have so much talent."

"The media coverage of July fourth has been noticed by our company and they want me to direct their promotions. I think I might enjoy that type of work. Oh Rachel, here we are talking about my work, when the most important..."

Rachel placed her fingers on Derek's lips, then lowered her head to kiss him lightly on his lips.

"Forgive me for causing you all this pain and please pray that we can cope without each other."

Derek rose abruptly. "Rachel, I purchased thank-you gifts for the aunts. I guess they are now farewell gifts. I want to see them individually to say good-bye. And yes, I have a small jewel box here that I will not be giving to you." He paused to gain his composure. " I'll head to Boston for a few weeks to finish my holidays and to visit the regional office. I'll call as soon as I come back. You will be in my heart and mind always. " He leaned forward and kissed her cheek, then quickly left the room.

Rachel could barely find the strength to get up. She slowly rose and climbed the stairs to her bedroom, closing the door behind her. She went to the window seat, sat down, staring at the front yard and the harbour, seeing nothing, feeling everything.

After an eternity, she saw Derek leave through the front entrance. He quickly got into his car and drove out of the yard beyond the wall. He was gone from her. Her dream was gone! This time she had shattered the dream; she had made the decision.

She glanced at the harbour remembering her other dream of so many years ago. She had dreamed of sailing out into the harbour, up the Atlantic Coast to Nova Scotia, stopping at Northumbria.

She was filled with her own pain and with the pain she had caused Derek. She was once more alone! She sensed that she would live her life without love being fulfilled. Her soul was so chilled that she walked from the bedroom into the hallway searching for her aunts. She needed

to be surrounded by love, even if they couldn't understand what she had done.

She found the three aunts sitting in silence in the living-room. She feared they would be annoyed with her. As she entered the room, they rose from their chairs and rushed to embrace her. They shared a long tender group hug as all four released again the emotion that they were feeling...

*** * * * * * * * * ***

Robert gazed at Rachel's diary. She had given up an opportunity to be Derek's wife. Derek would have devoted his life to making her happy! What courage she had! The aunts were a tower of strength to her in the weeks following the refusal. Derek did accept the position at the regional office. It was months before he was able to visit the mansion again, but he and Rachel did occasionally chat on the phone. Rachel's wrist was a constant reminder of the love that Derek had shared with her.

Robert glanced at his watch. If he didn't abandon this sentimental world of diaries and letters, he would end up rushing to get dressed for the funeral at 2 o'clock. Yet, he had to complete his journey to prepare for the real beginning of his life! Rachel's other love was gone, but destiny was not without other surprises that would continue to influence their lives!

Chapter 6:

Breakin' In A Brand New Broken Heart

Robert withdrew a copy of Connie's biography, ***Who's Sorry Now:*** *Connie Francis*, from the book shelf that contained his collection of prized books. He skimmed the table of contents noticing that chapter nine was entitled, "Breakin' in a Brand-New Broken Heart". In the chapter Connie deals with the heartbreak she endured after she and Bobby Darin parted. She lived with the hope "No, the full expectation, really - that somehow, sometime, somewhere, some way, Bobby and I would be able to love each other again and be together, this time forever". Her dream vanished when he married Sandra Dee.

Robert thought of Rachel coping with her broken heart following her refusal of Derek's marriage proposal. The summer of 1976 in Flanders Cove was so very different than the previous year. It was not a time of romance but a time of heartache; it was not a time of celebration of heritage, but rather a time of defending the very existence of the Thomas legacy.

Robert withdrew Rachel's 1976 diary and turned to the summer entries.

- - - - - Flanders Cove, 1976

It was July 21, Rachel's 31st birthday. The aunts were gathered on the front lawn with Rachel as the guest of honour. The bouquet were trying their best to brighten Rachel's day, but the significance of the day dominated their thoughts. It had been a year since Derek had been denied his opportunity to become part of their family. They had done their best to comfort Rachel and indeed, her heart had slowly begun the healing process. Today, however, it was impossible to forget what she had done to Derek, to herself and to the aunts.

Rachel had written to Robert telling him that she and Derek had agreed not to marry, but she did not disclose any details. She realized that she was following the example of Robert's secrecy when he had suddenly married Leah, but she could not confess to a married man with an invalid wife that she was still in love with him. How could she confess that, despite all obstacles, she loved him too much to share her life with another? There could never be another love to replace his! She would have to keep that truth from him and yet learn to live without sharing the reality of his love.

The aunts had prepared a high tea to rival anything they had ever enjoyed in the tranquillity of their garden paradise. The silver tea set rested among silver trays of sandwiches, savouries and sweets. Although English trifle and Belgian galettes were present, it was the large birthday cake that was the focal point of the celebration. Fresh larkspur was featured in the centre of the cake and at the base of its supporting crystal pedestal. The aunts had hired the Flanders Cove Ensemble to play music from the gazebo. Rose had requested that the group include a few of Connie's happier hit tunes. Rachel's gifts were displayed on a white cast iron table near her.

With music in the air, the aunts entertained Rachel with family stories of the past. Rachel appreciated the effort that her aunts were making to make her birthday a happy one. She would have preferred to have let the day go by without any recognition of its importance, but she did not want the aunts to feel excluded from her, even if it meant that she would have to feign happiness.

On cue Marion, the housekeeper, arrived in the garden to indicate that Rachel had a long distance phone call. Rachel was apprehensive as she walked to the house. She feared it might be Derek. Although she and Derek had remained in contact and were friends, she did not think she could speak to him on this, the first anniversary of his proposal.

She went into the library to answer the phone, hesitating as she picked up the receiver.

"Hello, this is Rachel."

There was no response from the receiver. She repeated her greeting.

"Hello, this is Rachel."

"Rachel, this is Robert."

"Robert who?"

"How many Roberts do you know?"

The full realization of who was speaking to her filled her with an emotion that could only be expressed in tears. She gasped! Then she sobbed.

"Robert, this is such a surprise! I'm sorry, you caught me off guard, let me blow my nose."

"Rachel, I am sorry to spring this call on you. It seems ridiculous that we have never used the telephone to communicate with each other. We have known each other all these years and never once have I called."

"Robert, I have thought of calling so often myself, I know what you mean."

Robert had written to Rose to seek her advice on the advisability of him telephoning. Rose heartily recommended it. The aunts had intentionally delayed the beginning of the party until the phone call came through.

"Happy birthday, Rachel. We are both 31 now. I'd like to be there to taste that trifle and birthday cake."

"If you think I am sending you trifle by mail, forget it. A piece of the birthday cake might be possible. Robert, your voice sounds so...well, you sound like a radio announcer."

"Is that good or bad?"

"Oh, it was a compliment, I assure you."

"Rachel, we have the strangest relationship. We've been friends all these years and it is only today that we have heard each other's voice."

"Robert, I have long ago given up trying to understand us; I just enjoy the warmth of our friendship. It is my consolation in times of trouble, my joy in times of happiness. You have made my birthday so very special. I thank you."

"Rachel, mother and father and the famous trio of Gramma Horton, Miss Brown and Mr. Gordon are here. They have a message for you."

Northumbria sang "Happy Birthday" to their Robert's dearest friend.

Rachel's face was flooded with tears as she listened to the sung greeting.

"Thank you very much, it was terrific! Robert, that was so sweet."

"Rachel, we all feel a close bond with Flanders Cove now that we have read the two books and the photo article in *American Estates*. We watched the television program *Heritage Tours* last week that featured your estate. It was sensational."

"I was hoping you would see that program. We have copies on video, I'll send you one. Robert, thank your mother for sending me birthday galettes. We are about to enjoy them in a few minutes."

"We'll have some here to join in your celebrations with you!"

"Robert, it is so good to hear your voice..."

"Yes, Rachel, I can't believe that we...that we have waited so long. We always seem to...I guess, well, we just try to do what is right and in the end, we deny ourselves the closeness that...friends should have, are entitled to have."

"Robert, you have made my day. Thank you from the depths of my being."

"Rachel, I know that today is not only your birthday, but it is a year ago that you and Derek decided not to marry. I hope that the warm memories of your time with Derek will bring you comfort today."

"Robert, I guess you know from my letters that I have struggled. I have thought a great deal about Derek and the life we might have had, but life does go on. We can't cling to what was and what could have been. I guess we both have learned that lesson well. I think Derek and I are friends; I think we will continue to be friends. It is just difficult adjusting to such a drastic change in a relationship. You and I struggled in our relationship after you married. I remember the silent times when we...well enough of that."

"Rachel...writing is safer than speaking. Hearing your voice is wonderful. Your voice sounds familiar, as if I have heard it before. I do treasure our friendship, I hope you know that. I look forward to your letters...I...I don't know if I have ever really told you that...I have no other relationship like ours. I have lived with so many dreams that just didn't work out and I have eventually shared them with you. I am sorry that so long ago I was unable to tell you my real feelings, to tell you how special you had become..."

"Robert, perhaps speaking has its limitations. Your letters do convey more than words; I know what you are feeling, I really can read between the lines. I know that sounds trite, but it is true."

Rachel looked around her. She was in her grandfather's library. Her grandparents had often sat quietly in this room, exploring the wealth of literature, travel, religion, and politics. It was in this room that she and Derek had spent so many hours planning for the open house just a year ago. Now she was talking to Robert; his voice had joined those of others who were dear to her.

In correspondence, Robert and Rachel had always been separated. By the time she received a letter, things might have changed substantially in Northumbria, but Robert was here now with her. They were together for the first time! She felt excited, comforted. As so often happened in their lives, the unconscious memory of music quietly enveloped her, returning her to past memories when she and Robert were younger. She drifted, if only for a second, to a beach, they had walked together in her dreams, they had touched. Now she had his voice to add to her souvenirs...

The two friends chatted for half an hour, neither wanting to say good-bye, both realizing that they had waited far too long to talk to each other. Their relationship had never been ordinary, had never been easy!

Rachel was smiling as she rejoined her aunts. "I suppose the tea is cold by now!"

Daisy replied, "Marion will bring fresh tea in a minute."

Rachel resumed her chair by the gifts. "I guess you know who was on the phone!"

Rose responded for her sisters, "Yes, we do. Quite a surprise! He can never be accused of rushing into things, it only took him fifteen years to call."

Iris defended Robert, "Rose, that's terrible. Have we ever called Bertha to thank her? Has Rachel ever called Robert?"

Rachel laughed, "It's all right! We are all so reserved, so polite. Robert says that Mr. Gordon's favourite saying is: 'You can't do wrong by doing good'. It seems simple enough, but practising it is not always easy. I have wanted to call him so many times, but there was always a logical reason to prevent me from picking up the phone. Anyway, he has called, we have spoken to each other and we will do so again, soon."

Daisy clapped, "Bravo! Bravo! That's the spirit!"

Rose approached Rachel, passing her the first gift. "I was just teasing. We are too reserved! And he is just like us. That's why we like him so much. Now open your presents."

Rachel discovered the three gifts were theme related, three stuffed bears: a Winnie the Pooh bear, a polar bear, and a Paddington bear. She was delighted with the fanciful gifts.

Daisy was in charge of explaining their choice of gifts. "Rachel, at 31, it is time you became a collector. We decided you needed some company. I'm allergic to cats, Iris is afraid of dogs and goldfish are boring. We decided these bears would take little care and can't help but be excellent company. They never talk back."

Rose interjected, "Rocky is a bit jealous, but he'll get over it."

Rachel picked up Winnie, holding him so that he faced the aunts. "I have always wanted a Winnie the Pooh bear or a Paddington bear. And I love the polar bear as well."

At 31, Rachel was given her bear starter kit; it was the beginning of her bear collection that extended beyond stuffed bears to include ceramic, china and her 'cherished teddies'.

July 1975 was the year that the family had invited the world to visit their private domain. They dared to allow strangers to explore their gardens and to enter their home; to see where they enjoyed music, where they dined and even where they retired at the end of each day. Strangers had gazed upon the stained glass window from inside the home, they touched the famous quilt.

It was, however, the latter part of 1976 that saw the family venture into the wider community; they left the security of their home to defend their values, to become advocates, to provide leadership.The bouquet surprised even themselves with the resolution they displayed in crisis. Like their mother, they were more than lace and poise. They had inherited talents that their protective environment had never required them to develop. They proved to themselves and to the community that they were much more than a delicate bouquet of summer flowers!

The aunts were enjoying a leisurely breakfast in the dining-room following their day of celebrating Rachel's birthday. They were engrossed in a discussion of the new rector of their parish.

Rose looked at Daisy, "You weren't impressed with the rector during his interview for the position, were you?"

"No, I wasn't. He was so slow responding to each question. I wondered if he didn't really have enough intelligence to understand what was being asked or if he were trying to decide what answer would best please us. I have never seen anyone with such a blank expression. His interview was twice as long as those of the other six candidates."

Rose added, "But he did impress some of the other members of the search committee?"

"Oh yes, of course, they felt he was a good compromise. Two of the candidates appeared to be too progressive, one was too high church, one was a female and one wanted to come to the parish to have a lighter work load. There wasn't much choice."

Rose shook her head, "Didn't anyone support the female priest?"

"In all fairness, Rose, she had no experience. We felt that our parish was already into programs that she didn't have experience with, she couldn't provide the leadership we needed at the moment. Oh, yes, two of the committee members didn't want a female priest."

Iris questioned Daisy, "What is the parish council going to do about him? How can we get him to perform his duties?"

"It's not easy. He did sign a covenant with the council when he agreed to serve the parish. We have reviewed the covenant with him, but he just sits with a blank expression. As you know he hasn't been visiting the shut-ins at home or in homes for special care. When he was challenged about this lack of visitation at a parish council meeting, he claimed that he found visiting difficult. The parish secretary, Sarah Brown, asked him if he always had a problem visiting. He indicated that he finds visiting very stressful. Sarah then asked if he always had trouble with interpersonal relationships. He agreed he found it threatening to knock on people's doors. She pursued the matter further by asking him if he had sought help. He indicated he hadn't. But it's not just his lack of visiting, he is practising a ministry of total neglect. He is doing nothing except delivering a ten minute sermon on Sunday."

Iris sighed, "We have always been blessed with progressive rectors, rectors who cared about the parish. We have no experience with such incompetence and apathy. But Daisy, you are just the person to deal with the problem."

"Thank you for the vote of confidence. As chairperson of the committee, I'll have to see if we can find a solution. It is not a role that I am comfortable with. I never dreamed I would be in conflict with anyone, especially a rector. However, the other committee members are looking to me for leadership. Just because I wrote a book, they think I might be a leader."

Iris nodded, "Daisy, you are the only person in the parish who can deal with the situation. I'm here to help you in any way possible. I'm a good follower."

"We'll work on it together; the parish has come too far to suddenly regress now."

Looking concerned, Rose spoke. "Daisy, remember the doctor insists that you not put undue stress on yourself, so share the burden of your responsibilities with others. Are you sure you should do this?"

"I will be all right, and it is something I have to do."

Iris removed her glasses, "We are all under pressure. If we do nothing, we'll worry about what we could have done. We have no choice. But we do need to be sensible, to pace ourselves and to pray a lot. Daisy, you must make sure you get your rest!"

In the midst of the lively discussion about the incompetent rector, Marion, the housekeeper, rushed into the dining-room indicating that her husband, Walter, the gardener, had noticed surveyors on the property.

Rose rushed to the window, pushing aside the curtains. "Yes, I see them, I'll find out what they are doing."

Daisy and Iris both got up from the table to join her.

"Sisters, I'll go alone. We don't need a delegation because someone is surveying our property. Stay here. I'll be back in a minute."

Daisy spoke up, "Get Rachel to go. She'll be down for breakfast in a minute."

Rose chided her, "Leave Rachel alone. I have a tongue in my head. I can ask questions." With no further comment she left the dining-room and soon joined the surveyors in the backyard.

When she returned to the dining-room, she was furious. "A new highway! They are surveying for a new highway that will run through our property."

Daisy grew pale, "They want to build a highway on our property! But they can't!"

Rose continued, "They are only surveyors, they are only following orders. But it is a state highway project. I don't know know why we haven't heard about it before, but we'll not have any state highway running through our property, that is for certain." Rose stiffened her body as fire gushed from her nostrils. "By the gods of war, they'll never do it. Over my dead body!"

Iris nervously sipped her tea, almost in a trance. Finally she stood up, holding her cup in her hand. "Sisters, this is our home, it is threatened. We now need to fight for what is right. Remember, 'You can't do wrong by doing good'. We need to stand up for our rights. We need to protect our legacy. Father would want us to do so."

At this point, Rachel entered, sensing that something was wrong. "What's happening here? Marion is upset. What is this about surveyors on the property?"

After they recovered from the initial shock that their privacy and legacy might be threatened, they began plotting their strategy to gain the necessary information required to plan their offensive. Their neighbours on Melrose Road were caught off guard as well when surveyors arrived to survey their properties. Flanders Cove town council provided several information sessions at the civic building and orchestrated a media campaign; they also helped to co-ordinate a meeting with state officials.

Rachel and Rose decided to concentrate on the highway project; Daisy and Iris would focus their efforts on the rector.

****

Robert placed Rachel's diary on the table beside his wing chair and reached for the gold framed photograph of the three aunts that rested on the table. The three aunts looked every inch the Victorian ladies they were. They appeared delicate, sedate, and demure. Perhaps Rose who had always been the athletic and radical sister looked slightly less fragile. He smiled as he recalled the challenges they faced at a time when they were entitled to enjoy the tranquillity of their idyllic setting.

Robert reached for his 1976 diary, turning to the September entries. Margie and Howie were proud parents. Young Robert was ready to be christened; his parents had asked Robert to be the godfather.

Margie wanted to spend as much time with young Robert as possible, yet she did not want to give up her nursing career. Nursing was much more than a job for her, it was her calling; it provided another form of ministry. With Howie's position as bank manager, finances did not require her to work. As so often in the past, Bertha provided everyone with the solution to Margie's dilemma.

- - - - - Northumbria, 1976

Howie, Margie and Robert were enjoying watching young Robert play with his rattle in Leah's bedroom; Leah remained asleep in her bed.

Howie teased Robert, "Are you ready to be a godfather? Or have you seen too many mob movies to take on the responsibilities?"

Robert laughed, "I can handle it. Listen, if you can be a father, I can be a godfather."

Margie passed the baby to Robert, "Here godfather, do your fatherly thing. Remember godfathers are expected to be babysitters, so get in practice now."

Robert was tentative as he reached for the baby, treating him like a delicate piece of crystal. "No time like the present to learn, thanks." Young Robert looked into Robert's eyes, causing Robert to enjoy the wonderment of such a precious gift, a gift that he had been denied."

"Margie, what have you decided about returning to work?"

"I really don't want to work full time, actually I won't work full time. But I want to nurse. The hospital is not keen on having me part time so I guess I'll retire reluctantly."

"Mother and I were discussing your predicament this morning. Just a minute, I'll call her." He passed young Robert to his father, then left for a moment, returning with Bertha.

Bertha went directly to the baby, reaching out to hold him in her arms. The baby was perfectly at ease with everyone.

Looking at Margie, Bertha spoke. "Margie, you are a wonderful nurse. You have been so faithful in helping with Leah."

Margie tried to dismiss the compliment, "She's my cousin and best friend. I do it as much for me as I do for her."

"That may be so. The fact is that I have been dependent on you not just for Leah but for the attention you give to the other guests when you are here. Margie, I'm 64, beginning to think of retirement, but like you, I can't easily give up a way of life. The manor is about people, people we love, people who are entrusted to our care. If I don't obtain regular nursing help, I will have to consider closing the doors. I would like you to consider half time nursing responsiblities here at the manor. It would help if you could come most mornings. Would you consider it?"

Margie shocked Bertha by responding immediately, "I don't have to think about it, I'll do it. I am flattered to be asked. It is a perfect solution!"

"Margie, there can be a great of flexibility, some days you might want to come in the afternoon, or perhaps not at all. We can work out the schedule on a weekly basis." She passed the baby to his father, then hugged Margie. "We'll seal the agreement with a hug."

Howie responded, "I think the bank should consider hugs instead of all the red tape we are forced to deal with."

Robert looked mischieviously at Howie, "I never quite pictured you as the happy hugger, but who knows?"

Looking affectionately at young Robert, Bertha said, "There is no reason that young Robert can't come to work with you."

Margie smiled, "I was just wondering about that. I was not looking forward to dealing with a babysitter or housekeeper. I'll try him here, if it doesn't work out, I'll make other arrangements."

"He'll be fine, the guests love children. It will be good to have a baby among us. Believe it or not, Camille is excellent with children, if you are willing to risk exposing the baby to a television addict."

Robert broke into the conversation to tell his friends the latest Camille story.

"Last night father was watching a Perry Mason movie. The judge in the courtroom scene said, 'Court will reconvene tomorrow morning at 9:00 o'clock.' Father never watches television until the afternoon, but this morning he arrived in the living-room at 5 minutes to 9, waiting for the court to reconvene. Who said television is not real!"

Margie and Howie always enjoyed Camille stories. Camille endeared himself to everyone who met him. He was quiet, witty and charming. He said little, but what he said made an impression. Perhaps his lack of sophistication or his innocence attracted people.

Robert asked Margie, "I hope you are not considering giving up your position as organist and choir director."

Margie was quick to reply, "Absolutely not, that is my real ministry. I need my music!"

Robert sighed with relief, "We need your music!"

Howie looked at his watch, "Rob, it is eight o'clock, are we going to the fitness centre for an hour?"

"We should go, but Trevor is home for a few days and I don't want to risk meeting him there. Let's go jogging instead."

"Good idea, I'll meet you outside in a few minutes, I'll go home for my running shoes."

Margie and Bertha remained in Leah's room to discuss the details of Margie's employment at the manor. Bertha was a business woman and she wanted to ensure that they both understood the responsibilities and benefits involved even though they were friends.

Howie and Robert were not regular joggers, but on occasion they enjoyed a good run. As they jogged through the park at the edge of town wearing jogging pants and t-shirts, they met Trevor and a friend seated on a bench sharing a few beers. Trevor had had a few drinks, enough to fuel his anger but not sufficient to lower his performance. As Robert and Howie came near, Trevor stood in their path, forcing them to stop.

"If it isn't Robbie and his friend, Howie. Guess you're looking for a spot to be alone together? Hey, guys, I won't tell your wives!"

Howie responded, "Trevor, you've got a sick mind!"

Trevor held up his bottle of beer, "I'll drink to that. You two would make anybody sick. The two choir boys out for a good time together. At least you can't get pregnant!"

Robert had had enough. "Trevor, move aside. We don't want to argue with you."

Trevor pulled his friend by the shirt to draw him closer. "Jason, meet my brother-in-law and his dearest friend, Howie. Quite a pair. They live in church. Of course these days, that's where their type hang out."

Robert attempted to move away from Trevor but his adversary was determined to fuel the flames of the argument.

"Now Robbie, I hear you've been working out. Let's see if it does you any good when you have to defend yourself against a real man. I don't like to fight guys like you, but someone has to control the fairy population."

Trevor threw a punch aimed at Robert's jaw, but Robert was not the same inexperienced target he had been when they first fought. He quickly moved aside allowing the punch to go astray. Trevor was provoked, bursting forth with the vilest expletives.

"You son of a bitch, this time I'll finish you." He rushed at Robert but was unsuccessful in delivering any blows. He stumbled; in his frustration he kicked Robert's right ankle. Robert reached down to soothe his wound. Trevor coupled his fists, driving them down on Robert's back, knocking him to the ground.

Howie moved to help Robert, but Jason prevented him from doing so.

"Stay out of this, guy, or you'll need to deal with me."

"Stand up Robbie, I want to pay you back for killing my sister. You bastard, you ruined her life and now I hear you are romancing that American girl. Can't knock her up with your sweet letters though." He then threw himself at Robert once again. Robert remained calm, averting the blows but not striking out.

Howie broke his silence, "Robert, don't let him do this to you again. Defend yourself. Finish this once and for all."

Trevor laughed as he shouted, "That's it Howie, get him to hit me, if he can." He raised his right foot to kick Robert in the groin, but his foot missed its goal.

Trevor stood erect, placing his hands on his hips. "Here Robbie, hit me. I won't move! I can take it. I'm a man!"

Robert got his second wind, but remained immobile, staring at this crazed man, picturing Leah in his mind, knowing that she would not want him to fight her brother.

Howie broke the silence, "Rob, don't just stand there. Don't let him bully you. Do it for yourself! It's now or never!"

Trevor responded, "Robbie, listen to your choir boy cheer leader!"

Robert fixed his attention on Trevor, staring at him as the fear, anxiety, disgust and anger of years of abuse swelled within him. He felt himself charged with energy that propelled him into action. He threw a successful punch at Trevor's head, followed by another one. He pounded his adversary with all the strength he could muster. Although he was unaccustomed to using his fists, he thought of his father, remembering his advice about standing up for what is right. He heard Howie shouting for him to finish what he had begun. His mind whirled, his body was an explosive power house releasing years of pain and frustration.

His mind flashed back to that cold night so long ago near the church when he had promised himself that no one would ever physically abuse him again. He had trained rigorously to ensure that he could defend himself. He knew that he had to strike Trevor; he knew the time had come to show Trevor that he was not willing to put up with his threats any more. He remembered Trevor's letter to Rachel!

He struck blow after blow at Trevor who was no match for the brother-in-law he had provoked once too often.

Trevor fell to the ground and could not get up. Jason pulled Robert aside, "You've won! You got him, now leave him alone. Are you a professional fighter?"

Gasping, Robert replied. "No, my first real fight since high school."

Jason extended his hand to shake Robert's, "You won fair and square. I can tell you, I wouldn't tackle you and I've been in a lot of fights."

Robert looked down at Trevor who was trying to get up. "Is he all right?"

Jason leaned over to help Trevor up. "You guys leave us, he'll be all right."

As Howie and Robert walked away, Howie congratulated his friend. "Robert, you were terrific. I'm proud of you."

"Howie, he's Leah's brother!"

"He's a bully! Remember, he's the guy that wrote to you and Rachel about Connie's rape! He's a sadist! He's sick! You had to fight him!"

"I guess you are right, but it isn't any comfort."

"He'll think twice before he challenges you again! Good for him, he deserved it. I'm glad Jason was with him. Jason has a loose tongue so Trevor won't be able to hide his defeat."

* * * * * * * * * *

Robert closed his 1976 diary, exchanging it for Rachel's diary on the table beside him. Trevor maintained a low profile after his defeat. He did not visit his sister for several months and when he finally appeared again, he discontinued his usual harangue with Robert at the end of his visits. Robert no longer received letters with the black dot signature. It was a relief to have Trevor's interference curtailed, but Robert knew that Trevor would seek revenge; he knew it was only the quiet before the storm.

Robert enjoyed teaching senior high school English language arts. He used Shakespeare as his thematic approach to uniting reading, writing, listening, and speaking into meaningful experiences for his students. Each year the students were involved in a Shakespearean symposium in which they shared scenes from the Shakespearean dramas they were studying in class. They also wrote introductions for each scene focusing on the theme depicted in their scenes. All of the students were required to memorize a passage from one of Shakespeare's plays and to present from memory that passage in costume. Students were involved in dancing the minuet, baking such Elizabethan delights as maids of honour and Banbury tarts. Following a full day of activities, the students then performed the best of their scenes for their parents, relatives and friends in the evening. Through drama, song, dance, food and costume; Shakespeare came alive.

Robert always attempted to model what he preached to the students. If he expected them to write, he knew that they had to perceive him as a writer. He began writing short dramas for school and church. He never considered his writing to be of much value, but he felt it would be a suitable preparation for his first attempt at real writing, writing the novel he had thought about since his high school days.

He had just returned home after a rehearsal for the high school's one act drama festival. It was a particularly cold November evening. He found the famous trio in Leah's room entertaining each other with their familiar stories. As he joined them, Mr. Gordon was just completing one of his yarns.

"My four year old grandaughter came running into the house shouting, 'Grandad, Peter is saying bad words again.' I asked her to tell me what he had said, but she reminded me that it wasn't nice to use such words. I reassured her that it was all right for her to tell me. She said, 'He's using the R word.' I thought for a moment, trying to decide what the R word could be. 'Debbie, it's all right to tell me the word. I need to know what Peter said if I am going to ask him not to say it again.' She motioned for me to lower my head so she could whisper in my ear. With a faint whisper she said, 'Arse!'"

The ladies enjoyed Mr. Gordon's humour even if at times his language was slightly commonplace.

Gramma Horton glanced at Robert, "I think she spells phonetically. Would you agree?"

"I think you may be right. After all, Shakespeare never minced words! An arse is an arse! Why, Eliza Doolittle used it!"

Miss Brown waved her index finger at Robert feigning disapproval. "Such language from a custodian of the Queen's English. I am shocked!"

Gramma added, "And so am I. Wait until we tell your students the kind of language you use at home. We'll have to make a special trip to your class to inform them of their beloved teacher's colourful language."

Robert chuckled, "Thank you for mentioning a visit to my classroom because I have an invitation for you to join my students."

Mr. Gordon responded, "You want us to go to your classroom!"

"Yes, I do. Talk about being a risk-taker! Actually my students have just begun reading the novel *The Stone Angel* by the Canadian author Margaret Laurence. It is about Hagar Shipley who is in her nineties. The students are reading the novel from their teenage perspective. I have two favours to ask of you. I would like you to read the novel, then to come to class to discuss the novel with the students. It will give us two very different points of view. Would you be willing to do it?"

Gramma glanced at the others, "I don't know, Robert. I certainly don't mind reading the novel, but to be in front of students. How many students are there?"

"I have two grade twelve classes, a total of seventy students. We'll meet in the library."

Mr. Gordon exclaimed, "Seventy students, three of us and seventy of them."

Robert turned on his charm adding, "Well, you three have entertained the elementary students for years. Some of these grade twelve students will already know you. Do you mean to tell me that with all your experience dealing with people you are afraid of seventeen-year- olds. Now that I can't believe! You are always asking me if there is something you can do to help. Now there is! Come on, be a risk-taker."

Mr. Gordon was the first to reply to the challenge. "If the ladies will, I will!"

Miss Brown and Gramma put their heads together to confer. It was Gramma who gave their consent.

"We'll give it a try, but we'll be nervous."

"Thank you, I have the novels in my brief case. I'll get them."

Miss Brown inquired, "How long do we have to read the novel?"

"Three weeks!"

Mr. Gordon pointed to the doorway, "In that case, you'd better get them immediately. Like everything else I do, I read more slowly than I used to."

When Robert returned with the novels, the trio left for their individual rooms to begin their reading assignment. During the three weeks leading up to the seminar, Leah was subjected to a constant discussion of *The Stone Angel*. The trio could understand Hagar running away from her overprotective family; they felt her horror as she struggled with a seagull in a confined room. They knew what it was like to give up independence, to rely on others and at times to be considered children again.

Finally, the day of the seminar arrived. The ladies wore their very best dresses; Mr. Gordon wore a suit and tie. The three guests sat with Robert at a table in the school library facing the students who were seated in a semi-circle.

The seminar was a fantastic success. At the conclusion of the exchange of views, numerous students spoke individually to the trio.

Philip, the brightest student in the class shook Mr. Gordon's hand. "I really appreciate the time you took to read the novel and to share your viewpoint with us. I understand the heroine far better now."

Trish, the flighty student every class contains, stared at Gramma Horton. "You are exactly as I pictured Hagar, only you look better than she did in my mind."

Bob, who was by far the most offbeat grade twelve student, stood directly in front of the trio exclaiming, "Cool! You guys are cool! You're really with it!"

It was Sally, the most timid student in the class who provided the finishing touch. She was an average student who often used poetry to express her feelings; she was a most conscientious student. She approached the trio with a poem, passing it to Robert. "I...I wrote this for them." She left before they had an opportunity to respond. Robert read the poem to his three guests:

You came to share your thoughts with us,
But you shared so much more.
With age, you have gained wisdom,
With experience, you have mastered patience.
With hardships, you have become strong.

In denying yourself, you have found others.
You came, you shared, you cared.
You touched us; we have grown.
Hagar is now a real person,
Because of you, she will live with us.
Thank you for giving us meaning!

Robert could hardly believe that Sally could pen such lines, but he realized motivation is the key to all successful writing.

For days the conversation at the manor focused on *The Stone Angel*. The students' comments were repeated time and time again. December had slowly crept upon everyone with its promise of new life in the birth of the Holy Child. Robert tried to convince the trio to do a joint reading for the Christmas Eve family church service. They had almost agreed, but it was not to be.

On December 5th, Miss Brown suffered a severe stroke. She was rushed to the hospital where she lingered for a day before slipping quietly to her eternal rest. She had devoted a lifetime in the service of her God. She had been a missionary in Africa, she had always served where the need was greatest. She was ever the servant, following her Lord's example. Robert was asked by the family to read one of the lessons at her funeral and to deliver the eulogy. The family wanted only a simple eulogy befitting their loved one who had always walked the humble path, preferring to stay in the background unnoticed.

As he stood to read the lesson, Robert surveyed the congregation, his eyes resting for a moment on the family members, but then lingering on his mother, his father, Gramma Horton, Mr. Gordon and the other manor guests who were able to attend. Howie and Margie remained at the manor to look after Leah and the other guests who were confined to bed. His heart was breaking, but he was determined that he would not falter. He wanted to give Miss Brown his very best presentation, to honour her in death, as she had touched everyone she had met. Robert had suggested to the family the passage he wanted to read. They had agreed with his choice. He opened his *Good News Bible* to the familiar passage:

"A reading from the Book of Isaiah, chapter 40, verses 28-31

Words of Comfort

Don't you know? Haven't you heard?
The Lord is the everlasting God;
He created the whole world.
He never grows tired or weary.
No one understands his thoughts.
He strengthens those who are weak and tired.
Even those who are young grow weak;
young men can fall exhausted.
But those who trust in the Lord for help
will find their strength renewed.
They will rise on wings like eagles;
they will run and not get weary;
they will walk and not grow weak."

"Miss Ethel Brown devoted her entire life to serving others. She often became weary and tired, exhausted in her efforts to reach out to the endless faces that needed her. She found her inspiration in this book." He held up the *Bible*. "The passage from Isaiah was one of her favourite readings. May it be a comfort to us in our time of sorrow that Miss Brown would remind us, if she were here, that if we trust in the Lord she so faithfully served, we too, 'Will run and not get weary; walk and not grow weak'."

"It is always difficult to say good-bye to someone who has touched one's life, but her inspiration came from this book, it was her roadmap, her guide. The more often we open this book, the closer we will draw to her and the One whom she served."

Robert glanced at the congregation; they like him, were hurting because she was no longer with them. But all of them would mount on eagles' wings for their dear one had, as Bertha reminded them, gone from the land of the dying to the land of the living. She and Mrs. Ford would be together.

****

Robert replaced his diary in the banker's box, but he held onto Rachel's 1976 diary. He wanted to review the December entries. He looked at Miss Brown's plaque hanging on the wall beside his desk. He had never travelled to Africa, yet he felt a bond with those whom Miss Brown had served overseas. She treated everyone the same. It was now over 20 years since she had passed away, but her influence would forever be with him.

The doorbell rang, causing him to leave his memorabilia. It was Margie who wanted to check on the bridegroom. They entered the living-room.

"I see you have some of your Christmas decorations up, Rob. I love the garland above the fireplace." She approached the mantle, touching some of the golden objects. "These are mountain ash berries. You spray painted them gold! Clever. Now why wouldn't I think of that? These angels are so adorable. What are these clusters of dried flowers?"

"They are hydrangea, I spray painted them in the fall, too."

"The golden accents against the green garland really are attractive. The pewter nativity scene in the centre is exquisite. Interesting contrast between the gold and pewter." Now, Rob, how are you doing? Nervous?"

Robert pointed to a Queen Anne chair, motioning for Margie to join him as he sat down. "No, but your husband called an hour ago to check up on me. I'm beginning to think I'm supposed to be nervous. It's not as if I'm 25 and getting married. When you are over 50, it's easier."

"Maybe you are right."

"Margie, thank you for playing for the wedding; it means so much to Rachel and me. Howie is my best man again. I don't know what I would have done without you two; you've stood by me through so many difficult times."

"Rob, that's what friends do. You now have a second chance at happiness, one that was denied you when you were so much younger. Dear, sweet Leah, we loved her and lost her. But you bore it all without complaining."

"Enough of that, I have spent the morning reading letters and diary entries, feeling sorry for myself, laughing to myself and feeling the closeness of everyone who shaped my life. I was just looking at my 1976 diary entries. Remember the year that young Robert was christened. I can still see the priest passing you and Howie the lighted candle saying:

**"Receive the light of Christ,
to show that you have passed from darkness to light."**

"Twenty years ago, and to think that Robert is now in his second year at university. Rob, Robert has always been so close to you. Without your influence, we might have lost him when he turned to drugs in high school. You knew how to reach him. Howie was too forceful, I was too compensating; you helped him to see the light of Christ that had been with him from his birth. You risked your life for him when you jumped into that freezing water to save him. I have never felt comfortable about snowmobiles since that accident. In a few years he will pass baptismal candles to parents as he reminds his congregation that each child is baptized into the household of God."

"I am delighted that Robert will be an usher today, Margie."

"Rob, I have a confession to make, and I might as well make it now."

Robert wondered what secret could possibly need to be shared on the day of his wedding. Secrets had too long been unspoken during his relationship with Rachel. He smiled at Margie, "Go ahead, confess".

"Don't worry, it's no big deal, but you never know!"

"Confess!"

"Rob, I know how important Connie Francis has been to you and Rachel, so I wrote her a letter telling her the story of how you met Rachel and the great influence she has had on your life. I...I took the liberty of suggesting that she would be most welcome to attend the wedding and reception. I gave her my telephone number and home address."

Smiling, Robert asked, "And have you had a reply?"

"Not yet!"

"Margie, it was sweet of you to invite her. Rachel and I did think of her, but soon dismissed it as a silly notion. She doesn't know us. She would hardly fly to Nova Scotia to attend the wedding of two fans."

"Rob, you two are devoted fans, she has shared your lives. She introduced you."

"Exactly. If she had to attend weddings and other family events for all the people she has influenced, she'd have no life of her own."

"I guess you have a point. Anyway, I feel better having told you. Wouldn't it be great if she appeared?"

Robert shook his head, "Let's not set a place for her at the reception. I hate empty seats! Is the soloist ready?"

"Betty and I rehearsed the two solos for the church service and Glenda is singing a medley of Connie's hits as requested at the reception. Glenda's voice was so-so last night. Getting a cold, but she'll come through."

"We are looking forward to the music; your music always inspires."

"Rob, I want to play the best I have ever played for your wedding this afternoon. It is too bad that the wedding had to be delayed for the funeral, but it is all working out."

"Yes, two weeks ago, we thought we would be married this morning. The funeral had to be today, we had no choice. The rector leaves for his European trip early tomorrow."

"Rob, you mentioned you were recalling events of 1976. Wasn't that the year that the aunts were struggling to save their estate?"

"Yes, it was the year that Daisy and Iris gave up their comfortable pew to challenge their inept rector. Let me get Rachel's diary to read you a few passages. Do you have time?"

"Enough time to share that memory with you."

Robert returned with the diary, opening to the November entries. He noticed a letter from Derek included within the November pages. He felt he could share the letter with Margie.

- - - - - Flanders Cove, 1976

Rachel had survived her heartbreak but it had not been easy. She sat at her desk writing a letter to Derek. Their correspondence had been irregular; she hadn't heard from him for six weeks, but she wanted to drop him a few lines before she was faced with sending him a Christmas card and having to apologize for not writing sooner. She knew he was busy with his new career.

Rose appeared in her doorway with letters in her hand.

"You have two letters to read." She glanced at the postmarks. "One from Nova Scotia, one from Boston." She passed the letters to Rachel. "Hope the news is good." She left without further comment.

Rachel held both letters in her hand. The two dreams! She had suffered a broken heart because of both of them. Robert's decision had ended her dream, she had ended Derek's. She suffered with the loss of

both dreams. After fifteen months without Derek, she was still breakin' in a broken heart. She knew the pain she felt would fade, indeed, she was on the road to recovery, but she would never be totally free from it.

She decided to read Derek's letter first since she was in the process of writing to him. She could reply to the letter at the same time. She opened the letter with her grandfather's opener.

Dear Rachel,

**It will soon be Christmas once again.
I have been thinking of Christmas celebrations in your home.
I can hear Rose playing carols in the conservatory,
taste Daisy's turkey and trimmings, and smell Iris'
freshly decorated garlands. I treasure those memories.**

**I think of you often. I was thirty before I really began dating.
I always lacked self-confidence. I guess my days of being overweight
took their toll. You gave me back my self-worth.
You made me feel attractive, made me feel loved.**

**I have been so lonely in Boston away from everyone
that I know and love.
I have been been dating, forcing myself to get out of the apartment,
searching for someone to fill the terrible void in my life.
I know what love can do and I need to have it.
I have been in love with you and in love with love.
Life without love is meaningless. I know you have
Robert's love to comfort you,
at least the dream of his young love for you and his friendship now.
I have been tortured by the love that I have lost; I have not really talked
about my loss to you before because I did not want to
cause you further pain.**

**It was because my need for love was so strong that I met Denise.
I had to be careful that I was not just using her
as a release for my overwhelming
need for companionship and love. We have dated for two months.**

I know you would like her. I guess I sought a replacement who not only
looked somewhat like you but would be similar in personality as well.
She works in my office. She is two years younger.
She had just broken up with her boyfriend before I arrived on the scene;
he had physically abused her so she was hesitant about dating anyone.

Denise knows about us and how deeply I have felt about you.
I now understand more clearly how it is possible
to love two people at the
same time. I find myself struggling with the dilemma you suffered.
Denise understands; it doesn't make it easier.

I am spending the Christmas holidays with Denise's family,
I haven't met them yet, so wish me luck with the inspection.

I wear my watch every day. It is a constant reminder of Flanders Cove,
of the dream that I shared with all of you. Please say hello to the aunts,
I'll write at Christmas.

Rachel felt the wrist band of her watch; she and Derek were bound together in time and by time.

Rachel, I thank you for the love we once shared and, I am sure,
continue to share in a different way. I have a copy of our photo
article in front of me with a picture of your desk.
I wonder if you are seated there as you read this...

The letter slipped out of Rachel's hand falling to the floor. She sat in silence. Derek had suffered as she had. She knew it had to be so. She had mixed feelings about his announcement. Part of her regretted that he had moved on without her in his search for love, but the greater part of her rejoiced that he had found someone to love. Her painful decision seemed to lessen as she thought of his second chance at happiness. She prayed that his second dream would be fulfilled.

She placed his letter on her desk and decided to continue writing to him. She was just finishing the letter when she heard the dinner bell. She freshened up, then joined her aunts in the dining-room.

Marion and Daisy were featuring lamb for dinner, cooked with lemon and garlic and served with mint sauce. Roast potatoes, creamed onions, glazed honey carrots, and a garden salad completed the fare. Marion had baked a cottage pudding for dessert.

As the meal concluded, Rose was brave enough to ask Rachel for Derek's news.

Rachel blushed as she replied, "Derek wishes to be remembered to everyone. He...he has been dating someone from his office, sounds serious. He's going to her family's home for Christmas."

The aunts dare not look at Rachel. Rachel realized how awkward her announcement was.

"My dears, I am fine; I have had a cry, I am really glad for him. And I know you are, too. If anyone deserves happiness, he does." She raised her glass of water. "To Derek."

The aunts in turn raised their glasses, "To Derek!"

Rachel quickly changed the subject, "We have agreed that tomorrow morning we will meet in the fan club office to discuss the progress we are making in our endeavours to save our property, our church and our community. Is that correct?"

Daisy nodded in agreement, "Iris and I are ready."

Rose raised the peace sign with her right hand and, pointing to Rachel, exclaimed, "So are we!"

As agreed, the following morning Rachel met with the three aunts in the fan club office. They were seated at a large round table with piles of papers placed in the centre of the table. Rachel assumed the role of chairperson for the discussions.

"Daisy, as chair of the parish council committee reviewing the rector's performance, please give us a progress report."

"Most of this you already know, but the committee composed of six parish council members and three members of the congregation including Iris have met with the rector on five different occasions. We also met with the chair of every church organization, including the choir and Sunday School. We placed all the names of the parish families in a box; each of the nine committee members selected at random ten families to visit. We discussed what was happening and not happening in the parish with the selected families."

Daisy held up a questionnaire. "We placed a copy of this questionnaire in the church bulletin for three Sundays. As you'll remember, the questionnaire divided church activities into five categories, each subdivided into ten questions. We received 278 completed questionnaires, a significant per centage of our regular attenders.

"We have met with Father Smith on five occasions to discuss the concerns of the parish. He has stated emphatically, 'If I thought any parish was regressing because of my ministry, I would resign long before things started to decline!'"

Iris interjected, "Of course, he can't resign, no one else would have him. He did say he'd resign before things started to decline; well, they have declined so I suppose it's too late for him to honour his pledge."

Rachel asked Daisy, "You were compiling a list of concerns; how many items were on that list?"

Daisy searched in her notes for the list, holding it up so Rose and Rachel could see it. "Nine major concerns, twenty-six if you deal with them individually."

Rose shook her head, "How can that man just sit there oblivious to what the parish is saying. The congregation is speaking with their purses and feet. I'm surprised you had so many questionnaires returned."

Daisy responded, "Only because we delivered them to homes and picked them up. Our average Sunday attendance used to be 477, in the last two months it has fallen to 230. There's a message there."

Rose asked, "What are the major concerns on that list?"

Daisy looked over the list. "The same ones we have discussed; lack of visitation, no involvement of laity in services, no *Bible* study or spiritual development workshops, no support for committee work, lack of support for choir and Sunday School, etc. Ministry of neglect is the common theme."

Iris looked disgusted, "We have met with the archdeacon on two occasions, but he's useless. He claims that parishes are so diverse today, that it is impossible to be everything to everyone. Of course, we have a few parishioners who are pleased with the rector. They know that there will be no further changes with him, he'll maintain the status quo."

Daisy added, "And for those who don't want long sermons or who don't attend regularly, they think he's fine, has a nice voice."

Rachel sighed impatiently, "Where do we stand? What can we expect from all of this?"

Daisy opened a letter. "I received a letter from the bishop yesterday. He has examined our surveys, questionnaires, and petition. He writes a typical bishop's letter from the security of his office in Hartford. Listen to this:

My Dear People,

Thank you for sharing your review of parish life in Flanders Cove. I regret that you appear to be experiencing some difficulties within the body of Christ.

I am sure that as you work within your committee structures and glean advice from your archdeacon you will find the solutions you need to address the increasing needs of the parish.

The church universal is under tremendous pressure as we deal with increased secularization and also with sweeping changes within our own structures. I know that as the parish continues to pray and listen for the will of God you will be given the grace required to help the parish through its perceived problems.

I am dismayed that your report indicates that some parishioners have gone elsewhere to worship. I remind everyone that schism within the church has always been a sin greater than heresy. I trust that no one is encouraging parishioners to abandon worship at St. John's.

Please continue to inform me of developments as you respond to God's direction in its fullest expression.

My prayers are with you.

Daisy threw the letter on the table, "We gather all the evidence, we organize it, we interpret it. He reads it and says he'll pray for us."

Rose spoke, "I guess we have lost that battle!"

Daisy stood up, "If he thinks we will let our parish fall apart because he's afraid to do anything, he's a bigger fool than our rector!"

Rose feigning annoyance, "Daisy, such language, you are speaking about a bishop of the church!"

Daisy was quick to respond, "When he acts like a bishop, we'll treat him like one! How many more parishioners will be neglected and offended before action is taken. The rector won't do anything, he's either too dumb or too lazy or both. Who knows? He thinks, if he does think, that we can't do anything. He believes that we are stuck with him. He has a copy of the bishop's letter so he'll now believe he's home free."

Rachel attempted to comfort her aunts, "Daisy and Iris, you have done everything you could. Sometimes we can't fight bureauracy, even in the church. Rose and I appreciate the leadership you have provided for the parish..."

Rose placed her hands on Daisy's, "It isn't worth risking a heart attack. He can surely see the writing on the wall, he'll leave."

Iris shook her head to deny Rose's observation, "There is no place for him to run." Looking at Daisy, "Daisy is fine, she can handle this. Besides she has a surprise!"

Daisy added, "I am fine, don't worry! We haven't given up. We are ready to put our faith into action! We worship a God of surprises! We have one for the bishop!"

****

Margie leaned forward in her Queen Anne chair, chuckling as Robert talked about the aunts taking on the bureaucracy of the church.

"Robert, can you imagine us doing the same thing with our bishop? It took such courage. We tend to believe in the sacredness of the office. After all, our clergy take solemn vows to serve."

"We have been so fortunate but remember the aunts had always had effective rectors. Priests and bishops are only human; some thought they had a calling, but it was probably a wrong number."

Margie smiled, "I guess you are right. Robert, tell me about the surprise once again."

Robert closed Rachel's diary. "I can recall the event as vividly as if I were there. With Daisy as chair, the parish hired four buses, filling them with over 200 parishioners. She arranged to meet the bishop at the diocesan centre for what he assumed was a meeting with her and a few parishioners. She called the diocesan centre to book their auditorium without the bishop's knowledge."

"The December trip to Hartford was risky, a two hour drive on slippery roads. Upon arrival at the centre, everyone was taken to the auditorium. Daisy and Iris went to the bishop's office; they led him to the auditorium. Daisy asked him to sit down while she delivered the message on behalf of the parishioners."

Robert opened Rachel's diary once again. "I guess I had better check on the details. Here, let me begin with her prepared speech to the bishop."

"Bishop Harold Matheson,

We are here today to tell you that we have lost faith in our rector. We have documented our concerns. We have met with him on five occasions and twice with the archdeacon; no progress has been made. We have written to you and you have indicated you will pray for us. We appreciate your prayers.

We intend to remain at this centre until you tell us that our prayers have been answered. We are praying that our rector will be relieved of his duties in our parish immediately."

The bishop was mesmerized, confounded, bewildered. Never had such a thing happened to him! Daisy called him to the microphone. He was dressed in a suit and his purple clerical shirt. Without his robes he looked so ordinary. With the parishioners waiting for a response, he looked so fallible!

He rose and walked slowly toward the microphone. As he did so, the parishioners shouted. "We want action! We want action! We want action! No talk! No promises! Action! Now!" They had rehearsed their message on the bus trip.

The bishop was visibly shaken by the outburst as he moved closer to the microphone. "I hear what you are saying, but I cannot remove a rector without due course being followed."

The parishioners stood up. "We want action!" They repeated their slogan over and over until the bishop raised his hands to silence them. They resumed their seats.

"I hear you, my people. I hear you! It will be as you will. You may carry my letter of removal home with you!" He walked slowly back to his chair, looking much as Pilate must have after conceding to the crowd who wanted action not words.

The auditorium became silent. It was eerie! All heads were lowered in prayer, then quietly everyone walked reverently out of the auditorium in silence. The bishop was stunned!

After the last parishioner had left the auditorium, Daisy suggested that she accompany the bishop to his office to obtain the required document. And that is how Flanders Cove cut through the bureaucracy of the church. Daisy and Iris became advocates for change, they led the parish out of their wilderness to freedom.

Margie clapped. "That is quite a story! It would make a great documentary!" Looking at her watch, "Oh Rob, I do have to leave, I must have one more practice with Frances who is singing a solo at the funeral. Thanks for sharing those precious moments with me. Now don't you spend much more time with those diaries, you had better start getting ready. You have less than two hours before the funeral. I'll see myself out."

She kissed him lightly on the cheek, then departed.

Robert looked at his watch, hesitated, but returned to his seat in the living-room. He just had to read the details of the struggle with the Connecticut Department of Transportation. He flipped to the pages that described the meeting held at the Flanders Cove courthouse when Rachel and Rose spoke in front of the Transportation Commission.

- - - - - Flanders Cove, 1976

Rose had chaired a community support group to provide opposition to the proposed route of the new six lane highway. Thirty-three Flanders Cove presentations were scheuled for the Transportation hearings. The community support group requested that Rose and Rachel deliver the final brief. Rose had invited Governor Wallace and Senator Smith. The mayor and town councillors of Flanders Cove were all present; the town itself had presented a brief opposing the route suggested for the new highway. The bishop was there to support St. John's brief to protect the church property from bulldozers; the church itself as well as the rectory and a portion of the graveyard were threatened. The bishop would probably not have attended, but he had learned not to ignore requests from the Thomas sisters. Rose had also invited the media who lined the entire back wall of the historic building.

Rachel and Rose had each chosen to wear a navy blazer with a grey skirt. Rose selected pink accents, Rachel blue. Rachel spoke first on behalf of the Thomas family. She was poised and unrattled by the flashing of cameras, the hum of private conversations, and television cameras following her as she walked toward the members of the commission who were seated in a semi-circle facing the audience. Every other speaker had stood at the podium to deliver briefs, Rachel and Rose had decided beforehand that they would not be confined to one spot; they wanted to get as close to the powers-that-be as they could. They had rehearsed their speeches in front of Daisy and Iris.

After Rachel had finished her opening remarks, she methodically stepped in front of each member of the commission, looking at each of them, smiling, but saying nothing. The members were obviously not sure what to make of this; they appeared uneasy. She then walked in front of the audience, most of whom had already presented briefs. A silence fell upon the room; it lasted less than a minute but its effect was electric. She returned to her position in front of the commission and pointing to the audience began her impassioned plea.

"I am sure I speak on behalf of everyone here. We are proud of our civic and state leaders. We appreciate the valuable work done by our Department of Transportation. We know that Flanders Cove has become a unique tourist area. We recognize also that our lakes and ocean frontage have attracted metro dwellers to build summer homes here and that we have become a prime area for retirees. We welcome everyone to our community as we were welcomed by those who are no longer here, but whose legacy we bring before you today."

"We realize that progress means change. As more people come to enjoy the beauty of Flanders Cove, the increased traffic must be accommodated. You have already heard from others the concerns we have regarding the route you are presently supporting. That route would require the moving of a two hundred year old church and a sacred burial ground. Twenty homes will be affected, ten of them the oldest homes in Flanders Cove. The new highway will bypass several of the most scenic spots we have; that issue has already been addressed by our mayor."

"We realize that the decision for the proposed route is based solely on economics. We believe in stewardship as well. The question here is, What is it that we value?"

Looking once again at the members of the commission, she walked toward them as she posed rhetorical questions:

"Is an historic burial ground still sacred in the state of Connecticut?

Do we still revere the past?
Is a home more than a building?
Do government officials still listen to the will of the people?
Is there a place for sentiment in decision-making?
Are people more important than asphalt?
Do highways exist to serve us or
Do we exist to accommodate highways?"

"Today, you have heard Flanders Cove speak. It has been a united voice. We welcome a new highway, but we cannot and will not allow a highway to destroy the community that has inspired the need for more traffic and consequently a new link to our community."

"I live with my three aunts at 355 Melrose Road. The original house is over a hundred years old. Through the years, renovations have enlarged and modernized the building we call home. The house was featured last year in *American Estates*. You may have seen a copy of the September issue. Our home has been declared a state heritage property. The heirlooms it contains are part of the Thomas Trust that will ensure that the property and most of its contents will one day become part of the state's historic homes, a living museum."

"The issue before us today is a simple one. Is the state of Connecticut willing to sacrifice the heritage of Flanders Cove in order to save money in the construction of a highway? What is it that we value?"

Rachel continued her walk in front of the commission members as she delivered a second series of questions:

"Is your home your castle?
Is your church built on holy ground?
Would it bother you to dig up your forebearers?
How do you explain to your children reverence for the past?
Are some things in your life beyond price?
What do you value in life? At what cost?"

Without further comment, she sat down as Rose walked toward the commissioners. She was calm and poised.

"I am one of the infamous Thomas sisters." Turning around to face the audience, she raised her voice. "Would my two sisters please stand." Once they had been identified by everyone, Rose motioned for them to be seated and continued.

"Until last year the three of us had lived rather secluded lives behind the walls of our home on Melrose Road. Last year our home was featured in a national magazine and we hosted our first open house; it will not be our last. This year, we have had to defend the heritage we have prized. I am 67 years of age. This is only my second public speaking venture in a lifetime. It is not easy to be here in front of you, to know that you have the power to make a decision that will tell the Thomas sisters and our niece that our heritage and indeed the heritage of so many others in this room is important but not as important as a road."

She walked toward Rachel who passed her an envelope. She withdrew a letter.

"I want to conclude by reading one paragraph from a letter that my father wrote to Governor Harrison in 1944 when the world was threatened by tyranny."

"Flanders Cove is a small community; I suspect you may not even know of its existence. In this community of five thousand people, we know each other. We work together, pray together and play together. We come from different backgrounds, but we believe in each other. Together we have built a community that values our past and is building for the future. Our country is now at war. We understand that the important things in life must be cherished and defended at all costs. We revere our heritage, we want to preserve it and we are honoured to defend it..."

Rose paused, returned the letter to the envelope, looked at the commissioners and lowered her voice.

"Nothing of value is without cost! What do we value in the state of Connecticut?" She paused, lowered her voice further, repeating, "What do we value? We await your decision." She quietly sat down. The audience instantly rose to their feet, giving her a thunderous ovation. One by one the members of the commission rose to their feet; some had mist in their eyes.

The commission took only two weeks to convey its decision to Flanders Cove. The mayor requested everyone who had made a presentation to gather at the courthouse. Only he and the town council members were aware of the decision, and none of them had betrayed the confidence that they had sworn in the council chambers. When everyone had gathered, the mayor welcomed them and showed them the letter he had received that morning. He asked Rose to read the contents of the letter as highlighted by the town's solicitor.

Rose was somewhat startled to be given such an honour, but she did manage to maintain her usual composure as she turned to face her friends, the members of the community to whom she was no longer a stranger.

"The Department of Transportation must provide highways that are built according to state specifications; ensuring durability, easy access, safety and financial prudence. The proposed highway structure via Flanders Cove is deemed to be the most economical one. However, the commission has decided to build the new highway, project number 5432, using the alternate route that crosses Flanders Cove at the north end of the town."

The townspeople rose to their feet clapping. Rose returned the letter to the mayor. The mayor had the last word.

"Please be seated. In a conversation this morning with Mr. Frank Taylor, chair of the commission, he asked me to convey to you the commission's recognition of the spirit that exists in our community; it was that spirit that swayed their decision. May I remind you of a quotation we heard in this very room just two weeks ago..."

'What is that we value in the state of Connecticut?'

"We now have our answer!"

December 1976 was such a hectic month in Flanders Cove. The three aunts and Rachel had waged two successful campaigns. They had risked leaving their private world and in so doing they had gained the admiration of the community that they had too long avoided. No longer were they the mysterious Thomas sisters who lived in the big mansion surrounded by the forbidding wall; they became Daisy, Iris and Rose. Rachel was asked to be a member of the town's heritage group. The bridge that had been built to the community continued to exist for the remainder of their lives; they continued to reach out and the community was given ample opportunity to enjoy Thomas hospitality.

Rachel enjoyed the peace and quiet of the days following Christmas. The birth of the Christ Child was always celebrated with lessons and carols in the conservatory. The entire house was decorated with tasteful garlands, wreaths, candles and creche sets. Holly, poinsettias, Christmas cacti and pine cone arrangements could be found throughout the house. It was a Victorian delight! A large pine tree dominated the conservatory near the piano. The living-room contained a large Jesse tree decorated with Christian symbols that Iris had created. The customary floral arrangement in the foyer was replaced with Advent candles that reminded everyone who entered of the peace, joy and love of the season. The Christ Child and his parents were nestled in the centre of the wreath.

Rachel delighted in wandering throughout the house during the season, enjoying the decorations, smelling the homemade garlands, hearing the familiar carols, watching the aunts become child-like once again.

December 28 was a bitterly cold day with snow falling gently creating a winter postcard scene. Rachel had just heard the grandfather clock strike two o'clock as she placed logs on the fire in the living-room. Every time the fireplace was used, she regretted that it was not used more often. She had just settled down to examine her Christmas mail when the doorbell demanded her attention.

Nothing could have prepared her for her visitor.

As she answered the door, a woman who appeared to be in her late twenties wearing a fur coat and fur hat smiled at her as she extended her right hand.

"You must be Rachel; I am Denise LeBlanc. I know that this is an intrusion, and I know that one should never visit without telephoning first, but I felt we should meet. May I come in?"

Rachel was flabbergasted! She was unable to think. She muttered, "Yes, come in. You are Denise! Yes, Derek has mentioned you!" Perhaps because of nerves, she giggled, "Oh Denise, this is such a surprise, but a delightful one! Let me take your coat and hat."

After boots had been removed, Rachel led Denise into the living-room. Denise was gracious, complimenting the furniture, the decor and the Christmas touches. They each sat in a Queen Anne chair. Rachel was still not at ease; Denise seemed to be perfectly comfortable.

"Rachel, you will think I am forward, taking liberties that I should not. May I assure you that I have given this visit a great deal of thought. Yes, I did think of writing. Actually, I have several unfinished attempts on my desk. I have dialed your telephone number on several occasions, but I didn't feel much would be accomplished chatting with someone I have never met."

Rachel continued to stare at her uninvited guest not knowing what to expect.

"Denise, it is good of you to come. Are you in the area? Is Derek with you?"

Denise shook her head. "No to both questions. I took the bus to Flanders Cove this morning. Derek knows I am visiting but he is back at work. I still have a few days holiday. I have a room at the New England Inn; it is a charming place."

"Yes, the Inn is a wonderful place, warm and cozy with a friendly staff."

"I know you are wondering why I have come." She sat back in her chair, paused, then continued. "I am aware of the special relationship you and Derek enjoyed and continue to enjoy. You were his first love, and yes, he still loves you."

Rachel blushed with embarrassment. She studied this woman in front of her. Denise was stylish. Her hair was immaculate; brunette with a short curled hairstyle. She wore a seasonal red dress with gold accessories including a three inch gold bracelet. Rachel wondered if the design of the bracelet featured angels.

"Rachel, Derek has asked me to marry him. I believe you know that I was engaged to someone this time last year. I discovered before it was too late that my fiance was not the charming man he had pretended. Anyway, that is in the past. I now have an opportunity to fulfil my dreams. You would know how precious Derek is. I know he loves me, but I also know that you have claimed part of him."

Rachel was beginning to feel more at ease with Denise even though the conversation was so personal. She knew that Denise was a remarkable woman. Here was a modern woman who was cut from the same fabric as the Thomas sisters. She admired her courage in coming to visit.

"Denise, forgive me for being startled. I think I'm all right now. I do welcome you. I have tried to picture you."

"Rachel, a very dear man has asked me to marry him. He has held nothing back. I have somewhat the dilemma that you faced last year. Can I marry someone who can never be fully mine? I know that many people marry realizing that we are all part of past relationships. I had to meet you, to get to know you, to hear you talk about Derek before I can make my decision. I don't believe in secrets; I don't believe in hiding feelings. I am naturally somewhat envious of the bond that you and Derek share. Yet, it has also endeared him to me."

"Denise, I have a special love for Derek." She smiled at Denise. "Do you have a favourite singer?"

Denise returned her smile. "Yes, the Beach Boys were always my favourites. But you are wondering if I ever listen to the New Jersey singer and the answer is yes. I followed carefully the careers of Brenda Lee and Connie Francis as I was growing up. I must admit in the last years, I have not really kept in touch with their careers. So we share to some degree an interest in Connie. Derek recalls that one of our first conversations centred on pop music. When he discovered my interest in Brenda and Connie, he felt he had enough background to impress me with his knowledge."

Giggling, Rachel said, "I'm surprised he didn't convince you that Petula Clark was by far a better singer. Well, you will probably be familiar with many of Connie's hits. It is interesting how the heartache expressed in Connie's songs can be the very same feelings we are experiencing. Do you know the lyrics of "Breakin' In A Brand New Broken Heart"?

Laughing, Denise confessed, "All too well! I can identify with the sentiments expressed. I guess that is why some of Connie's singles have become such hits; we can identify with them."

Connie's music had always been a comfort for Rachel. It was interesting to have Connie's music fulfill still another purpose as the two strangers shared common experiences benchmarked by the songs of their past. Rachel was amazed that Denise who was so polished, so stylish, so precise, enjoyed the very same music that she treasured.

It was five o'clock when the two strangers realized that evening was descending upon the household. Denise stayed for dinner. The following day she checked out of the inn and remained at 355 Melrose Road for two days. She and Rachel became close friends.

* * * * * * * * * *

Robert closed the diary, looking at the calendar on his desk. Over twenty years had passed since Denise had visited Rachel. Mr. Gordon's

words echoed in his head. "You can't do wrong by doing good." Mr. Gordon had been very wise. 1976 was the year that risks were taken! The ensuing twenty years were filled with joys and sorrows as life tends to be. Nothing could have prepared Northumbria and Flanders Cove for the events of 1981 when once again their lives were threatened by a silent force more destructive than anything they had ever experienced. It would unite them, but at what cost?

Today, however, his dearest friend, Howie, would be his best man; Denise was to be Rachel's matron of honour. Margie would play the organ for their wedding. Young Robert and Derek were to be ushers. What a combination! What a day it promised to be!

Chapter 7:

I'm Me Again

Robert struggled with his emotional journey into the past. He thought about his life in Northumbria and Rachel's in Flanders Cove. How differently life might have unfolded if Leah had not become pregnant. What might have happened had they not lost their child? He knew, of course, that everyone has 'what if's' in life. Connie's life was also filled with traumatic events that destroyed many of her dreams. The difference between the events in Connie's life and theirs was a simple one; theirs were private, Connie's were given full media coverage. The world knew that Connie's marriages failed; that had suffered a miscarriage, had adopted a child, Joey; knew that she had been raped and knew that her brother, Georgie, had been murdered by the mob. The world knew that Connie had temporarily lost her singing voice, had lost her confidence, had lived in fear. Her doctors had told her she would never sing again! It seemed that Connie was destined to a life of pain and struggle. Her personal life and her professional career had changed dramatically from the golden days when she was on the top of the charts, making hit movies, appearing at the most popular nightclubs, and entertaining television audiences with guest appearances on all the major shows. It was no longer the accolades of a flourishing career that the media covered, but the tragedies that befell and overwhelmed her.

In her autobiography, *Who's Sorry Now? Connie Francis*, Connie states. "I've learned, the hard way, many sorrowful lessons." In an interview with a national magazine in 1958, Connie had indicated that she felt she was protected by a guardian angel because her life was free of major problems. She discovered in the years that followed that her guardian angel may not have protected her from hardships but had provided her with the strength to survive; and she has proven that she is a survivor!

Robert looked at his wrist watch; he realized that he must leave the past and begin his day of days. He did, however, want to spend just a

few more minutes reminiscing. How could he leave these precious memories without recalling the events of 1981, the year of the silent threats?

- - - - - Northumbria, 1981

Robert was seated on the bed beside Leah. It was March in Northumbria. The ground was still covered with a layer of ice and snow, but spring was definitely in the air. He looked at his dear Leah. She was ever the sleeping princess. If only he could wake her with a kiss. He left her bedside, returning to a wing chair near the bedroom window. He looked at the trees with their barren branches. Soon the warmth of the sun would transform bleakness into soft tones of green as nature once again brought forth its yearly resurrection. Once again, spring would heal the wounds of winter, bringing new life with its promise.

He looked at the stand of oak and birch trees that lined the driveway. He loved the trees; the oak trees were so solid, so straight, so dark; the white birches were more fragile and all of them leaned at a different angle. The birches always seemed to be shedding their outer bark. Robert had started a tradition after Mrs. Ford passed away of naming each oak tree in memory of his departed extended family members; a small bronze plaque commemorated each loved one. The first oak at the entrance to the driveway was Mrs. Ford's memorial. He reviewed the plaques, pausing at Gramma Horton's as he thought of eagles' wings. In 1977, he had had to name a tree for Miss Brown and in 1978, Mr. Gordon had claimed his tree. Robert had such wonderful memories of the trio. So many other guests had come to reside at the manor since the passing of his three dear 'grandparents'; he treasured each one of them, but none of them could replace the famous three.

Soon, the trees would burst their buds again. When the leaves rustled in the cool breeze, he was certain that he could hear his beloved friends reminding him of their presence. They were his guardian angels. He had first learned of guardian angels from Miss Brown who was fond of quoting "Psalm 34":

"His angel guards those who honour the Lord and rescues them from danger."

Miss Brown had enjoyed reading Daisy's chapter on angels. Daisy had begun the chapter referring to a quotation from "Hebrews" that stated:

"Remember to welcome strangers,
because some have welcomed angels without knowing it."

It was a lesson that Robert tried to remember. The oak trees reminded him of so many lessons; Mr. Gordon's - "You can't do wrong by doing good" and Gramma Horton's - "The garden is the key to health". She knew that gardeners not only enjoyed the fruits of their labour but communed with creation as they dug, tilled, planted, hoed, watered and nurtured. Iris and Gramma Horton knew so well the blessings of the earth.

Robert smiled as he thought about the rich legacy he had been privileged to share with the manor guests. He thought of a passage he had read in Connie's autobiography, where she mentioned her belief in guardian angels. She felt that her brother, Georgie, had become her guardian angel, loving and protecting her in death as he had in life!

He returned to his wing chair to finish writing an article on educational change that he was sending to a professional education journal. He was reading his completed draft when his parents-in-law arrived. He was very fond of Leah's parents, Ellen and Ken MacDonald. Without reservation, they had accepted him as their son even though they had never been told of his sacrifice. They knew that Trevor was a thorn in Robert's side, but they did not realize how Trevor had persecuted his brother-in-law. Robert was careful to protect them from discovering the full extent of Trevor's hatred for him.

Robert rose to greet his in-laws. Ellen sat on the bed beside Leah; Ken claimed his favourite resting place, a rocking chair near Robert. Ellen looked younger than 68; she was fastidious about her dress. Her petite figure was always fashionably displayed with the latest styles and colours. She was a capable seamstress and was able to sew most of her wardrobe. Ken liked nothing better than to wear his favourite cardigan and checked shirt. Like Camille, he had been a miner. He and Ellen had recently celebrated their fiftieth anniversary.

It was Ken who began the conversation. "Robert, Leah has been confined to bed for eleven years. You have spent that time at her bedside; you are now 36 years old. We have all waited for Leah to improve. She has been examined by specialists, subjected to the newest treatments at the provincial infirmary, and Margie tells us that regular laying on of hands has occurred. Ellen and I never give up hope, but time is passing."

Robert was uncertain where the conversation was going; he decided he would simply wait to discover what was on his in-laws' minds. "We have had expert medical advice. Prayers have been offered here and elsewhere; I guess our answer has been the strength to endure Leah's lack of progress."

Ellen looked lovingly at Leah. She leaned over to kiss her daughter's forehead. Looking at Robert, "Robert, I am sure you know how much we respect you and love you. We know that Trevor has never accepted your marriage; he wouldn't have accepted anyone as a brother-in-law. We love our son; in many ways he is good to us, but we are not blinded. He is stubborn and we know he can be cruel."

Robert was not sure how to respond. "I'll admit that we don't get along. It is too bad, but just one of those things."

Ken responded, "Ellen and I appreciate the planning that you did for our recent anniversary, even if Trevor was not co-operative. You do everything so efficiently, so quietly. Ellen and I are getting on in years. I will be 73 my next birthday. We hope to live to celebrate many more anniversaries, but nothing is ever certain in this world. We have decided that now is the perfect time to get things in order."

Ellen continued, "A number of our closest friends have passed away recently and it is a reminder to us that we should enjoy the health we have and the life we have. We are having our wills updated and we have decided to sell our home."

Robert was startled, "Sell your home, but you have done so many renovations over the years. Are you sure you want to give it up?"

Ken responded, "It is hard to leave the home that we have enjoyed for over 40 years, but we want to sell it while the market is stable and the house is in good shape. It is a decision that most people our age have to make, even if it is with regrets."

Robert stared at his in-laws. They had had their share of hardships. Ken had wanted Trevor to go to college, had saved for his education. When Trevor left high school after his suspension due to hitting the physical education teacher, Ken was devastated. Both Ellen and Ken had wanted grandchildren. Trevor had not married and Leah had been unable to bring their only hope into the world. Ken had suffered a mild heart attack a year ago; perhaps that had caused them to reflect upon the uncertainty of life.

Looking at his parents-in-law, Robert asked, "What can I do to help?"

Ken replied, "We want to ask you to be our 'business manager" and to be the executor of our wills. We'll understand if you would prefer not to. You may want time to think it over."

Robert shook his head, "No, I don't need time to think it over, I would be only too pleased to help in any way. I have just one reservation...What will Trevor think about this?"

Ken glanced at Ellen, then returned his attention to Robert. "Trevor has many good qualities; you probably haven't experienced them, but he has trouble managing his own finances. He seems to spend all his money on those frequent trips to Toronto. You know he drinks and he is gambling as well. We will tell him that we have made a decision and he will have to accept it. We'll look after him, don't let that bother you."

Ellen added, "Robert, we feel so close to you and we want you to know that half of our estate goes to you and Leah. When Leah goes to her reward, you continue to be the beneficiary. Should anything happen to Trevor, you and Leah receive his portion."

"I am grateful for your confidence. Where do you intend to live once you have sold your house?"

"Ellen and I have investigated the new apartment complex in Garden Estates. There are two bedroom units available that are attractive and functional. There is a central recreation area, including an indoor pool. It is within walking distance of church. We like it!"

Ellen elaborated, "Robert, leaving home is not easy. Even though you and Leah did not have the best of times in your apartment, I remember you telling us how difficult it was to leave it. After forty years, we have so many memories stored in our home; we'll just pack them up and take them with us to the apartment."

Robert knew that Trevor would not welcome his parents' news; he didn't have to wait long to know the full extent of his brother-in-law's displeasure. Trevor's response came in the form of a parcel that arrived two weeks after Robert's in-laws had discussed their moving and business affairs with him.

As was his custom, Robert opened his mail in Leah's room after helping with the clean-up from dinner. He recognized Trevor's script on the address label of the parcel. There was no return address, but it bore the familiar Halifax postmark. He hesitated opening the parcel; it had been several years since he had received one from Trevor; the last one had contained condoms. He knew that the contents would either be Trevor's way of striking back at him for Leah's confinement, or his response to his parents' news.

After tearing away the brown paper covering, he discovered an attractive box used by a provincial pewter company to ship their creations worldwide. He was confident that Trevor was not sending him a choice piece of pewter. There was a note taped to the top of the box.

I did not enclose the real thing because you already have one!
Didn't know you knew how to use one?
I have one ready for you!

Robert opened the cover of the box, withdrawing a toy gun with another note, attached to newspaper clippings!

Hey, guess you couldn't stand your singer loving her brother so much.
Couldn't rape him, so you shot him!
I'm ready for you!
O

Robert placed the gun back in the box; he didn't need to look at the clippings to know that they would focus on the death of Connie's brother, Georgie, who had been killed by the mob. Robert realized that as disgusted as he was, he might have expected this type of letter from Trevor. He was uneasy with the overt threat to his life contained in the letter. Jason had not kept Robert's fight with Trevor quiet. The locals all knew that Trevor had lost his fight with his brother-in-law. Trevor had stopped frequenting the local tavern when he was home on the weekends because he couldn't handle the teasing of his drinking buddies. Robert felt that Trevor was capable of shooting him. He agonized about whether to tell Howie or perhaps the police, but in the end, he decided that he would not share the threat with anyone. He knew, however, that his life would always be at risk!

He was disappointed that he had not received a letter from Rachel, so he decided to call her. Rachel and the bouquet had all had a severe case of the flu in February. The aunts seemed to have recovered more quickly than Rachel. Rachel complained of being tired, her joints ached and she had lost her appetite.

Although there was a telephone in Leah's room, Robert never used it when telephoning Rachel. He realized that he felt guilty talking to his dearest friend in Leah's presence, even if Leah were not seemingly aware of her surroundings. His conversations with Rachel were intimate, but not romantic; they fulfilled his need for a confidant, but not a lover. However, the unspoken truth was there, he loved Rachel and he knew that love was returned. He was a married man; he had pledged himself to Leah and he would never abandon those sacred vows. His heart, however, did have a mind of its own and he could not control his dreams.

He entered his bedroom, closed the door behind him, and dialed Flanders Cove. He sat on his bed as he awaited an answer.

Rachel answered with a weak voice; she, too, was in her bedroom. She was wearing a blue turtleneck sweater with a matching cardigan. She placed a tissue in the pocket of her culottes as she answered the telephone. "Hello, Rachel speaking."

"Hello Rachel, Robert here. Thought I would check with you to see how you are feeling. Your voice sounds husky."

"Thanks for calling, I am tired of this flu. I have been to the doctor's office for a check up. He thinks it is just the flu hanging on, but he wants to be certain that there are no complications so I'm to go to the hospital for a battery of tests next Tuesday. The aunts are fussing, of course. But really, I'm just tired. I'll be all right. I am sorry I didn't write."

"A lot of people have had the flu here, too. Same symptoms that you describe. Mr. Gordon always recommended a hot toddy."

"Sounds good to me, what does it contain?"

"Hot water, sugar and a good shot of rum!"

"I might just give it a try. We always have a good supply of spirits. Grandad maintained a well-stocked liquor cabinet and a small wine cellar. As you know, we often have wine with dinner and the aunts enjoy an evening liqueur. They claim it is all medicinal."

"They may be right. Margie says a daily drink is beneficial and she certainly knows a great deal about maintaining healthy bodies."

"Robert, we have had such high winds the last few days. If it were autumn, we would probably be calling them hurricanes. I can see the front yard from my window as we speak. The trees are really bending in the wind. A good thing they are without leaves. I think we need to get Arthur to cut down a few of the oaks nearest the house. The trees are enormous and absolutely beautiful in full foliage, but I worry about them crashing onto the house. Several of our neighbours actually had a few trees that were raised from their roots during the hurricane season last year."

"We are fortunate at the manor, most of the large trees lined the driveway. I was just looking at 'memory lane' as I call it, the trees that have plaques on them as remembrances of our departed guests. Trees serve many purposes!"

"I guess our stained glass window and quilt serve the same purpose. Robert, you should write an article on the manor. The idea of the 'memory lane' is just the type of focus that magazines would like to feature."

"Thanks for the suggestion, but I have not tried that type of writing."

"What do you tell your students when they are not willing to try something different?"

"Touche! I'll give it some thought."

"Robert, when Iris and I wrote the article on the quilt, the real pleasure came from the process of writing. We enjoyed the sharing! You have mentioned in your letters that schools are moving away from a fixation on the products produced to a balance of process and product. I think you will find writing an article on 'memory lane' will be good for you even if it is never published. However, once it is written, be a risk-taker, send it to a magazine. I'll be waiting to read the article."

"Rachel, I'll give it a try! I guess it would help to have a few photographs. Howie is not a bad photographer, I'll get him to help. Now what is the equivalent in Canada of *American Estates*?"

"I'm glad I suggested it. I'll give you Derek's address, he can give you suggestions for photography and contacts for publishing. Would you be comfortable writing to him?"

"I...I never thought of it before. No, I think I would feel relatively comfortable. It might prove an interesting contact. Sure, send the address."

Rachel looked at her dresser. It contained a photograph of Derek and Denise's wedding. They looked so happy. In the years since their marriage, the couple frequently visited Rachel and her aunts. Denise and Rachel had become close friends; it was Denise who had taken the initiative to ensure that the bond that Derek and Rachel had created would not be lost. Now that Derek was married, he and Rachel were able to relax with each other and enjoy the warmth of friendship. Rachel greatly admired the empathy and confidence that Denise possessed. Denise did not believe in skirting issues; she practised what she called 'polite bluntness'; she was more than candid, but never harsh.

After the telephone conversation, Robert returned to the window, looking with nostalgia at his 'memory lane', allowing his imagination to begin the process of creating the story of the manor. The trees were a source of life; the plaques did more than suggest the end of life, they were a celebration of life. Each tree had its own story, but together they were so attractive!

Throughout March, April and May, Robert spent hours standing by Leah's bedside glancing out the window at the memorial trees. Howie had captured the trees in beautiful prints. A late snowstorm in March had provided a winter scene. Robert looked at the trees with their fresh green covering; spring's promise was slowly becoming summer's delightful shade.

He had completed the draft of his article on the manor, using the sun porch as the setting for his narrative. He had shared his draft with his parents, Howie and Margie, and naturally Rachel who had been his inspiration.

Robert took his draft outdoors to read it on one of the benches located on the front lawn. He sat for an hour reflecting upon the family that had given him so much. He thought of Rachel and her aunts. He was distressed that Rachel was still not well. She had had every possible test. The specialists could not diagnose her ailment. There had been discussions about a viral infection, but nothing was confirmed. She remained weak and suffered dizzy spells. She claimed her joints ached continuously.

He rose from the bench to check a detail in his article with his father who had been working in the garden. He found his father resting in a wooden lawn chair near the vegetable beds. Camille appeared to be enjoying a nap. Robert decided not to disturb him; instead he returned to the manor to check the details with his mother. His mother who was wearing a floral apron, was seated in the living-room at a small desk in one corner looking at her accounts.

"I see you are attempting to balance the books!"

His mother removed her glasses, "Yes, but not month end accounts. I am preparing a financial profile of the manor. Sounds impressive, doesn't it?"

Robert pulled a chair close to the desk. "A profile?"

Bertha smiled at Robert, "Robert, I am 69, it is time to retire! I am about ready to enter a manor myself!"

Robert knew that one day his mother would retire. She had gradually employed more help at the manor; Margie was invaluable.

"You have mentioned retiring a number of times. Have you decided to close the doors of the manor?"

Bertha looked around her, her glance fading into memories. "No, we have nine guests who call this home, I cannot tell them to leave."

Robert looked confused, "But how can you retire if the guests remain?"

"Not an easy solution; I think we should have your father join us."

"I can't imagine father leaving his home! Have you discussed this with him?"

"Yes, we have had discussions. Well, I talked and he listened. Go into the garden and tell your father to join us. I will find Margie."

It didn't surprise Robert that Margie would be included in the conversation, but he could scarcely know the real reason for her inclusion. He went to the garden to find his father, discovering him in exactly the same position he had seen him in earlier. He was unable to rouse him. His father had slipped away to his eternal rest in his favourite spot, among his raised vegetable beds.

Camille was 89 when he returned to the earth. He had cursed the cruel earth when it claimed his son, but his garden had soothed his wounds as he watched the seeds he planted produce a bountiful crop for the manor's table. The silent one in the family would be heard no longer, but his presence would continue to be with them, not only in their memories, but in the sound of rustling leaves in Robert's 'memory lane'.

Robert had known that his father could not live forever, even if Camille had been in good health, vowing to live long enough to celebrate his centennial. Although Robert had learned to say good-bye to loved ones at the manor, it did not seem to ease the pain of losing his father.

During the two evenings of visitation at the local funeral parlour, Robert and his mother were able to begin the grieving process as they shared with family and friends memories of their beloved Camille. Camille's miner's hat and a lantern were placed on the top of the casket. At Camille's head was a family pillow of flowers. One floral arrangement was placed beside the guest book. It featured roses, irises, daisies and larkspur. Flanders Cove had remembered the Mascaux family in their time of grief. Robert thought of Rachel and the aunts as he touched each of the four types of flowers in the arrangement. Seeing the floral symbols helped him to feel closer to the Americans whom he had never met, but who had come to be such an important part of his life.

There were chairs along three walls of the funeral parlour's viewing room. The older Belgians occupied these chairs. They were dressed in darker clothing and for the most part sat in relative silence. They looked solemn; they had lost yet another Belgian patriarch, miner, friend. For them there was the realization that in just a few years, there would no longer be any native born Belgians left in Northumbria to mourn. Their memories of life in Belgium were theirs and theirs alone. They had not passed on to their families a false glorification of the life they had left in their native land. They had embraced Canada as home and had instilled within their children a respect for Canada's promise. They were never bitter about their former homeland; they had simply moved on to a new and better life. They had no regrets. However, funerals were a time to reflect upon their lives and to recall but not linger in the past. Their children were their gift to their adopted country.

Bertha and Robert welcomed so many friends during the two days of visitation. Robert wore his navy blazer, blue shirt, blue striped silk tie and grey trousers. Bertha wore Camille's favourite dress; the dress she had worn for their fiftieth anniversary. It was a blue silk dress with a lace collar and pearl buttons on the full length sleeves.

The two visitation evenings were a time of sharing the humour, the gentleness, the kindness and the mischief that was Camille. Everyone had a Camille story to share.

Howard MacGregor who was ninety years young recalled the times he and Camille had walked the old road to the mine for the midnight shift. The miners were a superstitious lot and stories abounded of ghosts and forerunners. The first Belgian miner to be killed in the Northumbria mines was a young man of 24 who had been married only two months. Many miners claimed that they saw him walking along the deserted road leading to the mine; he was always carrying his lantern. His widow had committed suicide three months after her husband's tragic death. The miners claimed that she, too, wandered the road searching for her husband. She wore a kerchief in her hair just as she had in life. The miners believed that on nights when both husband and wife were seen searching the road, it was an omen of an impending disaster; they would refuse to enter the mine for the midnight shift.

Howard was bent over with age, but his eyes had lost none of their youthful sparkle. He kissed Bertha on both cheeks. "He was a good man, your Camille." Looking at Robert, "I was his first buddy. We shared the same tunnel for a year. We shared our lunches, chewing tobacco and our dreams in that dark hole. Son, you never had to work in the mine, a lucky one! But your father, until his Arthur died, he was a great miner. No one loaded more coal! No one knew the mine like he did. He knew the earth. He could hear it move before the rest of us. He could feel a disaster coming! I can remember him shouting, 'Get to the wall! Get to the wall!' Within seconds, the roof would let loose, dumping its black earth on us. Yes, he saved many of us from an early grave. Robert, he died when he realized that he wasn't able to save his own son. That was cruel!"

Robert placed his hand on Howard's shoulder; he had often listened to Howard and his father talk about life in the mine. They had chosen to be miners and accepted the risks that were involved. Camille could never accept the price his son, Arthur, had paid to share his father's way of life.

"Howard, you and father were such good buddies. Do you remember the night you both saw the young couple on the pit road?"

Howard looked intently at Robert and Bertha, drawing closer to them. "I will never forget it. Betty was her name, you know. We met her near the creek just as we began climbing the hill to the mine. She held her kerchief in her hand. She walked slowly toward us, waving the kerchief at us. We were frightened, but as always she faded as we drew closer. I felt chills in my bones. As we came to the entrance to the mine, we were met by the young miner. He lifted his lantern, stopping in front of us as we approached the mine. He had her kerchief around his neck. He was shaking his head."

Howard seized Bertha by the hands, "Your Camille stopped in his tracks, telling me to be quiet. We stood in the dark, there was nothing to see except the young miner, shaking his head. Suddenly he vanished! Camille hit my arm to signal for us to continue walking. When we reached the spot where the ghost had stood, we found a kerchief lying on the ground, covered with blood. Camille picked it up. We didn't know what to do with it. Camille tied it to a tree near the road. We both turned around and came home."

Bertha nodded at Howard, "That was the night of the cave-in in your tunnel, wasn't it?"

"Yes, we would have been killed! And some people don't believe in forerunners! Your Camille knew that we had been saved from death. The next day when we went back to get the kerchief, it was gone. We never saw either of them again! Nor did anyone else."

Later Robert shared a few minutes with his father's two sisters, Mary and Oliva, who reminded him of the special role Camille had played in their lives, recalling the mischief that their brother had enjoyed creating.

Oliva hugged Robert, "Your father spent his life digging the earth, under the ground and in his garden. Now it is time to dig the ground for him. I miss him already. He was the quiet one!" Looking at Mary, she continued "Our older brother came to this new land with our mother just after papa died. He became the head of the household; he protected us."

Mary was more emotional than Oliva, she could not keep back the tears. "No matter how hard times were, he smiled. He worked in the mine so that Oliva and I could go to school. He did without so that we could have things we needed. He laughed when we all wanted to cry. In the early days, he loved to play his accordion, he played at so many weddings and baptisms. Oh, the grand parties we had! Camille would play his accordion as we placed our hands on each other's hips forming a musical train that weaved its way from one room to other. We sang, we laughed, we were so happy then." She paused for a moment, smiling as she continued, "He liked to play music with a fast rhythm. I remember Father Brown visiting on one occasion, your father was outside playing "What A Friend We have in Jesus". He claimed it was 'une belle air'. It was only after Arthur died that the music ceased."

Oliva embraced her sister, "Will we ever forget the night Camille stopped playing his accordion? The night you lost your brother, Robert. Camille was so proud of you; you did not have to spend your life in darkness. You are a teacher!" Looking around at the visitors in the room, she whispered, "He was so proud when he heard that you stood up to the MacDonald boy, that muscle guy."

Robert put his arms around both aunts as they shed a few tears together. It was Oliva who changed the tone of their discussion, "That Camille. There were times I could have killed him myself! Remember those prune pies!" She instantly realized that she had made a faux pas in front of Mary, but fortunately Mary did not appear to have heard the comment.

Robert winked at Oliva. "Will we ever forget father dunking his galettes in his coffee? What a mess!"

Oliva interjected, "Galettes I could stand, but dunking my apple pie. Who ever heard of such a thing?"

Mary wandered back into the conversation by asking, "What did you mean, Oliva, the prune pies?"

Oliva smiled as she glanced at Robert who raised his eyebrows..." Once...Camille dunked his prune pie!"

Mary smiled, "Oh, I see." She noticed Bertha kneeling at the casket and went to kneel beside her.

Robert smiled at Oliva, "That was a close call!"

"Robert, I can still see your father licking his fingers behind Mary's back. He was such a tease. And those terrible jokes he told. And he told them so often, yet he changed them each time he told them. At the parish dinner when we celebrated the church's 150th anniversary, he told the story of two people at a banquet. Your mother was furious!"

"I don't think I know that one."

Just as Oliva was about to tell the story, Bertha and Mary joined them.

Oliva smiled at Bertha as she hugged her. "Robert wants me to tell Camille's banquet story. Do you mind if I tell him?"

Bertha shook her head, "No, tell it, but I'm sure he must have heard it."

Oliva motioned for Bertha, Mary and Robert to join her in one corner of the room where there were empty seats. Oliva was a heavy set woman with a rounded face that always radiated warmth. She was dwarfed by her sister, Mary, who was tall and slender, but bent with age. Oliva loved storytelling as much as her brother had and was just as capable of embellishing the plot with her own details.

Looking at Robert, she began. "I'll tell the story as if I were Camille. Once I was at a miner's banquet seated between two gentlemen that I had never met. On my right was a distinguished fellow named Frank; on the other side, a guy named Pete who looked like a labourer, just like me. Pete was a union man who was to speak to us after the banquet. Just as we began to eat, his dentures broke. What a fix! He couldn't eat and just think what he'd look like delivering a speech."

Robert chuckled, "Nothing to bite with!"

Oliva smiled mischievously, "Frank noticed Pete's problem and said, 'Don't worry!' He withdrew a pair of dentures from his coat pocket and passed them to Pete. Pete tried them but they were far too small so he regretfully returned them.

"'Try these.' He passed a second pair to Pete, but they were too large. Pete was disgusted that neither of the pairs would fit. Frank didn't seem to mind at all; he passed Pete a third pair and they were a perfect fit."

Robert added, "I guess it helps to sit beside the right people at banquets!"

Oliva continued, "Pete was able to enjoy the meal and delivered his speech with a beaming smile. At the end of the evening, he went to the washroom and cleaned the dentures. He returned them to Frank."

"'Thank you, Frank, I appreciate your kindness. Are you a dentist or denturist in the area?'"

"Frank replied, 'No, I'm the mortician!'"

Robert laughed out loud as he pictured his father telling the story at the parish banquet. It was good to share such memories with family as they prepared to say good-bye to someone who had cared for them, teased them and often frustrated them.

Ellen and Kenneth MacDonald joined Bertha, Robert and the aunts as they continued to recall Camille's legacy. It was Ken who wanted to share a story with the family.

"I worked for a short time with Camille just before he retired. Danny Rankin was our other close buddy at the time. You must all remember, Annabel, Danny's wife. She was a case! Never quite knew if her head was screwed on right. Camille said she had a few vacant rooms upstairs that needed plaster."

Bertha nodded, "He would say that."

Oliva continued, "Camille said that Annabel would pick up things and take them home, no one considered it stealing, but you know there's a fancy name for those people. It seems the guys had a spit bowl that they used in their cardshack where they played poker on the weekends. Guess they used the pot for almost anything. They used to put it outside of the cardshack to air during the week. One day it went missing."

Robert smiled, "Let me guess where it went?"

Ken would not be distracted from finishing the story, "A few days later, Danny invited your father for a supper of corn chowder. You know your father did not like to eat out very much, but Danny was a good buddy and although Camille wasn't sure what kind of cook Annabel was, he agreed. They had a great serving of corn chowder." Looking at Robert, "Your father had seconds."

Robert asked, "There must be a twist to this story! Or is that it?"

Ken leaned toward Robert as he delivered the conclusion of the incident. "As Camille left through the back door, he noticed the chowder pot was the missing one from the cardshack.

Bertha exclaimed, "Camille didn't eat corn chowder for years!"

As they were sharing Camille stories, the young couple, Bert and Brenda Johnson, who had recently moved into the company house across from the manor entered the room. The couple looked ill at ease as they came toward the family. The husband spoke first as Bertha and Robert rose to their feet.

"We are very sorry that you have lost your father, Robert and you, your husband, Mrs. Mascaux. We have only known Mr. Mascaux for five months. I guess you know that our four year old son, Donny, has recently been confined to bed for a month. We placed his bed by the living-room window so that he could see the street; as you know, the window looks out on your backyard.

Mr. Mascaux entertained Donny everytime he was in the garden. He would bring him treats. It was just two weeks ago that Donny woke up to find plastic birds attached to his window from outside. He thought it was magic. We knew it was Mr. Mascaux."

Brenda Johnson's voice quivered as she spoke, "We have never really chatted very much with your husband. He seems...seemed so quiet, but he has become Donny's adopted grandfather. Both sets of grandparents are on the West Coast. I can't tell you how much Donny enjoyed the accordion; he loves music and to have Mr. Mascaux play just for him was so special. We haven't been able to tell Donny where his 'grandfather' has been the last few days." As tears streamed down her face, her husband comforted her.

Robert placed his hand on Bert's shoulder. "Thank you for coming this evening. I'm sorry I haven't taken the time to visit. It means a great deal to have you share my father's kindness to your son."

Brenda withdrew a single red rose from a plastic bag she was carrying; it had a plastic bird attached to it. "We wanted to return the kindness with this rose that grew in our garden. Your father helped us to get the bush growing; said he was better at vegetables and not to tell Bertha he liked flowers, too." She passed the rose to Bertha.

Bertha accepted the rose with tears flowing down her cheeks. "Camille loved children." She placed the rose between the miner's cap and the lantern on top of the casket.

The funeral service was memorable in the parish because it was the first time a contemporary eucharist service had been used. The service included the extension of the peace. Margie was the organist; Frances, the soloist sang "What A Friend We Have in Jesus" and "Seek Ye First The Kingdom of God".

Bertha had selected a passage from "Ecclesiastes" which Howie read:

"To everything there is a season,
And a time to every purpose under the heaven:
A time to be born, and a time to die;
A time to plant, and a time to pluck up that which is planted;
A time to kill, and a time to heal;

A time to break down, and a time to build up;
A time to weep, and a time to laugh;
A time to mourn, and a time to dance..."

During the service Father Brown began a different tradition in the parish. At the end of the service, he lit a candle and presented it to Bertha, saying, "The light of Christ has come into the world, Camille has passed from the world that Christ lighted to the home of eternal light."

Camille had not been a regular attender at church, but he was a man of faith and his actions bore fruit of his faith. There is, indeed, a season for everything. The family knew that it was their time to mourn, but they knew that together they would once again mount on eagles' wings.

A month after the funeral, Bertha and Robert met with Howie and Margie. Bertha wanted to discuss her retirement; she had already spoken to Margie on several occasions about her plans.

They were seated in Leah's room.

Bertha began the conversation, "Camille would have found it so difficult to leave his home and yet he knew one day we would have to do so. To think that he was spared that..." She paused to regain her composure. "It is time for me to retire! Margie, you have given careful consideration to my proposal. What have you and Howie decided?"

Margie reached out to take Howie's hands in hers. Looking at Bertha, she replied. "We have decided to take over the manor as you requested. We will be ready to move in as soon as you would like. Howie plans to take early retirement from the bank. We will do some renovations to the manor, extending the north wing of the house. We love gardening and young Robert will enjoy the freedom of the large yard."

Howie looked at Bertha, "Are you sure you will be comfortable living in the apartments at Garden Estates?"

"Robert and I will be quite comfortable there. It is good of you to keep the bedroom in the basement for Robert when he wants to stay over."

Howie responded, "It will serve as a spare bedroom and our private fitness centre. Got to keep in shape now that we are getting older."

Smiling, Bertha teased, "Yes, you guys don't want to get love handles! Do you think you will have much difficulty selling your bungalow?"

Howie addressed the question, "Not at all, someone at the bank has already indicated an interest in looking at the house when we are ready. No, it won't be a problem. Bertha, we will look after the house and the guests."

Bertha was always the strong one. "I am grateful to you both. I don't know how I could have forced myself to leave this place, if I didn't have the assurance that it would continue to be a home to our dear ones." Glancing at Robert, "Your memory lane will continue to live. We have the newest plaque to place on a tree this evening. It will be the hardest one we have had to commemorate, but he will join the others who have given us all so much..."

Throughout the summer, Robert and his mother were busy preparing for their move. On August 14, they found themselves in their new apartment. Robert continued his evening visits to the manor to be with Leah, his 'grandparents', his godchild and his dearest friends. Bertha visited often as well to provide assistance with the numerous lighter chores that form part of the regular routines of a nursing home.

It had been difficult for both Robert and Bertha to say good-bye to Camille and at the same time to their home. Neither believed in living in the past; both of them found comfort in their memories. Bertha became more involved in church work now that she had more time; even at seventy, she had no thought of retreating to a rocking chair.

Robert was unsettled by the news from Rachel. She called on the telephone but her correspondence had ceased. Despite every possible test, she had not regained her strength. She was weak, her bones ached continually and she was often dizzy. She had wanted to come to Northumbria for the funeral, but her aunts would not hear of it and in the end, she knew herself that she was not well enough to travel.

It was September 16 that Rose called Northumbria. Robert had just returned from school. He answered the wall phone in the kitchen of the apartment.

"Hello, this is Robert speaking."

"Robert, this is Rose Thomas speaking. How are you and your mother doing in your new apartment?"

"Rose, this is quite a surprise, we are fine. But is there a problem?"

Rose hesitated for a moment. "Robert, two days ago, Rachel didn't arrive for breakfast; we discovered her unconscious in bed. She was rushed to the hospital. After two days of tests, the doctors are still baffled. They don't know what is causing her weakness. They have examined her for Lou Gehrig's, multiple sclerosis, leukemia, that new disease, chronic fatigue, and so on. They are sending her home at the end of the week. She can't walk at the moment. We are so worried about her. I know this is not an opportune time to telephone you and to burden you with our problems, but I wanted you to be aware of Rachel's condition in case she doesn't...doesn't improve."

Robert twisted the telephone cord in his hand as he thought about Rachel lying helpless in the hospital. "I appreciate your call, Rose. How are you managing without Rachel?"

"Rachel has our business affairs in order and she has transferred ample funds to our chequing account so that I can pay our routine bills. A learning experience for me. Of course, I don't need to fuss with the investment portfolios."

"Rose, I'll call you on the weekend to see how Rachel is; if she is no better, perhaps we can decide how best I might help."

After two weeks and numerous telephone calls to Flanders Cove, it became apparent that Rachel was slipping away from her loved ones. Robert called Rose on September 30.

Rose answered the telephone from the library. "Hello, Rose Thomas speaking."

"Rose, mother and I would like to visit you, Rachel and her other aunts. We could be in Flanders Cove on October 2; would that be convenient?"

"Robert, I could not bring myself to ask you to come, but it has been our wish that you visit Rachel. We won't tell her that you are planning to come; we don't want her to think she is dying, but we are so afraid; she is not responding to any treatment."

"We will have the spare rooms prepared for both of you. It will be wonderful to finally meet you and your mother. We feel we know you so well. Regrettably, the visit is precipitated by unfortunate circumstances. I know this is not a convenient time for you to visit. You are at school."

"Don't worry, I have made all the necessary arrangements. I have never missed a teaching day in my career. I have a good substitute teacher so everything will be fine."

"Is your mother feeling well enough to travel?"

"Yes, she wants to come for a number of reasons. We'll discuss those over tea one afternoon."

- - - - - Flanders Cove, 1981

When the taxi bearing Robert and Bertha drove along Melrose Road, Robert could hardly contain his emotions. He couldn't help feel excitement about being in Flanders Cove. Within minutes he would enter the world he had seen in *Amercian Estates*, had read about in the aunts' two books, had seen on television and had dreamed about for over two decades. As the taxi passed the houses on Melrose Road, Robert thought of Smith Avenue in Northumbria where the more exclusive houses were situated. The houses on Melrose Road were definitely executive style homes with their formal gardens, orchards, wharves, boats, stables and swimming pools. The houses on Smith Avenue would look so out of place on this prestigious road.

Bertha was returning to New England after an absence of 40 years without her beloved Camille. After all these years, the guardian angel bracelet was still around her wrist. She would soon walk through the home of Henry Thomas, her benefactor. She thought of standing in his library, looking at Iris' quilt, preparing a meal with Daisy in their kitchen, walking with Rose through Rocky's garden of delights.

Uppermost in their minds was Rachel. Robert had longed for the day when they would meet. He had imagined the meeting a hundred times. He could picture Rachel standing at the top of the winding staircase, descending to his waiting arms. He had imagined walking into the library to find Rachel seated at her grandfather's desk. He had fantasized Rachel walking through the gardens only to turn around as he walked toward her. He had imagined them "walking the lane together" in so many ways, but of course, he knew that he was a married man. He felt his body grow cold as the taxi moved closer to 355 Melrose Road. He knew that his Rachel was gravely ill, he knew that he might be too late; he knew that he had lived too long in his dreams.

As the taxi reached 355 Melrose Road, it slowed down. The driver commented, "Here is where the Thomas estate begins; it is the largest in the area. Have you seen the write-up in that magazine?"

Robert responded, "Yes, we saw the article, very impressive."

He and Bertha studied the view of the estate as the taxi continued, finally slowing down to turn into the driveway, then proceeding past the gazebo, the gardens and stopping at the front entrance. The Canadians were mesmerized by the estate. It was more grand than they had imagined. The house was picture perfect. The autumn flowers were beautiful; the lawn was manicured. The famous stained glass window was breathtaking, surrounded on both sides by stately oaks. Both Robert and Bertha thought of their oaks, their memory lane.

As the taxi pulled away, they were met by Marion and the three aunts who rushed to embrace them as they entered the foyer. Marion helped to carry the luggage to their rooms. Robert was given a rare privilege; he was assigned to Henry's room; Bertha was given Violet's room. The spare rooms had been set aside for other guests.

Once they had freshened up, Rose took them to Rachel's room. She was sleeping. She looked as frail as she was! Unlike Leah, she did not appear to be a fairy princess. Robert and Bertha stood at the foot of her bed; perhaps it was five minutes, perhaps an hour. Their hearts broke as they looked upon the young woman who had inspired her aunts to share their gifts with the world; had transformed 355 Melrose Road from a museum to a state treasure, had reached out to them across an international border.

Following dinner, everyone retired to the living-room for coffee and a liqueur. With everyone comfortably seated, Robert was given the task of adding wood to the fireplace. Everything about the house was on a grand scale. The living-room was the size of at least three of the rooms at the manor. The walls were twelve feet in height with elaborate floral plaster designs in the four corners and in the centre of the ceiling surrounding the chandelier. The hardwood floor was a work of art, carefully preserved, with the centre covered with an oriential rug. The room reminded Robert of the grand reception rooms in the foyers of the more expensive hotels he had enjoyed in his few trips to Halifax.

Rose studied Robert as he stared at his surroundings. Perhaps she was reading his mind when she spoke. "Robert, do you find the house large?"

Realizing that he had been caught staring, he replied, "Actually, I do. I knew, of course, there were twenty-three rooms, but I guess I hadn't really imagined that one room might be the size of two or three rooms in houses back in Northumbria."

Daisy looked at her Canadian friends, "The house is large, I can tell you every corner has a dust story. Houses are never homes because they are large. My father always said he and my mother were never happier than when they had a small apartment over the offices where he started as a clerk. I don't know what I would do without Marion and Walter; they are so good to us. They have moved in with us for the next few weeks. It works out perfectly for us and they are having renovations done to their home. Marion is delighted to get away from the dust and noise. We enjoy our home, but of what value is all of this when our dearest possession is slipping away from us..."

Bertha spoke to the aunts. "The magazine article was wonderful; but it could never have captured the grandeur, the elegance, the coziness of the house. We have only been here a few hours, but it feels so comfortable. I love the conservatory, Camille would have loved it as well. Thank you for allowing us to share your home."

Iris looked at the bracelet on Bertha's wrist. "You are wearing a most attractive bracelet, Bertha. Does it commemorate a special event?"

Bertha realized that the aunts did not know the bracelet's story. She felt that a sin of omission was not possible as she shared the warm hospitality of these gracious ladies. She told them the story of how Henry Thomas had reached out to her when she was so young, so lonely, so poor.

It was Rose who spoke first as Bertha concluded, "Bertha, I fully understand why Rachel didn't tell us. She was simply respecting the code of ethics that has always dominated this household. We never questioned father and mother; we never pry, we are so reserved. In the last few years, we have come to realize that families need to be more open with each other. We have slowly begun to share among ourselves and, of course, we have opened our home to share with others. Rachel came into our home as our niece, she was an orphan. Within such a short time, she became our guardian. She runs this estate. She protects us by allowing us to live as we have always done, without financial worry. She would assume that if father had wanted us to know about the bracelet he would have told us. We respect that decision. However, we all need to learn to allow truth to stand on its own!"

Robert thought of his own guarded secrets over the years. "Yes, truth must stand on its own. I agree with you, Rose."

Bertha looked at the aunts, "To everything there is a season. Perhaps sometimes we want to protect our loved ones from truth. It never gets easier to tell the truth. Robert, you have learned that lesson so well yourself."

Robert confirmed Bertha, "Yes, I guess experience is a great teacher."

Rose asked Bertha, "May I look at the bracelet?"

Removing the bracelet, Bertha passed it to Rose, who shared it with her sisters.

Bertha spoke as the Thomas sisters looked at the gift their father had given to a stranger so many years ago. "I have worn that bracelet almost every day since it was given to me. It has been my guardian angel. It was crafted in New England; it has lived in Nova Scotia, but it has returned home. I intend to give it to Rachel when we are able to chat."

Robert was startled by this announcement. "You are giving up your bracelet?"

"Yes, Rachel needs the guardian angel more than I do. Her grandfather would want me to give that hope to his grandaughter."

Rose spoke on behalf of the aunts. "Bertha, that is so very kind of you, but I'm not sure Rachel will...not sure that she will ever be well enough to wear it." She passed the bracelet back to Bertha.

Placing the bracelet back on her wrist, Bertha paused before continuing, choosing her words carefully. "I realize Rachel is not well. It is not so much giving her a piece of jewellery as it is a gift of love. Your father gave me a costly gift and I have always been aware of how expensive it is, how beautifully it is crafted. In this house, it doesn't look out of place at all. In my manor, the bracelet may have appeared extravagant. It has been admired by everyone who has seen it. Its real value has been the spontaneity that caused your father to give it to a stranger; the unselfishness of the benefactor. We knew each other for three hours; we didn't even know each other's names. Yet, he knew how I much I admired the bracelet, knew that it was well beyond my reach. He gave me more than a bracelet; I give Rachel more than a bracelet. It will be her hope, her guardian angel, too."

"Forgive me, Bertha," responded Rose. "I understand what you are saying! It is so very generous of you."

Daisy rose and approached Bertha, placing her arms around Bertha, hugging her. "We Thomas sisters make perfect Episcopalians, we have earned the title, 'God's frozen people'. Bertha, to think that you have been connected to this family for forty years and we knew nothing about it. We have grown so fond of all of you. Thank you for coming to us. We are helpless. The doctors cannot find the real cause of Rachel's illness; they have hunches, but nothing to cure her. We are all people of faith. I know you have just lost your husband, your father. God doesn't always spare our loved ones. Sometimes he blesses them by taking them home. Rachel is young; she has done so much for us. We have made up our minds that we cannot allow her to leave us without trying every source available to us to obtain a full recovery. We believe in the medical staff, but we have more faith in the Great Physician. We know that you, Robert, have had experience in the healing ministry. We want to shower Rachel in prayer! We want to do it together, to bring all the individuals who have been an important part of her life together, to pray for her recovery. I know you have prayed at home, but we wanted to have everyone present in Rachel's room so that she would experience together the communion of the Spirit."

Robert was overwhelmed by Daisy's comments. "Daisy, I guess we all feel so helpless. It has been so difficult being at home wondering what was happening. Yes, we have prayed. Yes, we believe in the power of prayer for healing. We know that God answers all prayer and sometimes the answer is 'No' or 'Not yet'. We have prayed so often for Leah and yet she has slipped away from reality; she sleeps most of the time. We are thankful to be here."

Iris could not contain her tears. "It is too bad that tragedy always brings people together. After all these years we meet you at a time when Rachel can least appreciate a visit, but perhaps a time when she most needs to have you with her. After you confirmed your visit, Derek and Denise called to indicate that they would be here this weekend. The weather forecast is not good; we are to have high winds and rain, but they still expect to come. I hope you don't object to this arrangement. You haven't met Denise; she insisted that they meet you. She is a loving individual, but definitely speaks her mind. She and Rachel enjoy each other's company; she has become Rachel's closest friend." She realized she might have excluded Robert from the last comment and tried to redeem herself. "What I mean is...oh Robert, you are in a category by yourself with Rachel, I...you understand, don't you?"

Robert smiled, "I understand. You know that I love Leah but our love has been a delicate flower that never bloomed; my love for Rachel is the same, it is there, it is always restrained, but cannot be denied. It was easier before we spoke on the telephone and it was easier before we arrived here. If truth must be told, then you will know that I have loved two women for most of my adult life. I have struggled to deny my love for Rachel, but..."

Bertha interrupted, "Robert, I am sure Rachel's aunts know exactly how you feel."

The aunts nodded in agreement. It was Rose who spoke. "Robert, will you be uneasy meeting Derek?"

"The bond I share with Derek is Rachel. I truly wanted them to find happiness together. I was tortured when Rachel refused his proposal; tortured because I wanted her to find happiness, to be loved and yet, I was envious that they would find the happiness that had eluded me. Derek and I have corresponded regarding my photo article of the manor. I have several copies of the article upstairs. It was featured in *Canadian Treasures*, a magazine that features antiques, homes and interesting Canadians. Derek was a great help with the photography and he has given me some editors' names for possible publication here in the States."

The first evening together was a rich sharing of concern for Rachel, the power of faith, the legacy that shaped the families and the enjoyment of finally being together. It was the next morning before Rachel met her guests.

Rachel was awake when Robert entered her room alone. She had only known that Robert and Bertha were coming the day they arrived. She looked less frail as she smiled warmly to greet him; she slowly raised herself in the bed.

Robert stood in the doorway, frozen with emotion. He felt his heart beating furiously in his chest. He wanted to run to Rachel's bed, collect her in his arms and show her how much he loved her. But she was too weak for such a greeting and it was their first moment alone together. He knew that someone else was lying in a bed in Northumbria; someone who wore his ring on her finger. He had come to Flanders Cove to help

Rachel, not to satisfy the surpressed desires that he had buried and controlled for so long.

His mind flashed back to the photo of Rachel and Connie that he had looked at so many times; he thought of the first time he had heard Rachel's voice. Now he was here with her; they were alone.

Finally he spoke, "Rachel, it is so good to be here, to see you."

Rachel was wearing a rose coloured nightdress and a heavy pink sweater that helped to give her colour; she did look less gray than the previous day, but it was only a touch of make-up that was camouflaging her inner weakness. She wanted to muster every ounce of strength to make their greeting a pleasant one.

"Rachel...I...think your aunts are wonderful, just as you described them. The house is so elegant, so spacious, so Victorian. I can truly say, it looks as if it stepped out of a magazine."

Rachel enjoyed the humour, "And you look as if you stepped out of a fashion magazine. You are taller than I imagined, although I knew you were almost six foot. I see you are wearing your vest and silk shirt. I remember you telling me that you liked to wear vests. See, I do read your letters carefully."

"Thanks for the compliment! I've never been told I look like a model before. Your eyes must be blurred." Realizing he should not have referred to her eyesight, he tried to backtrack. "What I mean is..."

Rachel saved him from any further embarrassment, "Robert, do you intend to stand in the doorway, or are you going to come closer. I assure you I am not contagious!"

Robert blushed, "Oh, I wasn't afraid of catching anything, I..." He chuckled, "I guess I am so glad to be here that I'm afraid if I move, I might wake up." He walked directly to the bed and kissed her on the cheek, then sat in the chair next to the bed.

Rachel giggled, "Robert, I have had better kisses in my life!"

Robert smiled, "I'm sure you have!"

"Rachel, tell me how you are feeling. I want the truth."

Rachel sat upright, "I don't know how I feel. I just feel numb and I am cold all the time. I know everyone is worried about me. I am worried! I think I may be dying! I guess that is why you are here." She tried to be strong, but her voice broke. "I...am sorry...we must meet like this..."

Robert took her right hand in his; it was cold. "Rachel, our lives are filled with regret. There are so many things we should have done. I am here. I know Rose would jokingly say that I could never be accused of being too forward or aggressive."

Rachel laughed, "And she has said exactly that."

"Rachel, on the evening before Leah confessed her problem to me, I dreamed that we were together at a beach. Connie's hit "Together" filled my thoughts and my dreams; I saw us so vividly, holding hands, embracing, kissing. I was sure we were destined to be together for life and yes, I had fallen in love with you. The next morning I discovered Mrs. Ford had passed away. That afternoon, my life was frozen in time! Now that I see you, I know what I have missed. I do love you." He leaned over to kiss her lips.

Rachel kissed him back. "Robert, thank you for coming."

Robert returned to his chair, "Rachel, what can I do to help?"

"Robert, you have done the only thing you can, you are here. The aunts are thrilled to have you and your mother visit; I can't tell you what it means to me." She grew faint as she spoke. "Robert, I think I need to rest, will you forgive me if I close my eyes? Will you sit here with me?"

Robert remained beside Rachel for an hour while she drifted off to her private memories. He sat quietly looking at his American dream. He knew she was gravely ill; he could not accept the possibility that she might not recover. He wanted to believe that one day, they would be together. He thought of the hours he had spent at Leah's bedside. He wasn't sure if he should feel guilty. Was he betraying Leah; was he breaking their marriage vows as he confessed his love for another woman?

He was awakened from his reflections by Rachel. "Do I smell Aramis cologne?"

Robert blushed, "I guess you do. Do you like it?"

"It is sensuous!"

Robert smiled as he looked into Rachel's eyes, "Then I'll splash more on the next time. Of course, I don't want your aunts chasing me!"

Rachel chuckled, "Be careful of Rose!"

"I will."

The two intimate friends continued to recall memories they had previously shared only through correspondence and in later years through telephone calls. Bertha brought their sharing to an end when she appeared in the doorway. She had just come from the kitchen. She was wearing one of Daisy's aprons.

"Hello, Rachel, I'm Bertha." She walked slowly toward Rachel, kissing her on both cheeks. "How are you feeling today?"

"Tired, but so happy to meet you!"

Bertha stood beside Rachel's bed, moving toward the head rest so that she was not blocking Robert's view. "Rachel, we have been so worried about you. We have prayed for your recovery, but you will know all this. Rachel, I have had a guardian angel for forty years." She removed her bracelet. "I want you to have this."

Rachel exclaimed, "Bertha, I couldn't accept it!"

"Rachel, it was given to me by your grandfather. He didn't ask if I wanted it; he knew I needed it! I am not asking you if you will accept it. I am giving it to you." She took Rachel's left hand in hers, and placed the bracelet around the thin wrist. "The bracelet has been returned to the Thomas family. It will be your guardian angel! It will give you the promise of hope that it has given me throughout my life."

Rachel's eyes grew misty. "The angel is so delicate, the bracelet is wonderful! I love it! Thank you."

Robert looked at Rachel and his mother. His two favourite people meeting each other. He admired both of them, loved them and rejoiced that they could finally be together.

Bertha twisted the bracelet on Rachel's wrist so that the invalid could enjoy the engraved design. "It is a marvellous creation, isn't it?"

Rachel nodded in agreement. She attempted to straighten herself in the bed; Bertha helped her to become more comfortable by adjusting the pillows behind her.

"I am sorry that you lost your husband. I had hoped I might meet Mr. Mascaux one day."

Bertha attempted to lighten the conversation. "He was a character, let me tell you. You would have liked him, I am sure. He was a flirt, you know, not like his son." She placed her hand on Robert's shoulder.

Rachel smiled, "Was he as good looking?"

Within a few minutes Rachel had once again faded; she had consumed all of her strength. Robert and Bertha slipped quietly out of the room after she had fallen asleep.

That evening Bertha and Daisy cooked dinner. The menu included veal cutlets cooked with garlic, thyme and prunes; applesauce, red cabbage, carrots, asparagus, mashed potatoes, and a tossed salad. Bertha had carefully packed her homemade chutney, beets and pickles for the trip to Flanders Cove; each was featured at the dinner table. Bertha's brown sugar pie was the special dessert.

Following dinner, Bertha and Daisy announced that they would do the clean-up. They had cookery secrets to share. Bertha wanted the pleasure of washing the Florentine china. Both women were relaxed with each other, laughing and chatting as if they had known each other for years. Bertha washed while Daisy dried the dishes.

"Daisy, your book is so inspirational. I have read your poetry and songs so many times. Your descriptions of parish life are so graphic; I could identify with many of the concerns you raised. I have had too little time for involvement in the church and Camille was not a good attender. But the church has always been important to us. Robert, Margie and Howie are very involved."

"The church cannot survive without dedicated people. For so many years, I sat in the comfortable pew, but gradually I realized that my voice was as important as anyone else's. For years I was a good follower; I never imagined that I might lead. Scriptures are filled with the least likely leaders. Moses stuttered; Abraham and Sarah were ancient when they became parents, and who would have thought a young shepherd named David would be one of the greatest kings of the Old Testament, all because he had a slingshot."

"Was it difficult to convert your diary entries into the format required for your book?"

Daisy placed the dry dinner plates on the round table located in the centre of the kitchen. She and Bertha would later return the Florentine dishes to the built-in china cabinet in the dining-room.

"No, I often write my entries as poems, songs, and even in short anecdotes. It was difficult to accept the fact that others might find my ramblings of interest. I haven't read as widely as Rose and I am not a real writer but..."

Bertha stopped washing for a moment, turning to look at Daisy. "A good writer is not necessarily someone with a degree in journalism or even someone with an extensive vocabulary; a good writer is someone who has something to say, feels it strongly, and says it simply. Your book doesn't preach; it isn't filled with literary devices; it communicates its message. The reader identifies with what you are saying; that's the bond that all writers need to achieve."

Daisy blushed, "You are very kind, Bertha."

"Daisy, we don't know each other very well, but I can tell you I don't mince words, I believe in telling it as it is."

Daisy placed her arm on Bertha's shoulders, giving her a gentle hug. "I can't believe you are here. Cooking dinner this evening was a treat for me. I enjoyed watching you prepare the cutlets. Thank you for bringing the herbs. You do use more garlic than I normally do and the prunes were delicious. I will use more red cabbage, too. The apples and vinegar really give the cabbage a different flavour."

Bertha held up a Florentine cup. "Robert told me about this pattern. I went to the local china shop to check it out. They had a few pieces, but it was too expensive to maintain large supplies. It didn't matter, one cup and saucer was all I could afford."

Daisy looked at the figure beside her. They had so much in common. They loved to cook, they were both short and full bodied; they both wore aprons with large bibs. They were united in the bond of affection that existed between son and niece.

While Bertha and Daisy were in the kitchen doing dishes, Robert wandered into the conservatory where Rose was seated at the piano. She was playing a medley of Connie's hits, including, "Many Tears Ago," "My Happiness" and "Who's Sorry Now?". He was carrying a cloth bag with a few Connie albums he had purchased for Rachel. He sat down beside the piano in a wicker rocking chair. Rose stopped playing as he joined her.

"Oh, please don't stop. It is so good to hear you play those familiar tunes. You play so well."

"I play, not very well, but thank you for the compliment." She continued playing as Robert sat in the chair looking at the lush greenery around him. He thought of the manor's sun porch where the guests enjoyed the view from the picture windows with a few plants growing on the window sill. What would his trio have thought of this room? Gramma Horton would have known the names of all the plants. He was aware of the rain beating against the windows on the south side of the conservatory; the predicted winds were tossing the autumn flowers to and fro. Many of the blackeyed susans, giant marigolds and cosmos had fallen to the ground with their broken stems. He withdrew one of the albums he had purchased for Rachel; it was Connie's newest release. It was entitled, "Connie Francis: I'm Me Again"; a silver anniversary album released on the familiar MGM label. The album jacket had a gorgeous picture of Connie looking refreshed and so very youthful. The main track was the title song, "I'm Me Again" (Alan Roy, Scott and Ed Fox) Ragtime Music, 1980 (ASCAP) which reflected Connie's attempt to put the past behind her, to resume her career, to be the entertainer she had been and was meant to be. The opening verse of the hit tune said it all:

"When all the easy times
Turned into long, cold nights,
I let myself take the blame.
I felt so numb inside,
And lost my sense of pride-
Now I'm no longer ashamed
I'm me again,
I've conquered all my fears,
Now I'm at peace again."

Robert read the album cover as Rose continued to play. He studied Rose as she filled the conservatory with Connie's music; the music that had been his constant companion. Rose sat so erect on the piano bench, her long fingers flowing gracefully over the keys. Perhaps she was the most intimidating of the aunts to house guests, but at the moment two strangers were brought together by timeless music; music of love. Robert had known too little the promise of Connie's songs and Connie herself had discovered that life is often more tragic than romantic.

Robert wondered if Rose had ever been in love. Rachel had never mentioned any of the aunts having had a romantic liaison; but that did not mean that they did not have dreams or even secrets that Rachel had not uncovered. Rose looked up, giving him a faint smile.

So many of Robert's family members and friends had commented on his ability to handle stress; to deal with Leah's condition, to cope with Trevor's threats. Howie often called him 'the rock'. He was stoic on the outside, but his heart, like Rose's, was a tender one. To survive, he and Rose had created a calm outer appearance.

Rose stopped playing, turned to face Robert. "Enough sad songs for one day."

Robert passed her the new album. "I thought Rachel might enjoy this album."

Glancing at the album, Rose commented. "There are some of her newer songs here: "Milk and Honey" and "What Good Are Tears" as well as some of the old hit tunes like, "Don't Break the Heart That Loves You" and "Where the Boys Are". I Know Rachel will enjoy the album when...when she is feeling better." She rose abruptly from the bench, placed the album on Robert's lap, then walked toward the patio doors.

Robert was not sure what was happening. Had he said something wrong?

Rose turned from viewing the outside garden, walked toward him, and sat in the chair beside him. She stared at him before speaking. "Robert, I speak my mind, don't believe in skirting issues. Hope you don't mind if I talk to you about your relationship with Rachel?"

Robert was not unaware of Rose's forcefulness; Rachel had shared numerous stories of Rose as the aggressive, undiplomatic aunt.

"Rose, speak freely, I want to hear what you have to say."

"You may regret this, but I have given you and Rachel a lot of thought. I respect your values; I respect the sacrifices you have made. Now that I have met your mother, I know where you have learned the lessons of life. You and Rachel are the strangest couple. Nowhere in fiction is there an equal. I sometimes thought you must be like the brooding heroes in the Austen novels. I love the Victorian novels, but life was so simple in those days. You and Rachel have known each other for over two decades. It took fifteen years before you talked on the phone; and twenty years before you met. Are you just good friends? What are your feelings for her?"

Robert might have blushed if anyone else had requested him to disclose such private thoughts, but he was neither embarrassed nor annoyed by the request. "Rose, whenever I look back on my relationship with Rachel, I marvel that it has survived. We are both so afraid of assuming too much, of hurting each other and yet our silences and our politeness have caused us to suffer unnecessary pain. I am a married man! I will have Leah as my wife forever; I can have no other. Yet, I have always loved Rachel. I struggle constantly with my feelings.

It was easier before we telephoned, it was much easier before I came here."

"Robert, have you shared with Rachel the depth of your love?"

"Yes, we have begun to speak more honestly..." He paused, looked at Rose who showed no emotion. "I cannot see a solution to our dilemma. I cannot betray Leah, but I cannot deny my heart. I don't know what to do, I...I..."

Rose placed her hands on Robert's. "My bark is worse than my bite, I assure you. Robert, I admire you and it is only because I know that your feelings are so strong for Rachel that I ask these questions. Rachel's love for you has sustained her through these many years; she has never complained."

Robert looked at the album he had placed on the floor. "Will Rachel ever be able to say, 'I'm me again!' Am I to lose Rachel as I have lost Leah?" He lowered his head, staring at the floor.

Rose remained still. Silence permeated the room, generating itself, bringing its uneasiness to the two occupants. Finally, Rose shattered the uneasy quiet, "Robert, the doctors do not offer much hope; they have tried everything they can. We have asked for Rachel to be at home with us; there is nothing that can be done at the infirmary. Rachel has given her aunts life; this house became a home again when she came to reside with us. Her laughter, her affection...have enchanted us. We were given new life! Now that lifeline is threatened. I am afraid! Don't tell my sisters that I have confessed my fear. They look to me for strength."

Robert smiled at Rose as he gently touched her shoulder. "Your secret is safe with me. I am so afraid myself. My faith has sustained me through so many crises, but of late, I have lost my peace, lost my hope! I haven't told anyone, because I cannot deal with it. I cannot accept that the God I have spent my life with, can expect me to bear any more. Where is the comfort?"

Rose nodded, "Robert, Daisy is the one of faith. I have read her book several times during the last week. I, too, cannot understand our God of love rejecting us. I know Daisy would remind us of the Great Sacrifice and tell us to put our trust in the divine plan. But Rachel is getting weaker; medical science has no answers; prayer is not working."

"Rose, is Rachel paying a price for the love I share with her?"

"Robert, I don't know what to think. Love cannot be denied. I cannot see that your love for Rachel is wrong! I wonder what I have done that has separated me from the strength I need to endure this!"

Robert trembled, attempted to gain control of himself but could not; he exploded. "Why does it have to be this way? Why would God allow it?" He pounded his fist on the arm of the chair over and over again. "Damn it, I am so angry! We are going to lose her and all the praying in the world is useless! Useless!"

Rose knew that Robert was releasing the pain he had bottled up too long; she let the anger flow without attempting to soothe him.

"I feel betrayed! I don't have anything to hold on to; nothing! If only she would get better, I would gladly pluck my love from my heart, deny it, confess my sin..." He paused, raised his head to look at Rose.

Rose reached for her tissue inside the sleeve of her sweater; she wiped the tears that she could no longer control. "Robert, it is only when I hear you blaming yourself that I realize how foolish it is for any of us to blame ourselves. You have done nothing wrong. Your love has been Rachel's joy, even though she has been denied..." She could not continue, she cried.

Robert was overwhelmed by Rose's sorrow, he too, could not keep back the flood of emotion. Together they shared the fullest expression of their fear and sorrow. Rose leaned over to hug Robert.

"Robert, we can't blame ourselves. It is good for you and me to share these tears...I have cried too little." Straightening herself in her chair, she once again took Robert's hands in hers. "These hands are special. You have used them to write of your love to Rachel. Place these hands on her in prayer; let your love and the love of our Father flow from you to her. I just know that she will feel its power."

Robert raised his hands, staring at them, moving his fingers. "Rose, I don't have the faith required to use these hands for healing. I know that we can all be agents of God's healing power, but..."

Rose smiled warmly, "Oh, I have read and reread Daisy's chapter on healing and my sisters have discussed healing a great deal in the last few days. I know that there are no healers capable of restoring Rachel, except the Great Physician. Perhaps we need to heal ourselves first...and these tears..." Wiping her eyes..." these tears will help."

Robert withdrew his tissue from the back pocket of his trousers; he wiped his eyes and blew his nose. He looked lovingly at Rose, he smiled. She returned the warmth of his feelings by kissing him on the cheek.

With a twinkle in her eyes, she spoke to Robert with a southern accent."Young man, I want you to know, it is not my custom to kiss gentlemen whom I have just met, but I have made an exception just for you. I trust you are not one of those gentlemen who delights in revealing to the world such indiscretions!"

Robert feigned a southern accent for his reply, "My dear, your secret is as safe as mine. We'll just have to honour each other!"

Rose picked up the record album and studied Connie's photo on the cover. "Connie has had enough troubles for several lifetimes, but she is indomitable, a real survivor. You know, I came to admire her in the early years when I helped Rachel with her thriving fan club. Over the years, the fan club numbers have dwindled; I think we still keep in contact with about fifty fans. If Connie can survive all her ordeals, we can surely do the same. Let's put our trust where it belongs. Let's expect that Rachel will also say to us, 'I'm me again'!"

Robert repeated Rose's statement, "I'm me again!"

The weather station was not calling the heavy winds a hurricane, but Flanders Cove seemed destined to bear the brunt of the storm that was lashing the harbour with its gale force gusts and drenching the already sodden earth with its torrents.

Derek and Denise arrived after midnight on Saturday evening; they were welcomed by Marion and Walter and settled into the main guest room. The rest of the household had already retired for the night.

The wind and rain pounded the sturdy house. Robert could not sleep. He put on his housecoat and descended to the library. He had not yet explored the Thomas collection. As he approached the library, he noticed that someone was already in the room. He was about to meet Rachel's other love.

As he entered the room, Derek stood up immediately. The men looked at each other; it was only a moment, but men are always uncomfortable when caught staring at each other. Derek extended his right hand to shake Robert's.

"I'm Derek, and you are obviously Robert."

Robert looked at Derek. He had seen photos of Derek with Rachel, but Derek was more handsome than he had pictured. Derek was impressed with Robert's physique; Robert's years of working out had produced impressive shoulders, chest and waist proportions that even a loose housecoat could not conceal.

The men sat in wing chairs, attempting to deal with the awkwardness of the moment. A gust of wind threw its force against the library windows, causing the window panes to vibrate.

"Derek, it must have been wild on the highway this evening."

"Yes, the roads were slick, and a lot of debris was flying around." He smiled, "And you have never travelled with Denise. She isn't fond of high winds and is nervous travelling in any kind of storm."

Robert wasn't sure how to react to Derek's statement regarding Denise so he changed the subject. "The library is impressive, isn't it?"

Derek left his chair to approach the leather-bound books behind Henry Thomas' desk. He pointed to the books. "You would be interested in this collection. One hundred richly bound leather books, the one hundred most popular classics." He withdrew one book from a shelf, raising the book to his face to smell the leather.

Robert joined him at the collection. "Oh, *Pride and Prejudice*, *The Sound and the Fury*, The *Scarlet Letter...The Three Musketeers*. What a collection!" He opened a copy of *The Iliad*. The gold edging on the pages sparkled as he flipped through the pages. The blue ribbon bookmark fell from the centre of the book. He looked at the vast collection occuying the other walls. "A lifetime would be too short to enjoy these books."

Derek returned to his chair. He held up the book he had been reading before Robert had joined him. "I was reading a chapter from Daisy's book."

As Robert reclaimed his wing chair, he felt comfortable enough to ask Derek, "Are you reading the chapter on healing?"

Derek blushed, "Actually I am. I guess healing has been on our minds a lot these days. Robert, I know you are very religious...what I mean is...you have a strong faith just like Rachel."

Robert was uneasy as he reflected upon his earlier conversation with Rose. "Let's just say, I attend church regularly and try to make sense of our lives through...through a trust in a divine plan."

"Before I met Rachel and her aunts, I never attended church and didn't really think much about God. Knew someone was there, but wasn't sure who. I learned a great deal from this house. God is everywhere here. I found him in Iris' gardens, Rose's books, Daisy's faith and Rachel's love...Am I getting too melodramatic? Living with Denise has made me less reserved than I used to be."

Robert shook his head. "Derek, we both have loved and continue to love Rachel. I am happy that this house has touched your life; it influenced me greatly long before I arrived on Wednesday. I understand what you mean. The house itself has an atmosphere, an aura...not sure what word can describe it, but it is a special home."

"I am really pleased that we have met, Robert. I have admired you, been jealous of you and I would have to confess that I have detested you because you claimed Rachel's love. Do you understand what I am trying to say?"

Robert admired Derek's frankness. "Derek, I have had the same feelings for you. I am glad that you have found happiness with Denise."

"I guess you know that love has many expressions and it is possible to love two women at the same time without violating the codes of trust, devotion and faithfulness."

Robert hesitated, reflecting upon the struggle he had with balancing his love for Leah and Rachel. "Yes, it is possible. I am so pleased that you and Rachel have remained close friends; I know that Rachel really enjoys Denise's friendship as well."

Derek studied Robert's face before continuing. "Robert, you have been so devoted to Leah and I know that until recently you and Rachel have not really talked about your love for each other; it has always been understood. May I ask a rather personal question?"

The bond that had always existed between the two men was instantly strengthened as they sat together in the library. They had never considered themselves competitors although they had desired the love of the same woman. Each had been loved by Rachel; each had matured in that love. And each had been influenced by the bouquet and the charmed life that existed in this special home on Melrose Road.

Robert was about to reply to Derek's question when they were interrupted by a crashing sound that penetrated the entire house. As they rushed from the library to the foyer, they were greeted by wind and rain streaming through the broken panes of the revered stained glass window. There were fragments of the treasured glass everywhere. Several large oak limbs were lying near the window seat. Walter rushed into the foyer, followed by Marion and the aunts. Denise and Bertha were the last to arrive. Marion, with assistance from Denise and Bertha, was able to take the distraught aunts to the safety of the library. Walter assumed responsibility for repairing the damage and keeping the storm from creating further havoc. The men were able to place sheets of plywood over the broken sections of the window.

In the morning stillness, the sun shone through the upper portion of the window. The bottom four sections of the window had been smashed by the impact of two large oak branches that the wind had thrust through the family heirloom. The family crest in the centre of the window had not been damaged. Those who viewed the window from the outside were as dismayed by the damage as those inside the home whose hearts pondered the real loss that extended beyond the pieces of broken glass.

The local media gave full coverage to the freak storm and featured the broken Thomas window as the focus for their review of the storm's impact. Although trees had been uprooted on other properties, the local wharf had received considerable damage and one of the downtown streetlights had been damaged; it was the famous window that dominated the news.

A gloom descended upon the household. No one dared mention the fears they harboured in their souls. The window was more than glass; it was the legacy of the house. Only Iris' quilt rivalled the window in sentimental value. The window dominated the house. It was impossible to avoid its presence. It had provided light and beauty for the family in their joys and sorrows, in their triumphs and defeats, in sickness and in health, and in death.

There was the question that no one would ask, but everyone feared. Was the broken window an omen? Was this the end of the Thomas legacy? Did the shattered window signify that to everything there is a season and now a time for saying farewell?

The aunts displayed remarkable fortitude in the midst of the confusion that enveloped their tranquil household. They had guests to entertain. They were invaded by insurance investigators, the media, members of the heritage society, carpenters, stained glass craftsmen and cleaners. Perhaps they might have agonized more about their broken treasure had not their dearest possession been threatened by death. The home was more than heirlooms; Rachel was their lifeline. Without her, the priceless artifacts were worthless. They had always been grateful for the material things they enjoyed; they had never taken them for granted, and they had never worshipped them. People were more important than possessions.

Marion and Walter assumed responsibility for dealing with the clean-up. Derek, who was familiar with Flanders Cove, was able to help the aunts in the restoration of the window after the insurance company had settled their claim.

It was Sunday afternoon before the household had returned to a degree of normality. Daisy had spoken at length with Robert concerning the laying on of hands for healing. They had discussed their plans with Rachel who had expected that her family and friends would join with her in prayer at some point during the visit. Daisy had acquired oil from the bishop which had been blessed during the previous Holy Week.

It was at three o'clock on Sunday that the aunts gathered with Rachel's Robert and Derek, Bertha and Denise to offer prayers for divine healing. Rachel was propped up with pillows. She was wearing a blue sweater, shivering with the cold despite the excessive heat in the room.

Robert and Derek stood on opposite sides of Rachel's bed. Denise stood beside her husband; Bertha beside her son. Rose stood in front of the bed with Iris beside Denise, Daisy beside Bertha.

Robert served as the officiant. "Rachel, we are here so that all our prayers can be united with yours for healing."

Rachel's voice was weak, "Thank you, it means a great deal to have each of you here."

Everyone in the room was stoic; no tears appeared, no voices broke. There was a peace present that passes all understanding. The afternoon sun broke through the clouds, shining through the three full length windows in the bedroom.

Derek read the first passage of scripture from *Matthew 18:19-20:*

"Jesus said: I promise that when any two of you on earth agree about something you are praying for, My Father in heaven will do it for you. Whenever two or three of you come together in My name, I am here with you."

Denise read the second passage from *James 5:13-15* in which St. James is speaking:

"If you are having trouble, you should pray. And if you are feeling good, you should sing praises. If you are sick, ask the church leaders to come and pray for you in the name of the Lord. If you have faith when you pray for sick people they will get well. The Lord will heal them and if they have sinned, He will forgive them."

The message, "If you have sinned, He will forgive you" echoed through Robert's being. He silently confessed his lack of faith, asking for forgiveness.

Daisy looked at Robert and Derek. She knew the worth of these young men; she knew that their love for her niece was so strong that it could move mountains. She knew that the Spirit of Pentecost was present with them; she knew that they were never alone, would never be abandoned.

Denise looked at Robert, seeing in his eyes the love that he bore for her friend who could barely stay awake as they raised their minds, hearts and souls to the Great Healer.

Robert placed the index finger of his right hand in the vial containing the blessed oil. He formed a cross in the name of the Trinity on Rachel's forehead. He and Derek then placed their hands on Rachel's head, joining their other hands with the others present. A circle of love and faith was formed as Robert led everyone in prayer. Rachel had her family, friends and her guardian angel bracelet to comfort her and, above all, the faith that she had practiced from her childhood.

"Dear Father, we know that you are present with us. In the name of Your son, Jesus Christ and in the power of the Holy Spirit, we pray that you will continue to answer our prayers that Rachel will experience Your healing grace. When Your Son was with us, He was the Great Physician, the Divine Healer; we now pray that we might serve as channels for that same healing grace to be present with us. We ask this in confidence knowing that Your risen Son is present with us at this very moment..."

Following prayers and the singing of one verse of a hymn for healing that Daisy had included in her book, Rachel's family and friends stood looking at Rachel as they concluded their time of sharing by joining together in saying:

"The Peace of the Lord be always with you, Rachel."

Rachel whispered, "And also with you."

Daisy went to Rachel's desk, returning with a lighted candle. "This candle is a reminder to us that the Light of Christ has come into the world. Darkness has given way to a light that can never fade." She placed the candle on the night table beside Rachel.

Everyone who has prayed for healing would like to experience the instant healing portrayed in the gospels. More often than not, faith is tested further as prayers take time to be answered or are answered with far different results than anticipated.

As prayers were offered in Rachel's room, she felt a warmth move throughout her body, a tingling sensation that gently carressed her being; but she remained in her weakened state; there was no instant healing. On Monday at three o'clock, Rose answered a telephone call from a specialist at the infirmary; he had spoken with a medical researcher in New York who recommended that Rachel be given an experimental drug that would have no negative side effects and might be the remedy that was required.

The following day, Daisy was thrilled to announce that Rachel had requested her sweater be removed. It was the beginning of a gradual healing that led to her full recovery. Rachel did receive injections of the experimental drug. She remained confined to bed long after Robert and Bertha had returned home. It was difficult for her to say good-bye to Robert. She had been too unwell to really appreciate his presence, but she treasured among her souvenirs every moment they had shared. She had seen him, smelled his cologne, felt his warmth and love bestowed upon her lips; she had finally met her prince charming.

The house seemed so quiet after the Canadians had departed. The aunts spent most of their free time with their niece. Iris had just come to Rachel's room carrying a faded photo in a tarnished silver frame. She sat beside Rachel on the bed.

"You are feeling better today?"

"Yes, I am getting stronger. I actually ate most of my breakfast this morning. I know Marion was pleased. I feel like a child."

Iris patted her shoulder, "No harm in that; we are all children. Who would have thought that Rose could be so childlike with Rocky?"

"I hear Rose and Rocky entertained our guests with their newest story, "Rocky takes on City Hall"."

"It may be the best story yet. As soon as you can come to the living-room, we are promised a repeat performance."

"That will be worth waiting for."

Looking at her niece who had begun to regain her natural colouring, she spoke softly, "Rachel, what an experience it has been to have Bertha and Robert with us. I cannot remember a time when we have had two strangers become so quickly a part of our household. When they left it was like saying good-bye to friends we had known for a lifetime. I know we have heard about them for years and we have all chatted on the telephone, but it is truly remarkable."

"I am glad we have met. I'm sorry that I will never have the opportunity to meet Camille, but I have met his son."

"Rachel, it was so inspiring, so emotional to see Robert and Derek together; especially in this room, placing their hands on you. I had chills up and down my spine. They are both fine young men. And now that I have met Robert, I know that whatever happens, you two were destined to be together. His eyes convey his love for you."

Rachel reached for her tissue, "Thank you, Iris..."

Iris hugged her niece, "There I go making you cry. You must miss him a great deal?"

"I feel blessed that we have met, even under the circumstances that prompted the visit. I am grateful for the brief visit. Now that I am beginning to feel better, I will not allow myself to descend into self-pity. Love is different for every person. I would like to have time to be with Robert, to get to know him better and to experience life with him, the ordinary things; but I care for him and he cares for me, that will sustain us."

Looking at the photo in her hand, Iris lowered her voice. "Your aunts have spent most of our lives together; we know each other so well and despite this familiarity we have still managed to guard a few private moments from each other. Have you ever wondered about the romantic entanglements of your aunts?"

Blushing, Rachel replied, "I have wondered, but I know how private the three of you are."

"Rachel, I don't think my sisters know the full story of my one romantic involvement. I want to share it with you now for a number of reasons." She showed Rachel the photo of a young man wearing a poorly fitted three piece suit. "This is Adam Harrison from Hartford. As you may remember, I spent six months in Hartford attending a secretarial college. I was only eighteen; he was a twenty-six year old bachelor. We dated, and within two months I knew that I was in love."

Rachel kissed her aunt on the cheek, "Please tell me more, if you are comfortable."

"Adam was originally from South Carolina, a farm boy. He was tall, dark and as you can see, incredibly good-looking. He lacked polish, but his natural charm was infectious. He was working in a factory, but taking university courses to improve his chances for advancement into management. I was afraid to tell father of my love for Adam so I procrastinated. I had mentioned Adam to the family, but I never told them the depth of my feelings. In those days, father could be merciless and I feared that he would soon dispatch Adam as an unworthy suitor. I struggled with my lies of omission."

"What happened to him?"

"Just before I was to return to Flanders Cove, we had a quarrel. It was my fault, I loved him, but I feared father more. I had to decide and yet I couldn't. He had been so patient. I left Hartford with a broken heart so I do understand the emotions you have felt. I have lived to regret my decision. I never heard from him again. Years later, I heard by chance that he had been injured at the factory. He spent five years in a private hospital before dying. I regretted that I was not able to be with him, to comfort him; but he was such a proud man, that my presence would not have comforted him. I have often wondered how he could afford to stay at a private hospital all those years."

Rachel was stunned; she realized that Iris had solved for her the second mystery contained in her grandfather's records. She wrestled with the decision of whether she should reveal her secret to Iris.

Iris solved the dilemma for her. "I know that your aunts and my parents probably suspected that Adam and I were more than friends, but we are a family that does not pry; and we had little discussion about Adam upon my return. I wrote to him, but received no replies. When I heard about Adam's confinement in a private hospital, I did wonder if father might have been involved, but that was such an absurd idea, a fantasy that I hoped might be the consolation for my immaturity."

Rachel looked at the photo. "Iris, I can tell you that your father did pay Adam's medical bills. I have discovered payments for a five year period at an infirmary in Boston where Adam was transferred after his accident."

Iris gasped as she clutched the photo to her breast. "Father paid Adam's bills!"

When Rachel's health had improved considerably, she showed her grandfather's records to Iris, thus confirming Adam's benefactor.

It was December before Rachel had fully recovered. A week before Christmas she wandered throughout the house looking at the festive decorations, enjoying the bracelet that adorned her wrist. Derek and Denise were to spend New Year's in Flanders Cove. The family had sent Robert and Bertha special Swiss wrist watches as Christmas gifts; Denise was given one as well. Rachel placed the album, *Connie Francis: I'm Me Again* on the stereo. As Connie sang the lead song, Rachel waltzed around the conservatory, shouting, "I'm me again! I'm me again!"

Chapter 8:

Who's Sorry Now?

Robert returned the 1981 diaries to their banker's box. He looked at his watch, the gift he had received from Rachel and the bouquet at Christmas following his first visit to Flanders Cove. He could scarcely believe that he had spent five hours reminiscing, recalling the individuals and events that had separated and united Flanders Cove and Northumbria. He sighed with regret, realizing that he could not complete his journey into the past; the present could no longer be denied. The funeral, the wedding and the birthday party would now weave a time for mourning and a time for joy into the fabric of the life he shared with Rachel. They had survived their separation; now was a time to mount on eagles' wings!

Before leaving his den, he once again picked up the photo of the three aunts, the precious bouquet. They would not be attending the wedding. Daisy had passed away in January of 1995 after suffering a heart attack; Iris did not recover from falling down the central staircase in September of the same year. Rose had outlived her sisters but welcomed her final journey in November of 1996.

As he looked at their photo, his hand trembled as he felt the love they had given him warm his entire being. He could hear them chattering, smell the aroma of Daisy's cooking, see Iris' floral masterpieces in the foyer, hear Rose playing one of Connie's hits in the conservatory. He could see in front of him the Thomas crest etched in the restored stained glass window; he could see each block of the quilt that preserved the Thomas legacy. He smiled, then chuckled. The aunts would be at the wedding! There would be so many touches to remind their niece and her husband of them. He knew that he and Rachel would feel their presence.

Robert and his mother had flown to Flanders Cove numerous times following their first visit. They spent several months with Rachel following Rose's passing. There were so many details to settle. The estate was transferred to the Connecticut Heritage Trust. Rachel was able to remove any furnishings and belongings that she wished to have. She had claimed her bedroom furniture and a few of the living-room Queen Anne chairs. She had come to Northumbria for the first time in November of 1997, in time to plan her wedding. She stayed at the manor in an unoccupied guest room. She enjoyed having time to explore the Northumbria that had been Robert's home for over fifty years; the place where they would begin their life together.

Robert returned the photo of the bouquet to the table. He realized that this was not his first marriage; he had exchanged sacred vows with his dear Leah. Leah had slipped away quietly in the summer of 1995, five years after her father had gone to his reward. It had been difficult for Robert to say farewell to Leah. He had spent much of his life at her bedside; he had struggled with his love for her, his promises to her.

He knew that he must leave the valley of the dead and embrace the celebrations of the day.

When he and Rachel were planning the guest list for the wedding, they had wanted it to be a short one, but as most couples discover, it is difficult to exclude friends from sharing such an important event. They were expecting 185 guests to share their wedding and reception. They had agonized about whether to invite Trevor. In the end, they had decided that Mrs. MacDonald would expect Trevor to be there, so they relented. Trevor had sent a brief note in his reply:

"Miss your big day! Never! I have a gift that will shock you!"

Robert had gone to school with Northumbria's police chief; he shared with him his concern that Trevor might pose a problem at the wedding. The police chief assured Robert that he would see that Trevor would not spoil the events.

Robert left his den to shave, shower and dress for the funeral. When he returned to the den, he was wearing a dark suit with a gray tie. He went to the closet in the foyer to find his overcoat and boots. He was to pick up his mother and mother-in-law who shared an apartment at Garden Estates. They had lived comfortably together since Robert had purchased a mock Tudor home on Smith Avenue. He had always admired the stately homes in the older part of town. After Leah had passed away, he knew that he and Rachel would eventually marry. He had video taped the interior and exterior of several houses for Rachel to view so that she would not feel excluded from the selection of their future home. Rachel was too engrossed with business affairs in

Flanders Cove to even consider travelling to Northumbria. She had insisted that Robert use his judgement. They had agreed that they would spend at least a year in the house and if it was not satisfactory, they would search for a replacement together.

As he put on his winter boots, the telephone rang. It was Mrs. Garrison calling from Halifax to send her regrets at not being able to attend the funeral; she had a severe case of the flu and could not leave her bed. As he placed the receiver in the cradle, his mind flashed back to the events of December 3, 1997. He and Rachel had just reviewed their wedding plans with Bertha and Ellen MacDonald when he received a telephone call from the Halifax police department. Trevor had been killed in an accident on a major highway. The roads were icy; his truck had skidded on a portion of the highway labelled, 'death row'. Numerous lives had been claimed by the treacherous curves that funnelled drivers along side a deep cliff descending to the shoreline. It was the most picturesque spot on the highway, and the most deadly.

Mrs. MacDonald, who was now severely crippled with arthritis, was not capable of going to Halifax to deal with her son's affairs and to make arrangements for his funeral. Robert had served as her business manager and trustee for years; he had made all the arrangements for her husband's funeral despite Trevor's protests.

- - - - - Northumbria, December 3, 1997

Robert had mixed emotions as he talked to the Halifax police on the telephone. He was shocked by the tragic news; he looked at Mrs. MacDonald knowing that her heart would be crushed with the news. He sighed with relief knowing that Trevor would not spoil his wedding, would not fulfil his promise to destroy him. Immediately he was angry with Trevor for causing him the inconvenience of arranging a funeral within a few days of his marriage. Was this Trevor's surprise? He hated himself for thinking ill of the dead, for not mourning the loss of his brother-in-law, for being selfish in the midst of a tragedy.

As Robert drove to Halifax early on December 4, he attempted to cope with the crisis Trevor's accident had created. He was surprised to learn that Trevor had willed his organs for transplanting. Trevor had also requested cremation, and that seemed strange since his mother was not aware of her son's intention. He had come to fear and to dislike

Trevor more than any other human being. He knew that hatred was not a Christian virtue and that it was destructive for the person who harboured it in his soul. He could not forget the letters, the parcels, the condoms, the gun, the threats and Trevor's determination to use his appreciation of Connie and his relationship with Rachel to further his evil desires. He had struggled to forget and to forgive, but it had been impossible. Trevor was his lifelong adversary. He couldn't let his guard down; he knew Trevor was capable of harming him and those whom he loved.

Robert recognized the irony in the role that had been thrust upon him. He could not disappoint his mother-in-law and he knew that Leah would want him to do what had to be done to see that her brother was given a proper funeral. Bertha and Rachel understood his dilemma. Rachel had offered to travel with him, but he wanted to spare her the ordeal that he expected to face in Halifax.

The Halifax police were extremely helpful. It was apparent that Trevor's truck had gone out of control on icy roads; no one else was involved in the accident. An approaching car had seen Trevor's pick-up leave the highway, crashing through the guard rail, tumbling over the cliff to the the rocky beach below. The truck was totally demolished; Trevor's seat belt kept him inside the vehicle. He had died instantly in the crash.

The police escorted Robert to Trevor's apartment building in a relatively quiet housing complex in the older part of the city. After a brief conversation with the police in the apartment parking lot, Robert sat quietly in his car waiting for the courage to begin his first visit to his brother-in-law's apartment. The brick structure contained sixteen well-maintained apartments, each with a small balcony. He was not sure what he would find in Trevor's apartment, but nothing could have prepared him for Trevor's surprises!

As he looked at the intercom listings for the superintendent's office, an elderly lady bundled in a winter coat, hat and scarf and carrying a cane approached the main door. He opened the outer door to let her in.

"Thank you sir. Very kind of you to help an old lady. " She looked up at him with a twinkle in her eyes. "I like gentlemen with manners."

Robert looked affectionately at this wrinkled winter pippin, recalling his 'foster grandparents'. "It is a cold day!"

She searched in her purse for her key, passing her cane to Robert. When she finally opened the inner door, she asked Robert if he wanted to join her inside.

"I was just going to ring the superintendent."

"Oh, he works outside the apartment building Monday through Friday so there will be no response. Try Betty Graham's number on the intercom; she acts as the assistant superintendent."

Robert tried to reach Betty Graham, but there was no response. "I guess I have come at a bad time."

"Betty must have just gone to the convenience store, because we chatted earlier and she said she was baking this morning. Are you wanting to rent an apartment? We haven't had an empty apartment for quite some time. Of course..." She paused, lowered her head, sniffed, then proceeded. "Mr. MacDonald's apartment will be free...oh, dear, such a tragedy. It's like losing a son."

Robert could not believe that this dear soul was talking about Trevor. "Do you mean Trevor MacDonald from Northumbria?"

She raised her eyes with interest. "Yes, do you know him? I mean did you know him?"

"Yes, very well. He's my brother-in-law."

She leaned over to hug him. "I'm so sorry for you. He was a perfect gentleman. Now, if I had only been thirty years younger, I would have set my cap for him. I could never understand why he wasn't married." She pointed to the empty chairs in a small alcove in the foyer. "Would you like to join me for a few minutes? You might as well be comfortable while you wait. If you don't mind my company, I'll stay with you until Betty returns. By the way, I'm Jenny Garrison."

"I'm Robert Mascaux. I would love to sit and chat with you." He assisted his companion to one of the chairs.

As she removed her scarf and opened her coat, she continued chattering about Trevor, providing Robert with a very different view of his arch enemy. It was apparent that Trevor was the resident expert on plumbing and electrical work. Even the superintendent relied upon his expertise.

"Mr. MacDonald has come to my apartment in the middle of the night to help me. There are a lot of elderly people in these apartments. He often scrapes windshields for the old folks before he goes to work in the morning. Whenever we have heavy lifting to do, he is there for us.

You know, on his days off, he almost runs a taxi service for us to the mall. Never takes a cent. Doesn't sound like the city, does it?"

Robert was bewildered. He knew that Trevor must possess some redeeming features locked away in that sinister muscle-bound frame; but he had experienced too little of its expression. Although he did acknowledge that Trevor had always been devoted to Leah and his parents, he had convinced himself that Trevor's decency was confined to these three people.

Robert stood up to remove his jacket. "It's getting warm here."

"You can thank Mr. MacDonald for that. When I first moved to this apartment building ten years ago, it was poorly run. The owners never did repairs, nearly froze my first winter. Things changed after your brother-in-law moved in. We all complained, but no one listened. He organized us, had a meeting with the owners. We all threatened to move out. That's when we got this new superintendent...I guess he's not new anymore, been here eight years." Looking at Robert, she leaned toward him to pat his knee. "You must be heart-broken to lose such a fine relative!"

Robert hesitated to reply. His companion assumed it was an emotional moment for Robert. She patted him once again. "It's hard to accept such tragedies. When you are my age, you've lived long enough, but he was so young and gave so much to people...I know how you must be feeling."

Robert felt that he had to respond. How could he tell Jenny Garrison that the man she revered had caused him nothing but pain? It was not acceptable to speak ill of the dead; even to tell the truth as he knew it. He answered as best he could, "Trevor was very devoted to his family."

"Please convey my sympathy to each of them. Tell them that we have lost a real friend..." She searched her purse for a tissue to wipe her sunken eyes. "I grew to depend on your Trevor, I will be lost without him." She sneezed several times. "I hope I am not coming down with a cold; I've had the shots, you know."

Robert spent forty minutes with Mrs. Garrison, listening to a profile of Trevor that was filled with accolades. He was touched by the impact that Trevor had had on Jenny's life and indeed, on the lives of the other apartment dwellers, especially those of more advanced years.

Their conversation ended when Betty Graham arrived. Betty appeared to be a woman in her early thirties; her hair was windswept, her coat partially open as she entered the foyer. She was carrying a bag of groceries in each hand.

She led Robert to her apartment on the second floor; it was directly opposite Trevor's. Before providing him with Trevor's key, she invited Robert to share coffee and fresh biscuits. Robert accepted her kind offer. As they sat at the kitchen table, Robert was provided with a further confirmation of his enemy's other side.

"My husband, Andy, works on the oil rigs off the coast of Newfoundland; he's gone for long periods of time. He and Trevor are good buddies. We have twins, Donnie and Trish, two lively seven year olds. Quite a handful! Trevor is a great father substitute; takes the kids to sports events and does all the things Andy does when he's here. I often wondered why Trevor didn't have kids; he was a natural with them. Robert, do you have kids of your own?"

Robert lowered his coffee cup to the table. "No, Leah and I never had any children."

"Trevor never said much about his family; oh, he talked about his parents, but I can't remember him mentioning his brother-in-law."

Robert was uneasy responding. "We...we weren't very close, one of those things that happens in families. We just lived our lives apart from each other." Once again, Robert found himself struggling with the growing awareness that he had perhaps misjudged Trevor, he had created an arch enemy that was devoid of feeling; someone who had no virtues. It was easier to dislike Trevor by imagining that Trevor was cruel to everyone.

He wondered if Trevor should have been told the truth of Leah's rape. Would he have accepted the truth? Could he and Trevor have spent their lives supporting each other rather than detesting each other? He had broken his promise to Leah when he told the truth to his mother; later he had shared the secret with Rachel. He had rationalized that Trevor would never accept the truth. Now he was not so sure.

Betty left the kitchen for a moment, returning with a framed photo featuring Trevor receiving a plaque. "Trevor attends the same church that we attend. Andy and Trevor co-ordinate the Saturday program for teens, sort of a drop in centre. They started with just themselves and a handful of teens. Now there are twenty adults who work with over two hundred city youth, helping to provide a place to hang out on Saturday, arranging sports events, camping trips, and so on. Trevor is there fulltime when he is not working in construction. This photo was taken last September at a reception given by the church to honour Trevor's work. That's the bishop presenting him with the award. Are you Roman Catholic, Robert?"

"No, I attend the Anglican Church."

"I thought you weren't because this photo appeared on the cover of our diocesan newsletter so you would probably have seen it. Strange his mother didn't have a copy?"

"As I mentioned, Trevor didn't share a great deal with us about his life, a very private person."

Betty poured herself another cup of coffee, lifting the pot to see if Robert wanted a refill. Robert passed his mug to her. "I guess he was private. We knew he went to Northumbria some weekends and he frequently flew to Toronto for holidays; never really discussed his time away. I suspected he might have a girlfriend in Toronto, but he would never admit it."

Robert sipped his coffee, thinking of Trevor, wondering if he had ever been in love. He was discovering a Trevor he had not known existed. Perhaps Trevor had more than a girlfriend in Toronto; perhaps he was a father. He looked at his watch, realizing that it was now early afternoon. He was grateful to Mrs. Garrison and Betty for helping him to see Trevor in a better light; he would need time to sort out what he had learned, to reappraise his estimation of Trevor. He wanted to share his revelations with Rachel and his mother; to understand how Trevor could be so loved in Halifax and yet so feared by him.

Leaving Betty's apartment, he stood at Trevor's door, hesitating to push it open. He felt like an intruder. He knew that of all the people in the world, Trevor would not want his brother-in-law to enter his home, to look through his private papers, to make any decisions concerning him. Trevor would not want more contact with Robert in death than they had had in life. He had spent his life trying to second guess Trevor in order to protect himself. As he entered the apartment, he thought of soldiers entering enemy territory. He wondered if he should check for traps; he walked cautiously, almost afraid to touch anything.

The apartment was immaculate. He had imagined empty beer bottles would be strewn everywhere, clothes would be on the floor and dirty dishes piled in the sink. He felt so uncomfortable that he simply wandered from the living-room to the kitchen, stopping to open the refrigerator door. The fridge was empty; it apparently had been recently cleaned. He entered the bedroom and found the bed neatly made; the closet was filled with Trevor's jeans and dress pants hanging in an orderly fashion beside dress shirts, T-shirts, casual shirts. A faint smell of Old Spice aftershave lingered in the closet, floating into the bedroom as he stood with the closet door open; the splash-on scent was one of Trevor's trademarks. He claimed it was the "only real male scent". A large crucifix hung over the headboard of the double bed. The dresser contained a number of framed photos, including one of his parents' fiftieth anniversary, another one of Leah and Trevor taken at Leah's graduation from Teachers College. There was a photo of an elderly woman seated in a rocking chair, with a blonde teenager beside her; Robert did not recognize them. There was also a photo of Andy, Betty and the twins.

He was amazed at the orderliness of the apartment but perhaps it was what he did not see that puzzled him most. He had fully expected to find girlie pin-ups everywhere, and to see evidence of Trevor's coarseness. He found instead an apartment that was cozy and inviting.

Robert entered the second bedroom which Trevor used as his office and workout room. Sets of weights, barbells, dumbbells, cables and a workout bench occupied one portion of the room. A computer, printer, scanner, bookcase and desk lined the remaining wall of the room. Robert was not surprised to see the workout equipment, but he had never thought of Trevor being interested in computers. He sat at Trevor's desk, opening the main drawer. He withdrew a white envelope bearing his name. It shocked him to discover a letter addressed to him. He decided that Trevor had failed to mail his latest threat. Now that the battle of the brothers-in-law had ended, he thought of simply dropping the envelope into the wastepaper basket near the desk. He held the envelope in his hand for a few moments, relented, and opened it. The content of the letter was even more startling than the revelations he had already discovered about Trevor! The letter had been written on a word processor.

Dear Robert,

You know so little about me. We have never been friends. You have every reason to hate me. I have hated you all my life. I have made your life miserable and in so doing, I have made myself miserable. I have tried to make up for the feelings that I could not control, but every night I had to wrestle with myself.

I loved Leah; I guess I loved her too much. I wanted my sister to have a happy life, instead she had no life. I now realize whose fault it was! That realization has caused me to take certain actions; I don't expect you to understand them or to condone them; but I entrust them to your privacy.

I have recently learned that no one guards a secret more faithfully than you.

I hope you are seated as you read this. You will judge me harshly as you continue to read; I can expect nothing but your scorn, your revulsion.

I have led three lives. You are familiar with the Trevor who grew up in Northumbria and you detest that person. You may discover that the Halifax Trevor is a kinder, more respectable person; I hope that you will know that I did think of others and in some way tried to make a difference in this world. You would not have discovered the Toronto Trevor unless I had chosen to reveal him to you. He will shock you and revolt you, but bear with me.

I know you were never fond of Big Al from your college days; the guy who dated Leah. You will remember that we became friends and you may know that our friendship continued. Al moved to Toronto shortly after graduation. I have spent all my holidays with him since he moved to Toronto.

We are more than friends; we have been lovers. Hard to believe? This isn't the place to explain the lifestyle I chose and the person I chose to share it with.

I had a few other gay encounters in my life; none of them have been in my native province. In the last ten years, I have not had any other contacts than Al; Al has not been as selective.

Al is an educational administrator in the metro area; he is discreet about his lifestyle even if he doesn't mind sharing his apartment with numerous friends.

It was Al who fed me lies about your relationship with Leah. He told me that you had drugged her and taken advantage of her. He fueled my temper each time we met. Of course, until last week, I had no reason to doubt him.

Al has a computer and has been online with internet for two years.

He has teased me about being an illiterate tecky! I decided in October of this year to give the net a try. I thought I would surprise Al by becoming familiar with the net before letting him know that we had another means to communicate with each other. The telephone is costly!

I knew that he frequented some of the more popular gay internet chat rooms and he always used his handle, "Big Al". We liked to play practical jokes on each other so I decided that I would create a fictitious handle and identity for the net, engage him in a relationship, then surprise him. Guess who got the surprise?

Al has never been to the United States. I assumed the handle, "Boston boy", suggesting that I was a college guy, age 20, looking for a friend in Canada. It didn't take long to find Al on the net and because I knew his interests, I created a real interest in this hot stud called Boston boy. I purchased several books on New England so I could mention a few places and sites to whet his appetite for a visit.

I was able to get a printout of our online chats. You wouldn't enjoy any of them, but I have attached one that you need to read.

Big Al: Well, stud. We need to get together soon. How about you visiting me for the Christmas holidays?

Boston boy: Sounds good, but I can't afford the air fare.

Big Al: E-mail your address and I'll see that you get the air fare.

Boston boy: Al, can I ask a personal question?

Big Al: Shoot. Ask anything you like.

Boston boy: Have you ever had sex with a woman?

Big Al: Ya, I've tried it, when I was in college.

Boston boy: You didn't like it?

Big Al: It was ok, but I discovered I liked guys more. Hey, I had my first sex with a college gal I drugged and raped. Found later that her brother was better in bed than she was.

So, Robert, you see what I now know. You were innocent. The man I have shared my intimate life with raped my sister. I am not using the language I want at the moment because I know it would offend you and I've spent a lifetime offending you.

I hate myself for what I did to you. I have had several weeks to examine my life. I realize how blind I was. You have always been so faithful to Leah and to my parents; I resented your goody good efforts, felt you were just trying to show me up. I apologize for everything that I did to you. I was cruel to you and to your American sweetheart, and I know that I was malicious in using your singer friend's misfortunes to my advantage.

You also need to know that a month ago I had to have routine medical tests; I have tested positive with the AIDS virus. Al has been my only contact in ten years. I have wanted to kill him and I had actually begun planning the deed. In the end, I have decided that I have harmed enough people in my life. Al is a bastard, a filthy swine; he deserves to get his dues, but he will get it as he decays with his disease.

I am a coward; I cannot face a lingering death; especially now that I realize what I have done to you. There can never be forgiveness for my cruelty.

I have been to a lawyer and drawn up my will; all my business affairs are in order. I have seen my parish priest, Father Bernie at the basilica, to make my private confession.

Robert lowered the letter to the desk. He sat staring at the workout equipment in front of him. Trevor had been a fanatic about keeping himself in shape. He was obsessed with body building, yet he had been careless in his relationship with Al, knowing that Al did not restrict himself to a monogamous relationship. He stood up, walked over to a set of barbells, lifted one in his right hand for five repetitions, then dropped the barbell to the floor. It was a waste, all this effort.

He paced from the bedroom to the living-room, trying to understand this brother-in-law that he had so misjudged. They should have been friends. Leah had wanted them to get along, but instead they became obsessed with their hatred. He was as guilty as Trevor.

He was filled with remorse as he thought of the agony that Trevor must have endured since his discovery of Al's deed and the knowledge that his own body had been invaded by the killer disease. Al was Trevor's downfall.

Robert had never liked Big Al, now he found himself hating him more than he had ever thought possible to hate one of God's creations.

He understood why Trevor had contemplated killing Al; Al deserved no less. He paced and he paced, his mind bombarded with the most vile thoughts of revenge. He stormed into Trevor's bedroom, turned on the overhead light. The crucifix over the headboard picked up the light sending its image deep within him. He knew that he was overreacting, he knew it was his own guilt that was causing him to focus on Al. Trevor was dead, nothing could bring him back. A few hours ago, he had almost been contented to think that Trevor would no longer be a threat to him and Rachel.

He returned to the desk, picked up the letter to continue reading Trevor's last words to him.

"I apologize for making arrangements without getting your permission and I am asking for your assistance in an important matter. You are listed as my executor. Since I gave up gambling at least ten years ago, I have made sound investments. I have left part of my estate to you and mother and various charities.

I know the kind of person you are! I trust you to help me do something right. There has been one special person in my life that was the son I never had, the nephew I had wanted! His name is Jason Forbes, he lives with his chronically ill grandmother. He has no parents. I have left part of my estate to him. He and I met at the church. He is only twelve years old; very intelligent, a good student despite the rough life he has had. He is good in sports, but really likes drama and writing. I think you would like him. I beg you to at least keep in contact with him. Tell him how fond I was of him.

I won't be at your wedding! I'm sure you are sighing with relief. I know you will want to share this letter with your mother and your wife. I hope you will not share it with anyone else, especially my dear mother who deserved more than she got from me.

'Death row' is such a treacherous spot on the highway. You know I always worry about having an accident on it. But it would be no loss! A dying man!

A cursed man! A guy who hated the wrong man and loved the wrong man!

All I can say is I am sorry; I know it isn't enough. Robert, forgive me!

I have read your singer's autobiography; she rose to fame with her hit single, "Who's Sorry Now?". I'm the one who's sorry now, believe me!

Trevor"

Robert held the letter in his hand; he wasn't sure which emotion he wanted to release. He was filled with the guilt his silence had helped to forge. He thought of the heart that had reached out to so many in the apartment, at the church and to a twelve year old. He remembered the Trevor who had sat beside Leah...He wanted to swear, wanted to throw the workout equipment through the window of the apartment, wanted to call Al on the telephone and tell him what he had done.

He was beside himself with grief, guilt, and hatred, all fighting for control of him.

His inner battle was interrupted by a knock on the apartment door. It was now five o'clock in the afternoon. It was Betty who wondered if he had heard the storm advisory warning.

Betty noticed that Robert was upset, she would have expected nothing less from a relative of Trevor trying to cope with grief.

"Robert, you had mentioned that you would likely return to Northumbria late this evening. You probably haven't heard the storm advisory warning. We can expect fifteen centimetres of snow, followed by freezing rain and high winds. Maybe you should consider staying overnight?"

The last thing Robert wanted to do was to spend a night in Trevor's apartment, but he was not about to risk his life on the highway either. He thought of going to a hotel, but realized that he had work to do at the apartment and some of it could not wait until after he returned from his honeymoon in January.

"Thanks, Betty. I...I guess I will stay over, there's lots to do here."

"Robert, why don't you join us for supper around six-thirty, it's just myself and the twins. Nothing fancy, corn chowder."

He smiled, thinking of his father's story of Annabel's corn chowder. "Corn chowder sounds great!"

"Robert, I called Andy to tell him about Trevor. He really would like to attend the funeral; he and Trevor were close buddies. He can't get back to Halifax until late evening on December 11th. Is it too much to ask that the funeral be delayed?"

Robert thought of the request. The earliest the funeral could be would be December 12, his wedding date.

"Let me make a few calls, we'll see what we can do."

They were interrupted by the telephone ringing. Betty left to prepare supper; Robert returned to Trevor's desk to answer the phone. The telephone featured number and name display. It was Al Phillips calling from Toronto. Robert fought with himself as he reached for the phone. This was his chance to set the record straight, to tell Al what he had done, to tell him what a monster he was. He stood frozen looking at the name of the caller, hearing the ring pierce his ears, feeling his anger rage within. He walked away from the phone, pounding his fist in his left hand.

His life had been filled with gentle people who placed their faith in a God of love. He now faced the greatest challenge to his faith. He knew so well the scripture verse from Leviticus, chapter 19, verse 8:

"Do not seek revenge or bear a grudge against one of your people, but love your neighbour as yourself."

He shook his head in disbelief as he recalled the passage. Sometimes he wondered about his God. Perhaps looking from above makes it easier. He returned to the bedroom and once again was confronted with the crucifix, the symbol of forgiveness, of God's grace. He thought of the words in the most famous prayer ever written, the prayer that Jesus had taught. "Forgive us our sins as we forgive those who sin against us."

He spent the next hour on the telephone with Rachel, sharing with her the shocking insights he had discovered. Rachel had a calming effect on Robert and helped him to realize that they needed to celebrate the good that Trevor had accomplished. They wrestled with the wedding plans. Rachel called Father Sampson to discuss the funeral and then Father Brown to discuss the wedding. She knew that Father Brown had travel plans for December 13. It was agreed to have the funeral at 11:00 o'clock on December 12th; the wedding would be postponed until 3:00 o'clock.

Robert enjoyed his supper with Betty and the twins, and the corn chowder and biscuits were delicious. Later in the apartment the telephone rang as he was preparing the sofa for his bed. It was Al once again. This time he lifted the receiver.

"Hello, Trevor MacDonald's apartment."

There was silence at the other end, so Robert repeated his greeting.

"Trevor MacDonald's apartment."

"Is Trevor there?"

Robert hesitated but continued. "I'm sorry to break bad news to you, but Trevor was killed in a highway accident two nights ago, due to slippery roads."

"Trevor's dead! Oh man!"

"I gather you were a close friend?"

"Yes, very close! I'm calling from Toronto. When is…the funeral?"

"Not until December 12, in Northumbria at 11:00 o'clock."

"I see, I won't be able to make it, but…may I ask whom I am speaking with?"

"Certainly, it's Robert Mascaux, Trevor's brother-in-law."

The receiver clicked; Al could not talk to the man he had betrayed. There was never any further communication between them.

The next morning it was eleven o'clock before Robert was able to leave the apartment. He had called Jason Forbes' grandmother the night before to arrange to meet Jason, suggesting that with her permission he would arrive with lunch for everyone. He checked with Mrs. Forbes to see what he should bring.

It took him a few minutes to find the apartment located in a senior citizens' complex. He was greeted by Mrs. Forbes who was in her late seventies; she walked with a cane. She wore a wig to cover her hair loss as a result of treatment she had received. Jason was a skinny runt with blonde hair and vibrant blue eyes.

The apartment was small, but did have two bedrooms. They sat at a wooden table covered with a white tablecloth. Robert had taken fish and chips for Mrs. Forbes and himself and Jason's favourite burgers and fries. Before eating, Mrs. Forbes asked Jason to say grace. After offering thanks for the food, the three individuals seemed to relax as they chatted about Trevor and Jason.

Mrs. Forbes smiled at Robert. "This is good fish, haddock, I believe. Thank you for bringing us a treat."

Robert swallowed before replying, "How are the burgers, Jason?"

Jason was having trouble handling the giant deluxe burger he held in his hand. His mouth was covered with mustard, ketchup and relish. Beaming, he replied, "My favourite food!"

After the meal was over, the three continued sitting at the table.

Robert asked Jason, "What are your favourite subjects in school?"

Without hesitating, Jason replied, "English, writing class is the best. I want to be a writer when I grow up."

His grandmother's eyes beamed, "Jason writes all the time. Jason, bring Mr. Mascaux the letter you wrote to Trevor's mother." Looking at Robert, she asked, "Would it be inconvenient if we asked you to take the letter to your mother-in-law for Jason?"

"No, by all means. I'd be happy to deliver it."

Mrs. Forbes passed Jason a hand towel to wipe his hands before sending him to his bedroom to get the letter. Upon his return, he sat at the table to read.

Mrs. Forbes laughed as she cautioned her grandson, "Don't put the letter on the table, I think you may have dropped some of the mustard from those huge burgers."

Jason held his letter above the table, reading in a soft voice:

"Dear Mrs. MacDonald,

My name is Jason Forbes. I live with my grandmother in Halifax.

Trevor was very kind to both of us. He took me to the rink to see hockey games and purchased a pair of skates for my birthday. He helps my grandmother get groceries and works around the apartment.

We are sorry that Trevor was killed in an accident. We know you must love him as much as we do. We'll miss him a great deal.

Trevor was going to get me a dog for Christmas, a black Lab. I will have to wait for my dog, but when I get it, I'm calling him Trev, if that is ok with you.

My grandmother checked my spelling!

We hope you will be all right!

Love,
Jason"

When Jason finished reading, he had tears in his eyes. He lifted his head to look at Robert. "Gramma said it is ok to sign the letter with love since Trevor was my best friend. I don't have any parents. Trevor was like my father." His eyes then met his grandmother's, "I guess we are all alone again, gramma."

Robert was deeply moved by Jason's respect and love for Trevor. He saw in Jason the son he had been denied. His god child, young Robert, would be a perfect big brother for Jason. His mind went into overdrive as he tried to sort out all the ramifications of Trevor's legacy. He wondered how he could ever ensure that Trevor's trust in him would be justified. Yesterday he had driven to Halifax, annoyed that his adversary was causing him distress a week before his wedding, now he wanted to ensure that his brother-in-law could rest in peace, knowing his final wishes had been fulfilled.

Before leaving the city, Robert stopped at the basilica, hoping to meet Father Bernie. As he entered the main office, he was met by a secretary who was escorting visitors to the chapel. She informed him that Father Bernie was expected back in his office within a few minutes; she left Robert seated in a chair while she went to the chapel. Robert examined the contents of the office. There was the usual photocopier with shelves housing the paper, two desks, each with a computer, a magazine rack featuring various Roman Catholic publications with one section reserved for periodicals from other denominations. He reached for a copy of the current Nova Scotia diocesan journal. He was reading an article on the struggle of inner city youth when a priest who appeared to be in his late twenties arrived. The priest extended his hand, speaking in a clear resonant voice, "Hello, I'm Father Bernard Davidson, commonly called Father Bernie. And you are?"

Robert replied, "I'm Robert Mascaux from Northumbria."

Father Bernie shocked Robert with his response. "Oh, yes, Trevor's brother-in-law. I have been expecting you."

Robert could not conceal his surprise, "You have been expecting me?"

Father Bernie motioned for Robert to join him in the office nearest to them. Once inside, the priest closed the door and asked Robert if he would like to remove his jacket. He suggested that they sit in two arm chairs separated by a stand which contained several lush plants.

Father Bernie was obviously good at pastoral work; he had the ability to make total strangers feel comfortable in his presence. His warm friendly smile easily broke down any barriers that might separate him from even the most reluctant guest. He was wearing his black clerical suit with the familiar white collar.

"Trevor and I have known each other for six years. We have worked closely together on the youth programs at the basilica. He is a natural with young people. The boys admire his build, his strength, his no nonsense approach. He speaks their language, accepts them for who they are. Until Trevor got involved with our youth ministry, it was a failure. We failed not because we didn't attempt to do the right thing, we wanted to do too much. Trevor taught us how to trust the youth with responsibility; it was a hard lesson to learn. Our first attempts backfired, but he insisted that the church above all other agencies had to be the home of trust, of faith. It worked!" He glanced at his guest. "Ah, but you did not come to hear about our youth ministry."

Robert feigned a smile. "No, but I am interested to hear about Trevor's leadership in the parish."

Father Bernie looked compassionately at Robert. "Robert, I guess your friends call you Rob, is that correct?"

Robert nodded in agreement.

"And I know you detest being called Robbie!"

Robert blushed as he nodded again.

"I guess you can tell that Trevor and I have had a long discussion about his relationship with you. You will know that he made a full confession prior to his accident. He paused, searching Robert's face for a revelation. "It was such a coincidence! Nevertheless, we chatted about the major issues beyond the confessional booth and it was Trevor who assured me that you would seek me out. He instructed me to share anything we had discussed with you."

Robert fidgeted in his chair, feeling uncomfortable and yet wanting to relax so that he could share his own feelings with this compassionate man of God. "I am confused by all of this. Yesterday, I came to Halifax knowing a Trevor that I felt had no real value in life, he was my constant tormentor. I think I had learned to loathe him. In the last twenty-four hours, I have been introduced to a Trevor who sounds like a candidate for sainthood." He was annoyed at his choice of words and the tone he had used. "Sorry about that, I didn't really mean to diminish Trevor's good deeds here..."

Father Bernie did not wait for Robert to conclude. "Robert, you have reason to be confused and bitter, but I pray that you will learn to forgive your brother-in-law. He is a tragic figure. I know about his Toronto life and it shocks me and appalls me because it has destroyed him. I do not condemn his lifestyle; I applaud his good deeds."

Robert found himself becoming emotional, but straightened in the chair to gain control of himself. "You have no idea how cruel Trevor has been. Next week I am to be married. I...we have had to change our wedding time to accommodate Trevor's funeral. Isn't there great irony in that? Even in his death, he haunts me. Oh, I am sounding bitter and I don't mean to be. I have been touched by all the testimonies I have heard. It is just overwhelming."

Father Bernie reached for a *Bible* that rested on his desk. Showing Robert the *Bible*, he spoke in a reassuring tone. "Robert, you have been wronged by Trevor. You have reason to dislike him and to be skeptical of the revelations you have discovered about his devotion to others. No one would expect you to fully appreciate the Trevor we have come to admire and respect. This book, as I know from Trevor, is not unfamiliar to you. This book is the story of people who often meant well but failed time and time again to be what their creator had intended. There was nothing in them that could redeem them; it was only God's grace that set them free. Trevor has confessed his sin, he has repented, he has been given the assurance that he is pure in the sight of God. God doesn't keep a record of confessed sins. He forgets and forgives. He asks us to do the same."

Robert was unable to control his tears. He sobbed; he could not speak. Father Bernie laid his hand on his stooped shoulders.

"Robert, you are a person of faith, I knew that before you entered the room. You are wearing a ring on your right hand that features a cross. That cross will be your source of strength in the days ahead. I know you are not Roman Catholic. Would you, however, join me in the chapel in prayer for Trevor? Perhaps we could light a candle in his memory."

Robert was barely able to respond, "Yes...I would like that."

Priest and guest went to the chapel where the silence, the radiant light shining through the beautiful stained glass window featuring Christ as the good shepherd enveloped them. Prayers were said, candles lighted. It was a time for forgiveness and healing.

Following their quiet time, Father Bernie indicated that he would like to assist at Trevor's funeral in Northumbria. He would check with

Northumbria's Father Sampson, if Robert approved. Robert felt it would be most fitting to have Trevor's priest present for his final rites.

As Robert drove back to Northumbria, he was in awe of what he had learned about Trevor and delighted that through Father Bernie he had begun to heal the wounds that his relationship with Trevor had carved in his soul year after year.

- - - Northumbria, December 12, 10:30 a.m.

Robert started his car while he scraped his windshield to remove the heavy frost. He was headed for Garden Estates to pick up his mother and mother-in-law and Rachel. Rachel had moved in with Bertha and Ellen after they had received the tragic news. The ladies were waiting for him as he stopped in front of the apartment. Ellen MacDonald was heart-broken; she had stayed for an hour alone with Trevor after the visitors had left the night before. She had said good-bye to her son; now she did not want to spoil the celebration of Trevor's life by dissolving in tears. She knew that others would look to her for their strength.

As Robert drove into the church parking lot, he could not dismiss the image that invaded his thoughts. He noticed a bench on the same spot where he had quarrelled with Trevor and had lost. His mind instantly flashed back to the park where he and Howie had encountered Trevor. This time Trevor's challenge backfired! He saw fists flying, heard the insults he endured. He helped his mother-in-law out of the car, seeing in her eyes the son she mourned, the son that resembled more closely the Trevor he had discovered in Halifax.

As they entered the church, a bus from Halifax arrived bearing forty-six mourners from the city. Andy and Betty had arranged to provide transportation for church workers, residents of the apartment and youth who would have had difficulty getting to Northumbria.

Robert entered the church with his mother-in-law leaning on his arm. Rachel walked behind with Bertha. The church was almost full; once the bus was emptied, there would be few pews vacant.

Margie had been asked to play for the funeral although she was organist at the Anglican Church. Her music filled the church as they walked down the aisle. Father Bernie and Father Sampson stood behind the altar waiting for the family to be seated. Frances, a friend of the family, sang two solos, “Ave Maria” and “Here I Am Lord”. It was Andy Graham who delivered the eulogy.

Andy was a tall stocky man with curly brown hair that hung over his forehead. He had a boyish look even at thirty-five. He stood to one side of the lectern to speak to Trevor’s family and friends. His deep voice and capable projection did not need a microphone for enhancement. He concluded his eulogy by saying:

“We have come here today because we have known Trevor MacDonald. He has touched our lives; we are better people because we have known him. I ask you now to search your memories, to recall the reason you are here today.

Do you recall -

the child who made you laugh as he took his first steps, said his first words?

the teenager who wanted to prove his maturity?

the son who loved his parents; the brother who adored his sister?

the construction worker who was a buddy?

the youth worker who knew when to lead a prayer and when to hit the ball courts?

the guy who provided free taxi service?

the leader who turned an apartment building into a place we could call home?

Do you recall the friend we knew as Trevor MacDonald? If you do, your life was better because he was here among us.”

When Andy resumed his seat, there was a moment of silence for the congregation to reflect upon his message. Of all those present, no one mourned more openly than Jason. Jason wept throughout the entire service. His body shook with emotion. He was seated beside Betty who placed her arm around him and provided the necessary tissues.

Everyone was invited to the church hall following the service for refreshments served by the ladies’auxiliary. The time of fellowship was a time for Northumbria and Halifax to be united in their sharing of memories. It was good for Northumbria to hear about the Trevor they had seen too little of, and had never really known.

Mrs. MacDonald was delighted with the affection shown for her son. She sensed too that Robert had come to see some merit in her son despite the abuse he had borne at Trevor's hand.

Robert had made arrangements with Andy and the bus driver for an extra passenger to be included on the return trip to Halifax. Just before the bus was to pull out of the church yard, Jason was asked to go to the back door of the glebe house. Robert escorted him.

As they walked toward the back of the house, Robert informed Jason he had a gift for him to take back to Halifax.

Jason was excited, "A gift for me! But why?"

Robert placed his hand on Jason's shoulder. "It is a gift that Trevor would want you to have; it is something for you to remember him by."

As they reached the back of the house, the door slowly opened, allowing a black Labrador Retriever pup to gain its freedom. The pup ran frantically in all directions, spied Jason and ran directly toward him.

"Trev, Trev, my own dog!" He ran to the excited puppy, lifting him high above his head, then tenderly holding him in his arms.

From the bus, the passengers watched the transformation in Jason's face. They knew that he was grieving for the loss of his friend; they, too, felt his pain. They watched his face light up as he held the black puppy, allowing the dog to lick his face and hands. This time, the tears were of joy!!

As Jason returned to the bus with his new friend, everyone clapped to show their approval. Trev was the focus of everyone's attention on the return trip to the city.

It was after twelve o'clock when the bus departed; the bride and groom had little time to change from their mourning clothes to their wedding attire. They had said good-bye to Trevor. Robert no longer had an antagonist; he had forgiven and was forgiven. He was now ready to begin his life with his bride. Together they would exchange their vows, share their love, and spend their lives together. The day was not over, it was just beginning; a wedding and a birthday had yet to be celebrated. After their honeymoon, they would settle in their new home, they would be husband and wife. There might even be an extra room in their Tudor home one day for a dog and his young master.

Chapter 9:

The Wedding Cake

Northumbria, December 12, 12:30 p.m.

Robert had shaved and showered for the second time on this day of days. He stood in the foyer of their home on Smith Avenue adjusting his pink silk tie in front of the full length mirror. He had chosen to wear a white double breasted sport coat for his wedding even though no fashion magazine would have recommended such a choice for a December wedding. He and Rachel had decided that their lives had always been dictated by convention; they were determined that their wedding ceremony, reception and honeymoon would not be restricted by concern for tradition. He checked his navy trousers for lint, glanced at his black patent leather shoes; then walked into the den for one last look at the memory boxes.

He looked at the two boxes of diaries and letters that had consumed his attention and at the souvenirs of their lives that filled the room. His glance lingered as he scanned the book shelves housing his treasured classics. Daisy and Rose had become published authors late in life. He and Rachel had already had articles published; perhaps it was not impossible to think that one day *With Love, With Connie* might find its way into print. Perhaps one day, others would read of their journey with Connie, would be introduced to the bouquet, and the manor.

Robert gently closed the door of the den, lingering, maintaining his hold of the doorknob, recalling the memories that were preserved within the room. He glanced at his new cufflinks; it was only two days ago that they had emerged from their secret dwelling place. He recalled their discovery.

- - - - - Northumbria, December 10, 1997

Robert and Rachel were seated in the living-room of the house that would be their home when they began their married life together. Each was seated in a Flanders Cove Queen Anne chair.

Rachel was wearing a red pullover sweater decorated with a delicate pattern of snowflakes embroidered with shimmering gold thread; a delicate golden snowflake with a diamond centre hung from each ear. Her black pants draped over her gold slippers. Even with the gold accents, she was wearing her silver guardian angel bracelet. Robert was wearing a mauve silk shirt with his favourite black vest, black trousers and his comfortable deerskin moccasins.

Robert and Rachel both liked decorating. They had enjoyed unpacking the festive decorations that had become traditional expressions of the season on Melrose Road in Flanders Cove. Many of the wreaths and garlands were lovely creations, crafted by Iris with assistance from her sisters. Robert and Rachel were somewhat disappointed that they would not be at home to celebrate their first Christmas together, but they had always dreamed of going on a Caribbean cruise for their honeymoon. They had studied the travel brochures, searching for the perfect cruise. Their choice provided a ten day cruise with a connection that enabled them to spend five days in Bermuda. They would then fly to Toronto for a few days.

Today they were enjoying the fireplace and Christmas music; the music they would have too little time to savour during the season itself. One of Connie's Christmas albums was playing. Now that their record collection was combined, they had duplicates of most of Connie's singles, albums and CD's. Robert examined the covers of the three Connie Francis Christmas albums they had collected. The earliest MGM albums were entitled, "Connie Francis: Christmas in My Heart", featuring a youthful Connie wearing a traditional European country costume with a mop cap, her hands folded in prayer to the side of her face. The more recent version of the album was produced by Sessions records, featuring a far different cover photo of Connie, reminiscent of photos used for some of Connie's Jewish albums, featuring her with a lace shawl draped over her head, with Connie gazing upwards. The album was entitled, "Merry Christmas: Connie Francis". Although there was little variance in the songs included on the two different releases,

Rachel was pleased that the 1981 release featured Connie's hit, "Baby's First Christmas". Both she and Robert had seen Connie perform the song on the "Ed Sullivan Show" many years ago. Robert was fond of Connie's hit, "Blue Winter" which the newer release also included.

As Connie sang "Adeste Fidelis" Robert chuckled. "This is the earliest I have ever decorated for Christmas, and I know the bouquet did not decorate for the festive season until a few days before Christmas. Decorating for Christmas is time consuming, so why not enjoy the house trimmed with angels, the creche, candles and garlands as long as possible? I love the smell of a fresh fir tree."

Rachel agreed, "Robert, I think we will always decorate this early! Even if Margie scolds us for rushing the season. I know that Advent is a special time to help us prepare for the birth of the Christ Child, but I do love the decorations and the music." She moved toward the wooden Advent candle stand located on a round table near the fireplace. The stand featured three purple candles and a pink one surrounding a white one. "Let's light all of our candles, we'll really rush the season."

Robert took a long wooden match from a brass container on the hearth, struck the match on the bottom of the container and proceeded to light the five candles. Rachel joined Robert at the table as he continued, "Let's see if I can light the candles in the correct order: hope, peace, joy, love and the white candle for the Christ Child."

As he finished lighting the Christ candle, he held up the burning match for Rachel to blow out. Rachel placed her hand on his. "The Advent wreath is one of the special ceremonies I love about this season and lighting them with Christmas music is a wonderful touch." She placed her index finger over her lips. " Shh! I won't tell anyone that we are rushing the season!"

Robert winked, "If I see Margie coming, we'll turn off the Christmas music! I understand the church's stand, we can't enjoy Christmas fully without Advent, and I know the secular world plays Christmas music to increase sales, but the music is so beautiful!"

Rachel got up, walked toward the mahogany table in front of the bow window. An enormous Christmas cactus housed in a brass jardiniere was just beginning to flower. She held one of the pink blooms in her hand. "Iris would be pleased that her favourite plant survived a trip through Customs."

She rushed toward Robert, throwing her arms around his neck, kissing him over and over again. "Just making up for each Christmas we didn't share together."

"Rachel, it is incredible to think we are finally together! And we are alone in our own home, if only for a few hours!"

Rachel stood up, sauntering around the room, touching the furnishings. "Oh Robert, there are so many reminders of Flanders Cove in this room and I just love this refurbished settee from the manor. I'm also glad we purchased a few new pieces of furniture, especially the curio cabinet to display our prized treasures, including some of the awards our families have accumulated."

Robert extended his arms to his loved one, "You are my treasure. Come here and we'll make up for more of those missed Christmases. Let me see, we must have reached 1963, now that was a good year!" They embraced and kissed...He returned to his Queen Anne chair.

Rachel allowed herself to fall into his lap, to feel his inviting arms surround her, to feel his gentle touch, to be enveloped in his love. They had spent a lifetime apart; they had dreamed of such moments. They were together!

Robert enjoyed teasing Rachel; he and Rose had often inflicted Southern accents on the family at times of celebration. "Excuse me, madam, but if you do not pour the tea, it will be cold. No lady of the house should serve her gentleman friend cold tea, it is just not done, I assure you!"

Rachel abruptly withdrew from his embrace, and stood, mimicking his accent. "Why sir, tea would be preferable to the kisses I have had the pleasure to share with you in the last few minutes. Cold tea would be as inviting!" She began walking to the tea wagon that was near the stereo.

Robert pursued her, causing her to turn. He wrapped his arms around her, pulling her to him. They kissed passionately, unaware of the tea waiting to be poured and the music playing. Time stood still, memories faded, intimacy was shared as they embraced and allowed their lips to speak for them.

The telephone interrupted their intimate moment. Rachel answered the call. It was Margie. Connie was singing "Baby's First Christmas". Rachel giggled.

"No, you are not interrupting." She blushed as she winked at Robert. "We are just about to have tea and check on last minute wedding details."

Margie teased, "Do I hear Christmas music?"

Rachel confessed, "Oh! It's Robert, he just can't get enough Christmas music!"

Robert pointed his index finger to Rachel, raising his voice for Margie to hear. "Don't believe her, she forced me to put the Christmas albums on!"

Margie had called to check on the time for her and Howie to meet Robert and Rachel at the church to decorate the angel tree for the wedding. As Rachel hung up the receiver, she moved toward several large cardboard boxes resting in the foyer.

"Margie was confirming our arrangements for decorating the angel tree. Rob, if nothing else, our wedding gifts will be unique!"

"Rachel, we are doing the right thing! We certainly don't need wedding gifts, just look at all the stuff we have! We already have two of most things! How many coffee pots and electric kettles do we need?"

Rachel returned to her Robert, dragging one of the cardboard boxes. "I think our guests really appreciated our suggestion for wedding gifts. Instead of giving us something we don't need, they can make a donation to the local food bank which desperately needs funds for this season."

"I know the food bank is pleased; Gloria Baxter, the co-ordinator, called to thank us yesterday; she had already received over 170 wedding donations."

"Rob, I'm glad we added the second suggestion; I thought some of the guests might think it frivilous, but they have complied with our wishes."

"How many wedding invitations ask the guests to make a donation to a food bank and forward an angel decoration for an evergreen tree to be featured in a church. Father Brown was thrilled with the idea and so were the ladies of the altar guild; it will be the beginning of a tradition."

Rachel withdrew three delicate white crocheted angels from the box; each was beautifully crafted, starched, and each held a floral bouquet in her hand. "Your mother and Ellen did a marvellous job on these angels. Look at these little bouquets. This angel has roses, this one daisies, and just look at these irises."

Rob approached Rachel to examine the angels. "You saw the two mother sent this morning?"

"There are two more?"

Robert went into the foyer, searched through the other boxes until he found a plastic bag. He returned to Rachel with the bag. "Two more angels, same craftswomen! Two different bouquets. Can you guess what flowers they have in their little hands?"

Rachel giggled, "Let me see...lilies and violets?"

Robert beamed, "How did you guess?" He passed the bag to Rachel.

Withdrawing the angels, Rachel exclaimed! "Five special angels for the tree! Made with love, remembering love! Oh Rob, it was so thoughtful of your mother and Ellen to remember my family."She placed the angels with their bouquets in the cardboard box. "I am amazed at the variety of angels our guests have sent." She lifted up a silver angel with wings spread out; the angel carried a banner with 'joy' etched on it. Another angel was a handpainted ceramic one. Several pewter angels from a nearby factory were included.

Robert reached into the box to examine a glass angel who was carrying a harp. "The music of angels." Connie was singing "Ave Maria" as the couple delighted in examining each of the delicate creations.

Rachel laughed as she held up an angel made by a five year old. "This is adorable! I think we can call it, "A Charlie Brown angel'. It is so sweet, just look at the legs, dangling below the white fabric of the dress. The halo is crooked and she looks..."

Robert couldn't resist interrupting. "She's a night angel!"

"A night angel? I don't get it?"

"She's struck on moonshine!"

Rachel tapped Robert gently on the head with the angel, "You may be right! Oh Rob, the angels will look wonderful on the tree. I am so pleased Father Brown agreed to have us decorate the tree for the wedding; I know he is sensitive to this whole issue of rushing into Christmas."

"Don't forget we usually have a Jesse tree during Advent; an angel tree need not necessarily be a Christmas decoration."

Smiling, Rachel responded, "Rob, you don't have to convince me!" Rachel extended her right hand to the bottom of the box and giggled as she lifted a chubby angel from the box. "Now this one is a masterpiece. I almost want to keep it for myself!" She held up a small white teddy bear with burgundy wings. "Rob, this is adorable!"

Robert couldn't resist adding, "He looks as if he's eaten too many galettes! Must be a Belgian angel!"

After the angels had been carefully returned to their resting places, Robert reminded Rachel that tea had not been served. Earlier Rachel had made English trifle, following with accuracy her aunt's recipe; Robert had made fresh galettes so that their tea would have their two favourite desserts. They were using the Florentine china, knowing that the bouquet would have approved of their choice.

Robert held in his hand a crystal stemmed dessert glass filled with English trifle. The whipped cream with crushed walnuts and red maraschino cherries covered a blending of custard, raspberry jam and cake laced with sherry. He looked at the dessert, recalling the many occasions when he had enjoyed the same dessert at Flanders Cove. He raised his dessert glass to touch Rachel's, "Here's to Daisy!" With eyes closed he savoured the first burst of flavour. "All desserts should have three ingredients: they must be moist, contain whipped cream and reveal a touch of sparkle! Rachel, this is delicious...not quite up to Daisy's, but good, nevertheless."

Rachel laughed, "And may I return the compliment?" She passed Robert a galette. "I tasted one of your galettes earlier; they, too, are delicious, but Bertha's always have that extra ingredient!

Robert nodded in agreement. "We'll just have to do our best to improve. Perhaps the second serving will be better!"

Following their enjoyment of Flanders Cove trifle and Northumbria galettes, it was time for them to return to the past, to open a gift that Henry Thomas had sealed in a strongbox long before there was any thought of Rachel getting married, a gift that had intrigued Rachel since she first discovered its existence in 1967. Mr. King had known what was inside the strongbox; she knew it wasn't a gold pocket watch, but she had no other clues. It was a moment of nostalgia as she and Robert sat together, so many years removed from the day when her grandfather had closed the lid of the strongbox concealing its treasures. The time had come for Rachel to open the box that her grandfather had requested she open on the occasion of her marriage. As she looked at it, she remembered the times when she had been certain she would never experience the joy of opening the box. She thought of Derek and the love they had shared. For a brief time she had thought she and Derek might savour this moment together. She threw a kiss to Robert, whispering to him.

"I love you. I have always loved you. In two days we will be married. I can hardly believe I am here in Northumbria, in our home, alone with you, sharing this precious moment."

Robert left his chair to sit near Rachel on the floor. He held her hands in his as he kissed them tenderly. Looking into her eyes, his face glowed with his love as he spoke. "It is almost eerie, isn't it? Your grandfather placed something in this strongbox decades ago, a gift for our wedding. He could never have known the journey that the box would take, in time and across an international border. He had never met me, but he had met my mother. I am so glad I am the one to share this with you." He raised himself to kiss her lips.

Rachel hesitated as she placed the key in the lock of the strongbox. "I really can't imagine what is here, but the time has come to find out." The lock clicked, she raised the lid, discovering an envelope and two burgundy velvet jewellery boxes. She opened the envelope, held the letter in her hand for a moment, hugged Robert, then began reading.

June 17, 1956

My Dear Rachel,

Congratulations on your wedding! I am sure the man you have chosen
to love will have recognized the treasure he has been blessed to share.
I pray that you both will enjoy the happiness that
Violet and I experienced
in our life together. Trust each other and honour each other;
but above all cherish each other!

You will know that Violet transformed me; she saw the goodness
that needed to be released and she did so,
not always with my cooperation.
In the early days, we struggled with finances as
I speculated and invested.
By the time we celebrated our twenty-fifth anniversary, our investments

were at the peak of their performance. We have enjoyed our home
and the benefits of being financially secure. Violet was the instrument
that led us to share our blessings with others;
we rarely thought ourselves extravagant.

For our twenty-fifth anniversary, we did allow ourselves to purchase
tasteful gifts which were more costly than the ordinary personal gifts
that we exchanged on other special occasions.
The gifts were given in love,
an expression of twenty-five years together, with a prayer
that we might enjoy another twenty-five.

It is the gifts that we exchanged as we celebrated our quarter of
century together that I now give to you and your husband. Enjoy them,
remember the bond that you share with your family;
remember to cherish not gold and silver, not even memories,
but each other.

God bless you as you begin your life together!

Love,

Grandad Thomas

Rachel withdrew a tissue from the sleeve of her sweater. She wiped her eyes. "Rob, I can't help the tears. I hate tears; I've cried enough for three lifetimes, but I can picture grandad writing this letter."

Robert kissed Rachel's hand. "Rachel, there are tears of joy and tears of sorrow. We can expect to share tears of joy in the next few days. Let's just enjoy them!" Taking the letter from Rachel's hand, "Rachel, this gesture is unique, it was so long ago that he locked these jewellery boxes away and yet your grandfather has come to our wedding with his gift, with their gift. I think we need to open them, to allow them to speak to us."

Rachel placed the larger burgundy box on her lap, and gently opened the cover, revealing a sparkling necklace. The necklace featured four diamonds set in a silver weave of ornate leaves and flowers. The four diamonds surrounded an angel who looked remarkably like the guardian angel on Rachel's bracelet. The angel lifted up to reveal a golden heart placed in the centre of a cross. The craftsmanship was absolutely exquisite. Rachel withdrew the necklace, held it against her sweater, giggling. "Doesn't go well with the gold accents, oh, but it is so beautiful. Diamonds, silver and gold! A gift of love! I now have two pieces of jewellery to treasure and one more to come." Rachel returned the necklace to the jewel box. She then withdrew the smaller box. "Robert, this must be grandmother's gift, I suspect it is intended for you. Open it." She passed him the burgundy box.

Robert opened the cover to find a set of gold cufflinks, each with a diamond centre. The diamonds sparkled in the morning light. "Rachel, they are handsome!" He lifted one of the cufflinks out of the box to examine it. "I'll just have to wear them for our wedding, but I don't have a shirt with French cuffs, threw them out years ago."

Rachel looked puzzled, "Oh yes, French cuffs. You are driving to Halifax tomorrow morning to meet with Trevor's lawyer. Let's call a few of the men's shops to see if they carry shirts with French cuffs, I am sure the formal rental places will have one, even if we can't purchase one."

"Great idea! Rachel, your grandfather has given me a gift; cufflinks for my wedding; long ago he gave a bracelet to my mother! I just think the coincidence is unbelievable!"

"Rob, you once said that nothing about our relationship was ordinary. Rose certainly thought so."

Robert laughed as he remembered Rose's comments, "And she told us so!" Mimicking Rose, "'You'll never be accused of rushing into a relationship, Robert!' I constantly reminded her that the legendary tortoise wins the race, but her comeback was, 'But a tortoise can live for several hundred years!'"

The gifts were returned to their containers until December 12, when they would sparkle as the church lights and candles reflected their beauty, enhanced their beauty; and endowed them with the light of the moment, the light of joy and love!

Robert and Rachel continued to enjoy looking at the fire, listening to Connie, remembering the past that had blessed them, the past that had just reached out to them.

Robert got up to put another log on the fire. As he returned to his position on the floor beside Rachel, he smiled mischieviously. "Any chance of having a cup of coffee?"

"Coffee, we just had tea!"

"Father always said tea was for the British; the Belgians all drank coffee with a touch of chicory."

Feigning annoyance, Rachel added, "And tea is definitely for ladies! Well, if you want coffee, you shall have it. I'll wait here while you make it. I'm sure I would never get the correct blend!"

"I guess I walked into that one with my eyes open." Robert picked up the tea tray as he left the room. "I'll be back in a minute."

Rachel rose from her chair and once more walked around the room, looking at the Christmas decorations, remembering the bouquet fussing over the garlands as they added each ornament.

She went to the stereo to put on another album. She chose, "Connie Francis Sings Bacharach and David" featuring such songs as: "The Look of Love", "This Girl's in Love with You" and "What the World Needs Now (Is Love, Sweet Love)". She thought of the media's recent coverage of wars, political unrest, economic instability. It would soon be Christmas, the stores were bustling with shoppers. Somewhere amidst all of the commercialism and world unrest, a child would be born once again with a promise that the world would be a better place. The world did need the gift of love; the world had already received the gift of love. It was time for the annual reminder of what really matters in life. She looked at the boxes containing their gifts; she knew they were expensive, but they were priceless, they were given in love.

Robert returned with a pot of coffee and two Spode mugs on a tray. "I assume you would like coffee, madam?" he asked in a manner befitting a butler serving a gracious Victorian lady seated in a Queen Anne chair.

"James, I would love to have a cup of your freshly ground brew."

As they enjoyed the aroma of the coffee, Rachel showed Robert the cover of the album they were listening to. "Robert, we both have copies of this album. What association do you have with this one?"

Robert thought for a moment, "Oh yes, I first heard that album in 1970 just before I learned the secret of the guardian angel bracelet. When mother shared her secret, I shared mine, confessing the reason for my marriage to Leah. One of the songs featured on the album is

"Promises, Promises" from the Broadway production of the same name. I thought of the promises I had made, the promises I was breaking. Every time I hear the album I return to 1970."

Rachel shook her head, "Yes, it was 1970 when Mr. King gave me the information regarding the strongboxes. I guess it was more than coincidence that I should select this album to play today. Connie's music is filled with our private stories; filled with poignant memories. Rob, you'll remember that one of the hit tunes featured is, "Magic Moments". She walked toward him, reached up to kiss him on the cheek. "This is a magic moment!" They shared their magic moment as they embraced, expressing their love for each other.

Robert picked up the album jacket, looking at the cover photo of Connie. Connie was looking alluring in a long red dress with two front slits extending far enough to allow her to reveal a shapely leg. She was wearing a sparkling silver pin as an accessory. Robert had always liked that portrait of Connie.

Rachel smiled, "Rob, should I be jealous of Connie?"

Robert teased, "Jealous of the gal who introduced us and sustained us through our difficult times, never. Besides we are having a party for her on her birthday, the day of our wedding!"

Rachel chuckled, "We will have a birthday party and the guest of honour will be absent. I think it was sweet of Margie to suggest that we have a theme for the dance following dinner. The band will play Connie's hits and Glenda is going to sing. We'll have not only a wedding cake, but also a birthday cake to celebrate Connie's 59th birthday!"

"I hope Glenda's voice holds out. Margie has been worried about her cold!"

"I'm sure it will work out! Rachel, we both want the wedding ceremony to be a time of worship as we stand before the altar and are united with God's blessing; it is a sacred moment when we confess our love, confess our faith, share our rings, share the body and blood of a living God, and do this with family and friends. I am glad we have planned a rather whimsical reception! Hearing Connie's hits is a perfect way to end the evening." Blushing, "Well, to end the evening that we share with others!"

"Are you blushing? Mr. Mascaux, I am sure that the evening will just begin as we share our final dance at the reception!"

Robert held a galette over his coffee mug. "Here's to my father!" He dunked one end of the galette into the coffee, then enjoyed the dripping sweetness. "Now if only I had a piece of apple pie to do the same thing."

Rachel joined in celebrating Camille, she dipped one end of her galette into her mug. "To Camille!"

The couple continued to enjoy teasing each other, recalling fond memories, sharing the sights and sounds of the festive season, and thoughts of their approaching wedding; they were basking in their love, a love that was in reach of the wedding cake.

Northumbria, December 12, 2:15 p.m.

As Robert adjusted the cufflink on his left wrist, he could see Howie's car coming to a stop outside. He slipped on his overcoat and joined young Robert and Howie for the trip to the church.

Howie, young Robert and Derek were all wearing white double breasted sportcoats, pale blue shirts, pink silk ties, and black dress pants to complement the groom's attire. The men wore a single pink rose for a boutiniere. As Robert stepped outside, he was pleased that the ground was free of snow and ice. The sky was overcast, but no precipitation was expected for several days.

Meanwhile, Rachel was at Garden Estates with Bertha, Ellen and Denise who were helping her dress for the wedding. Denise stood back, looking at Rachel in her wedding dress. Rachel had purchased a full length ivory silk dress with a rounded jewel neckline and empire waist. Originally she had intended wearing a necklace given to her on her twentieth birthday, but she would now be wearing her grandfather's gift, Violet's necklace. Despite her age and arthritis, Ellen was a competent seamstress; she had taken lace from Rachel's mother's wedding dress and from the gowns worn by Lily's sisters to decorate the bishop's sleeves and the scalloped hemline of Rachel's dress. The bodice featured lace appliques; a large silk bow adorned the back of the dress beginning at the bodice and cascading to the floor. The bow gave the illusion of a train. Rachel had chosen to wear a subtle headpiece containing larkspur. Her bridal bouquet featured fresh flowers representing the special bouquet of aunts she had loved all her life. She wore ivory shoes, featuring a delicate bow with a small pearl in the centre.

At age 52, Rachel was to be a bride for the first time! Her brown hair was still worn short, but she had gone to a hairdresser to get a little curl that would give her more height and would lift her hair from her forehead. She had grown tired of her page boy hair style.

Denise checked every detail of the dress, then placed Violet's necklace around Rachel's neck, checking to see that the clasp was secure. "Oh Rachel, the necklace is stunning. It is a perfect accessory! My diamond earrings are a good match. Let me adjust your headpiece."

Denise leaned forward to look at the necklace. She took Rachel's left hand in hers to examine the guardian angel bracelet. "Rachel, are you aware that the angel on your wrist matches the angel in your necklace?"

Rachel looked at the angel on her bracelet, then raised her necklace to view the second angel.

"Yes, the angels are the same! I have two guardian angels looking after me." Looking affectionately at Bertha, "There are angels everywhere!" She hugged Denise. "Thank you for being here today; it means a great deal to have you and Derek share this special time with me and Robert."

Denise stood beside Rachel in her full length periwinkle blue dress with a mandarin collar, bishop's sleeves and empire waist. The dress featured delicate flowers embroidered on the sleeves and bodice. She wore silver shoes. Her bouquet of pink roses, her favourite flower, and baby's breath rested on a coffee table in front of the sofa where Bertha and Ellen were seated.

Bertha spoke to Ellen, "You did a terrific job sewing the lace on Rachel's gown."

Denise added, "The lace is so delicate! The stitches are incredibly fine, it has to be Belgian lace!" She had forgotten the Mascaux connection to Belgium as she contemplated the origin of the lace.

Ellen raised her hands toward Bertha. "There was a time when these hands could easily make a dress in a day, now I am content to even sew lace on a dress. Denise was fortunate to find such a tasteful dress that complements Rachel's. I love the empire waist." Looking at Rachel and her matron of honour, "My dears, you look as if you just stepped out of a Jane Austen novel, enchanting!"

Denise turned to face the two ladies. "You both look regal! Just wait until you put on your matching hats! The Queen Mother would be envious!"

Bertha had chosen a chartreuse linen dress accented by a long flowing jacket. Ellen was wearing a steely gray crepe-backed satin shirtwaist dress with matching pearl buttons running down the front and on the cuffs.

Bertha and Ellen enjoyed the compliment. Bertha responded, "At our age, we'll settle for looking alive! Let's review the four requirements for dressing a bride. Something old, something new, something borrowed, something blue!"

Denise chuckled, "Well, three of them will be obvious to everyone!" She pointed to the gown, "Something old, something new." Then pointing to Rachel's earrings, "Something borrowed. And there is something blue."

Rachel lifted her dress to reveal a blue garter.

Denise spoke, "There, all four items accounted for."

Bertha looked at her Swiss watch, "The limousine will be here in a minute to drive us to the church. Ellen, we had better pay a penny before we leave." They each hugged Rachel and Denise before leaving for the powder room.

Denise took Rachel's hands in hers. "May the peace of the Lord be with you today and always. I am honoured...Derek and I are honoured to part of your special day. When you return from your honeymoon we want you to visit us in New York so we can continue celebrating!"

By 2:30 p.m. the bride and groom had arrived at the church. Howie and Robert waited in the vestry with Father Brown. Rachel, Denise and Bertha remained in the ladies' parlour while the guests were being seated. Derek and young Robert served as ushers, helping family and friends to find seating in the church that had been a presence in the community for over one hundred and fifty years. The church was a white wooden structure with a steeple containing one bell that was still rung before every service. Robert and Howie looked at each other as the bell tolled, reminding the community that worshippers had gathered to share a special occasion. Margie's organ preludes set the tone for the ceremony that would unite the bride and groom who had come to receive God's blessing on their union. Sixteen choir members were seated in the chancel wearing their burgundy cassocks and white surplices; they would provide leadership for the congregational hymns and the sung liturgy. Derek had just escorted Ellen to her place when Margie began the wedding processional, "Joyful, Joyful, We Adore Thee".

Father Brown led Robert and Howie out of the vestry to stand at the foot of the chancel steps. Denise proceeded down the aisle in front of Rachel who walked with Bertha. Rachel realized that she was not a young bride who needed to be escorted down the aisle nor did she expect someone to 'give her away', but she wanted to be joined visually to their heritage by having the only surviving member of their families walk with her as she walked towards the man who would be her husband.

As Rachel walked down the aisle, she could see near the lectern the ten foot fir tree bearing over two hundred angels. Suddenly the five hundred tiny white lights were illuminated, adding their glow to the candles on the altar and on every window sill below the stained glass windows that depicted the life of Christ who is the light of the World.

As she and Bertha continued walking down the aisle she smiled at family and friends, many of whom had already shared a church service with them in the morning. There is a time for mourning and a time for celebrating! Feeling his heart racing, Robert turned to look at his bride coming toward him. Rachel paused as Bertha took her place in the front pew with Ellen.

As Robert faced the congregation, he did not see the family members who had joined them, he did not see the educators and students with whom he had worked, he did not see the friends that he and Rachel had shared their lives with; he saw only the woman who had won his heart so many years ago. As she joined him at the chancel steps, they exchanged a smile; then turned to face the priest who would give them God's blessing. They could see in front of them the magnificent four panelled stained glass window featuring the Nativity, Crucifixion, Resurrection and Pentecost.

The Old Testament lesson echoed through Robert's memory, "They shall walk and not grow weary, they shall mount on eagles' wings". The New Testament lesson was the familiar passage from Corinthians ending with, "For now there are faith, hope, and love. But the greatest of these three, the greatest is love."

The couple stood in front of priest, congregation and God as they exchanged their vows, made sacred promises to each other, were united in their love, sanctified by the God who had given them their life, His son and their joy! As they exchanged rings, the priest placed his white stole over their hands, signifying their union.

Young Robert led the prayers of the people; he had written a supplement to the prayer found in the liturgy. During the signing of the register, Betty sang two hymns written by Daisy Thomas; one of which had been sung when the three sisters had invited the world to join them on Melrose Road. The choir joined Betty for the chorus of each hymn. The second hymn was entitled "Our Prayer"; the chorus touched the bride and groom's souls:

You have created us, sustained us;
You gave us all that we have.
We stand in awe before You.
Shine Your Light upon us.
Unite us in Your love!
Holy One, hear our prayer!

Robert and Rachel had opted to have eucharist with their wedding liturgy. After they had received the blessed sacrament, they knelt in prayer as the congregation moved to the altar to receive the blessed elements. The couple spent time acknowledging the wonder of their faith as they stared in awe at the story depicted in the four stained glass panels that filled their view. They looked at the angel tree, noticing that someone had placed two angels holding hands at the top of the tree. They watched in silence as their guests walked to the altar, the friends who had shared their journey with them, who knew of their heartaches, knew of their triumphs. There were some individuals that Rachel did not recognize. They both failed to recognize a stylish woman in her late fifties whom Derek escorted to the altar.

They tried to savour each moment; they were almost startled when Margie began playing the recessional, "Trumpet Voluntary"; the organ was joined by two trumpeters for the finale. As the music played the two couples walked down the aisle leaving candles, angels and sacred elements to find a place in their memories.

Following the ceremony, Robert and Rachel were driven in the limousine to the manor so that they could drive slowly past "memory lane", to acknowledge those who were in their thoughts on their special day. The car paused when it came to Camille's tree.

Later they joined their family and friends at the Northumbria Lodge for the reception. The lodge was a large rambling older two-storey wooden structure that featured ceiling to floor windows overlooking the harbour. The banquet room had been reserved for dinner and the ball room for the dance and birthday party. As the bride and groom entered the banquet room, they delighted in seeing the combination of wedding and festive decorations. The room was a sea of tables covered with white linen, china, crystal, and silverware. Each table seated eight guests; each contained a striking centrepiece featuring a set of pink candles, clusters of holly and heather to highlight pink and white roses. A tiny angel stood at the base of one candle; a teddy bear at the other.

It was the centre of the room that attracted everyone's attention. Two round tables covered with white linen cloths served to display the wedding cakes and an elegant floral arrangement of fresh flowers. Robert and Rachel had enjoyed discussing the type of wedding cake they would have. They rejected having the traditional dark fruit cake, opting for two separate cakes, one pound and one chocolate. Both cakes were heart shaped with a vase of larkspur and pink roses separating them; framed family pictures were placed around the vase, linked with white and pink ribbons. The pound cake was covered with rolled fondant frosting, the chocolate cake with Belgian chocolate frosting. Each cake featured an array of flowers cascading down its sides.

It was the second round table that intrigued the bride and groom. It featured an enormous crystal vase with a pedestal containing a stunning floral arrangement, rivaling even Iris's creations. The bride and groom realized that the arrangement had to be a gift. As they approached the arrangement, Rachel held on to Robert's right hand as she reached for the card that was attached to the white bow surrounding the pedestal. She looked affectionately at Robert as she read the brief message to herself, then held the card so he could read it for himself. 'Best wishes of your first day together; I wish you all the happiness you deserve. Trevor." Robert squeezed Rachel's hand as he commented on the gift. "It is sad, it is touching, but it was so thoughtful..."

Margie came rushing up to the bride and groom looking a bit harried but also resembling the cat that had just devoured the canary. "Good news and bad news. Glenda has laryngitis, won't be able to sing the medley of Connie's hits after dinner, but I can assure you, recovery is all that matters. No one will argue with the replacement, no one!" Without a further word, she was off to greet some of the guests. Robert and Rachel moved toward the head table.

The head table had seating for the bride and groom, the matron of honour, best man, young Robert, Derek, Margie, Bertha, Ellen and Father Brown. In one corner behind the head table stood a nine foot pine tree decorated by the lodge staff with large pink bows, white poinsettias and small white lights. In the opposite corner behind the head table stood a large birch tree, a Jesse Tree, decorated by Margie with assistance from the church ladies' auxiliary, featuring symbols from *Bible* stories including: Noah's ark, Jacob's ladder, David's star, Paul's epistle, etc. The tree was covered with tiny white lights. On the wall facing the head table, was a large bulletin board which Margie, Howie and young Robert had decorated with snapshots of Rachel and Robert, their families and friends.

A pianist played light classical music during the meal which featured a hot and cold buffet with wedding cake, English trifle and galettes for dessert. Howie served as master of ceremonies. As the guests were enjoying dessert, he asked Bertha to speak on behalf of the bride and groom's families.

Bertha left the head table to go to a microphone located at a lectern near the Jesse tree. She was calm as she began to speak. "It is my pleasure to bring greetings to the bride and groom, to my son and my daughter, greetings not just from the Mascaux family, but also from the Thomas family."

Robert and Rachel exchanged glances as Bertha continued. "During the last visit that I enjoyed with Rachel's three aunts in Flanders Cove, they presented me with a priceless gift that I was entrusted to deliver when Rachel and Robert married. The bride and groom have been unaware of this gift until now." She smiled at them. "We are a family who know how to guard secrets. I know that they will enjoy having this gift shared with their guests today." She briefly surveyed her audience, then continued. "Most of you will know that Daisy Thomas has written extensively of her faith; Rose Thomas has captured the whimsy in all of us with her stories of Rocky, the raccoon. Iris Thomas was not a published author; her legacy lives on in her famous quilt that captured the interest of so many magazine readers. The three sisters combined their talents to write a Rocky story that has never been published, never shared with anyone until this evening. I have asked Robert Patterson to read the story to us; it is entitled, "With Love, With Rocky".

As Bertha returned to the head table, she moved toward Rachel and Robert kissing each of them on the cheek. Rachel was moved to tears; Robert kissed his wife gently on the lips.

Young Robert stood in front of the lectern holding a Rocky puppet in his hand. "Hello, my name is Rocky. I have asked Robert to read my story about four of my friends. I'll just sit here on the edge of this table while he reads the story. Hope you like it!" Robert placed Rocky at the end of the head table, then opened his burgundy leather folder to begin the story.

"Once there were four raccoons who lived in the basement of an old country church. The leader of the four imps was called Big Guy; the smallest one was named Tiny. The other two raccoons were the twins, Frisky and Slow.

The basement was warm in the winter and cool in the summer heat. They had a secret entrance to the basement that their human friends had never discovered. They could rest in their hiding place in the furnace room during the day and then prowl at will during the night. They were very careful not to leave any evidence that they were nonpaying lodgers. They tried their best to earn their keep by eating leftovers from church suppers and bake sales. It did take quite a while before they learned to open that big white box that always contained such delicious treats; they were sure that the kind ladies had left them the food as a reward. After all all, they protected the church when no one else was around.

On one occasion, in the middle of the night they frightened three thieves who had just broken a window and were attempting to enter the basement. Big Guy scampered to the ladies meeting room where a large table lamp had a chain that turned the light on when pulled. He pulled the chain as hard as he could. Tiny knew how to turn on a little machine that played music. When two of the thieves saw the light come on and heard the music playing, they ran as quickly as they could, leaving their tough guy behind.

With the lights to guide him, the thief soon lowered himself safely through the broken window. As he landed on the floor, the lights went out and the music stopped, startling him. Suddenly he felt something land on his back as Frisky leaped from a shelf. Slow was attempting to get out of the intruder's way, but caused the uninvited guest to trip over him. The lights went on, the lights went off. The music blared! The thief shouted, "The place is haunted! The place is haunted!" He fled from the building without stopping to look behind him.

The following day the church people couldn't understand why nothing had been taken. Probably that was the reason they so often left food for their unpaid guards.

One evening when the church was very quiet, the four raccoons sat near the altar munching vegetables that the ladies had brought that afternoon. They were always careful not to eat more than their fair share, knowing that humans liked to eat as well. The foursome were trying to figure out what the real purpose of the church was.

Big Guy slapped his front paws together to get the others' attention. "It seems to me that our human friends don't live here and they only come to visit on special occasions. Well, some of them come once a week, but not most of them. The building must be here for those flower times."

Slow couldn't understand what flowers had to do with anything they were talking about. He gazed at Big Guy as he said, "Flowers, I don't get it!"

Big Guy just shook his head. "Haven't you noticed that the church has more people when it has flowers? Humans must like flowers. I wonder why they don't have lots of flowers more often, then they would get more people."

Slow just could not understand. "I still don't get it!"

Big Guy poked Slow in the ribs, "Slow, let me explain. Once a year, humans fill the church with those red, pink and white pointed flowers; that's when they have that baby in a wooden box. Do you remember seeing the people wearing those funny costumes. The mother picks up the baby to show him to the shepherds; then those three guys come with gifts for the baby."

"Ya, I remember that! So is that why the church was built?"

Big Guy frowned at Slow. "You aren't listening. That's only one of four times the church is filled. Maybe it's those tall white flowers that attract everyone. That's when everyone sings 'alleluia' a lot. They sang so many alleluias last year I got a headache listening to them echo through the pipes that come to the basement."

Frisky sat up straight. "If it isn't the pointed flowers or those tall flowers, what else could be attracting people here?"

Big Guy looked smug. "We always have the church filled when we have those artificial flowers stuck on the ends of the pews and those big baskets of flowers spread out in front of the altar. The women always carry flowers in their hands and the men wear flowers attached to their coats."

Tiny spoke up, "Yes, that's when they throw those little bits of paper and rice when the couple leave the church."

Big Guy patted Tiny on the head. "You have been observant!"

Slow looked up at Big Guy. "But you said there were four occasions when the church is filled with people. What's the other time?"

Big Guy spoke confidently, "It's that strange time when the guest of honour gets to lie down. They roll the person in, talk about celebrating life but everybody cries. Once everyone has a good cry, they wheel the person out but they don't throw bits of paper. Maybe this is the main reason we have a church because the flowers are not only in baskets but they come in compact arrangements, too. See, the church is always filled when we have flowers. No flowers, no people!"

Slow looked puzzled. "Why haven't humans figured this out!"

Tiny looked at Slow. "A good point Slow, maybe they haven't taken time to smell the flowers!"

Big Guy didn't appreciate sharing the limelight with anyone. "We still need to solve our problem. Why do the humans have this church? Is it to celebrate the birth of that baby, to sing alleluias, to have couples walk up and down the centre aisle or is it to make people cry while someone gets wheeled in and out?"

Slow's eyes brightened as he spoke. "The church is filled when there are lots of flowers! Maybe the church was built to display flowers!"

Tiny frowned, "No, there has to be something else besides the flowers!"

Young Robert stopped his reading, looked at his audience who were very attentive. "You know, there must be something else besides the flowers." He walked to the head table to pick up Rocky.

Rocky waved his front paws to the audience. "The story is not over, it has just begun. There is a solution, but we want you to read it for yourself. We have the full story for you to take home with you. Iris, Daisy and Rose want you to know that I am a master detective because I had to solve the problem for my friends, that's why the story is called, "With Love, With Rocky". I will give you one hint. Flowers are beautiful! They not only look nice, but they smell nice and they are soft to touch. They always remind us of love. Look at the fresh flowers in this room. Don't they make you smile? Don't they help you to celebrate life! Take time before you leave today to smell the flowers and you will have a clue how I solved the mystery of why the church exists!" Rocky leaned his head forward, "Pssst! Don't tell anyone the solution because next Sunday we could have traffic jams at every church!"

Young Robert carried Rocky to the head table. Rocky leaned forward to kiss Rachel on the cheek, then Robert. He waved to everyone, then gracefully lowered his head.

The guests had been enthralled with the simple story read so passionately by Robert. They clapped as Rocky bowed. The story brought the bouquet to the wedding; it reminded everyone that there is a child in all of us. All of us have need of a Rocky! The theme of love that had been so obvious in the wedding ceremony had weaved its way into the reception, reminding the guests that faith and love are what life is all about! No wedding floral arrangements have ever been more admired than those adorning the tables on December 12, 1997 at the Northumbria Lodge. Trevor's flowers became united with the gift from the three aunts; bouquets of love!

After Robert and Rachel had cut the first pieces of their wedding cakes, they circulated, talking to their guests. For cake lovers it was a celebration, chocolate and pound cake smothered in delicious icing. As the guests relaxed, listening to the piano stylings and greeting old friends, meeting new ones, the mood suddenly changed. George Harris, a 'younger' friend of Camille entered the room with his accordion. He began to play a lively tune as he approached Robert and

Rachel, motioning for them to form a train behind him. The guests followed. The train wandered throughout the banquet room, winding slowly past the Jesse tree, the fir tree, the bulletin board and circling twice around the centre floral arrangement.

George led everyone from the banquet room to the ball room. There was a small stage at one end of the room. A four piece band was already in place. The room had plush chairs scattered around its perimeter with a few festive decorations. As George led the train into the room, the lodge staff wheeled in the round table with Trevor's bouquet and another table with a large birthday cake. As soon as the flowers and cake were in place, George stopped playing. Immediately the band began playing hits of the late fifties. Twelve high school dancers dressed like teeny boppers with cool guys, their hair slicked back in duck tails, entered the room. They scattered themselves on the dance floor entertaining everyone with the freshness that was rock'n roll of the fifties.

Robert looked at Rachel, kissing her as they watched the young dancers recall the music of their youth. They were transported to the beginnings of their friendship. Robert whispered to Rachel. "It has been a perfect day!" He looked around at all the guests who were sharing these precious moments with them. The wedding would become a treasured part of their prized souvenirs, their happiness.

Rachel hugged Robert. "The wedding music was wonderful; Margie's playing was so inspirational and I still have chills thinking of Betty singing Daisy's hymns. I felt so close to you in church; the peace that is beyond understanding was there. The warmth of our families and friends was with me throughout dinner as the music of the piano floated around us. Robert, music weaves magic in our lives; I have always known it, but today the music actually became a part of me."

Robert agreed, "I was really moved by the power of music as George led us from the banquet room to the dance floor playing the accordion. The musical train has always been a part of Belgian celebrations."

Margie, Howie, Derek and Denise approached the bride and groom. Young Robert arrived with Bertha and Ellen on each arm. The band ceased playing for just a moment...then the familiar sound of "My Happiness" filled the room.

Robert and Rachel looked at the stage as a female singer stood at the microphone. She was wearing a red floor length gown with slits revealing a shapely leg. She wore a silver broach. Robert and Rachel were mesmerized as they stared at the singer. The music mounted, the singer began the opening lines. The voice was so familiar!

Rachel looked in shock as she hugged Robert, "It can't be! Robert, it just can't be!"

Robert glanced at Margie who was crying. She beamed as she nodded her head and winked.

Robert leaned over to kiss Rachel as he whispered, "With Love, With Connie"!

References

Much of the information referring to the life of Connie Francis exists in the public domain. A special thank you to Michael Motta and Thomas Hughes who like Rachel in the story served as presidents for Connie Francis Fan Clubs when the singer's career was flourishing. Their newsletters and annual yearbooks were an invaluable source of information. A special thank you to John A. Donatelli, Jr. for his assistance with discography information.

Who's Sorry Now? Connie Francis. New York: St. Martin's Press, 1984.

Song titles used for the Chapters:

Among My Souvenirs: (M. Nicholas, E. Leslie) Chappell & Co., Inc., 1927,1959 (ASCAP)

My Happiness: (B.Bergantine, B. Peterson Blasco) Happiness Music Inc., 1958 (ASCAP)

Everybody's Somebody's Fool: (J. Keller, H. Greenfield) Screen Gems-Columbia Music, Inc., Mandan Music Corp, 1960 (BMI)

If My Pillow Could Talk: (Jim Steward Jr., Robert Mosley) Longitude Music Company, 1963 (BMI)

Drownin' My Sorrows: (Hank Hunter, Stan Vincent) Longitude Music Company, 1963 (BMI)

Your Other Love: (Claus Ogerman, Ben Raleigh) Helios Music Corp (BMI) Ben Raleigh Music Company, 1963 (ASCAP)

Breakin' In A Brand New Broken Heart: (H. Greenfield, J. Keller) Screen Gems-Columbia Music Inc., Mandan Music Corp, 1961 (BMI)

I'm Me Again: (Alan Roy, Scott and Ed Fox) Ragtime Music, 1980 (ASCAP)

Who's Sorry Now?: (T. Snyder, B. Kalmar, H.Ruby) Mills Music, Inc., 1958 (ASCAP)

The Wedding Cake: (Margaret Lewis, Myra Smith) Ragged Island Music, 1969 (BMI)

Album jackets quoted from in the novel:

More Greatest Hits: Connie Francis: MGM Records, 1961.
All Songs BMI except: Mama (ASCAP), God Bless America (ASCAP), Among My Souvenirs (ASCAP)

Connie Francis Sings Bacharach and David: (Burt Bacharach/Hal David, Arr. Claus Ogerman) MGM Records, 1968.
All Songs (ASCAP) except: The Look of Love (BMI)

Connie Francis: I'm Me Again: Silver Anniversary Album: compl. Pat Niglio. MGM Records/Polydor Inc. 1981.
All Songs (ASCAP) except: Milk and Honey, No Sun Today, What Good Are Tears?, Comme Ci, Come Ca, Where the Boys Are (BMI)

About the Author

George R. Henaut has an abiding interest in language—its power and its beauty. His career as an educator provided many opportunities to enhance and share this passion with others. Since 1990 he has written, directed and produced ten dramas for audiences in his native Nova Scotia. His plays and short stories have been influenced not only by life on the Atlantic seaboard, but also by his Christian spirituality and appreciation of traditional family values. All of these influences have culminated in his first novel, With Love, With Connie, which also reveals his enduring appreciation of the music of Connie Francis. His greatest desire is to share this romantic, yet turbulent story of Robert and Rachel with others.

Printed in the United States
905100002B